Uncharted

Ellie Pond

MOUNTAIN KEEP PUBLISHING

Chapter 1

Overhaul

Haley

"What do you want me to do with this vine rope?" I cup my hands and yell up at Zane. I know what he wants me to do with it, but I want to see if he'll come up with another answer. One that we could have a little more fun with.

"She puts it in the basket."

I glare at him. For the last week, we've been snuggling at night while Zane retells us old movies. Last night was *Silence of the Lambs*. I wasn't a fan. I coil the rope and put it in my newest basket. This one has a handle and can actually hold more than a pound or two. All thanks to the reed-like plants Calvin found on the other side of the island. I watch as Zane pulls it up.

"How's it going?" I call back up again.

"Get on up here and take a look." I put another log on the stove. Dante will want it hot for dinner tonight. I give Pepper a scratch behind her ears. She's getting so big, like a gangly teenager. Her ears are too large for her head, and she's all paws—and only a little bit of claws.

I hold on to the rope and use the few footholds we've made to get to the platform. This one is mostly finished, and when the other ones are done, it will be our living room. There's a corrugated tin roof from the ship over most of it. The other side, with the least amount of wind, has a palm frond covering the top of the tarp. Calvin and Zane are working on the bedroom platform, a few steps above this one. It's going to be something when it's done. It's a lot bigger. It will have solid walls that the guys are convinced will hold through the rainy season. A few more boards, and the base will be finished.

I climb up the steps to the bedroom and poke my head in. "It's looking amazing." A soft brush of fur rubs up against my legs. "Look at you, Pepper. You're such a big girl getting up here on your own." I pick her up and nuzzle her to my face. I know it's going to take a while for her to get back down on her own. But it's a step in the right direction. "Can I come up?"

"Yes. Don't step over there. We're still getting it secured." Calvin points to the far corner.

Maybe it's all the time I spent working in yacht ship interiors, but I'll swing a hammer if they need me to. We only have one hammer. We found it in the locked chest on the fishing boat, along with two wool blankets that were remarkably not moth eaten. There were a few other tools, a saw and a hand drill, along with a picture of a woman wearing a flower in her hair. We've brought the chest into the kitchen area. It's where we keep all the supplies we want to keep dry. The hardest thing we've done is cut the raft apart. It was starting to leak. And I don't care what happens. I'm not leaving this island in an inflatable raft. Even if we could get it past the breakers, the thought of being thrown about with no way of knowing where we were going or being able to steer? Yeah, I'm not interested in that. I did spend a few hours yesterday straightening nails. But most of my time has been spent trying to make things better for us. I made more mats for the roof above the living space. Swept the dirt and sand out of the kitchen area. But I'm ecstatic about the sleeping loft. "When can we move into it?" The floor is almost done, and the roof was in place at almost the same time the support timbers were put up.

"It needs the rest of the sidewalls up. It's going to take a bunch more trips to the derelict to get the supplies we need." Zane has a sharp stick behind his ear. It's one he uses to draw in the sand when he's trying to convince Calvin to build something his way. He looks just like the architect I think he should have been. "We can't sleep in it until we know we won't fall out."

I nod. Bringing the supplies from the ship has taken a long time. We even talked about building it closer to the derelict, but there aren't any trees there as good as these.

"Hey, Sassy. We're home," Dante calls out, and something large thuds to the ground.

Zane crouches and looks through the last hole in the floorboards. "Excellent. They've got the support beam." He hops up and zips down the tree ladder.

I stand at the railing of the living room. "Hi, guys."

"Haley." Easton brushes his hand on his pants. "Is that a new basket?" He takes the swinging basket in his hands.

I'm down the ladder a lot slower than Zane. "Yeah. What do you think?"

Dante gives me a hug as he makes his way over to the stove. "Perfect temperature, Sassy."

"It's good. You're really improving." Easton kisses the spot below my ear. The one he knows makes me squirm.

"Hey, you two. We've got work to do. There's a few

more hours until it gets dark." Zane examines the new beam. To me, it looks like one of the ribs of the ship. But I've been wrong about my guesses before.

"Tide's going out. I'm going to go to the beach and check the fish weir," I say.

"I'll come with you." Calvin's down in three long steps.

"We're losing light." Zane kneels next to the beam, taking measurements with his pencil stick.

"And we'll have sunrise tomorrow," Calvin responds.

Dante puts his hand on Calvin's forehead. "Who are you and what have you done with taskmaster Green?"

Calvin pushes Dante's hand away. "Let's go see what's for dinner, Haley."

"Bring something good back. I don't want to make jerky stew again," Dante threatens. It's the only thing of his that we all had a hard time getting down. And it was only once.

"You coming, Easton?" I hold my hand out to him.

"No, I'm going to stay here." He looks at Zane, and I get the subtext. He's going to see if he can get Zane to chill out. Which lately has been next to impossible. He's excited. And I get it. But he needs to take a break.

"You all know where we'll be." I give them each a kiss before I go. It's become this little ritual we do. And I didn't even start it. It was Zane, or Easton. I don't remember.

I start with Easton since he's next to me. His kiss is tender and sends a zip to my toes.

"Me next, Sassy." Dante's waiting in line. He pulls me close and takes my breath away.

I move next to Zane. He's not looking up from the peeling green-painted beam. "Zane?"

"What?" He's deep in envisioning land.

"Give your girl a kiss," Dante calls over from where he's chopping up a coconut.

"Shit, Little Bird. Sorry." He pops up and wraps his arms around my neck. He kisses me and dips me deeply.

"Show off." Easton punches playfully at Zane's arm when he rights me.

"Take a break, Zane."

"I will, Little Bird."

When I turn back, he's measuring the other side of the new beam. I point at Zane's back to Easton. Easton nods. Maybe he can make him sit and take some of the pressure off his foot. The wound is healing, but not well. It's not infected, but the scab doesn't look right.

Calvin takes my hand in his. He has one of our oldest mats and a hunk of the plastic from the raft under his other arm. The trail to the beach is well-worn. And while we don't man the signal fire on the beach often anymore, we do sometimes. I kind of figure that once the shelter is done, we'll get back to it. Watching the horizon. Or maybe we'll just watch from the top platform, when it's complete.

"Look." I run down the beach, dragging Calvin along behind me. The fish weir is a lot bigger now. And we've discovered the far side of the beach works a lot better with the currents of the waves. Some days we have so many fish we throw a good portion of them back into the ocean. Other days there aren't many, but enough for dinner. "Holy crap, is that a sea bass?"

Calvin picks it up. The thing is two feet long. "It's huge." Calvin wades in.

"I'll toss the rest back." I pick up a small reef fish and toss it over the weir fence. We've added a lot more stakes over the last few weeks.

"Good job not squealing, Haley."

I roll my eyes. "I've been practicing. Still don't like picking fish up. But I don't want the poor thing to die for no reason." I gather more of the small fish, setting them free. "Go Willy, you're free."

"So help me, Haley, if you have Zane telling us the *Free Willy* story tonight . . ."

I hold my breath and wait for his reaction before I turn slowly to him. He's tossing another fish back. "What are you going to do if I do?"

He shakes his head. "It's not punishment if you like it, Haley." He picks up the sea bass again. It's huge. "Shit, this thing has to weigh over ten pounds. It's a good thing we came down here now. We're going to need the smoker going tonight."

We walk back shoulder to, well, mid-chest. "Want me to carry the fish for a while? You're not getting tired."

"Not tired. Contemplative." His eyebrows furrow.

"Really, Mr. Green? What are you thinking about?" I know the answer before I ask. While I love Zane's story time, he picks movies that he knows I'll like and will drive Calvin batshit crazy. He's done *The Devil Wears Prada, The Notebook, How to Lose a Guy in Ten Days,* and *The Proposal.* Calvin hated all of them. How you can hate anything with Sandra Bullock in it, though, is beyond me.

"A punishment."

"Oh. Well, if I'm going to be punished . . ." I take off running. I know I'm not going to beat him back, but I'm going to give it a try. I'm almost to them when he thunders beside me. "I won't, I won't. I won't make Zane tell us *Free Willy.*" Calvin picks me up and throws me over his shoulder——he's got the sea bass under his other arm. "Zane," I scream.

Dante's looking at me oddly, or at least I think he is. It's hard to tell when you're upside down. "What am I, chopped liver?" Dante shivers.

"What?" Zane races out of the jungle.

"Do you know the plot to *Free Willy*?" I'm out of breath from running and holding in my laughter. Dante bursts out laughing. Easton too. "Do you?" It's childish. I know, but pushing Calvin's buttons is necessary to keep him from going back to being a workaholic. Something I hope I can get Zane out of too. I'm a hard worker. But sometimes enough is enough. We have a roof and food. It's okay to relax.

Zane shakes his head, and he's back to whatever measurement or plan he was making.

"Nice try, Sassy."

Calvin drops the bass on Dante's new work surface. It's waist-high with a slab of worn, smooth lava rock on top. "Holy shit, that's a beauty." Dante slaps Calvin on his back.

"You got it? I've got some punishment to pass out." Calvin slaps Dante back.

"If I say no, do I get to help with the punishment?"

"No." Calvin laughs. "I need Rockwell for this."

Did Dante just wink at Calvin? I gulp.

Chapter 2

Giving Chase

Easton

"Which way are we going?" I nod at Calvin.

"You're taking his side on this?" Haley crosses her arms over her fabulous tits. She's playing it up. But she's not mad. I'm betting if I was to pull down her leggings right now, she'd be wetter than the ocean. I give her a wink, and I swear she blushes. She's playing right along.

"Rockwell's a lot of things, but he's not dumb, Haley."

"No, no, I'm not." My throat tightens. Calvin giving me even an offhanded compliment is odd. He's up to something, that's for sure.

"You're giving up your positions tonight," Dante yells over his shoulder. He's cut open tonight's dinner with the precision of a surgeon.

"Done." Calvin handles the negotiations without consulting me. "It's going to be worth it." We've been doing a rotation of who gets to sleep next to Haley. Who gets to have some one-on-one time with her next. After the waterfall, when we decided to move inland and away from the raft, it was like a dam burst. We all wanted Haley all the time. For her own preservation, we had to come up with a system.

"You're going to let me walk." Haley's eyes are wide. She might complain when Calvin throws her over his shoulder, but she told me in confidence last week she really likes it. But being the caveman is his thing. We've all got our own thing. Dante's the comic relief. Zane's the tenderhearted one. Or at least he was. Cal's the brute, and I'm . . . well, I don't know how I fit in. I know I do fit in. What's my role? I have no idea.

A few days ago, I found myself sitting around the campfire smiling. I'm happier here than I've ever been. It's weird. This place is dangerous as hell, but it's so much better than anywhere else. There's no four a.m. practices. But there are middle-of-night checks of the fish weir. There's no board meeting, but there is gathering boards for the shelter. No junk food, pasta or gourmet coffee, but there is Haley. And that's enough. More than enough. She has a way of making us all feel like we're the most important, that without us, our whole group would fall apart.

Calvin sweeps Haley off her feet and tosses her over his shoulder. "Calvin Green." She slaps at his ass. But that only makes him laugh. "Yes, my chief stew. How can I help you?" His tone is deep, and I wonder if he's got a plan, and if he does, if he's going to keep me in the dark too.

I'm also wondering why in the hell he didn't ask one of the other guys. Things between us all have settled down into a rhythm after the waterfall. But do I actually think Green and I are going to be best buds? Fuck no. Then again, Dante was making dinner, and Zane is crazy with the shelter. If his plan takes three, I'm the only one around to do it. Why in the world wouldn't he want to be alone with Haley?

I'm walking shoulder to shoulder with him, contemplating snatching her from his grasp and taking her for myself. "Are you doing okay there?" I cock my head sideways and give Haley a smile.

"I'm getting used to the blood pooling in my ears." She gives a quick giggle and grabs Calvin around the waist. It stops her from swinging side to side.

We're at the waterfall before you know it.

"You ready to get down, Chiefie?"

"Yes, Green."

He grunts and sets her down on the large smooth rock next to the waterfall. Chiefie? She doesn't notice or doesn't mind it. Her arms wind around Calvin's neck. She gives him a quick peck and then zips away. "You didn't think this was going to be that easy." She tears up the path that parallels the stream, laughing and giggling. Stealth isn't in any way her worry.

Neither Calvin nor I move—I'm stunned. Calvin's hand lands on my arm. "Give her a head start, Rockwell, or the fun will be over too soon."

"This was your big punishment plan?" I cock an eyebrow at him.

"No, but it certainly adds to it." He takes a few steps, and from behind a rock near the waterfall, he takes a small coconut wrapped in a piece of the plastic from the kit on the raft.

"What's that?" My brow furrows, and my eyes flick to the path Haley ran down.

"She's not going to go far. Are you scared your Olympic ass can't track Haley running through the jungle, leaving a trail a toddler could follow? Look." He hands me the plastic package.

I unwrap it. The coconut is cracked in half. I pull it

apart. There's a slurry of oil and paste in the bottom half of the coconut. I look up at him. I'm missing something. "Oh, fuck." The light pops on.

Calvin cocks his head.

"Lube." There are other things we can use, but this should work.

"Ding-ding. Now let's go get her." He takes off walking. And it's fucking terrifying. My heart is beating rapidly for her. But also, I can't wait to get her back here. I wrap it back up and set it on a dry rock. I take off past him. I might not know how to read the signs of a trail, but I know which way Haley took off. The lava rocks on this section going up the mountain are scraggly and jut out. There's clearly an animal trail, but it's nowhere near as defined as the ones lower. I'm up the trail about twenty feet from Calvin. He's still doing his whole slow walking horror movie thing. "You planning on catching Haley or going to pick some pomelos, Rock-well?" Calvin takes a sharp left off the trail into the low scrub of the jungle.

I pivot-turn and make my way back down to where he turned into the jungle. My palms are sweating when I catch up to him. He crouches. "Here." He points to a broken fern. He doesn't move. He's like a deer listening in the woods—I can almost see his ear twitch in the wind. Then he's up. Long strides take us parallel to the side of the mountain. And now I wonder if this wasn't a mistake. This could put Haley in danger. It makes me want to find her even faster. We round a grove of trees. These are different from the palms and the map tree. My hand runs along the loose bark as I go around it. The smell is familiar. I lean in and take a deeper breath. It smells like my dad's back deck on Nantucket. Teak. Is this what a teak tree looks like? I peel a piece of the long bark and breathe it in. I turn around, and

Calvin isn't behind me. Double fuck. Maybe getting rid of me was his plan. I shake my head and turn back the way I came from. This time I try to see things like he does. Well, from a little closer to earth instead of charging in. I wait, scan the forest floor. At first, I don't see anything, but then up ahead I make out some leaves not facing the sun. It's not a broken branch, but it's something. I head toward them, and when I get there, I stop again. To the left there's some scratches in the dirt.

Damn, I might be following a wild boar. I stop and listen, but nothing. At the bare dirt, I stand and search. Off in the distance, I find an area of moss with a footprint in it leading off to the right. When I get there, I see Calvin. His hands are calm at his side. He cocks his head to the right. I look, but I don't see anything.

Green rolls his eyes and points to a grove of straight, tall trees with shaggy bark. Then he does some Marine hand signal shit that I can only interpret as stay where I am while he flushes her out. I scan the grove. But I don't see anything. Certainly not Haley.

Calvin rounds the corner, his face without emotion. But then I see it flicker. A smirk. He's got eyes on her. A squeal erupts from the grove, and she charges right at me.

"Fuckkkk!" She takes a sharp left, but it's too late. I wrap my arms around her middle. But she rolls to the right and slips away. She tears off the way we came.

"Damn it, Rockwell. We had her."

"Well, you could, I don't know, run?"

"I don't run when I can use my brain and walk."

I take off after Haley, but Calvin doesn't move. "Whatever." I wasn't invested enough that time. But now I want to catch her. The idea of a little pleasure in her punishment is making me hard. She's fast. She missed her chance as an

Olympic runner. She's zipping in and out of the trees, but I'm catching up with her. I think. But then she's gone when I go past a clump of palms that have thorns. These are horrible. They have little spikes that cling to each other and the surrounding trees. In parts of the island, they're almost impossible to get around without ending up torn up and bloody. I'm not going through them, and there's no way Haley would have either. I circle around counterclockwise, my eyes flicking from side to side. That's when I spot a broken palm frond, one of the ones with spikes coming out of its trunk. No fucking way. She wouldn't be that reckless to dive into thorns. But then, Haley's not one for losing. A few steps ahead, I see a small opening underneath a larger palm. It's a hole in the dense thicket. Lightly padded footsteps come behind me.

Calvin, for his size, can have stealth when he wants to. He makes hand signals that he's going around. I should stay there. And then he adds an extra glare, which I take to be "don't fuck this up again." I give him a salute, and he shoots me back the middle finger.

I laugh, but silently. Because he's taking this seriously. When Calvin circles to the opposite side of the thicket, I can't see him at all anymore. It feels like an eternity, but Haley eventually pops out of the hole.

"We've got you, my Firefly."

She giggles in my arms. "Darn it. I thought I was going to get away." Her hair is covered in burrs, and there are two long scratches on the side of her arm.

I kiss her neck. "You're never going to get away now, Firefly. Let's go get you cleaned up so we can make you dirty again."

She kisses me and tries the same trick on me that she did on Calvin the first time. But I'm expecting it, and when she tries to slip out of my hands, I've got a hold on her. I toss her over my shoulder. Holding her there, I smack her ass. She squirms in my arms but stills when I rub the cheek I spanked.

"You got her this time. Good." He holds out his hands to take her. And as much as I want to carry her through the woods, he's got a lot more practice. The last thing I want is to stumble and hurt her. "You hurt yourself with your little game. That's not good, Chiefie. That's definitely going to cost you some more punishment."

"I can take it." Calvin's got her in a different grip. Her face is a lot lower. Instead of in the middle of his back, its right above his ass. "But can you?" She bites his cheek and turns to me, a sparkle in her eyes.

Chapter 3

Astern

Calvin

I grip my molars together without a flinch. The little vixen bit me. I turn to Easton, and he's glaring at Haley. She's obviously looking to him for support. "Don't go looking at him for help. He's on my side. Aren't you, Rockwell?"

"This time, yes." Rockwell's staring at the long scratches on her arm. When I found her, she'd wedged herself into the thicket. I didn't know if she'd come out in one piece. The few marks on her body are a lot less than she's going to have when we're done with her. Her eyes had gone wide, and I pointed at her to go back the way she came in.

Haley laughed. But I sure as hell didn't. Later, we're going to have a little talk about how far it's okay to take these games. Because sometimes the girl has no common sense.

"How did you even find me?"

"Calvin gave me a beginner's lesson on how to find a trail."

"One you're going to get tomorrow. And also how to run without making noise." I grunt.

"You're giving away all your trade secrets to the enemy." She laughs and gives my ass a quick pinch. I hike her up to how I normally hold her.

"Not secrets, Haley, they might keep you alive someday."

"I doubt I'll be able to hide from a boar. But okay."

I'm not going to bring up that she might have to get away, not from us, or from a boar, but from something or someone else. "We'll start tomorrow." While I'm sure it felt like a long way from the pool for Haley and Rockwell, we weren't even a quarter mile from the main trail. I go straight back to it.

"Whoa, we were close."

"We'll work on directions and orientation too. Rockwell can sit in on those lessons. I don't need to be rescuing him too."

"I can take care of myself. Although I'll be forever in your debt, Haley." Rockwell runs his hand down her leg.

I let Haley down again, then turn and glare at her.

"What? Fine, you win. I'll take my punishment and like it."

That has me smiling, and damn it, I can't hide it. "Hands in the air."

She lifts her hands, and I strip off her shirt. Her breasts wiggle. And fuck, it's hard to control myself. But this has to happen nice and slow. "Turn." She turns. And I pull down her pants.

She's facing Rockwell. He's got his clothes stripped off before I can toss her pants up on the dry rock. The coconut with its golden liquid sits right where we left it. I tug off my shirt and pants. I'm as anxious as Rockwell. I've been fucking thinking about this for a week. I whispered to Dante, and he agreed to make us something to play with.

Having all of us here for the first time might be the right thing for them. But not her. Not for me. I don't want Dante anywhere near her ass with his monster cock. Damn. Not now, most likely never.

"Kneel before your queen, Rockwell," I say.

He flashes a smile and takes her hand as he walks backward a few feet into the water. He drops to his knees and throws her leg over his shoulder. I move in close to her back.

I trail my fingers up the side of her arm to her neck. She tilts her head. "Good girl, are you ready to pay the consequences?"

"Yes," comes out with desire. She tilts her head back as Easton's tongue plays with her pussy. I pull her back onto my chest, taking her standing weight. We need her to be good and wet before we even start playing. I'm here for all the time it takes.

"Damn, Haley. You're so hot standing there taking his tongue. Does it feel good?" I growl in her ear and nibble my way around it.

"Yes," she gasps.

I hold one hand on her belly, and the other rings around her neck. My dick swells between her ass cheeks.

Haley picks up a sway that takes me to rock hard.

She moans. Easton's working his fingers in and out of her pussy.

"Need more." She's got her hands in Easton's hair. Damn, she's pulling him out by it, but I'll give it to him. He's not letting her get away easily. It's not until she grabs the side of his head and pulls up that he stops tonguing her.

"You're such a naughty girl, Haley." Easton grabs the back of her neck and pulls her in for a kiss. The smell of her on his lips has me dripping.

"Damn." He drops to the water. "You want more? Take

more, Haley. Just know you're giving more. Fuck me like you mean it, Haley. You take your more."

She pulls on my hand to go to him, but I stop her, spin her. The water sprays over Easton. He's working his cock, watching her, watching us. I need to taste her. I kiss her, tasting her and him. All of it. My cock twitches. I drop my hand, and she wobbles backward. "Do it, Haley. Take what you need."

Sucking in her lips, she looks at me like she knows this is a trick. "It can't be this easy."

"Oh, darling, there's not going to be anything easy about this." I spin her toward Rockwell. He's like a greedy puppy waiting for his meal. She straddles him and sinks onto him. The sound of relief fills the jungle. She sets a pace. I let her. Then I'm on my knees behind her, my finger dipped in the coconut lube. I push on her bud. A slow pressure at first.

Damn, she looks good. Her ass in the air. She turns her head and looks back at me. "You ever done this before, Chiefie?"

She shakes her head. "No."

"You know what I'm about to do?"

She nods. "Yes." It's soft. Too soft.

"You want to do this, Haley?"

"Yes," she says, louder.

Sounds come from Haley, sounds we've only started to know. Mews and cries I want to memorize. I push in a little more and work a full finger in. "Slow down Haley. Easton, don't you dare come, you rich, arrogant, entitled brat." I'm doing what I need to do. "Make him last. You want us to be a team, a family. We're doing this together. Understood?"

"Yes." She hisses, her movements strained.

Another finger in, more lube, more time. I go wider, deeper, watching, listening for her reactions. The coconut oil is thin. It's not the right texture, but it's not stopping me. "You doing good, Haley?"

"So good."

I knew she would.

Rockwell's thrusts become more in sync with her movements, and I work on her eager body. Intoxicating noises from Haley make me drunk with pride for her, for us. This is fucking unbelievable. My finger stretches her, and when I can hold three in her, matching Rockwell's rhythm, I pull my hand out and douse my cock in the remaining coconut oil and position myself at her ass. "You ready, Haley?"

"Yes, yes." Her back stills, but her shoulders slope down to Easton. He's holding her in place.

With a deep breath, I ease in, feeling the tight warmth engulfing me. So slowly I move forward. Until I reach my balls.

She throws her head back, a mix of pain and pleasure reflecting on her raised shoulders and in the way she's rolling her neck. I can feel all of her. It's so deliciously tight. She cranes her neck sideways. Haley's eyes meet mine, and I can see her determination to make it through this experience. As her body adjusts to the invasion, I hold back, allowing her to take control and set the pace.

"Do you want me to stop?" I ask, my voice low and gentle. Fuck, she needs to say no. I'm not sure I can stop if she wants me to. I need this. So fucking much. It's like a dam of emotion is waiting to break out of me.

"No," she gasps out, her body fighting for each new movement we make. "Don't you dare stop. Fuck me."

The dam cracks. I grab her by her waist and take control. I fuck her into Rockwell, sliding backward.

There's not a beginning of me, no end of her. We're one. Fuck. I don't want to be this tight. This is out of control. But my thrusts erupt out of me. I can't stop them. One, one, one over and over.

Haley moans as I continue to pound her from behind. The feeling of Rockwell's dick sliding in and out of her, coupled with my cock deep inside her ass, is something I could never have imagined. My mind races, trying to make sense of the sensations coursing through my body. Easton's hands are right above mine on her hips. We're pushing and pulling on her. It's her I need.

"Oh shit, this is better than I could have—"

Easton's got his hand between the two of them. I want to swat his hand away from her clit. I want this to go on fucking forever, but then it's too much. She needs to come.

"Please!" Haley cries out, her hips bucking beneath us. She tenses up, her shoulders rising. Her ass grips me even tighter. We're so close to release. I hold her steady, not wanting to come until she does. My cock throbs inside her ass, pleading for ecstasy. It's not easy holding back my own desire, but I know she needs me to be strong for her right now. "Do it, Easton," I grunt through clenched teeth. "Let her come."

Easton's fingers find her swollen clit.

Haley screams as she orgasms beneath us. Her body shudders violently forward and back. Her walls clench around our cocks in a way that sends shockwaves of pleasure throughout my entire body.

"Hold tight, Haley." I thrust into her again. My pace is frantic as waves of her aftershocks take me over into my own orgasm. Rockwell's doing the same. Haley's body continues to spasm, milking every last bit of pleasure from both Easton and me. Her cries of triumph and satisfaction reverberate through the jungle, our bodies still connected in a primal tangle. I'm holding her up. Adrenaline still surges through my body.

"Fuck me. I can't believe we did that." Easton pants, still holding Haley tightly around her waist. I pull out of her, an odd pride filling me as my cum leaks down her leg. I help her off Easton. There are bruises on her knees and hips.

"Let's get you cleaned up." I step back off the rock, Haley in my arms.

"Ahh." She screams. "Cold, no, not cold. Can't talk. Too tired, so sleepy. Like I've taken ten thousand melatonin tablets."

I avoid Rockwell's stare. The little shit better not think this makes us friends. It's something I wanted, and his dick was the right one, other than it being attached to him.

We float for a long time. Easton washes Haley's hair with some of the soap Haley and Dante are trying to figure out how to make. Then we float some more. Until I pull her out of the pool onto my lap.

She bites her lip. It's getting dark. We need to get back. I thought I'd feel relief, that this obsession would be cured. But it's not. I'm sick with her. I'm not going to ever get over her. Fixated doesn't even begin to describe it. I'm addicted. Dependent. I'll never be able to breathe without her again.

Easton holds out her shirt. I smooth her hair out of the way and help pull it down. Easton holds up her pants. She's already closed her eyes, her head on my chest. I shake my head no.

"Mosquitos are coming out," he reminds me.

"Haley, give Easton your legs." I help her turn.

She grunts but lets Easton put her pants on and then curls back up in my lap. I stand with her and walk back to the map tree. Easton's got my clothes.

Chapter 4

Liberty Call

Zane

"Where the hell are they?" I pace down the trail and back to Dante, who is cleaning up from the bass. The smoker on the beach is ready to turn the leftover fish into jerky. Fish jerky isn't something I thought I'd want to eat. But it's not half bad. I check on it several times, watching my steps as I go between the beach to the smoker. It's an almost moonless night, but there are no clouds in the sky, so there's enough light to almost see.

I'm back at camp for a few minutes when I hear them coming down the trail. I want to fucking punch Calvin in the face. But my mother didn't raise a fool. When they come around the corner, I freeze.

Calvin's holding her against his chest. Her eyes are fluttered closed. She's asleep and not sort of asleep and faking it. No, she's unconscious.

"What did you do to her?"

"Good," she mumbles. "So good. Tired. So, so tired."

I glare between Calvin and Easton. But then Dante pops up. "Did it work?"

"Sort of." Easton drops Calvin's clothes on the makeshift table. "Thicker's going to be more useful."

Dante nods. "Oh, it separated. Did you shake it or stir it?"

"You didn't say anything about stirring it." Calvin raises a single eyebrow. I wave at him to give me Haley, and he remarkably does, pulling on his clothes afterward. Easton hangs up the towels.

"I didn't? Yeah, sorry about that." Dante tosses some small scraps to Pepper.

"Can you make it up here, Little Bird?" I hold her limp body next to mine. Calvin and Easton have used her so hard, I'm not sure she can lift her head.

"She needs to eat first." Dante's holding a bowl.

"Upstairs." We're so close to having the sleeping plat-form done. I fucking wish we'd finished it. Haley needs the space to sprawl tonight. But it's not ready yet.

"I can do it." Haley opens her eyes. "You can put me down. I want to go up to sleep, and you can't carry me."

"Don't tell him he can't do something, Haley. He'll have to prove you wrong." Dante pats Pepper.

"I can do it." She looks from Calvin to me. I put her down slowly.

"I'll be right behind you." I rest my hand on her lower back. "Take it easy."

After they leave, I spend time cleaning the living area, changing it back into the sleeping room. "It looks good," Haley says through hooded eyes. "Thank you."

I pull back the woolen blanket. She always gets the cushions, and the guys next to her for the night end up getting some blanket. We're all using our life vests as pillows. It's not much, but even a little makes it feel like home. I tuck her in. "Anything you need, Little Bird?"

"Stay with me."

"I need to go check on the smoker. And talk to the guys about what we're going to do tomorrow."

"No. Stay with me."

"Haley, I have to—"

"Stay with me." I shake my head even though I know she can't see me. "I'll be back."

She exhales. She won't even know I'm gone. I quietly sneak down the ladder.

"What are you doing?" Calvin stops me on the bottom step.

"The smokers are going and then we need to talk about—"

"Tomorrow is Sunday. Crew day off," Calvin barks.

I furrow my brow and glare at him. It's not Sunday, it's . . .

"Ah, he's still in there." Dante feeds Pepper another bit of fish.

"You're working too hard. We can take a day off." Easton's got his hands on his hips.

"We need to finish the sleeping room before the rainy season."

"We will or we won't, man. But you're pushing yourself too hard. And by yourself, I mean all of us. You need to chill." Easton drops to the wood stove and puts another log on.

"What are we going to do?" It comes out before I realize what I'm saying.

"Do or do not . . . actually that doesn't work here. We can lie on the beach, and you can retell the plot of the entire

Star Wars universe or Marvel if we want to take two days off," Dante says.

I raise my eyebrows at Dante.

"Or we can go for a swim in the ocean and then at the waterfall," Easton adds.

"We can hike up the mountain. I can show those of you who haven't seen it what it's like." Calvin nods at me. "But we're not working on the shelter, and we're not making jerky or fishing. I'll open the back end of the weir. We won't even have to check it." Calvin points at me. "No cooking. We have fruit and jerky. No one works."

"I don't know who the hell you are anymore, Calvin Green." Dante laughs.

He smiles his lopsided grin. And it hits me. The fucking asshole is in love. I don't say it. I can't say it because I am too. Only I'm trying to show her how great things can be with making the best-most-homelike-home we could ever have. Show her that I'm a provider too. That she needs me as much as she needs the rest of them. *Stay with me*, she said. I nod at Calvin. "You can finish up the jerky tonight?"

"I've got it," he says.

"I'll help too." Easton stands.

"I'm going to go to bed."

"Good idea. The stars are coming out. It's a good time to just lie there and breathe."

I climb the ladder. Do nothing tomorrow. Haley will like it. It's not my idea, but she'll like it, anyway.

"You're back." Her voice is sleepy.

"Aye."

"You're not Scottish." She lets out the softest of laughs.

"No, but everyone says Scots are sexy."

"You're sexy." She lifts the edge of the blanket. "Can we snuggle?"

"Always." She turns her back to me, and I spoon her.

"Do you really know the plots to all the Marvel movies?"

"Aye."

She laughs.

"Did you hear everything?"

"Yeah, the walls aren't exactly walls."

"We thought you were asleep. I'm sorry if we woke you."

"You didn't, and it's fine. I like the idea of a day off. If you're okay with it."

"I can be."

"I can't keep them all straight." Pepper jumps up the last step and curls up in the crook of my legs.

"Can't keep what straight?"

"I got completely lost somewhere after Hulk 2."

"Oh, that's not hard to do."

"I'm waiting." Her voice vibrates through my chest.

"For?" I give her a squeeze.

"Marvel." Her voice is already sleepy.

"I don't know if we have time for all of it tonight, Little Bird. But in the beginning, there was Captain America . . ."

Somehow, I wake last. It's like my body knows. I push myself back, leaning against the giant trunk of the map tree. Everything we need to do pulses through me, but I take a moment and breathe through it.

Haley's dirty blond hair pops up the ladder. "Hey sleepyhead. I'm proud of you for taking the do-nothing day seriously, but we're going to do something now. Nothing productive, just a little jaunt up the mountain."

I stretch and come down the ladder after her. The rest of the guys are standing around the stove. "What happened to no cooking?"

Dante shrugs and hands me a cup. One of the ones Calvin carved out of a hunk of wood.

"What's this?"

"It's pretend tea." Haley jumps up and down. "Last time we were talking about what food we miss the most—you said tea!"

"This is very much not tea. But it's not water." Dante laughs. "It won't kill you."

"I like it." Haley smiles at me.

I bring it to my lips. It's floral, with an undernote of coconut. But that could just be the cup, though. Everything we eat has coconut in it. I take a sip. It's hot, and that might be where the similarity to tea ends, but when I take another, it's pretty good. "What is it?"

"Young bamboo leaves," Dante says. "Drink up, it's time we get going. I've got the fire out already."

We've been keeping it going night and day. It's a heck of a lot easier in a stove than in a pit in the ground. If we ever see a boat or a low-flying plane, we can grab embers out of the stove and take them to the signal fire.

Watching Dante fill the bottom of the stove with sand, smothering the fire, is . . . well, it sends a nasty pain into the pit of my stomach. I'm not Calvin. I still have hope. Yes, we're well past the twenty-one-day mark. We're closing in on five weeks. Haley wraps her arm around my shoulder. "You ready for the hike?"

"Not a hike. I don't hike. Stroll through the woods.

We're forest bathing," Dante announces, dusting his hands on his pants.

"What the hell is forest bathing? We're in the jungle." Calvin turns to Dante.

"It's where you take the time out of your busy life to notice nature and fuck. It's an article I read on the plane on the way over. I couldn't sleep."

Haley laughs. "Okay, let's get this bath on the trail." We're a few feet down the path when Pepper follows. "No stay here, Pepper. We'll be back soon." Pepper meows and sits down.

"I still wonder where she came from." I shake my head.

We get to the pool and stop to run our hands through it. "Should we take a quick dip?" Dante looks about ready to strip his clothes off.

"I don't want to get sidetracked." Haley runs back to the trail. "Come on, a dip in the waterfall will feel a lot more fun as a reward after the hike."

I grab Haley around the waist and kiss her. "But if it's a do-nothing day, can't we just go straight for the reward?"

"I'm with the redcoat on this one." Dante's got his shirt off.

"No." Haley points to the two of us with her Chief Stew face. "Up you go."

"Right. Up, up, up I go." Dante adjusts himself and takes Haley's hand. "Fine, but I'm walking next to you."

It gets steeper with each passing minute. The vegetation actually changes some as well. There are fewer palm trees and more hardwoods. And when we hit a small clearing where there are only lava rocks, it's drier and a hell of a lot warmer.

I turn around and offer Haley a hand to get up to the ledge I'm standing on.

"Damn, this is a proper mountain."

"I told you, the island is a lot bigger than we first thought. Even after we saw it from the top of the map tree." Calvin nods.

"Whoa." Haley looks around. "What's that over there?" She points to the East. Among the dark rocks, I can see an inky black hole.

"I don't know. That way, though, has a cliff straight down. You can't see over the edge though. There's a wall that goes straight up. But I think it drops right back down on the other side."

"Do you think it's a cave? Like the one you and Easton spent the night in after the fight."

"I . . . maybe? Only one way to find out." Calvin reaches for Haley's hand and helps her up to the next level.

I follow right behind. Calvin's right, there's a sheer cliff that goes straight up. It's the way the rocks are stacked. It takes even more effort to work our way parallel across the mountain. But when we get there, I can hear the ocean on the other side of it. And even crazier yet, there's a cave. This one was a lot bigger than the one Easton and Calvin spent their night in the doghouse in. Haley takes a step into it.

"No," Calvin shouts.

Chapter 5

Reveal Bearing

Sam

Land. Fucking Land. There's a damn reef. And there's nothing I can do about it. Absolutely nothing I can do about it. The squeal of metal against rock tearing at the hull makes my stomach flip. It's raining again. It's like it doesn't know how to stop raining at night. That's great when you have guests on board but not when you're trying to navigate by the stars. Not that I've had control of the yacht for fucking forever. But this hunk of an almost ghost ship has at least had the decency to put me up on a reef next to an island. I've got one flashlight and one solar-powered recharger left. Other than that, everything is dead. I've spent the last weeks getting everything I can out of the ship. And I pitched a hell of a lot over the side of the boat. Anything I might need is here in the wheelhouse.

The wind smashes against the leeward side of the yacht. The waves push us up against the reef a little more with each one. I need to secure the ship. I've been dragging an anchor for weeks. I'm only fucking hoping that now,

now it holds. But I can't count on it. I pull my foul weather jacket closer around me. "Stay here." I point to Penny. She's lying on her bed. Her big eyes stare wide at me. "I mean it." I close the door to the wheelhouse and fight with the wind to latch it. It's fucking blowing. I hold on to the rail. With all the ship's power gone, we've been listing since the first night. Our first miracle, whatever reef grabbed the hull has made the Rock Candy almost level. I'm not naive enough to trust it. I grip the side rail with every step. Peering over the bow, there might be a rock under the surface I can tie off to. But not in these waves, not now. I'll have to wait for light. I fight my way back to the wheelhouse side door. I don't pull off my coat, but I grab a flashlight and head into the belly of the ship. Down the stairs to the engine room. I run the light over the floor. There's a small trail of water running down the middle to what should be to the drain. My light flicks over the silent engines, then I move to the walls. I can't hear any water running, but the stream on the floor is coming from somewhere. Following the line—I find it.

Fuck.

There's a foot-long crack in the interior hull. It's seeping water. It's not a lot. But even a single drip without the pumps running will fill the ship, eventually. This is more than a drip. Far more. I look around the space. Is there anything I haven't stripped out of here? I've got two options: try and patch it to slow the leak or seal the compartment. If I work on the leak, I'm down here in the bilge. Another rogue wave like the one that pushed the Rock Candy up onto the reef and I could be trapped down here in a flipped vessel.

Fuck. Fixing this is just a band-aid. It's got to look a hell of lot worse on the outside. I think of Calvin. He's a genius with things like this. But I didn't get to become captain without dealing with some shit. I can do this.

In the tool cubbies, I find an epoxy kit. It's still in the wrapper. Like so many fucking things on this boat. I tear it open, tossing the plastic and paper wrapper on the floor. Holding the flashlight under my arm, I mix the two parts. Then I smear it over the crack. It's water epoxy. It expands in the crack until the water slows and stops, but it's not a fix. Next to the cubbies, there are several collision patches. They're three-by-three-foot sheets that can be affixed on the outside of the ship with the same epoxy.

Fuck it. I grab one and the supplies I'll need with them. Outside of the engine room, I pull the hatch shut and seal it. If my temporary patch doesn't work, the hatch will slow down the flooding of the ship.

I put the kit down and second-guess myself. I go back and grab the second collision patch. The stairs going up top are straight, which is something I'm grateful for. Not having to fight the angle and the waves is fucking fantastic.

I leave the first patch sheet in the hallway behind the wheelhouse and go back for the second one. I'm sweating under my foul weather gear. When I get back to the wheelhouse, Penny is pacing. "Now? Now you have to go out?"

She jumps at the word out.

"It's raining." I look at her. She hates the rain almost as much as she hates swimming. "You sure?" She barks once and gives me half a sneeze. Her version of *damn human, I said what I said.* "Fine, let's go. I clip her harness on her and take her out the back way through the massive salon and out onto the patio deck. It's where guests would have had most of their dinners. The furniture is all slid to the side, and I've got the turf golf mat weighed down with two of the ugliest horse statues on the planet. Possibly. I might have already pitched the ugliest ones. That night is a bit hard to remember.

The killed tequila bottle lies on the end deck near the stairs to the swim platform. Rolling with the waves. "Go potty." I point.

It's raining sideways when I say it.

Penny looks up at me with her big brown eyes. And sits down.

"Oh, for crying out loud. It's a covered deck. You're hardly getting wet at all. Just go." I don't mean to yell. Really, I don't. I've gone through the twenty-seven stages of grief, and I'm circling back around to the beginning. So much of this feels like a dream. A never-ending nightmare. I've gone from thinking we'll be fine to knowing that I'm going to die to wishing we would just die. To thinking there's hope. To, well, now. At least I have land. But what land? Judging from the few days I've gotten a reading on the stars, we're in a completely different current. A direction no search party would ever look in when they find the rafts. They'll come to the obvious conclusion that the Rock Candy is at the bottom of the ocean. Lost, with no beacon in place.

I just fucking hope Rocky finds the asshole who did this to us. That they slam them in prison for the rest of their fucking life. And then he sues the Aurora Oceanic ship builders, taking them to the cleaners. I glance at Penny. Rain is hitting the side of my face and running down my neck. "Now." I point.

She moves over in slow motion and does her business. When we were on a regular ship, back in the day, one of the crew would take her twice a day to shore if we were able. And if not, she had a small grass pad on the swim platform. This is a big step up in the doggy bougie world.

"Let's go." Back in the wheelhouse, I decide to take one more trip out on the bow. I shine the flashlight at land but see nothing. There's nothing left to do but hang my gear up and hope for the best. I'll see what happens in the morning.

I've been sleeping in the wheelhouse on the floor with Penny. It's easier to wake up and take measurements of the stars. But why sleep on the floor now? "Come on Penny, let's go to a real bed." Whatever happens happens.

I open the door to my cabin. I've pulled so many things out that it's a shitty disaster. I toss the things off the bed and invite my dog up. She looks at me like I'm fucking crazy. Why have we been sleeping on the floor when we could have been in a comfy bed this whole time?

It turns out the sentiment of whatever happens happens is a lot easier to think and a lot harder to implement. I spend a good hour listening to the wind and watching the ceiling. Thinking about my brother Charlie. This is going to be hardest on him. He followed me into the industry. My parents, yeah, not going to think about my mom. Or my dad. Sure as hell not going to spend any time thinking about the round little cheeks of my sister's kids. Lucy's cute chubby toddler cheeks or Henry showing me his muscles. I don't think about Haley's smile or the smell of her hair. Fuck, in my head the rafts were found. They're all back in port. They've taken planes back to the states or wherever they were from. Rockwell has dropped a big check in all their bank accounts. Fuck. Haley's smile. Nope, none of that is going to come into my brain. The wind howls, and I try to not think about what I have to do tomorrow.

I'm up before the sun. Looking out onto the island in front of me is like looking at the wall of Gibraltar. Or the side wall of the Panama Canal. It's a sheer cliff. Straight up. The tide is out, and there's about two, maybe three yards of sand exposed. But that's it. Port and starboard of the ship are about the same, for as far as I can see. I'm on land but I'm not. And I'm leaking.

But there's a few rocks on either side of the reef. Rocks that I might—will—tether to. I can pull myself off the reef and patch the damn hole. I take a deep breath in. I'm not giving up. Not now. Not ever. I need to live. I need to get this boat into the hands of someone who can turn it over for evidence. That's what keeps me going.

I feed Penny more of the chicken. The freezers are now just barely cool. A few more days, and all the meat we have will be gone. But that's tomorrow's problem. "Eat up, fuzz face." I scratch her head and fill my stomach too. It's the last apple. I'm not going to have an issue with food. There's enough canned goods for a year. I might be eating just tomatoes and canned beans, but it's fine.

I change into my wets and find a snorkel and fins and jump into the water.

Penny barks and chases me alongside the swim platform. I know she's not jumping in. She hates water that much. I wave to her, and she settles.

I kick over to the rocks. The water is warm and clear. Reef fish dart about. The water is warm. Another day, I'll swim along the edge of the island and find how far the wall goes. I've seen plenty of islands that are pillars into the sky and nothing more.

Around the other side of the Rock Candy, I see it. The crack in the side. She's resting on the reef. The spots aren't huge, but any hole in a ship isn't good. At low tide, the hole is out of the water. It's going to be tough to patch. But what else can I do? I swim over to the stern of the boat and pull myself up onto the edge of the swim platform. I sit for a moment, my feet dangling over the edge while I take my fins off and look at the ocean behind the Rock Candy. I've come a long way. Stopping now isn't an option. Penny puts her head in my lap, and I ask myself what would Calvin do? Not sit here. "Let's get to work, girl." This going to take a fucking long time. Ropes first, then crash kit.

Back in the water I go.

Chapter 6

Rockfall

Calvin

"No? Why not?" is Haley's response to my telling her she can't go into the cave.

I shake my head. "Come on, if there's something in there, like a boar or a snake, I don't want you getting hurt."

"Cool, I don't want to be hurt. I don't. I don't want you hurt, either. I can carry a sharp stick. But there's no way a boar is up here. Those rocks were loose. If a boar were coming around here, there would be a path. Like on the rest of the island. And we've been on the island a long time and haven't seen a single snake. It's a beautiful sunny day. Why would a snake be hiding in a cave?"

"She's got you there," Zane adds.

"Don't care. Humor me." I cross my arms. If Haley gets hurt, fuck, I can't even think about it.

"I don't like it, but fine." She drops her hands to her sides and sits down on the rock.

"Zane and I will go in and check it out." I have my sharpened walking stick and my knife. Zane has the same. I step in. It's darker than hell. But we didn't bring the flashlight with us. Only the flint and our knives. Dante has a bag of jerky, and we all have one water bottle. We're super careful with them. They're more precious to us than gold. "Ready?" I ask but head right in. Ten feet in, I stand and wait for my eyes to adjust.

"Damn, this is a big cave," Zane says. He's a few feet behind me, and I can still make out his form.

"Yeah." I can practically hear Zane thinking from here. Maybe we should live here. We sure as hell shouldn't. He's almost killed us making our tree house. I'm not moving all our stuff to live in a dark cave. But that's the thing. I've been in caves before. Spelunking is a thing back home. I can see the faintest of light coming from the back of the cave.

"You done exploring? Let's head back out."

"No, I'm not done exploring. Do you see the light from the back of the cave? That shouldn't be there."

"Nope, I do not. I don't see anything back there. It's dark." Zane's British accent gets stronger with any emotion, and right now he sounds like something off the BBC soaps my mom likes to watch.

"It should be pitch black. Let's go."

"Do you not watch movies? You don't go to the back of the dark cave and not expect something shitty to happen to you."

"It's not dark, so we're good."

"No, you're good. Anything back there is going to be scared of you and that mountain man's beard growing on your face. Me, I'm like a tasty snack. Come on." He pivots.

"Zane."

"Calvin?"

"I'm going back there." I turn.

"Fucking bloody hell. There is something totally mental about you Americans."

"You're not wrong. And you watch too many movies. We'll be fine."

"I want to be better than fine. Some do-nothing day this is turning out to be. Can you try not to stab me with your stick or your knife? Or anything else you have."

I grunt. "No promises." I feel bad that the machete stabbed his foot. But I'm not going to keep apologizing for it.

"Is there anything in there?" Haley's standing at the entrance.

"Give us a minute."

"There's nothing in here, Haley." Zane yells over his shoulder.

"Cool, I'm coming in."

A few seconds later, she walks right into me, her hands extended out in front of herself.

I want to grab her and march her out. But she's right. If there was something in here, it would already have come out of hiding. "Let your eyes adjust."

"Okay, what's back there?" She heads straight for the back of the cave.

"Hold on there, Little Bird. Just give your eyes a chance to adjust."

I take Haley by the hand. "Can you see anything yet? Just look into the cave, not back outside."

"Yeah, why isn't it completely dark back there? There's light coming in from somewhere."

"Yup. I was about to go back there when you came in."

"Let's do it!" She's got her pep back. I fucking hate pep. But not from her, which is damn weird.

"Hold on to my waistband. I'll lead us in." Step after step, we move in a straight line. The air cools, and the dampening silence hurts my ears. The three of us just naturally stop talking. The cave turns toward the ocean, slanting down. There's a dim light, just enough I can see my hand in front of my face. Patting the air in front of me, I keep from running into anything. With each step, the walls come closer until I have to duck, and then crouch, but the light gets brighter. Not so bright as to see. We go on and on. I'm crawling. And I stop.

"Can't you go farther?"

"Do you want to go more?" Haley asks. "Because I sure as hell do. This is the best do-nothing day ever."

"Right. I bet you I have a different description of what the best 'do-nothing' day is," I say, trying to lighten the mood as we move slowly forward.

"Oh, come on, Calvin," she retorts playfully. Her fingers wrap around my calf.

"This is fine," I insist, a little defensively. Damn, I would do anything for this woman.

"Fun, even," adds Zane from behind, his voice a bit muffled. "I'm having a good time." His tone changes subtly. "But then again, Haley can make any day better."

I swallow hard. The truth in his words rings. We inch forward, the atmosphere around us shifting subtly.

There's a breeze picking up from up ahead, ever so slight yet distinctly noticeable. It smells different, feels different—the air carries more humidity. The bottom of the tunnel even feels more sand-like and less gravelly.

"I think we're finding something. There's definitely something up ahead," I say, more to myself than anyone else. "There's definitely sky up ahead."

The tunnel we're in continues forward, narrowing even further. Now I'm army crawling, leading the way. I might not be the best person for this, but I'd never let Haley take the lead. If anyone's going to tumble into an unknown crevasse, it'll be me, not her. Not that I'm planning on falling into the ocean today.

My knees are raw from the rugged ground, my palms speckled with little bits of gravel embedded in the skin. But I can still feel Haley's fingers brushing against my calves every so often, gently propelling me forward.

The tunnel shifts yet again, veering to the left. Now it's a little brighter, and I'm slithering like a snake. I can finally see my hands in front of my face.

"We're getting there," I call out, my voice echoing slightly. There are flashes of sunlight. It fucking hurts my eyes.

"Good, good," Zane replies, though his voice sounds far away. Given the length of our elongated bodies in this narrow space, he's probably not even around the last bend yet. He definitely wants this adventure over, but he, like me, would do anything for Haley.

Crawling forward, I come up to a section where a boulder has wedged itself, leaving a tiny sliver of daylight shining between it and the rest of the ceiling. I cock my head sideways, closing one eye to get a clearer view.

It's the ocean. Haley was right—this tunnel cuts through to the ocean. I can see waves crashing below. Curiously, I cock my head to the left, closing my right eye and using just my left.

And then I see something unexpected out there. "What the fuck is that?" I exclaim, my voice a mix of wonder and apprehension.

"What is it?"

"A fucking boat." Just the aft is all I can see. I think.

"You're kidding me?" Her voice rises. "You're not kidding. What kind of boat?"

I turn my head to the left, closing my right eye again. But all I can see is the aft. "It's got a swim platform." I turn my head the other way. But I can't see anything but the other side of the damn swim platform. And it's pissing me off.

"Is it the Rock Candy?" Her words come out in heady breaths.

"I . . . fuck if I know." Maybe. Probably.

"What other yacht would be sitting on the same island as us?"

I'm both hopeful and fucking fearful. Sam is my friend. I've worked with him for years, and honestly, he's more than my captain. I could have moved on a long time ago. But I didn't. He's good people. And we're all fucking Haley. He can't have her back. I'll fight him for what's ours. Is he alive, even? Damn, I hope so. I don't like a lot of people, but I like Sam, and his damn dog too.

I have no idea what really happened to the Rock Candy. I've been thinking about it for weeks, tumbling it over and over with no evidence. How the hell could I ever get a real answer?

I can't. Left eye closed. The same view. Right eye closed. Same.

"I want to see." Haley's tugging on my calf.

"Hold on. Back up a bit. I want to push on this rock. Maybe I can get a better view." They do. And I push. And no matter how much I strain against it, I can't make it budge. It's just a small sliver.

"Yeah, well, that's going to be hard. Back it on up." It takes a minute for us to get to a spot where we can switch positions. Do I want her going in first? Fuck no. The rock didn't move for me, but that doesn't mean they can't move.

"What did you see exactly?" Haley asks.

"The aft of a super yacht. But only this much." I hold my finger up. We're still lying on the ground.

Zane's nod is a dark blur. "Right. Let Haley go first. Her head isn't as swollen as yours." He laughs.

Haley climbs over me. And yes, I very much enjoy the process. And hold on to her a little as she does.

I roll back onto all fours and army crawl behind her. When she gets to the edge of the rocks, I have one hand around each of her ankles.

"Ease up a little there, Captain America. I need a couple more inches to see."

"What do you see, Haley?" Zane calls behind me.

"The swim platform. But when I squish my head up to the top of the cave, I can see a little green on the back. Like a . . . I don't know."

"A golf turf." Zane calls from behind me. "Like you might use to let a dog go wee?"

"Yes. Ow, fucking hell, that hurts," I say. I've got a nice scrape on my ear now.

"Come out, Haley. Let's try something else." We get to the place where Haley climbed over me last time, and as much as I liked it, I'm not doing it again. "A little more, Zane." We back up far enough to lie side by side. "I want to go back in and push with my legs. Zane can hold on to my hands."

"Fuck no. I've seen this movie too. I'm strong, but not strong enough to hold up your fat ass like some swinging trapeze artist. Or a cartoon."

"I'm not going to fall out."

"No." Haley and Zane say together.

I grunt.

"I can't see his face, but he's doing it, isn't he?" Haley says.

"Absolutely. Fucking yes, he is." Zane replies.

"He's not going to listen to us, is he?"

"Nope." Zane sighs.

"Fuck," Haley breathes.

We're back in position. This time my legs are on the rock. My back is to the ground. Zane's holding on to my arms, and Haley's gone outside telling the others. What a shithead I am. Like they don't already know. "Tell me again how you think pushing that thing out isn't going to make this tunnel collapse?" Zane asks.

I tilt my head in the sand. "No. One, two, three." And I push.

Chapter 7

Visual Bearing

Haley

"Sassy, slow the fuck down."

Right. I take in a deep breath and pinch my eyes shut. "We got through to where we could see the ocean. And there's a boat. We couldn't make out the whole thing. Actually, we could only see the aft."

Dante jumps. "It's the Rock Candy?"

"That's what I was trying to tell you. The hole, it's too small. Calvin had a boneheaded idea to get at it with his foot and kick at the rock. To see if it will move. Zane and I told him no. The only fucking thing that's going to fall is Calvin." I'm trying not to hyperventilate. Really, I am.

"What the fuck?" Easton's ready to charge by me. I grab his hand. "Stop. The spot next to the cliff only fits one person. No, go. Go. What if it collapses on Zane too?"

We all race in. I take Easton's hand, and we train in like I did between Calvin and Zane last time.

"Fuck, it's cold in here, Sassy." Dante's right behind me, his warm breath in my ear.

"Yeah, it gets warmer the closer to the opening."

"Zane, Zane." I call out.

"We're here. We're mostly okay, Little Bird." His voice is soft. "Stay there. We're coming out."

I cup my hands. "What do you mean, you're mostly okay?"

"I mean, we're coming now," Zane says.

Zane backs out first. It's dark, and while we can't see anything, I know it's him. Then Calvin.

"Fucking shit," Calvin says.

"You're hurt. Why don't you listen to me?"

"It's not bad. Nothing broken. I'm not even bleeding, just a bunch of bruises, Chiefie. I'm good. But we're fucking even better. That's no boat down there. It's the mother fucking Rock Candy," Calvin exclaims.

I'm so torn. I want to help Calvin, but I want to go see the ship. Sam. "Sam. The captain."

They all laugh in some form. Calvin grunts, I think, but that might be the bruises. "I didn't see him. But it's tied up to the reef. Someone tied it up."

"We need to get his attention. Make him hear us."

"Agreed." Calvin grunts. "I'm going back out to the mountain." He doesn't say it, but he implies to check out the damage to his leg.

"I'll go with you," Easton says. "This is fucking fantastic news about the ship." There's something in his tone that confuses me.

"I don't need your help, Rockwell."

"Didn't say you did," Easton answers.

"Good," Calvin grunts.

"Good," I say with more enthusiasm.

I can hear them grumbling to each other as they head to the front of the cave.

"There's a lot more rubble on the ground now, Little Bird. Be careful. And stay clear of the edge. I'm going to keep my hands around your ankles. You can go next, Dante. It's best if you stay here. You won't see anything, anyway."

"Aye, Aye—" Dante leaves off the captain.

My heart is racing as I crawl and then slither to the edge. My palms are getting cut up. The rocks are sharp, and there are far more pebbles than sand now. But whoa, the hole is a lot bigger. A few more months on the island with no pizza or ice cream and I might be able to fit through it. I'm not scared of heights, but I don't want to get too close. Calvin was right; it's the Rock Candy. She's tethered at three points, two on the reef and one to the cliff.

But there's no one on deck. Maybe Sam's climbed the wall and is on the island now. "Sam," I call out. It's like the wind picks up my voice and shoves it back down my throat. I might as well be a mouse crying at the bottom of the Grand Canyon. "Sam." I cup my hands around my mouth and try again. Still nothing. Over and over until my vocal cords cry out for help on their own. I take in a big breath and blow it out as loud as I can. "Helloooo."

On the wind, I hear it. A single bark. And from around the side of the ship, she trots. Penny. What a good girl. "Pennyyy." She looks right at me. And barks again. "Up here Penny." Good dog. "You're such a pretty, pretty princess. Up here. Keep barking."

I see her mouth move, but the wind is blowing between us against the cliff. Her head is up, and she barks and barks. I can't hear her. Maybe that means she can hear me better. "That's it, girl. Helloooo. Pennyyy." I can't hear a darn thing over the wind. And then Sam appears around the end of the boat, and I freeze. I can't. I can't. He's alive and walking around, and my heart just seizes. "Sam, up here. Up here."

Penny looks. She's staring right at me. I wave my hand out the hole, scooching forward. Gravel falls out of the opening.

"That's far enough, Little Bird. Keep yelling, but don't get close to the edge." Zane's voice rumbles around me.

"Sam."

He crouches next to Penny, and I will him with everything I have to look up. "Look up at me. We're here. I'm here. We're going to get you. You're not alone anymore. Sam."

He takes Penny by the collar and walks her to the wheelhouse.

"Nooo. Sam."

Penny turns. I see her pull on her collar. But he's not having it. He tucks her away in the wheelhouse and disappears around the side of the ship.

"Sam!"

"Does the captain see you? What is he doing?" Zane's talking, but I can't hear him. I can't process what he's saying. It's like I'm underwater. When I pull away from the hole, the quiet of the cavern takes over. It's pushing on my insides. I can't handle it. This is all too much. He's alive. Alive and alone. And how are we ever going to get to him? I take a breath. That's not me, that's fear talking. We can do hard things. I can do hard things. Easton is a champion swimmer. He might be able to round the side of the island. Or we can make something. Or . . . I take off my crew jacket. It's hard to pull the sleeves off, but I do. I tie them in a knot. I inch forward with care. There are jagged rocks around the outside of the hole. But I find one and push the sleeves tightly down into a crevasse and push the rest of the jacket out. It's not going to go anywhere. And if he sees it, I have a whole lot of clothes down there that smell a hell of a lot better than this thing does.

"Sam." I yell one more time. I know he can't hear me, but I have to try. I should let Dante see. It's a ray of hope. Not that the Rock Candy looks like she can take us anywhere, but she can sure make life a whole lot more comfortable. There's a twist in my gut because I know getting off the island isn't going to happen anytime soon. And I'm not naïve. Things are going to get awkward. Uncomfortable, messy. But I want him to know we're here. I want to see him. Touch him. Know that he's in one piece.

"No. He didn't hear me. I'm coming back. We should let Dante see." I crawl backwards. My knees are scraped, and there's a cut on my left hand. I make a fist, holding the blood in. Letting my palm fill in the darkness. I tell them everything I saw. "You should look, Dante. Maybe with your deep voice, he can hear you. Or maybe if Penny keeps barking."

"It's okay Little Bird. He'll see your jacket. That was smart. And you know we're going to find a way to get to him."

I nod, even though I know they can't see me.

"Wish me luck," Dante says.

"I'm staying with him. Is that okay? I want to hold his ankles."

"Yes. Please."

"I'm not going to practice cliff diving. I could have done that in Greece last year, and I passed on it." Dante's voice trails off as he crawls down the cavern.

I make my way out, first crawling on all fours, then crouching, then ducking. When I walk out, Calvin is sitting on a rock at the entrance. I blink at the sunlight shining behind him. His shorts are off. His shirt too. He's washing the side of his leg with water. I want to both hug him and kick him.

"I know. I know you told me I might get hurt. But it worked, and I'm just bashed up. I'm not really hurt."

I look at Easton because he's going to give me the truth. He shrugs. "He's not. It's just a deep bruise. This is exactly what I went to school for. I can even give him some exercises to speed up his recovery."

"Just what everyone wants, to be stuck on a fucking island and still have to do their physical therapy."

"I could push him down the mountain. We wouldn't really miss him that much." Easton laughs and quickly steps back.

"What did you see, Chiefie?" Calvin pulls his shirt back on.

"Penny barked at me. But Sam didn't see me. He came out onto the bow and took her back inside."

"She likes to bark at seagulls. Drives him crazy. He probably thought that's what she was doing."

"I've been thinking. You didn't want to use the flare gun before, but now? When there's a shit ton of more supplies down there on the ship. If we wait until tonight at dusk and bring the flashlight, we could get his attention. Shit, the flashlight alone should be enough." Easton crosses his arms over his chest. "We could run back to camp and get the supplies and do it tonight."

"Think about what you just said, Swimmer Boy." Calvin leans back on the rock.

"Right, Zane's foot, which is not injured as he says, your leg, Haley's ankle, Dante's hatred of hiking. Fine, I'll run back to camp and get the supplies."

"I don't like it. I'm not sure I want any of us up here at night." He's got that growly tone to his voice. The one that's all "you will listen to me." It drives me nuts because my body is like, okay, whatever you want, Calvin. But my brain wants me to clock him sideways with a rolled-up newspaper.

"You mean you don't want me up here at night?" I blink at Calvin and cross my arms over my chest. Two can play that game.

"Yes, that is exactly what I mean. It's going to get cold."

"So we start a fire. We brought the flint." There's not much firewood around here, but I'm not going to point that out.

"We only have enough food for one meal." He cocks his head to the sack he carried up the mountain.

"So Easton brings back more jerky." I'm going to have an answer for every darn problem he comes up with. "What if the boat's not here tomorrow?"

"Well then, Sam's a fool. If he has any chance of survival, he's trying to get the radios back online. And when he does that, they'll send a plane. We've got our SOS on our beach, and we've got our signal fire ready to go. We do this the right way."

"Your way isn't always the right way, Calvin." I turn to Easton for a little help.

"I don't know, Haley. He's got some valid points." Easton comes back.

"I swear, sometimes I liked it better when the two of you were at each other's throats."

"You like when we're down your throat better," Easton says. Easton. I'm doomed. Every day, they're a little more alike.

I glare at him.

But Calvin's laughing, and I can't keep a straight face. "Tomorrow, damn you both."

"I'm pretty sure that's already happened." Calvin wiggles his eyebrows at me.

Chapter 8

Warning Shot

Dante

She's down there—my favorite knife. I guess the captain too. Spices. Fuck, clean clothes, chocolate for Sassy. I'm drooling like a culinary student at their first Michelin star meal. Damn, the Rock Candy looks like shit. Even from here, I can see the mildew over her. It takes a full deck crew to keep a mega yacht looking like a mega yacht. And right now, she looks more like something that's ready to sink and make an artificial reef. There are lines tied up to her, keeping her aft from swinging. One rogue wave, and I'm not betting on them.

Thyme. No, chili powder. No, pepper. If I only had like five minutes, what would I grab? I tilt my head to the left. "Sam." I project with as much South Side attitude as I can. This boy who grew up with nothing knew how to yell. That's for sure. Haley's right. I can hear Penny barking. But she's inside somewhere. And it's just a faint yap. If I didn't know any better, I wouldn't be able to hear anything at all.

"Sam." It doesn't even feel like it's coming out of my

body. Haley's jacket is waving in the breeze. "Treat," I call out. I'm pretty sure the barking gets more intent. "Treat." I wait. I twitch my leg. Zane's sweaty grip is giving me an itch. It's taking a Herculean effort to not kick the Brit in the head. I'm not jumping or slipping. I'll give it one more try. "Cheese."

Fucking hell, that did it. It's like the dog has gone feral. I still can't see her, but she's making more noise than the five accountant passengers I had for my last cruise last season. Fucking accountants. It's the quiet ones who cause the most problems.

"Cheese."

The dog howls, long. But Sam doesn't appear. And the dog quiets down.

I want to bang my head against the wall. This isn't happening. Whatever Sam is working on has got him completely occupied.

I crawl back to Zane.

"Any luck?" he asks.

"I got the dog to bark. But nothing else."

I blink as we come out into the sun. Haley's eyes are wide. "Did you get his attention?"

"No, but if you say cheese, the dog goes nuts."

"That tracks." Calvin nods.

"Damn, your leg looks like shit, Green." I nod at Calvin.

"Thanks." He cocks his eyebrows at me.

I look around the group. "Now what's the plan?"

"Back home. We'll try again tomorrow." Calvin picks up the pack.

It takes us longer than it should to get back. And I'm definitely not used to being the fast one in a hike. It is not that I'm not fit. I go to the gym. I run on a treadmill like God intended. Not outside. But the way we are now, I'm the least fucked up. And that's only because they don't know I'm still getting dizzy spells. Which is fine. There's nothing they can do about them. So there's no reason to talk about them. And that's how I'm going to leave it.

The stove is cold when we get back, but Pepper is sitting waiting. She's got a dead mouse that she trots over to Haley and leaves at her feet. "Thank you?" Haley pets the cat behind its ears, and Pepper purrs and climbs up the tree.

"Someone's happy we're home." I give Haley a hug around her shoulder.

"I just think we should have stayed and tried to use the flashlight. He's never going to see us during the day." She blinks up at me.

"Easton and I could head back."

"No, I should go. You don't know morse code. How's he going to know it's us? He might think it's pirates or who knows what. In the dark, we're just going to be heads sticking out of the cliff side."

"I know morse code. Cool down, Zane should chill. But we should leave now." I turn to Easton.

Calvin looks at the rest of us like we're babbling in another language. "I don't like it. But fine. The flashlight's in the dry bag. I'll light the stove, then you can take the flint and the flashlight."

Haley hurries around, making us some food.

"If you're not back by midday, we'll come up to you," Calvin says as he hands me the pack of food that I made. I take it from him and try not to do a very Calvin-like growl.

We're past the waterfall pool and heading up the mountain by the time Easton starts to get talkative. "Do we have a plan?"

"I flash SOS with the flashlight until he sees it or we run out of batteries."

"Remind me how to do it." Easton asks.

"Short, short, short, long, long, long, short, short, short."

"Okay, got it." He does it.

"Good, we can take turns." I nod. I've been racking my brain what to signal if we manage to make contact. I'm figuring R-A-F-T might work the best.

Easton and I make quick work of getting back to the cave. On our way there, we gather as much firewood as we could. Maybe the smoke floating down over the cliff might get his attention?

I start the fire outside the cave's mouth. When I open the pack, Haley has thrown in a towel. I have a feeling if she could, she would have given us a cushion too. I hold the towel up for Easton to see.

He laughs. "I was wondering why the thing was so damn big."

I hand him a piece of jerky.

"Thanks."

I nod and eat one myself. I'm getting pretty damn good at getting a fire going. The two of us sit around it. It is going good and strong by the time the sun has started to set. It's dark but not completely. "You ready to do this?"

"Yeah. It's about time. I'm good if you're good," Easton says.

"Let's do it." The tunnel is long and dark but somehow a little less intimidating with a flashlight in my back pocket. "I'm in position," I say as much over my shoulder as is possible. "He's not outside, and neither is the dog."

I start off with a string of words, "Sam, hey, Penny, cheese, treat." Then I just start singing, loud and crazy. Bruce Springsteen's "Born in the USA" is the first thing that pops into my mind, so I just go with it. Then I switch to Gwen Stefani's "Hollaback Girl." Nothing. When I stop singing, I wait a minute and listen. It's silent. Maybe a bark, but I can't tell. The wind is blowing right at the cliff. Which fucking sucks for two reasons. One, I'm fucking done with lying in a dark in a cave with a rock sticking in my junk. And two, I'm shining the flashlight as much on the wheelhouse as I can. I've been at it for a long time, and it's getting darker and darker. There are no lights on inside the boat. If I didn't know that Haley had seen them, and if I hadn't heard the dog bark before, I'd really have thought it was a ghost ship.

I stop the rhythmic flashing of SOS and just wave the light around the glass in the cockpit.

Nothing.

I've scared some birds away, and that's about it.

I turn the flashlight off. "I think Sam must be sleeping or working down below on something." I say to Easton. I put my head down and rest my chin on my arm. This position is like holding a yoga pose for too long. I'm exhausted. Nature, hiking, it's not my jam. A forty-five-minute SoulCycle class is way more my speed. Plus, looking at nice, toned asses doesn't hurt.

"What do you see?"

"The ocean, a few seagulls, and a 200-million-dollar paper weight. No Sam, no Penny. It's fucking frustrating."

"Let me take a turn." Easton pulls on my ankles.

"Yeah, whatever, sure." I ease out of the little demon hole, scratched up. I'm sure I've got a layer of gravel pushed deep into my skin. I'll be picking at it for weeks. I get to the first spot where we can shimmy around each other. "Keep going. I don't need to feel your ass rub against mine."

Easton backs up to where we can maneuver around each other on our hands and knees.

"Here's the flashlight." I hand it off to him like a relay racer. I eye the small sack in his hand. "What's that?"

"The flare gun."

"Don't fucking point the flare gun at the ship. You could start a fire."

"I'm not stupid."

"Don't use it unless you really think it's necessary."

"Again, not stupid."

I blink at him. I've seen him antagonize Calvin when he knew it was going to make him explode. Not that I'm against antagonizing Calvin. I just do it with more finesse. "Right. Don't shoot yourself, either. Haley would be fucking pissed at me."

"Anything else, Mom?"

"Yeah, wear sunscreen and use a condom."

"We don't have either."

"Fair."

Easton crawls forward, and I lie on my stomach, gripping his legs. It's sweaty and gross. I'm looking up at his ass. It's weird. I've been bi forever. Sometimes I act on it more, sometimes less. But I'll always be bi. The guys here are all good looking, but I have zero interest in any of them. Haley's the only one that makes my dick hard at all. Fucking hell. Even thinking her name has me getting hard now. And that's not something I want. Seconds feel like minutes. Minutes feel like hours. I'm barely holding on to Easton's sweaty legs.

He's hollering something, but his words are lost to the wind. Then I hear it. Easton's singing rumbles back down the cavern—a sound so discordant, I swear he's going to scare away every fish and bird within a hundred-mile radius. But as long as he gets Penny's delicate ears twitching, I don't care. If only she would start barking again, like she did yesterday.

"Easton! Are you flashing the light?" I yell over the cacophony.

"I'm doing it!" he yells back. "I'm doing S-O-S, then R-A-F-T."

"Well, stop it. Don't waste the light if you don't see them. Just keep making noise."

His voice is relentless, a constant in the chaotic night. I catch only fragments of his words. "What's that?" I strain to hear him over the sound of the waves.

"The scarf song by Taylor Swift. Fucking love her."

"Of course you do. Everyone loves her." Only assholes rag on Taylor Swift. *"Teardrops on My Guitar," my ass*, my dad used to complain. But he was an asshole. "Keep going, keep singing," I urge him, desperate to maintain our presence in the overwhelming darkness.

His voice falters, then rises again in a shout. "Sam!"

"How're your lungs?" I ask, trying to gauge our chances.

"Good. I've got swimmer's lungs. I can do this all night if we have to."

"Oh lord," I mutter to myself. "I can't take it all night. But it is what it is? We have to get his attention."

Calvin theorized there's still an inflatable stashed in the back. The Toy Hauler room off of the swim platform was a mess. They never had enough time to organize everything, thanks to the negligent decision of Rocky not wanting to wait.

Sam has enough experience. He should have known better. We never should have left port. And I should have spoken up, should have walked away. But in the yachting world, reputation is everything. Become known as the chef who walks off a job, and you're finished.

"Keep singing!" I shout at Easton, gripping his legs for support.

"I'm doing it!" he replies.

We've been at this for an hour, Easton belting out every song from Taylor Swift's *Reputation* and half of *Red*, including the ten-minute scarf song, twice.

"How's the flashlight holding up?" I call out.

"You told me to stop using it," he responds. "Make up your mind."

A shiver of frustration vibrates through me. "We've got to call it. This isn't working. He must be down below. We'll try again some other time."

"He might come out," Easton says, hope threading his voice.

"We'll try again later. Tomorrow," I say, resigned.

Then, another popping noise. I swear, if that's what I think it is, Easton's going to have another thing coming—not Calvin's fist . . . but mine.

Chapter 9

Morse Code

Sam

"For Pete's sake, Penny. I fucking love you, but you need to calm your shit down. There are birds outside. I know you like birds. But just stop." I'm exhausted. Penny has been out of her mind. I had to keep her in my cabin yesterday while I worked tracing the electrical issue to bypass the motherboard. I had repaired a wire that the damn saboteur cut as well. Yes, I should work on the radios some more. But I'm not a fucking engineer. There's nothing in the manuals. And Penny. Even when I went to sleep, she was going crazy. I went as far to grab a pair of the engine room earmuffs. Lumpy as hell to sleep in. But when your dog goes completely batshit? What am I supposed to do? I'm fucking exhausted. There are five hundred things I could do. And none of them have worked.

She jumps up onto my chest and licks my face.

"What in the hell has gotten into you?" I crouch and rub her ears. "You want to go play with the ball?" I glance outside. It's low tide. Our whole five feet of sandy beach is exposed. I try to take her out every other day. It's a battle.

She hates the vest and the ocean. Hates being in the water. Retrievers and poodles are supposed to love the water, but not her. It's most likely because my ex's parents had a Shiba Inu when Penny was a puppy. They hate water, and Penny thought that dog was Taylor Swift and Oprah combined. "Fine, you want to go outside and run in the sand? Roll in some seaweed?" I wouldn't mind standing on some land myself. Even if the tidal sand is mushy. Being on terra-mostly-firma feels good. It makes me almost believe there might be a way out of all of this. I grab a few balls and put them in the back of my wet shorts.

I'd planned on checking the collision patch anyway. It's holding well, at least as of two days ago. Even still, the engine room is wet and I've been spending a few hours a day bailing. Fucking not fun. I certainly don't love it. I'm not going to lie. But it's keeping a roof over our heads until I can figure out how to get one of the damn radios working. So far, I've got nothing.

I check the solar battery panel on the back of the boat. The ones built into the ship were fried with the lightning strike. But one I found in the crew cabins works when the ship is in the sun. Which isn't often with the damn cliff blocking it for most of the day.

"Let's go, Penny." I snap her life vest on. She hates it. But it's the only way I'm getting her to shore. It would be a much shorter swim if I could get her to jump off the bow. But yeah. That's not happening. No way she would ever do it, and the reef isn't far enough under this to not be in danger of hitting it again. As it is, I'm adjusting the ropes every day. There's a sweet spot. At least it's been a sweet spot so far. I jump off the back and hold her leash. Some days I have to give her the slightest of tugs to get her in the water. Though not today. She splashes in like a toddler on a hot summer day.

"Who are you and what have you done with my dog?"

She's paddling with all her might toward the beach. Most days I have to part carry her, part tug her. Crazy. "Okay, slow down, you." But she's not listening. Her feet are on the sand. Before I get there, she shakes off the water. The vest rattles, and she sits and barks again.

"Enough with the barking, Penny. Cool it."

She glances back at me and then at the cliff.

"I told you, you can't get those birds . . . what the hell is that?" There's a piece of fabric hanging down from the cliff. I crank my neck back, but all I see is the white cloth flapping in the breeze. My head goes to possible answers. A helium balloon seems to be the most reasonable. Or a bird building a nest with trash. Like a really big bird. I glance up. I fucking don't need to be shat on by something that is big enough to haul that up there.

"What is it, Penny? Is that what you've been barking at? I take back all those horrible things I said about you. Well, most of them." I scratch behind her ears and take the ball out of my pocket. "You want this?"

She looks at me and then at the cliff and back at the ball. Her head cocks. I can hear her saying humans are so stupid. Then she jumps and runs, and I throw the ball—for a good hour, until our little bit of sand disappears for another twelve hours. "Time to go, girl. We'll play ball again tomorrow."

Penny takes another look at the thing on the cliff before we head back. I yank her up onto the swim platform. She's a sixty-pound wiggling dog with another twenty pounds of water stuck in her goldendoodle fur, equal to 200 pounds by my math. Then again, I did feed her almost a whole chicken a day for a few weeks. It's possible she's up ten pounds. I strip the life vest off and take her towel from the back of the deck. After the crew left, while the boat listed along for a while, I tried to keep the boat guest ready. Then I snapped. Threw almost every damn horse statue overboard. All but the few that are keeping Penny's pee pad from sliding off the back from a wave. Though the few big waves we've had over the aft have cleaned things up a bit.

"You ready for dinner?"

She gives a happy bark. It's like now that I've seen the thing hanging off the cliff, she's happy enough to go about her day. "It's back to kibble for you, girl." The fresh food is mostly gone. But she doesn't mind. I've moved her things to the chef's galley. I let her eat while I go out back and scrub my plates from yesterday in the ocean. I watch some reef fish grab at the few grains of rice that drift off my plate. And it's crazy. It sounds like someone is singing. That happened once before. In the first week, I found an old school mp3 player in one of the crew cabins. In the rolling waves, something had slid and clicked it on. But damn, I really thought I'd gone through the entire ship, that I'd collected everything I could find. I stand up and wipe my hands on my beach towel.

Penny's done by the time I eat half a can of beans from the can. I drink some water. I'm done with the tequila and the whiskey too. I lost a good few days to them. No, I need to go back to the electrical. Then I remember the thing on the cliff. In the wheelhouse, I grab my binoculars. The sun is starting to go down. Another hour and I'll light a few candles and spend some time reading the oh-so-not-thrilling ship manuals. It's an exciting life.

I pull on my crew warm-up jacket too and head out to the bow. I bring binoculars to my eyes. It's not a balloon or trash. It's cloth. That's . . . I put the binoculars down and look at my chest. Then I look at the white flapping fabric again. My heart thuds. What, how? That's a Rock Candy crew jacket in the middle of a cliff. Did one of the rafts land here? Did they fall from the cliff? Did a rogue wave carry debris up? I shake my head at the last one. Impossible, without a tidal wave, and that's something I would have known about. I focus on the jacket. There's a hole next to it. It's not big, but it's there. "How in the hell?" I scan to the top of the cliff. It rises another fifty feet. Then a light flashes. A mirror catching the last of the setting sun.

"I'm here." I wave. Like they can fucking see me. I don't know who it is. Or which raft, the first or second to launch. Honestly, I only know that Calvin, Dante, Zane, and Haley were on the second raft.

The mirror drops, and Rocky's son Easton's head appears. Which raft was he on? I have no idea. He waves his hand excitedly but then is gone. *Fuck, fuck, fuck.* I race into the wheelhouse and find the strongest of the flashlights I have and run back to the bow. I lift the binoculars to the hole in the cliff. I'm hoping to see either Calvin or Anders poke their heads out. Either one of them should know morse code. It's not required for certification anymore. But both of them are the type to go above and beyond.

My heart waits for the next beat. Part of me wants it to be Anders, which would mean Haley is safe. Or at least floating somewhere in the middle of the ocean. The other part wants to see the raft with Calvin, because with enough time, I know the two of us can get the Rock Candy going good enough to get her to limp to port. And that's all we need. Or a fucking radio. A radio would be amazing.

Nothing.

Finally, there's a little movement. And it's neither

Calvin nor Anders but Dante the chef. I make a mental tally—Zane, Calvin, and Haley. Haley. Fuck, I want her safely back on the mainland. At least she's not drifting in a raft.

Dante flashes a flashlight that's on its last bit of power. At first, I assume he's just randomly flipping it on and off. But no. He's using code.

dit dah dit dit / dit dit / dit dit dit dah /dit / dah dit dah dit / dit dah / dah dah / dit dah dah dit / dah / dah dah dah / dit dah dah / dit / dit dit dit / dah

Okay, okay. I look down at the beach. Five camps to the west. Five. Easton, Dante, Calvin, Zane, and Haley. Five.

I glare at the wall.

I send back: O-K. Then I pause. I haven't gotten the inflatable together yet. There had been no reason to.

I hold the binoculars up, and Dante gives me a big thumbs up. And starts signaling again.

Bring . . . then his head disappears. I can just hear the chef murmuring. He's yelling at Easton and whomever is with him.

He's back. "S-P-I-C-E-S, B-L-A-N-K-E-T-S, S-O-A-P, L-U—" He's gone again.

But then he's back. And fuck, I should be writing this down. C-L-O-T-H-E-S, C-H-E-F K-N-I-V-E-S, R-A-Z-O-R-S, S-H-A-M-P-O-O, T-O-I-L-E-T-R-I-E-S, T-O-O-L-K-I-T, T-H-E W-H-O-L-E D-A-M-N B-O-A-T.

I signal back. "Will try." He gives me a big thumbs up.

I've thought about inflating the spare inflatable for a while. But I haven't had the need to. I lost one of the inflatable docks to the sharp rocks on the reef. I figured if there was anyone on this island, I would have seen them by now. The only reason to leave the ship would be if I needed something, which I haven't. I debate if I should gather all the things on Easton's shopping list. Their camp might not be close by, and if it's not, it could take a lot of trips back and forth. Plus, with six of us living on Rock Candy, we would run out of water quickly. No, if they've made camp, it's better I bring supplies to them for now. Then we can figure out how to fix the Rock Candy and finally get off this hunk of rock. I look up at where Dante is, but he's gone. Probably to the west, going back to tell the others.

Excitement bubbles inside me. It's like the first day of charter or pulling off an amazing docking. This is going to be good. Oh, so good. We're going to get her running and out of here.

Chapter 10

Territorial Waters

Calvin

"Pass me that board, Easton." I hold out my hand.

"Here," He says. It's a green-stained one. The way they are fitting together makes it look like one of those bougie designs where everything doesn't match, so it looks good. Then again, Zane spent the last hour laying the boards out where he wanted them. For a guy who's never done this before, he's good at it.

"Glad you could do that without shooting off by mistake," I say taking the board.

"Listen, I didn't mean to fire the flare gun. I was trying to get the flashlight to turn off." Easton glares at me.

Right, he's told us twice. Whatever. It happened. At least he didn't set the Rock Candy on fire.

"Remind me why we're doing this again? Captain's coming, and we can head back to the ship." Easton crawls to the next position.

I stop and focus on Zane. He's marking and measuring

another board. We're almost done. Though if the captain brings the toolkit, we'll have a saw. A real one. Or at least a sharper one. The one we have from the derelict trunk is good, but dull.

And suddenly I can't remember if we've told him what a piece of shit the Rock Candy was before we left port. Anders spent most of the repositioning cruise trying to fix the problem with the electrical, and that was before the issue with the stabilizers hit. I can't even begin to understand why we had a complete system failure. Why did the power stop working and the engines shut down? It's kept me awake at night, as I comb through everything I remember. And because I don't forget much, it's haunting me. Day and night, when I'm not moving. Before the Rock Candy showed up on our island, I was getting close to pushing it out. But not now. Now, it's at the forefront, which is why I'm not with Haley and Dante. They're sitting on the beach waiting for the captain whenever he shows up.

"Fixing the ship isn't going to be easy. There's no unplugging it and plugging it back in. It's going to need an overhaul. We can't take it back out in the open seas, not with the issues we were having. Not to mention it sat for a long time with systems off. Things that worked when the engines shut down aren't going to work now. That's fucking nuts. The captain has been on board now for a long time. With us all on board, we'd run out of water in a week. What's troubling is that repairs aren't going to take a week. More like months, if we're lucky. If we have the parts. If I can figure out how to do it. So we need a place to sleep. That hasn't changed." I grit my teeth, because the need for sleep hasn't changed, but with the captain showing up, we haven't talked about how things are going to go. It's like we're all super excited to see him, but we also want him to go away. Which is fucking twisted. Sam is my friend. And I'm sure as fuck glad he's alive. But yeah, I saw the way he used to look at Haley when he thought no one was looking. The same way I did. We're all assholes.

"Okay, okay, that's logical. Why?" Easton's eyebrow cocks up.

"Excuse me?" I push the next board in and glare at Easton. I take a straightened nail out of the tin can from the wreck. Two swings of the hammer and the board is in place.

"I mean, why was the Rock Candy so broken?" He takes the hammer and straightens a nail out, then hands the hammer and nail to me.

Right.

Zane cuts me off. "Your dad pushed Sam to leave before we were ready to go. He paid the factory off to rush the finish-work. And by finish-work I'm not talking about installing the damn horse statues. We were unboxing the interior as you came on board. Checking systems too. That's not fucking normal."

Easton turns to me. "Was that so hard?"

"No. Give me that board." I point to the one sitting next to Easton's foot. He passes it over. I hold it up, mark it, and hand it back to Zane. He cuts it and gives it back. Nail, swing. Nail, swing. I'm not picturing anyone's face when the head hits the nail. Okay maybe Sam's a little. I'm thrilled we have the ship back. But Sam isn't getting Haley back.

"I think we can sleep in here tonight." Zane stands in the middle of the platform. He's right. It's almost done. We should have another layer of boards to bring it up higher to where we have the plastic from the raft cut. It's rolled up now like a shade. In the rainy season, we'll drop it. We can put the other boards up later. Do I think we're getting off the island alive now? Maybe fifty percent.

Fifty percent.

"I'm going to move the sleeping stuff up here." Zane hustles off to the living platform. I catch Easton's eyes and hold them for a minute. He nods. Yeah, Zane is moving around like he's getting ready for inspection. But Easton gets it. This is not going to be good. Not at all. Sam is not going to understand the way we've been living. Fuck, it feels so normal to me now. But . . .

"Is he going to make a big deal of this?"

I know he's talking about Haley, not the shelter. "His ex-wife cheated on him. So what do you think?"

"They weren't together. That's what I was told." Easton means Haley.

"No, but you spend that many weeks alone at sea and you make up stories in your head." I would have used the image of her to whack off, make it through another night, the next hour. Yeah, no way this is going to go down well. "It's going to be a fucking shit show." I say under my breath.

Zane moves around me, setting up the cushion. It's a while before he says anything. "Damn, you think he'll really bring things?" He's so fucking positive he's brushed everything I've said about this being a ticking time bomb off.

"Dante gave him a long list," Easton says.

"Right." Zane leaves to grab more stuff while Easton and I clean up the tools. When he comes back, he arranges the cushions and puts things in the cubbies he's made along the back wall.

"It looks good, Zane." I nod at him. We've worked really hard to get things done.

"Thanks. I . . . I was a lot." Zane stumbles over his words.

"Yes. You were an ass. But your design is solid." I smirk.

He glances up the map tree to where we'd planned to build a lookout tower. "Thanks."

"Have you ever thought of being a designer?" Easton's got a woven little hand broom that Haley made and is pushing sawdust off the platform.

"Maybe?" Zane shrugs.

There's more there. I know he was saving for a boat of his own. But I might be wrong. We all stand and look at the platform. It looks fucking good for a bunch of reclaimed wood. Some of the derelict's panels had carvings on them, and Zane has incorporated them. With some of those twinkly lights my mom used to scatter around the backyard screen porch, this place would look almost magical. There's nothing left to do. We head down.

Dante's got the fixings for dinner, some crabmeat and a bunch of small white fish from this morning's tide. We've got a few hours before the next tide cycle when we'll need to toss anything we don't need and set aside the things we want to keep.

"I guess we should go down and wait with Haley and Dante." Easton's got his arms crossed like we're going to the DMV on the last day of the month.

"Come on. I'm excited to see him. And, well, clothes that don't smell like shit." Zane nods, grabbing a pomelo from the basket.

"Hey." Haley jumps up from a log on the beach. "How's it going?"

Zane sits on the log next to Haley. He puts his arm around her. "Great."

"The platform looks good." Easton adds. Then we stare at the ocean watching the waves. No one's talking about Sam coming. What are we going to do?

Easton clears his throat. "We're going to need to tell him." His face is void of emotion. The asshole really is meant for a corporate boardroom.

"Right. Sure. But how?" Zane looks around the circle.

"Hey cap, just so you know, we're all fucking. And I'm not planning on stopping. That should work." Dante shrugs.

"Dante!" She purses her lips at him. "We do have to tell him. Or rather, I have to tell him. It will be better coming from me." She nods like that's the decision.

"No, it won't." I shake my head. "I don't want him coming at you."

"He's not going to come at me. What does that even mean?"

"He's a man, Haley. We're not great at not being possessive." I take a step toward her. My heart thumps as I do. I've done hard things in my life, walking away from my brother and my ex. Then coming home for Christmas and not pounding him into the ground for my mother's sake. Working for assholes who think they know what's wrong with an engine when they have no clue. Heck, finishing my bachelor's degree when all I wanted to do was explore the world. But this? This is fucking tough. The thought of losing her to Sam? Sam, who most definitely is a better man than me. How the hell do I fight that? Because I can absolutely guarantee there's no way he's going to get with the program and want to share Haley. He's going to make her choose. And I'm going to have to not fucking punch him.

Her eyebrows shoot up. "Then how do you explain . . . us?" She waves her hand around the circle. "Because you all seem to be able to—" She can't even say the word. Share.

"Having some of you was better than never having anything." Easton folds his arms over his chest. And Rockwell has never said anything more true. Then again, he's leaving at the beginning of things. I don't know about everyone else, but I was convinced we were never getting off this rock. But I wouldn't stop now. Even if I could. I'll do anything for this woman. She doesn't realize how in control she is, even with the amount of testosterone pulsing through the air. It doesn't matter; she's the boss.

Over the top of Haley, I see something on the horizon: it's small to start with, but with each minute, it's getting bigger. Sam. Pirates wouldn't be in something so small. "There he is." I point. And for the next ten minutes, we watch. The waves are big, crashing around the inflated hull of the tender. It's the smaller of the tenders. The one we would use to take Penny to the beach to do her business or run into port quickly to grab a case of champagne. Fucking rich people. I glance at Easton. He's not as bad as I thought. Still don't want to hang around them.

"Is Penny with him?" Haley stands next to me. Her hand is on Zane's back and her head on my arm. This is the last minute for us. The last minute before we're broken apart. I glance down at her. She's watching him come. And all I do is watch her watching him. My throat swells shut. I can't breathe. It's like the devil from all my dreams is driving toward me. Promising all the things we wanted. All the things we miss. And I'm going to have to pay for it by losing her. I can't think. I can't hear the waves. It's like the one time in high school when I was knocked unconscious on the football field. When the fucking Waterfield defensive lineman put his elbow inside my helmet and clocked my chin and I was knocked out cold. When I came to, I decided I was done with football and I was going to get out of my hometown no matter what.

Fuck it.

I've got two choices: pretend I don't give a fuck or tell

her the truth. I whip her around, turning her to me. I hold on to her shoulders and dip my head. My voice, though, I don't dip. "I fucking love you." I want to kiss her shocked face, but that's a bit too much like pissing on my territory— even for me. So I spin her back to the incoming inflatable.

Sam's got a Rock Candy hat on. I fucking want a hat.

Chapter 11

Changing the Helm

Haley

I want to scream. I glance up at Calvin and then back at the incoming tender. Then back at Calvin. Why the hell did he do it now? Why? He loves me. And he wasn't just saying some shit. He means it. I can see it in his eyes. Why now? I can't even focus on what I'm feeling. Not with Sam coming in. It's like some weird version of when we all line up on the dock and greet the incoming guests on the first day of charter.

Only, now that I'm seeing Sam coming, I've got more butterflies than I ever had meeting any guests. Even more than the one time I had a prince on board. It's more than Sam. Zane touches my back. I want to ease back into his touch, but I don't. My face is neutral, like it would be to meet a guest. A pleasant smile, nothing else, but when he gets closer and I can see his blue eyes shining out at me, I can't help but smile. I turn to Zane next to me. He's smiling too. But the rest of the guys have their serious faces on. I'm not naïve—I know they're worried. I'm worried. What is

Sam going to think? And then I start thinking about home. Home.

We can get home. Calvin will be able to fix things. He'll be able to get the engines going or at least a radio. I know he can. He'll be able to get us out of here.

I want to be happy. Going home is what we all want, right? Granted, until we had our do-nothing day and found the Rock Candy, found Sam and Penny, I was kind of getting used to, well, being here. With the guys. But in the long run, we need things. We need medical supplies. We need clothes. Pizza and chocolate are also two things I don't want to live without.

The tender bounces on the ocean, coming over the reef. It's rough. Sam is gaining air with each wave. He's got one hand on the outboard motor and the other on a stack of large plastic storage boxes. I'm standing on the sort of beach that guests always want to go to when they're lounging on the yacht deck. It looks so inviting. But I have to remind them that the ride in will be super rough, that they won't like it. They still go—the first time—but never a second.

A few more feet and Sam will be over the roughest part. He's twenty feet out when Zane and Calvin high-step through the waves to grab his ropes and get him set.

"Hello," he yells, but his eyes are on me. He hands Calvin a rope and then Zane one. "Thanks." Sam tilts the outboard up, and the guys pull the tender bow up onto the sand.

Zane and Easton gather some large stones to anchor their side. Calvin has it tied up to a large boulder near the mouth of the fish weir.

"Impressive," Sam says. He nods at the trap.

"It's keeping us fed." Calvin offers his hand to Sam, but Sam jumps out on his own.

We're all just staring at each other.

"Where's the dog?" Dante finally asks.

"I wasn't sure how rough it would be next to the cliff, so I left her on the Rock Candy. It also let me bring more supplies." He glances back over his shoulder.

"We should get those unloaded." Zane charges for the tender.

"Wait!" Sam shakes his head. "First, let me give you a hug."

We all kind of laugh.

Sam starts with Zane. "It's good to see you." He slaps his hand on Zane's back twice.

"Fuck, it's even better to see you, Cap. I didn't think we . . ."

"I know . . . I know . . . Same." Sam's lip trembles. "Calvin?" Sam pulls him into an embrace. "I've thought about you a lot over the last weeks, months—every time I try to track down a problem and another one appears. What would Calvin do? That's what I say to myself. I guess I've been talking to myself, or rather to all of you. No volleyballs, though, but a heck of a lot of chattering at Penny." Sam gives Calvin a slap on the back. "I'm really glad to see you." His lips purse, and I really think he might cry.

"Easton." He gives him a quick hug. "Good thinking with the jacket."

"That was Haley's idea." Easton points his thumb at me.

"Of course it was." His smile takes over his face. He turns to Dante. "Good to see you, Chef."

"Sam." Dante stresses his name. "I'm glad to see you too."

"I brought your knives."

Dante can definitely be bought—a smile breaks out over

his face. At the same time, the clouds break and part overhead and a beam of sunlight shines on the lids of several boxes in the tender. He slaps Sam on the back. And I wish they would start to unload those boxes because, right now, all eyes are on me and it's too much. Too much. I want to run into the jungle and find Pepper. Sit in a tree and hide away from all of them.

"Haley." He steps closer to give me a hug. I don't think he's trying to kiss me, but I turn my head away quickly. A brief hug. I don't want to make this weirder than it will be. My toes curl in the sand. He's alive and here, and that's an awful lot. The rest can be worked out later.

"I'm glad you're here, Captain." I swallow and take a step backward.

His eyes cloud over. "Yes, me too." He takes his own step backward. "Let's get the supplies unloaded and talk about things. I've got a ton of questions for you, and I'm sure you have the same for me." He's looking mostly at Calvin, but then he glances back at me.

"Right." Zane takes the largest black tote off the inflatable. "Damn, this is like the best Christmas morning ever. It's like you're Father Christmas."

"Want help with it?" Easton asks.

"No. It's light for its size," Zane says.

"Blankets and things. I only brought necessities for now. I don't think we can all live on the ship."

"Water?" Calvin asks.

"Yeah, and weight. I've got a collision patch on. One that I'm anxious to have you take a look at."

Calvin nods. "Me too. How'd it happen?"

"When I got thrown on the reef. It's not big. But any hole is big enough."

Calvin grunts.

I'm watching them banter and I'm so confused. I step around Calvin to go to the tender. He moves his hand back, and it brushes mine. It's not much, just a little touch. But I see Sam's eyes dart down and back up. I freeze, just for a second, then I shake it off, going to the tender. There's six or seven of the smaller boxes, the type the provisioner sends us perishables in. I stack two of them. They, however, are a lot heavier than I thought they would be.

"Careful, that's glass." Sam looks up from where he's talking with Calvin still. I can't hear them, but I assume they're talking about the mechanics of the Rock Candy.

I nod and put one back. I don't need to be a hero around here. I'm not trying to prove anything. I follow Zane up the trail to the shelter.

Dante and Easton are right behind me. They're carrying the largest of the boxes together.

"What's in that one?" Zane asks. He really is excited.

"I don't know," I reply.

"Well, open it."

I unlatch the salmon pink plastic box. There are six bottles: four bottles of hard alcohol and two of red wine. And Sam grabbed the good stuff. Wrapped in a dish towel is a bottle opener and two wine glasses. I laugh. But then I pull the dish towel to my nose and breathe in. It's a little musty, but it's clean and I want to rub it all over my body.

"You're a drug addict now? Addicted to huffing laundry —I would never have guessed." Sam's warm chuckle fills me, and when I look up at him, his laugh lines around his eyes are firing and I want to throw my arms around his neck and give him a real hug this time. I shake it off, temper myself.

"Wine glasses are a necessity?" I smile, holding one up.

"I tucked a few frivolous things into the boxes. I figured we needed a toast. But six glasses seemed like too much."

His lip twists sideways. That's when he looks up. "Whoa." He touches the bark on the tree and then moves around the kitchen space. The posts are up to finish closing it off. I want to keep animals out—well, other than Pepper.

She jumps up on the work surface next to the stove.

"You have a cat. And a stove? Where did you get a stove?" Sam turns, and that's when he notices the platforms stepping up into the canopy of the jungle and the twine rope hanging down with my latest basket attached. It's a lot better than the ones before it.

I look up at the top sleeping platform. "Holy crap, is the platform finished?"

"Yeah, Little Bird. What do you think? It's bloody brilliant, isn't it?" Zane puts his arm around my shoulder, and I give him a kiss on his cheek. I can't stop myself.

"You did amazing. You were a bit of a drill sergeant, but it's fantastic." I don't pull away from Zane. I can't. I would never hurt him. But as my spine straightens, I can feel the captain staring at me.

Zane takes something out of the tote he was carrying. "We have blankets and pillows. And two yoga mats!"

Sam nods. "I thought they might be good for cushions."

"Yes." Zane takes a large handful of cloth and darts up the ladder.

I turn slowly. The captain's blue eyes are locked on me.

"Well, I should go get another load," I say. "I'll be right back. To help unload things."

I'm taking long, fast steps when he catches up to me. "Whoa, you guys have really made the island a home."

I nod, but I don't slow or turn to look at him. "We didn't think we'd ever leave. We've hardly seen any ships. And those we have were going the wrong way, or they had their lights off."

"Pirates?"

When he says it, it gives me shivers. "That's what we were thinking. From the top of the map tree—"

"Map tree?"

"The tree with the bits and pieces we know scratched into it. It's the one that's the base for the shelter platforms."

"Right."

"From the top we can see a string of islands near us, but there aren't any signs of civilization. No campfires."

"You seem good. Actually, better than good. More relaxed." Sam nods and reaches for me but then pulls his arm back.

"It's crazy that I'm more relaxed now that I'm trapped on an island. I guess that says something about my chosen profession." Laughter erupts out of me, a short burst of nervous energy.

We get to the tender, and I take another small box. There are only a few things remaining. I pivot and flee. Keeping busy is a lot better than running into the woods and hiding with a cat on my lap. Maybe. Then again, it's probably not.

Sam catches up to me again. He's holding one of the small boxes. "Do you know anything about the other raft? Easton asked me if I knew anything, and when I told him no, he grunted and grabbed a box."

"Rocky made Anders launch the big tender with him and Candy on it. That all happened before I went up to the deck. The tender capsized, and only Rocky and Anders were rescued. We'd drifted apart from them by the second morning. We never saw them again. I thought we might. We watched . . . but nothing. Calvin hooked a big fish the second day, and as strange as it sounds, I think it pulled us into a different current pattern than them. I keep hoping they were rescued." It happened so long ago, it feels like a dream.

"Same. But then I was hoping for both rafts to be rescued. Hindsight is hindsight, but abandoning the ship was the right thing to do. I know the Rock Candy is floating upright now in the water, but up until I ran aground, it wasn't. It took a while for me to get the listing under control too." He looks away from me, and I get that there's something else but he's not saying it. "In good weather, it was a little less, but in bad weather, the Rock Candy felt like a damn sailboat."

"I can only imagine what the interior looks like."

"I had some time. I might have done some redecorating." Sam laughs.

"All of those horse sculptures?" I raise my eyebrows at him. I put the small box on top of the table and head back to the raft.

Sam follows me. "They're confusing some bottom-dwelling fish right about now." He stiffens. I turn and see Dante at his other shoulder.

"That's the only good thing you could have done with them. They were so horrible." I'm focusing on not looking at him because it's too hard. There's nothing left in the tender but a suitcase—my suitcase, or rather, the expensive suitcase that was left on a yacht by a guest a few years back. My suitcase I hadn't unpacked. The one with all my going-out clothes and my . . . my personal things. I have them in a small lock box. Okay, not that small. It's the type you would get at an office supply store, with a little spin lock with a code. And now I can't remember if it was locked or if Sam would have seen what's inside. Fucking hell, if he did . . . I smile. "Wow, you brought my whole bag."

"I didn't open it."

Chapter 12

Setting Battle Sails

Dante

Sam's eyes flick over her.

The guy totally opened her suitcase, and by the oh so lovely pink blush trailing up Haley's neck, I want to see too. "Let me take that for you, Haley. We don't want to strain your ankle."

"My ankle's fine. We don't want to overtax your strength."

I laugh and take the suitcase from her.

"Haley? We need your help," Zane calls.

"Excuse me." She eyes the suitcase but doesn't reach for it. She takes off for the shelter. Her limp is completely gone, but that's not the point. Sam needs to know that we've been through some shit.

He moves toward the path to follow her, but I step in front of him. I shake my head. The energy is weird, and I don't do weird. I clear it out, get the problem out in the open.

"We're all fucking. And by fucking, I mean it's more

than fucking. We are all into her." I cross my arms over my chest. Sure, I'm going rogue. Haley thinks she should be the one to tell him, but fuck that. I'm not having Sam making her feel that she's done anything wrong.

"Each other?" His eyebrows raise, he looks out over the ocean and a second later back at me.

"No. I'm the only guy here who's bi, but without Haley, I'm pretty sure Rockwell and Green would be going at it, given enough time—or they might kill each other. Guess we have to wait and find out. But no, just Haley. The thought of fucking the other guys makes me want to clean the grease fryer with my tongue. Just Haley." I give a little shiver at my own metaphor.

His face goes from ashy to red and back to ashen again.

"You heard the 'it's not just fucking' part?" Haley is going to be pissed, but Sam needs to know. And she's not going to tell him. Not without a big push. Not without too much time passing. She's too nice. She'd never want to hurt him, or us. Hence hurting all of us.

"I did."

"And?"

"What do you want me to say, Dante? Pass the fucking lube?"

"Well, that's up to you." Telling him I'm trying to work out the best consistency of lube isn't the right thing to do. Not yet. I'll save that gem for another day. "Are you hungry?"

"What?"

I've dazed him. Which I don't mind. Having him a little out of his element is a good thing.

"Like, do you want something to eat? I've made a crab salad with pomelo and seaweed. Along with a coconut cream fish chowder. We didn't know when you'd be getting here, so I wanted it to hold."

His jaw drops. "I ate half a can of beans and a scoop of cold rice. Yeah, I could eat. Thanks."

"No problem. You're welcome."

"I brought . . ." He's staring out over the ocean. I'm not sure which has stunned him more—the fucking or the food. He shakes his head. "I brought some bowls, plates, and stuff too. Your list was oddly specific until it wasn't."

"I suppose 'the entire boat' was leaving things pretty wide open."

"Yeah, I can bring more things back tomorrow or the next day. I'm hoping Calvin and Zane come back with me to start troubleshooting." He's talking to me like I have some sort of say. Strictly by age, I'm the closest to him. I've been on yachts for a hell of a long time. I have enough money saved that I've thought about opening a restaurant. But then I have to make fifty perfect table tops a night instead of one. And the same fucking thing over and over again. On a yacht, it's always something new. Well, except for the time I was cooking on a Russian 125 meter. He wanted me to make him a replica of McDonald's hamburger and fries every night. It was either quit or ask him to shoot me.

I nod. "We should all go back, at least for a look around. Clean things up. The freezers have to be rank by now."

"No, I thought of that. I cooked a good amount of the meat on the back grill. Penny ate well. As things turned moldy, I tossed them overboard."

I nod. "Smart." Calvin's not wrong; the guy's a good man.

"This isn't going to be a quick fix."

"I'm aware. Calvin mumbles about it in his sleep, and

when he wakes up, he talks about it until I want to stab him in the ear with one of the spoons he whittled."

Sam's still looking out over the ocean. We stand for a while.

"What are you going to do?" I ask.

"I'm going to fix the ship and eat dinner. Not in that order."

"All right then, let's eat."

When we get back to the shelter, most of the tubs are open. Zane and Haley are up top, and Calvin is tossing up pillows. Snow white pillows. And while I'm excited for them, I'm more looking forward to my knives and spices. I set Haley's suitcase down next to Calvin.

"What's this?" Calvin asks.

"Haley's." I wiggle my eyebrows. I'm not clairvoyant, but I've been accused of being it before. I'm just observant. Damn observant. I'm guessing Haley has a battery-operated boyfriend inside. And I can't wait to fucking see it. Nothing else would make her blush the way she did. "You doing all right up there, Sassy?" I call up.

"Yeah, it's so nice up here. And we have blankets!" She sings it like an afternoon talk-show host announcing the latest and greatest celebrity. "It's amazing." She does a small hop. Even more amazingly, the platform doesn't move.

"I'm looking forward to it. I'm going to get dinner finished. Twenty sound good to you, Sassy?"

"Works for me if it works for everyone else. I'll be down soon."

A chorus of yups and "sounds good" fill the shelter.

She takes another one of the pillows from Calvin. "Wait. Don't open my suitcase." She points at it and then to Calvin.

He wiggles his eyebrows. "Wouldn't dare."

I meander over to the counter where the crab is cooking in the citric acid of a pomelo. It's going to be fantastic, even better with some red pepper flakes and garlic. I wouldn't imagine Sam would have brought a clove of it, but the provisioner did send some of the powered garbage. Dried cilantro would be amazing too.

"Your stuff is in one of the smaller salmon-colored containers." Sam opens one and then another. "Here." He sets it down on the counter next to Pepper. She's cocking her head back and forth like she's not sure what to think. "Is she friendly?" Sam puts his hand out, and Pepper hisses and swats at him. "I guess that's a no."

"Pepper is a good girl. She just needs to get used to you. She might smell the dog. She's never met a dog before." Calvin scoops her up and tucks her inside his jacket. And I have to do a double take because it's not the same one he's been wearing this whole time—it's a new one. Pepper sniffs and ducks her head down before she sticks her head out of the zipper. She looks up at Calvin, blinks her blue eyes, then turns and glares at Sam. *Exactly, Pepper. We're not sure if he's a friend or an enemy, either.*

Sam sits on the stump next to the stove, a mug in hand. Like he's a guest. "Where did the cat come from?"

"Showed up one day. We haven't seen another one." I poke through my tub. It's fantastic. I love every second of it. There are some other things I'd love to have, but it's fine. I didn't expect him to know that half of my knives are still wrapped up and in a drawer, not hanging on the magnetic rack. But I've got a set of metal bowls, spices, and knives. I can grab other things tomorrow.

I add some freaking pepper to the stew and some chili flakes too. He's done pretty good with the spices. He did add sea salt, which is hysterical, as that's the only thing I have now. But I can fill up the grinder with the stuff I've been harvesting.

I add some more wood to the stove to get it ready for tonight, then take the pot off. "Soup's up."

"Oh, did anyone open the other black-lid container? Not the one with the pillows?" Sam asks.

Calvin finds it on the other side of the tree. "Here it is." He plops it down next to the stove and peels the lid off. "What's in here?" There's a canvas bag.

"I think it's a mosquito net. It's labeled 'birthday party.'"

"What?" Haley sticks her head out the window of the sleeping loft. "Oh right, yeah, it's like you would hang over beds. I was going to blow up the air mattresses and put little canopies over each one. I ordered disco balls and a giant . . . well, some fun stuff. But the canopies could totally be used for mosquito netting. That's a total score."

I crane my neck, watching Calvin go through the box. Under the canvas bag are boxes of crackers and a bunch of canned goods. "Soup and crackers." Now Calvin is roaring like Haley did a minute ago. Maybe we can get back to where we were. Sam's not a bad guy. Calvin and Zane talk about Sam like he's Superman. Not as much lately . . .

"Soup's getting cold." It comes out in my irritated chef's voice.

"We're coming," Haley says.

"That's what she said." Zane laughs, and eyes land on him. "Right." Fun's over is what he was trying to say.

Calvin grabs two coconut bowls.

"We've got the real stuff now, Cal." I hold the ladle out.

"I like these. They fit in the palm of my hand." Which was the same thing he said about Haley's breasts three nights ago. I'm not the only one who's thinking about it. I look over at Zane, and he's got a shit-eating grin on his face.

We're about fifty-fifty on coconut bowls to ceramic. I've got one of each. All of us but Sam are eating with the wooden utensils that Calvin made. Food just tastes better with them, especially the ceviche. The metal taste would bother me now.

We tend to eat in silence for the first few minutes, then lately we've been doing something that Haley calls roses and thorns. And I'm hoping to hell she—

"Should we do roses and thorns? I'll go first. There are so many roses: Sam being alive, the ship, spices, pillows. Who's next?" Haley smiles.

"Nope. You never let us get away with not having both a rose and a thorn. You need to fess up a thorn, Haley." Zane leans in and bumps her shoulder. "Am I right?"

"Okay, right? Right, the worst thing that happened today . . ." She looks at Sam and then around the circle. "I stubbed my toe going up the ladder."

"Which step?" Zane's ready to leap up and take it out on the ladder. The girl is lying. The worst thing that happened today was that our bubble burst.

"Zane, it was my fault, not the ladder's."

"Okay, well, thorn: Easton stuck his knee in my ball sack last night. Rose: all of you. This meal. And the captain, of course." Zane laughs.

I glance over at the captain, but he's a little too mesmerized by my ceviche. It's good, but not good enough to stare at for ten minutes.

Dinner is over; I gather the dishes and package them up in one of the smallest totes. Given enough time, I know Zane's going to come up with a solution for washing dishes. But for now, whoever's turn it is to wash them brings them down to the ocean, scrubs them with sand, and rinses them.

Calvin and Sam are lost in their world of wires and

power surges, and I just can't watch Haley in that much pain anymore. Her discomfort is palatable, and the fact that I can't do anything about it makes me want to scream, so I head for the ocean.

I'm down the path, my feet hitting the sand, when I hear Sam next to me.

I lift my head. "Hey."

"Thought I should help since I ate." He nods at me.

"I've got it." I want him to go back to Calvin and figure out what's wrong with the ship, but if it means giving Haley a rest, I guess I can stand in the fire I started.

"I want to help. Show me how you do it."

"It's washing dishes, not docking a 200 meter at Portofino in Italy," I say.

"Nothing would be that hard. Let me help."

"Sure." I find the large rock we normally sit on. It's past the tender and the fishing weir. "It's a little easier with the tub." I set the tub on my lap and fill it with salt water. "What do you really want, Sam?" I go about doing the simple action. But honestly, I just want him to go away so I can kiss each one of my knives. I missed them so damn much.

"You really are a chef."

"What do you mean by that?" I'm holding my ten-inch chef's knife.

He shakes his head. "There's no beating around the bush."

"I don't have time to mince words—I'm too busy mincing onions. So shoot. What is it?"

Chapter 13

Refitting

Sam

"Are you going to explain any more to me?" I look at the chef. I guess I'm in debt to him. He told me when no one else said a thing, though there have been plenty of weird looks. I wonder if I would have picked up on the way they all seem to touch her if he hadn't said something.

"Yeah, like I said, I'm not stopping it. I have a relationship with Haley; I'm not ending that because you're here. Going back to being friends with her isn't happening. She's mine." Dante nods.

"You mean she's everyone's." It makes my stomach flip when I say it.

"So help me, Miller . . . If you for one damn second think I will allow you to disrespect Haley, you're going to have to back yourself the fuck up. She's the best human I've ever met. She has feelings for you too. I saw it when I first met the two of you back at port, when you were sitting on that tiny bench, watching Penny."

"Did you? Then why didn't you stop her from fucking all of you?"

"Did you put a ring on her finger? Were you going steady?"

I purse my lips.

"'Exactly. Asking her to go touring with you after the season is over isn't the same as telling her you're exclusive. Telling the crew you're together. Being together. I had a captain a few years back marry his chief stew. It didn't work out, but that's because they were both narcissistic a-holes. But it's done, it's happened. You could have told Rocky. Hell, Candy would have been thrilled to know that Haley wasn't trying to dig around in her gold pot. But you didn't."

I shake my head. "No, I didn't."

"Why? Not that it matters now. But why?" Dante tips his chin up at me, and I'm convinced he's as much of a narcissistic asshole as his old captain. But he's got a point.

"She's young." It's one of the reasons I've told myself over and over again. It's shit.

He laughs. He does that a lot. "She's the most mature out of all of us. Including you, fucker."

I square my shoulders. If we were on board, I'd fire him. I'd have him off my boat so fast his luggage would have to catch up with him.

"I see that look. You're not my boss on this island. I might be cooking for my family, but that's because they're my family. We're Haley's. She's ten times more mature than you." He's not wrong.

I feel my eyes burn through him. Jennifer, my ex, used to say something along the same lines—I'm not mature enough—and I fucking hated her for it. Not mature enough to forgive her for fucking around while I was at sea just because she thought I was doing the same when I wasn't.

I nod at him. What else am I going to do? Hit him?

"Someone had to tell you. Haley's mortified. Zane and Calvin have some sort of weird hero worship thing with you. And Easton thinks you're going to be our savior. But you are just as fucking scared as the rest of us. You're not a savior; you're another liability. But I fucking love your dog." He turns back to the dishes.

I'm counting to ten in my head. If I were a decade younger, my knuckles would already be swelling. I wouldn't have been able to stop myself from taking a crack at his jaw. I'm more than that now. I was more than that then. I'm trying to see it as they do.

"They tell me you're great. And maybe you are. But right now, to me, you're yet another captain. One of my contacts at the yacht crew management company said you're good to work with. Reasonable. You're the guy who said yes to my résumé. That's all you are. And I'm the asshole who laid it all out on the table for you. So let's start there. We're on an island, just trying to survive without hurting the girl we love."

"Love?" It's like a slap across my face.

"Yeah, I fucking love Haley. I'm not going to tell her. Not now. Doing it now would make me a selfish prick." Dante glances over his shoulder at the shelter. "If you so much as mention any of this to her . . . well, that's your relationship with her. But know that it will crack her open. Break her. Let her not be broken for a little longer. It's taken a long fucking time to get where we are."

I nod, but I don't say I won't.

"For the record, I know the difference between edible mushrooms, hallucinogenic, and deadly ones. I'm the one who cooks all the food. Do you understand me?"

"That you're a fucking psychopath and I need to hire a new yacht crew management company?"

"Exactly. I'm glad we're on the same page." He smiles and slaps me across my back. He picks up the dish tub and heads past the fish weir up the path to the treehouse.

I walk back up the beach, slowing at the trap. It's ingenious. It's definitely been repaired, adjusted, and redesigned a few times. There are old posts in the sand that aren't being used and a pile of replacements in the dry sand next to the tree line. I'm examining it like my life counts on it. It helps push the conversation with Dante out of my head.

Damn. Looking at Haley's picture every day is what got me through being out there alone.

I'm standing there looking at the fish weir when Zane comes walking up. "Heard you and Dante had a little chat."

I nod. "You could call it that."

"Right, so Dante's heart—"

"He's fucking nuts."

"Aye, he is that. But what he said. I mean it too. I'm not going to let you get in the way of what I have with Haley. I mean, I'm absolutely chuffed to bits that you're alive, but I'm not going to move to the side to let you, well, take her from us."

It's a phrase my ex used, and it stands out in my memory. She said her new husband couldn't have taken her away from me if we'd already had a stable relationship, which at the time I thought was total BS. But now I'm wondering if that's true on either side of my relationship with Haley. If we'd really had something, would she have started anything with them? And on the other side, could I take her away from them? Would I want to?

What I need to do is stay away from her. I need the crew to help me fix the ship. They deserve a life. The evidence needs to get to the government. And really, the only ones I can tell about the broken motherboard are Calvin and Zane. I know them—they had nothing to do with it. So for now, I need to keep it to myself. Well, between the three of us. I need to keep the peace and stay away from Haley.

Easier said than done. I've made her out to be "the one" in my head for weeks. The one. Now she can't be the one. She can't be anything. Not when she has four guys drooling over her already. Four guys who glance at her like I do. I'm captivated by her.

Fuck. She's mesmerizing, and what the psycho said is true—she's wiser and kinder than anyone I've ever met. Then again, I've had a long time to think about her. In my head, I've aged the relationship far beyond what it is.

Zane has a crude basket in his hands. He takes some of the bigger fish from the weir and tosses them in it. Then he meticulously goes through the trap and throws anything too small or inedible back into the ocean. He turns to me. "Well?"

"What?"

"Everyone wants her."

"Right." I chuck a four-inch pink reef fish over the weir fence. "This is good." I touch one of the posts.

"Lots of things here are good."

And it hits me. No one has talked about getting the ship seaworthy again. No one but me. I've had conversations with Calvin about it, but no one has brought it up without me talking about it first. They've mentioned getting clothes, spices, a mattress, but no one has talked about wanting to sail away from this place.

"I need to get back to the ship. Do you want to help me and bring some things back?"

Zane gives me a look I can't read. "Sure."

"I can't leave Penny overnight."

"Of course." He tosses the last fish and heads back.

"This beach would be a far better place to keep the inflatable tender, anyway. Having it scrape back and forth over the reef all night wouldn't do it any good. You mind if you and Calvin come back with me?"

"Sure thing, Cap. You want to go now?"

"Yeah. We're going to lose light soon enough, and you guys should get back in time to secure the tender."

"Right. Right. I'll go get Calvin." Zane takes the fish basket from my hands, and I spend a few minutes helping a small reef fish find its way back to sea, but it looks stressed. Like me.

The tide will turn soon. It always does.

I look up, and Calvin and Zane are walking down the beach with the others.

I wave. "I'll see you three tomorrow. Everyone should come for a visit." I fucking sound like my dad standing at his door for an hour saying goodbye to the neighbors after a football watching party.

Zane gives Easton and Dante fist bumps, then he hugs Haley and kisses her on her cheek. It looks innocent enough.

Then Calvin grabs her and kisses her . . . and kisses her, and what the fuck? "Later," he tosses over his shoulder at the other two. "Anything else you want besides the list?"

"No." Haley waves. She can fucking barely look at me, and it makes my chest clench. I want to lose dinner. And dinner was the best thing I've eaten in . . . well, I'm not sure when I've had a better meal. I licked my bowl. I mean, I turned around when I did it, but I fucking licked it.

Calvin pulls the other rope and hops in.

"Captain, how come you hadn't inflated this before?" Zane cocks his head.

I grit my teeth. It's embarrassing really. "Honestly, I've been so busy trying to fix the boat. The patch is holding. It went through the storm last week without getting torn open again. And I only had enough water for another two months. Getting things working was more important than exploring. I figured if anyone lived on the island, they would find me. I had dreams that when I sailed around the corner I was going to find a modern city and want to slap myself. But then it's just so rare to not see any light in the ocean. Even when you're in the Caribbean and think you're in the middle of nowhere during the day, at night, you can almost always see the lights of a cargo ship. Of course, we can see them on radar too. But here, I've seen almost nothing. One night during the storm, I saw lights, but they were so far away. I sent two flares up, but they didn't see them. Then again, with all the pirates that were reported last season, I don't blame them for not stopping if they did see. I only thought of this tender a few days ago." I don't mention the pirate boat I saw. I want to talk to Calvin about it by himself.

Zane pushes us off and far enough out that I can put the motor down, then jumps in.

It's choppy getting back out, but we manage. When we get to the cliffs, the wind wants to throw us into the rock wall. But I steer us away.

"Fuck, there she is," Zane shouts into the wind. "She's horrible-looking and amazing all at the same time."

"Indeed." I pull up to the swim deck. I've got one of the

inflatable docks tied to the back of the ship. The reef has popped one already, but we have ten of them and some days I'm too tired to pull it in and put it back out again. I use it to float equipment around the sides of the ship to check on the patch.

The way Zane hops out is a thing of beauty, a little slice of normalcy in the way he does it.

"I know we don't have much time before we lose light, but I want to talk to you about what I've found. And this stays between us. Let's go up to the wheelhouse."

Chapter 14

Foundering

Calvin

A fucking mole. "You think someone sabotaged the ship? Why?" It doesn't make sense. But then, I've been wracking my brain for weeks and none of it made sense then either. "Why?"

"Right. That I don't know. But this? This I can hold in my hands." He pulls a plastic zipper bag out of the cabinet behind his chair and hands it to me. "I put it in there. When we get back to civilization, maybe they can pull prints off it?" It's a computer board, snapped in half.

I flick my eyes over to him. I'm still not confident that we're going to get this ship working again. But maybe I can get communications back online. I eye a shortwave radio on the table beside his chair. My soldering iron is next to it. "All right, well, we know Candy was off her rocker. What if she came in here and pulled it out and snapped it?"

"No," Zane said. "Haley went straight to get Candy and Rocky out. They were asleep. I mean, this would have been noticeable right away." Zane pushes on the back of the table.

"It's not just the motherboard. The ship's radios were all sliced. And boards pulled, wires cut. The water tanks were out of balance, but these stickers were making them look like they were." He flips through the captain's log and points to two stickers.

"But we'd been having problems with the stabilizers all along, ever since we left the dockyard." I can't take my eyes off the destroyed electronics.

"Right. But we had a new crew on board." Zane's staring at it too.

"Yes, but they were on board. Making an entire boat abandon ship with yourself? That's just crazy." I hand the board back to Sam.

"Who's stupid enough to do this and trap themselves on a raft just hoping for a rescue?" The words hang between us, charged with a mix of hope and disbelief.

"It makes no sense. Not with the cracked motherboard and the myriad of other issues you've discovered. This is beyond a mere stabilizer malfunction; it's a shit show. It's going to take months, and that's if I had replacement parts. I haven't even made it down to the engine room yet. If they spent this much time messing with the electrical, what have they done to the engines?" My stomach tightens.

"Look at this," the captain urges as he guides us down the corridor, past his quarters, and into the "Grand Salon." He's peeled a panel from the wall to find wires dangling like loose vines in a jungle. That's what we see: a nest of cables, some severed clean through. "Someone not only yanked on these but cut them, too, then put the panel back in place."

"This didn't just happen; it started back at the boat-yard." The sabotage is deeper than I ever imagined, reaching further than someone aboard. But someone on board finished it.

"I can only trust the two of you," he confesses.

I instinctively cover my mouth, stepping back as Zane fixes him with a steady gaze.

"And Haley?" Zane's question hangs there, fragile as a soap bubble.

"Yes, Haley." He purses his lips. He's playing it cool with Haley. We've got other things to worry about, and I understand. "I trust Haley, but there's no need to bring her into this." The captain's assurance is solid, but his next words are for our ears only. "But this stays between us." He snaps the panel back in place with a finality that echoes my pounding heart. "Understood?"

He looks at me; I nod. "Just us three," I agree, my voice steadier than my nerves. I don't like not telling Haley. I've given the captain my word, and I'm always a man of my word. But I might not be this time.

"What else do you need?" The captain's practicality is a lifeline. "You've got about thirty, maybe forty minutes before darkness swallows us whole. I don't want the reef ripping a hole in the tender during low tide."

"Copy that," I say.

"I'm going to check out the crew deck." Zane glances to the back stairs.

"I'll join you," I add. I'm curious about the state of my own cabin.

The yacht is a fucking disaster. The cushions from the sofa are on the floor, but better yet, there's not a horse in sight, not a pillow nor a painting—they're all gone.

Down the stairs to the crew galley, there's junk all the way. Bags, boxes. I kick a few to the side. The captain made a hasty search for provisions. I grab a scrub brush, dish rags, and some hand sanitizer and toss it in an empty grocery bag from the floor.

I make my way down the hall, all the way to the end, to where my cabin was—or I guess still is.

There, I look through my stuff. I grab my wets and my swimming shoes too. The captain brought us a couple of clean uniforms each, most likely pulled from the laundry room. I grab some of my own clothes—an old football sweatshirt from high school, threadbare in the sleeves, but it feels like home. My toiletries, toothbrush, toothpaste—I toss them in the bag. Then I duck into Haley's cabin and do the same for her. On the desk, there's a picture of her as a little girl with her mother. I wrap that in a plastic bag that I find on the floor and tuck it into my larger bag, as well as some slippers and her robe from behind the door. I grab a few things for Dante and a couple of boxes of biscuits that I know Zane has been talking about before I make my way up to Swimmer Boy's room. Everything has slid around in his cabin, and most of the contents are pushed up against the wall. I walk into it and, before the door can wedge itself shut, I shove a fake plant between the door and the doorframe, holding it open.

I rummage around in his drawers, grab a few things: his swimsuit, a pair of sweatpants that say Team USA with the Olympic rings on it, and a sweatshirt. That should make Dante laugh. I add a couple of pairs of shoes—tennis shoes and a pair of comfy-looking boots. Going up the stairs, I now have three or four bags over my shoulder.

I haven't run into Zane again, and I've yet to see Penny.

But on the back deck, I look at the big lounging cushions. "Fuck, those will be a lot better than a yoga mat," I say to myself. "Zane!" I call at the top of my lungs. "Are you ready to go?"

"I'll be right there," he calls back from the sundeck.

"What are you doing?"

He has a large bundle under his arm. He was thinking the same thing as me.

"Did you even get any of your own stuff?"

"A few things. But this is way more important," he replies. He has the big cushion from the top sundeck rolled up tight like a sleeping bag.

"Looks good. You ready to go?" I ask.

"Let's do it," he agrees.

Just as we're getting things into the tender, the captain pokes his head out. "Somebody wants to say goodbye before you take off," he says.

The dog comes racing down the stairs, flying at me. I barely have time to catch her, keeping her from knocking us into the ocean. She licks up one side of my face and down the other.

"Be a good girl," I tell her. She actually looks a little fat, but it's good to see her.

Zane loads up the rest of the tender.

I look up at the captain; Penny trots back up to him. "We'll see you in the morning," I say.

"Well, be here just after— Scratch that. High tide should be right around sunrise. Be back then. It should make going along the cliff easier," he says.

"Sounds good," I reply.

Dread fills me as we pull away. I can't help but wonder. It just feels like the ship might disappear.

Zane has a large sheet of plastic from the toy hauler room off the swim platform. "It's too bad we can't get the Skidoos down without powering the crane. We could zip back and forth to the boat a lot easier." He eyes them on the roof of the Rock Candy as we pull away.

"Yeah, that's not happening. Hey, make sure that grocery bag stays dry." I touch the one containing Haley's picture with my toe.

He moves it closer to the cushion. "What's in it?"

"I think it's a picture of Haley and her mom."

"Damn." He rolls the top closed. "You should have said that to start with." He scratches his head.

"You really think someone tried to sink us?"

"The evidence sure as hell looks that way."

"What I do know is that there is no fucking way Haley, Dante, or Easton have anything to do with it."

"I agree."

"And are we going to tell them?" Zane looks up at me with his expressive eyes. The guy can make Haley do anything with the way he looks at her.

"Let's give it a day. Let the captain come to his own conclusion that they're innocent."

Zane nods. "Copy that."

We're past the cliff in a relatively calm part of the ocean when Zane glares back at me.

I furrow my brow at him. "What?"

"You could have waited."

I know instantly he's talking about me telling Haley I fucking love her. "You could have said it too."

"And look like I was just copying you."

"Who cares what it looks like? She needed to know before Sam came and planted his flag on our beach."

"You're afraid of Sam?"

It's a good question. Am I? Fuck yeah. I'd take Sam over the lot of us any day. "No," I lie.

His scoff is loud even over the waves. "Right, well, you could have waited. Been more romantic about it."

"I'm not the romantic one—that's you." I slow the tender a little. "She knows you love her. Just tell her."

He nods.

It's getting dark when we approach our beach, but Dante is sitting out by our old fire pit with a nice-sized fire going. He jogs over and helps us pull the tender ashore. "What did you bring?"

"An even better cushion from the top deck and some little stuff. More clothes, bathing suits." I pass him a bag.

"I don't need a bathing suit."

"Yes, you do," Zane and I say together. I'm tired of seeing his monster junk.

"Right."

I dry the motor and tuck it up. Part of me wants to pull it all the way into the jungle to keep it out of sight.

Chapter 15

Swab the Deck

Easton

Haley stares in the direction the tender disappeared ten minutes ago. "They'll be back," she whispers to herself.

"Definitely, Firefly. They'll be back." I rest my arm over her shoulder and squeeze her to me.

"No need to worry, Sassy. The three of them are expert seamen. They'll be back before dark."

"I know." Her eyes glow light blue in the early evening light. She turns to me and then to Dante. The tension for the last few hours has made the air thick.

"You ready?" I hitch my head to the tree house.

"Yeah." She turns, and we walk along the trail.

"Sassy, you and Swimmer Boy should go get cleaned up at the waterfall. You know, with shampoo. Real soap?" Dante's got his head in a bin. He picks up a container of spices and then puts it back.

"No, I'll stay. We should get the sleeping platform ready for when they get back."

I smile down at her. "Yes, but not you. I've got orders

from the tree house czar that he wants to put the finishing touches on before you go up. So let's go get cleaned up."

"You sure?" She picks up a tub of Dante's stuff.

He eyes her and then the tub, and then he turns back to the bin he's sorting. "You know I like you an awful lot, Sassy," he throws over his shoulder, "but I'm still a territorial bastard when it comes to my kitchen."

The box thumps on the wooden plank counter. Her shoulders slump. "Right." Dante's oblivious. But then she rises on her tiptoes and kisses the back of his neck.

He twists quickly, catching her around her waist. "Go, Sassy, give yourself a little spa date with Swimmer Boy. I'm sure he's been to lots of spas. He must know how to help." Dante raises his eyebrows at me.

Fuck. I've never been to a spa. I've had plenty of massages, but they were all for physical therapy and usually hurt like fuck. Having someone dig into your muscles with a blade isn't something I would do for fun on a Saturday afternoon.

There's a box near the ladder that hasn't been taken up yet. I spotted some spa scrub and shampoo there earlier. "Let's go, Firefly. I'll be your esthetician." I take two clean towels, and I lift them to my nose. I want to strap the damn thing to my face it smells so good.

"So good." Haley's joined me.

"Right?" I laugh and hold my hand out to her. I move to the path. "You know, let's use the soap in the ocean and then rinse the salt off in the waterfall."

Haley nods. "Good idea. We won't want to get soap in our drinking water."

I take her hand, and we walk quietly back to the big rock. It's high-tide, and the water comes right up to it. I leave the towel there. I want to ask her how she is, what she's thinking about, if she's okay. I flick my eyes over her. I'm terrified. I'm more scared of losing her than I am of not getting off the fucking island.

Haley takes my hand. Then she wraps her arms around my waist, pushing her head into my chest. "Are you okay?"

I laugh. "I'm good. I wanted to ask you the same thing."

"I asked you first—you looked so sad just now. What were you thinking about?"

"The island." I smooth her hair, holding her tight against me.

"They'll be able to fix it. Don't you think?"

I nod.

"Don't you want them to fix it?" She looks up at me, her hair a golden brown in the waning light.

"Yes. I mean, that's the answer you want?"

"I want the truth." I feel her lips curl against my chest.

"It's a curse and the best thing that's ever happened to me. Damn. At night, after Zane's done with whatever movie he's going off about and you all talk about the foods you miss . . . Chocolate—"

"Chocolate," she sighs.

"Yes, chocolate, pizza, beer . . . things I've sworn off for years. Junk food, alcohol. I made a choice. When I train, I cut them all out of my life. Then the second whatever big event is over, I'm off the bandwagon. And it's like that now. I shut the things I can't have out of my mind, replacing them with what I can have. What I do have is fresh fish, no internet, no training schedule, no looming date of working with Rockwell Tire, no meetings, no expectations. It's the most amazing thing I've ever had." *And you.* I don't say it. She's kind, beautiful, responsive Haley. "And it's weird, but you all are some of the best friends I've ever had."

She lifts her head from my chest and cocks her head back. "You and Calvin are friends?"

"It was rough in the beginning, but now . . . it's good. I know more about the four of you than anyone else ever. My friends at home dispersed from my life when I was training. And when the training was over, the only thing that ever happened was me paying for parties, traveling. Now they're mostly settled down and married, kids on the way . . . gone again. Fuck, I wonder if they even know I'm missing."

"Of course they know you're missing. Why would you even think that?" She squeezes me even tighter.

"That's what I was thinking about. You asked."

"Thank you for telling me."

"How are you?"

"Fi— I don't know?"

"Thank you."

"For what?"

"For giving me a real response." I sit next to the towels on the big rock and pull her into my lap. "Do you want to talk about it?"

She's shocked. I'm not sure why.

"You don't have to if you don't want to."

She nods.

We're getting too deep for her. Today was a lot. She needs time. I'm not going to rush her. I stand and let her slide to the ground. "No more. You are keeping Monsieur Chocolat waiting for your hair appointment. And he does not like to wait."

"He doesn't?"

"*Non.*" I give it my best fake French accent. "First, we must get you out of *zese* clothes. Mademoiselle must tell me where she gets her couture."

Haley laughs and lifts her hands in the air. I pull her shirt off. "Why, do you like it?"

"No, we must burn them to the ground." I pull the bandana out of her hair and toss it on the backside of the rock near where the sand is dry. My hands trail over her breasts, and she cocks a smile.

"Really? I think it just needs a good wash."

"No, it must be burnt." I push my finger to the sky for emphasis at the same time I'm wiggling out of my shorts. Seriously, burning our old clothes might be too good for them. But then I guess she's right—we shouldn't waste anything.

Once I'm free from my shorts, I sweep Haley up with one arm. I take off running for the surf. I've thought about how today would go for a long time. Never did I imagine it would end with alone time with Haley. She clings to my arm, her head tilted back, laughing. I run straight into the water, and tonight it's warmer than normal. Not that it's gotten too cold. Once the rainy season kicks in, I imagine things will be very different. We're not too far off from it.

That's the thing: things change.

I stomp through the waves. When I get deep enough, I let go of Haley's legs and take her lips in mine. She tastes of citrus. I kiss her until I'm dizzy and a wave overtakes us. I grab her hand, tethering her to me.

She coughs. "Well, that's one way to do a pre-wash. Monsieur Chocolat, I'm going to have to talk to your manager about your strange working conditions."

"Strange? Well, you haven't seen anything yet." I grab her around her waist. "Ready?" I whisper.

"Yes." I toss her into the next wave. Her laugh is swallowed by the surf. She swims back to me, and I toss her at least a half dozen times before I haul her body against mine and kiss her again. My legs flutter, keeping us afloat. I've inched us out past the breakers, past the violent waves.

She's on fire, devouring me like she hasn't eaten. When she pulls back, her eyes are wild. Her hand pushes between us. Her fingers close around my dick. She strokes up once and then twice. And for a half second, I forget I have to kick.

"Damn, Haley," I hiss out.

"Do you want me to stop?"

"No." I grip her with one hand and use the other to make our way to shore. All the while, she's working me. When my toes scrape along the sand, I give one more kick and plant a foot in the shifting sand.

"I need you." Her eyes flash in the low light.

"I need you too. Here or on the beach?"

"Here."

"All right then." I hoist her leg around my hip, but she does the rest, guiding me home—into her. That's what she is, home. "I will always be here for you, Haley." Damn, that's as close as I can get to *I love you*. Everyone I say those words to leaves me. I want to say them to her. Fuck, I want to give them to her like Green did. No, not like Green did but better. Sweeter. Like Haley deserves. When she's ready. Because I don't think that she was ready when Green said them. The way he shoved them at her has sent her into a tailspin. Fuck, would I say it if I could?

She sinks down on me. It's tight, so tight. I take another step forward, getting a better footing to brace in the crashing breakers. She's riding up and down, timing her thrusts with the waves. I grip her hip and push my hand between us. I circle her clit, giving her more.

"Easton." She pumps on me. Her hair twirls wildly around in the surf.

Large steps have us out of the water, and I lower myself onto the rock at the shore's edge. Firefly doesn't miss a thrust. Her head rolls back when I put my thumb on her clit again. "There you go. Damn, Haley. I wish you could see how amazing you look."

"Like a drowned rat. A really turned-on drowned rat." She flicks her head back to me at the same time a large wave crashes onto our legs. We cling together, laughing.

But damn, she's like a mermaid. She arches her back, and I grab her to keep from falling into the water. She bends farther, her hair brushing the waves. And the fact that she trusts me to keep her from falling into the water makes me even fucking harder. I will never let anything or anyone harm my girl.

"Oh, right there." Her new position has her driving deeper onto me. My pulse pounds in my dick. I'm never coming back from this. I force my eyes open as she's teetering on the edge of her orgasm. It's the best fucking thing. With one hand, I grip her hip, and with the other, I rub her clit, coaxing her over.

She vibrates on top of me, her pussy flutters around me, and it takes me with her. I'm soaring into the early evening sky.

"Whoa. . ." She sits up. "Another inch and I would have flipped all the way over.

"I've got you." I rub along her hips. She's going to have a mark later. I had to grip pretty hard to keep her upright.

"I know you do." She leans into me, resting her forehead on mine.

"Are you ready for your appointment now?"

"Appointment?"

I pick up the bottle of shampoo from behind me.

Chapter 16

Onloading

Zane

"Holy shit." I look up at the sleeping loft, and the window is filled with mosquito netting. "That's fantastic."

Easton pokes his head through the window. "No, what you're holding looks fantastic."

"It's a great addition to the new yoga mats." I'm holding the new extra-large cushion above my head.

"Hold on, let me help you," Easton calls down.

"Can I come the rest of the way up?" Haley's waiting on the living room platform with Pepper curled asleep on her lap. It's still early, but it feels like it's the middle of the night. And I'm ready to go to bed. But more importantly, I want to fix our connection with Haley. I know we all showed how we feel during the day. I tried to, at least. The captain's eyes glared at every passing touch. But tonight is going to be different, and I sure as hell hope she's willing to let us prove how much we need her. I need it. We all need it.

"Give us a minute." I pass the cushion to Easton and kiss her temple. I charge up the ladder with two grocery bags over my arm. I found some of the solar charge twinkle lights that the interior uses for parties on the sun deck. They were brand new since we'd never had a party. They're not super charged up right now, having spent their entire existence in a box, but they've got a little glow around the mosquito net. There's also a few of the fake solar-battery-powered candles. I have them in the corner, on the three-legged stool that we found under the bed in the fishing boat. The best part is the new pillows and blankets on top of the new big cushion. It's perfect. Like a tree house in the movies. "Ready," I call out.

"Hold on a second. I need to add something." Calvin's hair is wet. When he pushes past me, he doesn't smell like shit. Having soap is a freaking game-changer. He puts the picture of Haley and her mom on the little stool next to the solar-operated candle.

"Okay, now we're ready." Calvin crosses his arms over his chest. And I don't even care. He's not stealing my thunder; he's being Calvin, a guy who was smart enough and brave enough to tell her he loves her. I fucking love her too. But I can't tell her now. Not today. Maybe tomorrow. She's freaking out about the captain. I mean, I understand why. He's a good man, and they had a thing first. I don't care about who was first. I just want to be part of the last. That's the only thing that matters to me. I want to be part of her endgame—and I don't mean the movie.

Haley comes up the ladder. "It's amazing. This, this is . . ." Tears roll down her face. "Sorry, happy tears. OMG, is that my picture?" She storms to it. "It's my mom. Thank you for getting it."

"Zane grabbed it. The lights, the cushion. It's all him." Calvin throws his arm around me.

I glance at Calvin. He's giving me all the credit, I guess because of our chat in the tender.

"Oh, he grabbed your wets, some shoes, and your robe too. They're in the bag over there."

"Really! Thank you for getting them, Zane." She throws her arms around my neck, and this time she kisses me. Her soft lips take me in, and I get butterflies. I pull her closer, but then Dante jumps next to us, landing on the new bed.

"Can we go to bed now? Damn, that feels good." Dante pulls back a blanket and lies on his back. He's naked because that's how Dante rolls most of the time now. Unless he's cooking, he's living his best nudist camp self. Him, Haley, the rest of us, and his massive dick. "Come here, Haley. This mattress is the same thickness as our two little cushions together. The idea of not rolling off it into a desert of sand is f'n fantastic."

She unzips her new crew jacket. And I can die now. Underneath isn't her old shirt. Haley has on a white lace bra. The rest of us freeze. No movement at all. Until Easton moves first, and then we're all pulling clothes off, in a race. Until we're all naked.

All but Haley, who has her hand over her mouth, laughing. "Really?"

"What else is in that suitcase of yours, Chiefie?" Calvin's the first to grab her around her waist. He dips his head and kisses her.

She pulls back and looks up at him. "Toothpaste. Do we have toothpaste?" She smacks her lips.

Calvin laughs. "I think Zane got you some. It's in the grocery bag with your shoes."

Haley looks between him and me. She holds her hand out for me, and I take it. With my other hand, I trace down the white satin strap of her bra, letting my pinky slip under the edge. Goosebumps rise down the side of her breast. She places her hand on my cheek and stares into my eyes. "You're a good man."

My heart stutters. "As long as I'm your man, I don't care what anyone else thinks."

She gives me a little nod, and I take her lips in mine.

She tastes of home. This place is more home to me than any home I've had with four walls and running water. The captain's arrival has done more than change the dynamic with Haley. It's made me question what I want out of life. I've been saving for years to buy my own boat. I pictured myself running day charters. Somewhere in the Caribbean.

Now I'm thinking I want to go back to school and get an advanced degree. In architecture.

Or maybe I want to be a househusband. My hands settle round her waist. "How you feeling? Okay?"

"As good as . . . No, I'm not putting on my stew face and pretending everything is okay."

"You're the same person you were yesterday, Sassy. You haven't changed. You were happy yesterday. Don't let someone else's expectations upset you. You've got a brilliant brain and a better understanding or moral compass than most people I've ever met. Definitely you're more pulled together than most of the misfits in this industry. Present company not excluded." Dante stands and puts his hand on her back. "If Sam can't see that, he's a fool. Screw him." Dante clears his throat. "Actually, don't screw him."

She nods, and her chest heaves. There's more she wants to say, but her head flicks to the picture on the stool. "Zane, there was another picture with this one. I'm standing with my college roommate at her wedding. Was it there?"

My lips thin, and I turn to Calvin lying behind her. He shakes his head no.

"Sorry, I didn't see it."

"You know, I really appreciate everything you've done. You've worked hard and made us a beautiful home. But just because Calvin tells a lie doesn't mean you have to go along with it."

I laugh. "Noted."

"It wasn't on the floor? I know you didn't have long. I'm just wondering."

Calvin breathes out. "I'm sorry, Chiefie. I didn't see it."

I turn my head away. I know if I was alone on a ship for months on end, I'd collect a picture of Haley. Penny's a pretty dog, but Haley's everything.

Chapter 17

Clear Skies

Haley

I swing around in Zane's arms, looking into his dark brown eyes. I know what he wants to talk about, and he's not wrong. We should talk about a lot of things. What Calvin said to me on the beach before Sam arrived. I've been pushing that down. Because how can I love all four of them and be attracted to Sam? The way Calvin's eyes shined with certainty when he said it . . . I've been feeling it too. But a voice in the back of my head says they care for me because I'm the only option. Then another part of me gets defensive. It's like the angel and devil on my shoulders from old cartoons my mom liked to watch with me. It's real; at least, what I feel for them is.

My arms loop around Zane's neck. I'm being selfish. But how can I not be? I want all of them. And I suppose, as much as I want to be positive, I've taken on a little of Calvin's pessimism. Now everything feels . . . weird. We haven't been rescued, but maybe there is a way off the island.

"Or . . ." I step up on my tiptoes and take Zane's lips with mine. His kiss is tentative to begin with, but it doesn't take long before his tongue is in my mouth. Demanding, possessing. I want all of him. I want all of them. Zane's hands hitch under my bottom, lifting me onto him. My ankles lock around his back, and he turns and pushes me up against the tree. It's not until I reach back that I realize it's not the cold tree but the warm muscular wall of Easton.

"Hey, Firefly." Easton's lips tingle along my collarbone, and his fingertips trail lightly down the sides of my arms.

Zane pulls back and lifts my freshly braided—and tied with a hair tie, not my bandanna—hair to his nose. "You washed your hair, Little Bird." I expect him to say something like *you smell better* or *good*, but he doesn't. His eyes flash. It's weird to even see his eyes. Sleeping on the lower platform, I've become accustomed to not seeing anything. It's not like on the beach where the moon can peek through. Here it's just dark. But not now—the little twinkle lights are doing their best to stay on, and there's a bigger lantern hanging under the middle of the mosquito net, a lone moth flapping around it.

"Do you not like how it smells?"

"No—yes. Yes, Little Bird, I like how you smell." He kisses my lower lip, sucking it into his mouth. "You okay?" He runs his finger under the strap of my bra, and I shiver.

I nod at him. "Never better."

"Oh, I think we can do better. You got her, Rockwell?"

Easton's grip on me tightens. Zane unlatches my legs from around his waist, and he melts to his knees in front of me.

Immediately, my fingers go to his hair. My own head pushes back against Easton's shoulder. "Zane." My breath rushes out of me. I lift my head and look beyond him.

Calvin and Dante are watching while Zane makes swift work of pulling my clean short shorts to one side. His hot tongue finds its way to my core, and I jerk back with desire. My hips are ready to take off on their own.

Dante's soft chuckle fills the night air. "That's it, Sassy. You like what the Brit is doing to you, don't you?"

I suck on my lower lip and nod.

"Come on, Zane. Have Easton put her on our new bed. Let us all have a chance," Calvin growls.

Zane gives my clit one more long lick, then rights my shorts. He stands with such force I tug on his hair.

"I'm sorry, Zane."

"No worries, Little Bird. You can pull on my hair if I can pull on yours."

"You know Sassy likes an edge of pain. I don't think that's going to be a problem."

"She does, doesn't she?" Zane wraps his hands around my waist and takes me from Easton like I weigh nothing. In two steps, he has me on the new cushions. I'm staring up over the tin and wooden roof. There's a layer of the raft between the tin and the mosquito netting. The fairy lights aren't bright, but there is light bouncing off the orange, giving the treehouse a cozy glow. And having the cushions below me? It feels like I'm at a five-star hotel in the best city in Europe. But then they don't have service like this anywhere.

Easton peels my shoes and socks off. Zane has my shorts around my legs. Dante and Calvin have the straps to my bra down.

"This is nice, Chiefie. Maybe we should leave it on." Calvin runs the pad of his finger over the satin edge.

"It's pretty, but a naked Haley is better." Easton reaches around and snaps my bra off.

It comes off the rest of the way, but then Calvin's large hands wrap a soft piece of fabric around my eyes. The dim evening light vanishes behind a blindfold. His breath warms the side of my ear as he tightens it over my hair. "I meant what I said." He kisses the soft spot behind my ear, and my skin goosebumps all over my neck. He meant what he said. He loves me. I want to say it back, but I can't. Not in front of the other guys because, well, I love them too. I think. No, I do. I love all of them. Each of them do something different for me. They say there's no such thing as the perfect person. Together they are.

"What are you thinking about, Firefly? You're getting all tense." Easton's hot mouth sucks on my breast, and my hips fly up, pushing into Zane's mouth.

Before I can answer, Zane hitches his arms around the underside of my legs, pulling my pussy into his mouth. He's off, his tongue flying around my clit. My head pushes back, and Calvin's mouth is on mine. He swallows down my moans. When I'm spiraling with the three of them, I remember Dante. And it puts me on edge. What is he doing? When is he going to join? I take my hand from the side of Calvin's ear and move it around me.

Calvin breaks our kiss. "What are you doing, Chiefie? Wondering what Dante is up to? Don't worry about anything. Trust me, you're going to like it. I won't let his monster dick hurt you." Calvin chuckles. It's low and warm and completely unexpected.

"I can't see anything through the blindfold. I want to see you."

Zane lifts his mouth from my core. "No, you want to know what Dante's up to. And that, love, is going to be a surprise." Then he's right back at it.

Even Easton is laughing, and now I'm really twisting, wondering what is going on.

"Open your mouth, Sassy. You're so impatient."

I reach for him, swinging my hands. But Calvin grabs one wrist, Easton the other.

"Now, no cheating, Firefly." Easton pinches my nipple, keeping the pressure on until I arch toward him. Dante is right when he says I like a little bit of pain, not too much, but Easton lets go before it really begins to hurt. I open my mouth, but then I hear a spoon scraping along a pot.

"Good." Calvin lets go of my hand. Easton too.

"Open up, Sassy."

I open my mouth, and all the guys pause their attack on my body.

It's warm, and with the first touch on my tongue I'm not sure what it is, but then the sugar and the chocolate hit my tastebuds. It's overwhelming. So weird—I'd almost forgotten what chocolate tasted like. I make a noise somewhere between a groan and a moan. I'm not sure which.

"You want more? There's a little left," Chef's voice is deep.

I shake my head. "No, you guys should have some."

"Firefly, you keep talking about how all you want is chocolate." Easton runs his hands over my stomach. "Have another taste. Dante mixed this up just for you."

"I've got another idea. Sassy's right—we should all have a little taste. Open up, Sassy."

I momentarily purse my lips and then open them. Another warm spoonful. And then Dante drizzles down my front, around my breasts, to my core. "Now we can all have a taste," he says. And the rest of the guys groan.

"What?" I push up onto my elbows.

"Come here, Chiefie." Calvin pulls my shoulder up onto his lap. "You'll know in a second."

Zane and Easton's tongues are trailing around my skin.

"Dig in, Green." Dante laughs.

"It's fine. I don't want you choking our girl."

And I instantly know where the rest of the chocolate went. I open my mouth.

"See, Green, Haley's not afraid of my cock." Dante rubs the tip of it against my mouth. "But I do appreciate the teamwork." He pushes it between my lips. "Fuck Sassy, that's so good."

Chapter 18

Thrusters

Dante

When I found the two squares of baker's chocolate and the small tub of sugar, I knew exactly what I had to do with it. Haley's been talking about chocolate nonstop around the campfires at night. *"Wouldn't it be nice to have a marshmallow s'more?"* Which I find gross, but I would make them for her if I had the rest of the ingredients.

Damn, her hot little mouth closes around my dick. She swipes up around the underside with her tongue and sucks me in deep.

"I'll make you chocolate sauce every day I can." I'm going to toss that damn yacht looking for chocolate.

Haley pulls at the blindfold, but Green catches her wrists again. "No, Chiefie. You need to feel us. Each one of us. We're yours. We need you to remember that in the coming days. I love you. And they might not have said it yet, but they do too."

I flick my eyes at Calvin. I would do anything for Haley.

And I love her, but I'm not going to have another say it for me. Those are my words to give and my words only.

The noises from where Zane is eating her out change. He's sucking on her clit. Her hips bounce; her back arches. Her greedy tongue flattens on the underside of my head. But I want her to come, let her thrash about with all of her reckless wildness. I pull out of her, and she reaches for me. "No, Sassy. Take what Zane is giving you." I can't. I can't take it. I lean down my head next to Green's knee. I suck her ear lobe into my mouth, and when I let it out, I whisper—and I don't whisper, ever—"I love you. Don't you ever fucking forget that."

Her head falls into Calvin's lap. She's shocked. I don't have to see her eyes to know it. How can she be shocked? It drives me batty that she doesn't know how special she is.

Calvin leans forward and kisses her. I sit back on my knees and suck on her breast. My hand wrapped around my cock, I pump in time to her hips grinding on Zane's face.

Her moans muffle in Calvin's mouth. She's close.

"That's it, Firefly." Easton runs his fingers over her breasts.

I need her. Fuck. From the far side of the platform, I find my new bowl of coconut oil lube. I scoop some into my palm and take one of Haley's legs away from Zane. She's not going to last long. Not with what I'm about to do. I coat my pinky and wiggle it under Zane and Haley until I find the bud of her ass. I push it in, and she flies off the cushion, bouncing. Calvin's mouth is long gone. She screams into the night. It's amazing. She leaves me breathless. I push my finger farther into her ass.

"Your dick isn't going in there," Easton says. I expected it to be Calvin.

"Not yet, but one day."

"Fucking never," Green adds.

"We'll see." I push my pinky all the way in. Zane's got two fingers riding her wave, his thumb on her clit.

She settles back on the mattress. What's the etiquette as to who gets to take her first? I have no idea. But my cock is out and I'm naked. And Zane's moved to get her a cloth. He's such a gentleman. I'm not. I'm a South-sider who sees an opportunity.

"Sassy," I say, and I grab her legs, wrapping them around my waist. My cock is balanced on her entrance. I push in. Shit, there is nothing better in the world than this girl. Sharing her is better than none of her. Actually, sharing her is better. I love watching her come apart. Her riding Zane's face. Shit. "You good, darling?"

"So good."

I push the rest of the way in, to the hilt. Even as wet as she is, I give her a little time to adjust to my size. It takes a special kind of woman to ride my cock. Oh, all the girls think they want a big guy. They squirm at the size. But actually taking it, riding it? Yeah, that's a special kind of girl.

"Dante. Fuck, is she good and wet?" Zane drops down to her side, his finger grazing her tit.

Easton's sucking on her neck, licking the last bit of chocolate from her pale skin.

"So wet, aren't you, Sassy?"

"Yes. It's good. Really good."

I yank on the side of her butt cheek, flashing it to Zane. I raise my eyebrows to him in the dim light, and he gets the message. His hand cracks down on the side of it.

Haley screams.

"Did you like that, Sassy?"

"Yes."

I lift the other side, and it takes Easton a second to get

the message and move away from his dessert. He evens her out. The noise this time turns to a moan.

Calvin takes her hair and pulls her face back to his. His lips devour her. Her moans are muffled by his Viking head. I slam into her harder, my relentless pace taking her and pushing her into the giant.

On each side, I see both Easton and Zane working themselves, their dicks rigid and ready to explode.

I lean back, and Easton works his hand between Sassy and me. His finger finds her clit. She rockets off with the second brush of his finger.

She screams, "Dante." Her pussy begins to flutter around me.

"Come for him." Calvin's voice is deep and hard, his eyes wide. Our Viking likes watching too.

Her voice echoes through the forest. Hell, they might even be able to hear it on the mainland, wherever that is. Her orgasm slams into me, and it takes me over the edge with her. It's never-ending, the waves that come over my body. Calvin rips off her blindfold. Fuck, it's exactly what I need.

Her sleepy blue eyes hold mine as I ride out the last wave, my hammering slowing to a rocking motion. "Damn, Sassy. You are the best. There's no doubt about it."

I'm slow to move away from her. My cock is still hard, and I'd like to keep it in her for longer, but I can't—etiquette and all. Sharing is part of the game here. Not that it's a game any longer. Nothing about this is a game. This is real.

I take the cloth Zane has gotten ready. It's weird to have washcloths and clean towels. Gently, I wash her before crawling up her body. I kiss her lips and work down her jaw to her ear. "I love you. And not because someone said I do but because it's true." I won't whisper it ever again. No, I want to shout it from the top of the map tree. And before she can answer, I kiss her again. She tastes of chocolate and Sassy, which is better than chocolate any day.

"Dante," she says. I see it on her face.

I shake my head. She doesn't have to say it back. I'm not needy like that. Not that I think in a million years I'm deserving of her love. No, she's a three-Michelin-star restaurant and I'm cold fast food takeout. I run my hand down her shoulder and move to the side. We're in this for the long haul. And I'm not talking about just tonight.

Chapter 19

Luxury Liner

Calvin

It's drizzling outside, like it does a lot of mornings. But damn, it's nice to have a roof over our heads. It's like every other day, but it's not. Through the mosquito netting, dappled light fights to break into our treehouse. The weak sunbeams play with the golden tones in Haley's hair. There's probably a rainbow out there. I should get up, but I've got a few more minutes before I have to. High tide can wait—Chiefie's head is on my shoulder, her warm body curled against my side. Zane's hand cradles her waist.

Down by the stove, Dante lightly whistles under his breath. I don't think he even knows he's doing it. Things are clinking. The stove opens and closes with a loud squeak. I need to remember to grab oil from the Rock Candy.

Zane slowly lifts his hand off Haley.

"I'm not asleep," her groggy voice huffs into my chest.

"You sure about that, Chiefie? You sound like you're talking in your sleep."

"I don't talk in my sleep."

Zane laughs.

"Wait? Do I?" She's awake now.

"No. You're good, Little Bird. It's not full-on talking. It's more mumbling. You're proper adorable, Haley. No worries."

She lifts her head, staring at my arm. "And I drool?" She wipes at the wet patch.

But I catch her and roll her on top of me. "I like your drool. I like everything about you. Because I love you." I reach up and take her lips in mine before she can respond. I don't need her to say it. She loves me and the rest of us losers too. She'll get there; the whole Sam thing has thrown her for a loop. I'm not worried. This isn't like my brother Jared and Trisha. Haley isn't anything like Trisha, and this whole thing is completely different.

"Calvin?" She sits up, straddling me, and I've completely forgotten all that had me worried in the first place.

"Chiefie?"

"You're thinking about the Rock Candy, aren't you? You get that gleam in your eye when you're trying to solve a problem." She pats my chest, but I take her hand and move it lower to my morning wood.

Zane clears his throat. "I'm all for a little more fun, but the sun is coming up and it's almost high tide. We should get going." He digs around next to the mattress until he finds his crew hoodie. He holds it to his nose, breathing in. "Who would have thought that smelling mostly clean laundry could develop into an addiction?"

Haley kisses the tip of my nose. "Not me." She smiles. "I guess we should get going."

"We?" Zane asks.

"Yeah, aren't we all going to the Rock Candy today?"

"Hmm," Easton says from the platform below. "Is there room for all of us? Maybe you and I should stay here, Firefly."

Haley pivots back to me. "Why? A tender like that can take five guests to the dock."

"Yeah, but if we want to bring more stuff back . . ." Zane scrubs his hand down his chin.

"I need more spices, my large skillet, and bowls," Dante yells up. "Oh, fuck we had a gross of eggs on board. They should still be good. I'd kill for an omelet. Fuck, olive oil. I can't forget the olive oil."

"Dante's going?" Haley's voice cracks.

"I can stay," Easton calls up. "Haley can go."

"No, we should all go." Haley's crawling around on the mattress looking for her clothes, and I sit up.

Zane finds them from the other side of the platform and hands them to her. She stabs her legs into her leggings and zips up her crew jacket, shoving her bra and a T-shirt into her pocket with so much force the zipper slides down to her bellybutton. Damn, it's a cute bellybutton. Sure, she was just walking around naked, but I'm not the only one staring. I'm even harder and she's put more clothes on. It's wacky.

Easton's standing on the ladder, his head a foot above the platform. "It's fine, Haley. I'll stay here and keep the stove going for dinner. We need more firewood anyway."

Now Rockwell becomes reasonable? What the hell?

"I can get my pots another day," Dante yells.

What has gotten into them? Or I guess what has gotten into me? I don't want her going. The less time around Sam, the better. Even though I know he's not like Jared and she's not like Trisha.

"If it's not too rough, we can blow up one of the towable tubes," Zane says. "We won't be going fast, and we can strap things down. Or someone can ride on it wearing a life vest, of course."

"Sure, that will work. Guess we're all going to the Rock Candy." I see it now. Me wanting her to stay is irrational.

"First you eat," Dante calls up.

It's a good forty minutes past sunrise when we're finally pushing off our little beach. Pepper trots down the path and jumps on the big rock. She mews loudly.

Haley shifts in her seat. "Oh, maybe I should stay. Pepper will be lonely."

"I left her enough fish for lunch and dinner, Sassy. She'll be fine, and you know I would miss you more."

"You are going to be far too busy gathering all your pots," Zane says.

Dante makes a noise that's in agreement. "But I'd miss you in here, Sassy." He puts his hand over his heart and slides it south.

She playfully slaps his knee as I'm getting us out of the breakers. "I do wonder what Pepper is going to think of Penny, though. When they finally meet." Haley hooks her arm over Dante's leg and sets her hand on my bare foot.

Easton twists back to the chef. "Breakfast was really good, Dante."

"Thanks." He salutes.

"It was amazing." Haley pats her belly, and I miss the touch of her hand.

"Anything for you, Sassy. But it's the spices. We've been

eating like a backwoods New Englander with our food just salted."

"It was still good."

"Fresh is always best, Sassy." He pulls on her so her back rests against his chest. He tilts the side of her head and kisses her ear.

It's a perfect day to be out on the water. The drizzle has stopped. I worried what it would be like next to the cliff, but it's not too rough, and the tender cuts through what little chop there is.

"I didn't think I would ever want to get in a small boat again after the raft, but this is kind of fun." Haley reaches back, touching me again. "You doing okay? Running over your plan of what to investigate first?"

"Yeah, you called it, Chiefie." Because that's exactly what I should be doing, not thinking about the conversation Sam and her are going to have when they finally get to be alone. What the hell am I going to tackle first? The wiring looks like cut spaghetti. The engines first. Damn, I hope they didn't do anything to the engines. But whoever did this had it planned out. Those stickers were diabolical. How the hell did they have them? I've gone over and over this so many times. At one point, I convinced myself that it was someone who just went crazy, like Candy, and they decided to take us all down with them. But making stickers and moving water from one tank to the next . . . Yeah, the best thing is to keep an open mind, let the evidence point to who did it. Hopefully that will help me undo what they've done.

The tender edges around the cliff, into the cove. Dante, Haley, and Easton cheer. I catch Zane's eye. Fuck, it isn't going to be easy keeping the truth from them—about how bad the Rock Candy is or the level of sabotage.

Haley looks up at me. "I know; she's a hot mess, but she's our hot mess."

"Just like you, Sassy." Dante's deep laugh carries on the waves, and Sam's head pops up from the back sundeck. "*That* he hears? But me singing for hours on end, nothing." He laughs again.

Haley rights herself in her seat, leaning forward. Maybe it's for docking and prepping, getting off the tender. But more likely it's so Sam doesn't see her touching me or the other guys.

I pilot closer, shooting wide and turning back to the swim deck. Sam's there wearing a crisp white polo—but then we all are looking and smelling better than we have in weeks. Penny's beside him. She sits back on her haunches and howls.

Haley laughs.

And damn, I can't help but smile on the outside. We are far from out of the woods. Really, we're in the eye of the storm—it feels calm, good, but shit is going to happen on the other side. The other side of the storm holds the power.

Sam holds his hand out, and Zane tosses the rope like the pro he is. He hops out and helps Sam tie us up tight. There's enough water now that the inflatable isn't in danger of getting ripped open by the reef. But low tide? I look over the edge into the crystal-clear water and at the reef below. Yeah, later we'll have to muscle the inflatable into the toy hauler space.

I'm the last one to step out onto the swim platform. Sam has a tray of drinks, and Haley's laughing.

"It's boxed orange juice, but I thought we needed a toast." Sam holds it out for me to take one. That's when I see the second tray.

"Towel?" Easton offers me one, a smirk on his lips.

"I'm good." But I shake my head and take one. Damn, it does feel nice to wash my hands and face.

Sam raises his glass. "To all of you. I'm glad we've found each other. I know together we'll be able to work through our issues and find our way home." Sam clinks his glass with Haley's.

"Cheers!" Haley clinks back and does the same with the rest of us.

Sam goes around our circle too. When he gets to Dante, the chef cocks his eyebrow at him. I'm growling on the inside. Dante totally said something to Sam about what was going on back at camp. My eyes flick to Haley, but she hasn't picked up on it.

I toss back the drink. It's not cold, of course, but damn, it tastes like home. The sugar zings at the back of my tongue, and while we've been eating pomelos, this hits differently.

"Salut." Dante drinks his and winks at me. That fucker; I'm not wrong. "I'll be in the galley if anyone needs me. Sassy, come see me in a while."

"I pulled a few tubs out of storage and left them there for you." Sam places his glass on the tray.

"Thanks, Cap." Dante slaps Sam on the back and jogs up the stairs. Penny follows. "Are you coming with me? Let's see what's left. I'm sure I can find a treat for you."

"I guess I'll . . ." Haley's jaw drops, and she looks at me. "What can I do to help?"

"I don't know yet, Chiefie. But there will be something. Why don't you have a look around?" Preferably far away from Sam.

"Yeah, I'd like that. Come get me when you have something I can help with." Haley's hand twitches toward me, but then she pulls it back.

"Sam, Green, just let me know how I can help." Easton sits on a chair in the toy hauler. It's a hardback one. "Oh, my damn. Sit down. This is amazing."

I'm cocking my head at him like a dog.

"No, seriously. Green, Firefly, just sit for a second." He pulls another chair over. There's a tackle kit next to it. Sam must be fishing out here. Zane has disappeared. "Two seconds. Tell me if this isn't the most comfortable chair you've ever sat in, ever?"

I nod. "I'll trust you on it."

Rockwell has his eyes closed, his hands folded over his stomach. "I'm going to take ten minutes and just enjoy the beauty of a backrest."

"There's more comfortable—"

"I'm not a guest, Firefly. You don't have to take care of me." He opens one eye and smiles. "I'll be up to help in a minute. Promise."

Haley nods and dashes up the stairs to the porch off the main salon. I start to follow her, but Sam steps in front of me. "Are you heading to the engine room first?"

"I thought I would."

"I'll bring the manuals and the flashlights down." He takes off after Haley. I watch him vanish after her.

"You doing okay, Green?" Easton's eyes are open.

"Yeah, peachy." I head through the latched door in the back of the toy hauler room to the engine room.

Chapter 20

Christening

Sam

Taking the steps two at a time, I'm in the main salon behind Haley a second after her. But now I take it in with her eyes. It's a disaster. There's stuff everywhere. Sure, I've picked up a bunch. Or I tried to, at least. But it's not fit for guests. Not that that's an issue.

"Whoa, this place is . . . wow. Guess the Rock Candy's not a sailboat, huh?" Things really moved around during the listing.

"I've swept up all the glass. I didn't want Penny to get hurt."

She picks up a pillow and puts it back on the sofa.

I do the same; I'm not sure why. Fuck. I've got her alone.

"I've got it. I'll have her looking good in no time. But the second you have something I can do that's more vital, I'll do it." She's hugging a pillow to her chest. Her blue eyes are dark in the dim light. It gets a lot brighter in here as soon as the sun pokes over the edge of the cliff.

I glance down the stairs. I need to get down there to talk to Calvin. But this might be my only chance to talk to Haley alone. They're all over her. Even in the tender on the way in.

I step toward the main staircase but stop myself. "Haley, can we talk in the wheelhouse?" It's a shit place to have the conversation. It's where I have the power, even now. She's been yachting long enough that I know she'll feel it.

"Oh, uh. Yeah, I mean. I need to make an espresso martini for a guest, but I'll be right there." She drops the pillow on the sofa, giving it a chop to make a 'v' in it. She's joking, but it still gives me pause for a second. "Lead the way." She bobs her head. And I can't read her. It's weird because I can read anyone. It's what makes me a great captain.

I make my way down the corridor. It's so odd being here with people. Even odder is not having Penny at my heels. I can hear her in the galley. Or rather, I hear Dante talking to her. His words from yesterday circle in the back of my head. *Don't tell her.* Damn, how am I not going to bring it up? *So, remember when we talked about exploring our attraction before shit hit the fan? What happened to that, and how the hell are you letting four guys screw you?*

"Take a seat." I close the door behind her.

"Sam?"

"You're not—" Then I see what she's looking at.

"Were you sleeping on the floor?"

"Yeah, until I hit the reef. It made getting up in the middle of the night to take star positions a heck of a lot easier."

Haley puts her hand on the wall behind the bench. "Your cabin is on the other side; it's like three steps away from here. It's not like you were down in the primary's cabin."

"Yeah, I would never. It was fine. Penny liked it."

"I imagine she did." Haley cocks her head to the side.

I glance at where I had her picture taped on the bottom of the console. It's in my room now, taped to my lamp. "Listen . . ." I step closer to her. "I took your picture from your cabin. I taped it up there. I talked to you. You kept me alive."

There's a knock on the starboard door. Zane's there.

"Come in," I grunt.

"Hey Little Bird. What's it like to be back? Weird, right?"

"So weird. But shockingly, other than not having a working engine, I think the yacht was in worse shape when I first came on board."

"What do you need, Zane?" I try to keep my tone light, but I'm not sure I succeed.

"I've talked to Calvin. He thinks it's okay to use a few gallons of fresh water to rinse the worst of the mildew off the port-side. It must stay in the shade most of the day. I'm going to pressurize the tank, if that's okay with you?"

"Sounds good. There's a foot pump down by the tank. When I run out of rainwater, I've been doing the same thing."

Zane stands there looking at Haley and then me. "I'll do that, then I'm going to go help Calvin. He said he wants a few quiet minutes to really study things."

"Good." I cross my arms over my chest. That gives me more time to talk to Haley too.

"All right, I'm going to go do the thing." Zane nods and backs out of the room. His eyes are glued to Haley.

When the door clicks shut, she blinks at me. "I bet Penny likes sleeping in your cabin better."

"Oh, yeah. I suppose. Would you like to sit? Easton seemed really excited about that hard chair."

"Sure, thanks." She slides onto the back bench and sucks in her lower lip.

"I . . . I wanted to make sure you feel safe."

Her head slumps forward, and I'm afraid I've been too direct. "Safe? Yeah, weird to say it. We've only had a roof over our heads for a night, and I feel safer than I ever have. More than safe."

"Okay, it's just . . . Did anything happen on the island?"

"Anything? Well, I guess lots of things happened. Zane and I were chased by a boar that wanted to eat us. But we ate it. I sprained my ankle trying to . . . fix something I shouldn't have. We built a shelter, found a cat . . . Oh, there's this amazing waterfall . . ." A blush rises up her neck, and now I'm having visions of what might have happened at said waterfall. Fuck, all night, that's all I could think about. Them touching her. At first, I was furious. But the more I thought about it, the more fucking hard I got, until I had to take myself in my hand. Tonight's going to be so much worse. I'm not sure I'll be able to handle it.

There's a thud on the starboard side, and Haley's head swings to the opposite door. I should have chosen a room with fewer windows. There's another knock, and this time it's Easton.

"Hey, fuck, that was the most comfortable nap I've ever had."

"Nap? It's been like ten minutes," Haley says.

"It was a great ten minutes, Firefly."

The three of us stare at each other. "Right . . . well, I'm going to go down and rummage around in the cabins.

Unless you have something else I can do that will help?" Easton cocks an eyebrow at me.

"I think we're good until Calvin comes up with a plan."

"Okay, then. I'll be around if you need me." He holds the door open like he's going to stay and chat more. Then he gives a firm nod and pivots away.

I don't even remember the carefully crafted talk I wanted to have with her. I was hoping to get her to bring it up without any assistance from—

The door to the salon opens with no knock. "Hey Sassy, Cap, I'm going to make some lunch. Is there still propane on the back grill?"

"Tons."

"Good. Noon sound good to you, Sassy?"

She slides off the bench. "Works for me, if that's okay with you, Captain?"

Fuck me, I'm back to Captain. "That's fine. Thanks for cooking, Dante."

"No problem, Sam." He taps the wall next to the door twice before he leaves.

There's a nerve in the back of my eye that just about snaps with the effort it's taking to not roll my eyes. When the door shuts, I'm gone. "Firefly, Little Bird, Chiefie, Sassy? Do they know you have a damn name?"

Her eyes fly wide open. "We've become close."

"I can see that." Fuck, not what I wanted to say, and certainly not at the volume I did. I grab my beard, a beard that wasn't present before the wreck, and I pivot back to her. I let my chest rest. "You went through something . . . something that no one ever wants to think about. Of course you all have become close. I imagine there would be only two options: close or at each other's throats."

"Oh, Calvin and Easton definitely went through that stage." She grabs her sides.

What Dante said flashes back at me. "It must have been hard."

"Yes?" Her blue eyes gaze at me. "It was hard, but also not. It's weird; somehow keeping ourselves alive is less pressure. Waking up and eating has become the goal for the day. It's weirdly freeing. Your experience must have been a lot different. Being on the ship, just you and Penny. Trying to figure out what went wrong. That's a lot of pressure."

I nod and smile at her. She's changing the subject to me. "More frustrating than anything else." I lean against the console. "Did anything happen that you feel you need to talk about?"

Her eyes flick everywhere but my face. "Are you asking that as the captain of the Rock Candy or as Sam?"

I smile. There's heat rising up the side of my neck. "Both, I suppose. First as the captain."

"No, everything was good. Calvin really kept things on the raft going. We all collected rainwater, and then he caught a big fish. That was a real win."

"Good." I nod. "I'll have to ask Calvin for fishing pointers. I haven't caught much myself." I give her the space to answer the other half of the question.

"I really like you. That hasn't changed." She sucks in her lips.

"Good, I really like you too." I cock my head.

"Right, and we hadn't said that we were . . ." Her cheeks are turning white.

"Haley, are you okay? Sit back down." I take her elbow and guide her back to the seat. Touching her sends a zing through me. I'm an asshole—I can see how much stress this causes her, but damn, that simple touch has me hard. I should step back, but I can't. Her knee brushes along my thigh.

"I'm okay. Sorry, Sam."

Damn, it's a small victory, but having her call me by my name fires more zaps around my body. "I'm glad you're okay, but I want you to feel good."

"I do . . . I do feel good. This is just . . ."

Again, I'm an asshole because I have no intention of telling her I know.

"I really was looking forward to us touring around together. And taking a step back was the right thing to do for work."

"For work," I repeat. "Right, for work. Well, I've thought long and hard about that decision. And I made it from fear." I push a chunk of hair away from her face and tuck it behind her ear, and I leave my hand on her cheek.

"Fear? Oh, I . . . You were afraid?" Her eyes flutter to mine.

My thumb rests on the inside of her neck, and the thud of her pulse races into my hand. "Very much so. Things are different now. When I started yachting, you couldn't date anyone on your crew. And those who did were usually doing it for not great reasons. My logic was stuck in the past. But I could have told Rocky—followed protocol. I'm sorry I didn't. I've thought about you a lot, Haley. I've never met anyone like you. When this is all over— Fuck, no, before then . . . I want . . . I want something with you."

Her eyes are dilated, and her pulse races faster. When I brush my pinky over her lips, she swallows hard.

Then she jumps backwards. "I need to tell you something."

Chapter 21

Come About

Haley

This must be what a heart attack feels like. My fingers are numb, and my breath catches with each rise of my chest. I've never blacked out before—maybe that's it. I'm blacking out. No, I'm not. How do I tell him?

"Are you okay?" He reaches for me.

I close my eyes and put my hand up. "Give me a second."

"Of course, take all the time you need." The heat from his body radiates into me; it cocoons me with his musk. I want to cling to him, snuggle against his chest. Breathe him in. Every time I've thought about this conversation, I've pushed it out of my head. It's too painful.

"I like you a lot." I need to open my eyes.

"I like you too."

"Right, so . . ." Rip it off like a Band-Aid. "Over the last months, I've developed a relationship with the guys."

"I see."

"No, no, you don't. Like, I'm having sex with all of

them. But not sex—it's more than sex. Well, it is for me and . . . no, it is for them too." I think of Dante's rough whisper to me last night. I open my eyes and look right at Sam. He's not . . . well, he's not reacting, and somehow that makes it worse. I don't know what I expected him to do. Scream and yell. Throw something like my dad used to do in the last years of my parents' marriage. But his face is calm and his hands are loose at his sides, no balled fists. And it hits me. "You already knew."

Now his brow furrows. "Yes."

My gut hardens. "You could have—"

"How? How and not make it about them instead of about me and you?"

"You and me?"

"That's what I said, Haley."

"You . . . you're not mad?"

"Didn't say that." He puts his hand back on my face, and I lean into it.

"Oh, right." And then it hits me. "I'm not choosing." I try to back out of his touch, but I can't.

"Life is full of many choices, Haley."

"I know. But I'm not going to stop being with them. I . . . I care about them." I almost said love.

"You can care about a lot of people, Haley. Doesn't mean you have to sleep with them." He closes his eyes.

"You think I'm a whore?"

"What? No!" His brow ridge thickens, and his touch goes firm. "I would never think that of you, and I hate that it came out of your mouth. You went through something—something unthinkable—and you made what you will of it. And I would never think less of you. You didn't make any vow to me. What we had was the start of something—something fantastic—but it was just that, the start. No, Haley, I don't ever want to hear that word out of your mouth again." His tone drops deep, teetering on threatening. "And if you think that about yourself, you need to scrub it out of your brain altogether. Understood?"

"Copy," falls out of my mouth. "I'm not giving them up."

His eyes dart to my lips. "Copy," he repeats. Sam moves his hand from the side of my face to the back of my neck, and he pulls me to him. His lips brush mine, just a whisper at first, but then he's like a starved man. His tongue teases against the seam of my lips, pressing its way into my mouth. My brain turns off. There's no Sam vs the guys. At this moment, there's only Sam. There's only his mouth, his hand trailing down my back, pushing me into his cock. I rise onto my tiptoes, rubbing his hard length where I want it. I want all of him. I'm acting on reflex. Automatically my hands trail around the nape of his neck. His hair has gotten longer; it brushes the rim of his collar. I grip the back of his head, wanting him even closer than he already is. I'm on fire. I've stepped onto the highway, and now I'm driving at the speed of traffic. Scratch that—I'm speeding, and I want to be caught.

I'm thinking too hard. Do I want to be caught? What are the guys going to think?

Sam grabs both sides of my head and pulls away. "Haley?" His deep voice fills the wheelhouse. He brushes my hair away from my face again. I'm lost in his eyes. "Darling, are you okay?"

I smirk.

"What?"

"Was that a nickname?" My lips quiver.

He smiles, and then his lips are on mine again. He's forceful and commanding, just as I remember. My clean panties aren't clean anymore. I squeeze my legs together tightly. His hands haven't roamed beyond my neck, and I want him to pull me in closer, feel me, touch me. Pinch me. I need more.

The port-side door creaks open. I'm not going to stop kissing Sam. I'm not going to flinch away from him like I've done something wrong. I haven't. That's getting easier to remember with each day. I haven't promised any of them anything. Because . . . there's a big part of me that doesn't believe any of this is real. They're saying things and doing things they don't mean. Who could ever be this lucky? Four handsome guys—five. Five.

The door closes, and Sam pulls away. He doesn't step back, though.

Calvin's eyes peer over the top of Sam's head, but I have no idea what he's thinking.

"Hey Chiefie, Cap."

"Calvin." Sam's tone has dropped.

"Do you have those manuals?" Calvin swings around the wheelhouse. "Right, here they are. I'll see you downstairs, in the engine room. I'm forming a plan of attack. I'd like your opinion on it." He nods at Sam, but his eyes are trained on me and my chest freezes. "Oh, whatever Dante is cooking on the grill smells amazing."

"Lunch," fumbles out of my mouth.

"I know it's lunch, Chiefie." He laughs. "I have no idea what he found to cook, but I'm here for it."

"Yeah, I wonder too." Sam doesn't step away from me. "You mind closing the door? I'll be downstairs . . . in a while to see your plan."

"Sure thing, Sam." Calvin winks at me. And you'd think that would give me some relief. But I'm on the point of passing out again. The door closes, and I'm not sure what to do.

"Haley? Are you okay? Of course you're not okay. Fuck." Sam scowls back at the closed door. "Sit." He drops into a squat between my legs, and the rest of the blood drains from my head. He grabs a steel water bottle from the table next to his binoculars. "Here, drink some."

I hold it with two hands and guzzle down some water. Sam hovers above the bottle. The water sloshes around in my gut. It's like my hormones are inside of a yo-yo today. I hand the bottle back to Sam, and he sinks to the bench next to me.

His head hits the back of the wall. "Damn, Haley. This is confusing to me." His eyes focus out the front of the Rock Candy at the cliff. "I can't imagine what it's doing to you." He pinches his nose and shakes his head. "I can't step aside and watch you have a relationship with all of them. Fuck, I should. But I can't. And I hear you. You're not going to choose me over them."

"I'm not choosing them over you, either." My chest tightens when I realize what I said. Shoot, shoot, shoot. Only I could have five guys one minute and then end up single.

"Yes, you said as much earlier." He's not looking at me.

I take his hand. "Are you going to—"

"Be okay with you . . . *dating* four other guys? Honestly, I don't know. If you'd asked me that three months ago, I would have laughed. Now . . . now I'm not sure. But if that's the only way I can have time with you, I'll try. I'm not saying I'll be good at it." He shakes his head. "No, fuck, I know I'm going to suck at it. Green is okay with it?" Sam waves at the door Calvin disappeared out of.

"At first, no. He was super jealous of Easton. But he's definitely come around."

"How . . ."

"How is Calvin not jealous? He and Easton had a bunch of fights—"

"I can totally see that, but no, how did it start? How did you start being with all of them?"

"I'm not really sure. It . . . it just happened." I never thought it would last, actually. I didn't think about what would happen next. "But I care for them all a lot now. I would never want to hurt any of them." I put my hand on his chest. "Or you. This whole thing was so organic. I'd hate to . . . well, tarnish it."

"I'll try not to be a killjoy. But that's kind of my job, normally."

"Sam, don't say that."

"It's true when you're in charge. I literally have to steer the ship."

I smile.

He grips the base of my chin and kisses me. I melt into his lips. Until he pulls back. "How does it work with the guys? Do I have to get on your calendar?"

"Calendar?" Now I'm really laughing. "We don't have a schedule."

His eyebrows rise.

"What? It's just organic. There's no schedule or tally." I slap my lips together. "And don't you start a tally. Because most of them are really competitive, and it might kill me." I shrug with another laugh.

"I guess that's one way to go." He pulls me onto his lap so I'm straddling him.

"What happened with going to talk to Calvin?" I play with the button on his white polo.

"It can wait a few more minutes. I've missed you, Haley." He stresses my name.

"What happened to 'Darling?'"

He pulls my head back to his again, and this time it's more than a dizzying kiss. His hands race around my back, down to my legs. His fingers play with the hem of my shirt, and then it's gone. A large hand cups my breast. Our kiss breaks. "This is pretty. I pictured you in it more than once." His fingers slide over the lace of my bra.

I playfully slap at his muscular arm. "Sam, you said you didn't open my bag."

"I lied. I couldn't help myself. I missed you too much. Do they know what else is in there?"

"No." I shake my head. My hair falls around his shoulders. The heat is rising up my neck. "Why did you say you hadn't looked in it, then?"

"I thought you would want to keep it private."

"Oh, well, thank you." I should have just thrown half of them away. I didn't. But I couldn't have left them in storage, in a garage where anyone could find them. A garage that's technically owned by me, but if they think I'm dead? My father would be the one to go through all of my stuff. I'm more than glad I brought the lockbox.

"No, thank you. I can't wait to try them out on you."

"They were locked up."

"I had time. There's only so many combinations. I used it as a solvable puzzle compared to the mess the boat's in. There might have been tequila involved too."

"A drunk Sam? That's something I want to see."

"Well, tequila and I are no longer on speaking terms." He nips at my lips.

"That bad?"

"You have no idea." He kisses me again.

It feels so normal. Like the radio could crackle with Shayla's voice asking if I want her to start on cabins or laundry next. I kiss him back.

"Fuck. Right, I really do need to go." He picks me up and sets me back on the bench, then races out of the room, leaving me with a raging lady boner. Is that a thing? Well, I know how to fix that. I pull on my shirt and make my way down the corridor, past the destroyed main salon to the galley to Dante.

Chapter 22

HMS King George V

Dante

"What are you singing?" Haley leans against the doorframe to the galley. "It feels like a year since I baked cupcakes for Emily."

"Sassy! Just the person I always want to see. Come here . . . I was singing? I didn't even realize I was." I put the knife down and pull her into my arms. I kiss the top of her head and then hold her away from me. I study her face. There's no residual red puffiness caused by tears. If anything, her lips look puffy. I run my thumb over her lip. She sucks my thumb into her mouth.

"Yummy, onions. There's something I never thought I would say." Haley runs her fingers through my hair.

I swing around and pick up an onion. "Oh, this is the base of everything good. Well, everything besides you. Damn, seeing you here . . . I had a lot of wet dreams of you and me and this kitchen counter."

She laughs.

"That's no laughing matter, Sassy. How did your talk with Sam go?"

"My talk?"

Now I'm feeling like my sister back in high school when she was trying to get all the tea about my friends out of me. I'd gone to the all-boys Catholic school, the one where all the boys she was crushing on went, while she was going to public school. Something else my SOB uncle decided had to happen.

I started the hard conversation; I might as well finish it. "You were in the wheelhouse talking to Sam." It hits me that I have to tell her that I told him. Because it's going to come out. And when it does, it will be better from me.

"He knew. At first . . . at first I was terrified. But then, once I realized it was Sam and not some scary guy, I relaxed. I'd figured he knew about Calvin, at least."

"Yeah, that goodbye kiss last night didn't leave any doubts, did it? But he knew." I say it as a statement. I raise my eyebrows at her, telling her without telling her that it was me who spilled the beans.

"How can you be so . . . Dante? I told you not to say anything."

"Yes, and I should say I'm sorry, but I'm not. Did it make the talk easier?"

"Dante." She stares at the cabinet above my head. "I mean, yes. But I said not to."

"Are you mad?"

"I'm not mad. I'm upset. I told you not to, and you did."

"Right. Have you ever had more than one boyfriend before?"

"No. You know I haven't."

"Well, you need to keep everything out in the open. It's

the only way. If you start to have secrets with one person, that's how things implode."

"Have you have you had more than one girlfriend?"

"I've had more than one partner before, yes, Sassy. But that was a long time ago. They're still together. I'm not big on social media, but the last time I checked, they were."

"Oh."

"Does that bother you?"

"I mean, no. But yes."

I give her a kiss on her ear. "That's the only correct answer, Sassy. But right now, for the record, I love you. And I'll try not to go and do anything drastic again. But no promises, because drastic is my middle name."

"I thought it was Saffron?"

"I'm like the King of England. I've got lots of middle names. Some you can even say in public." The wind changes direction, and I can smell the grill from the back deck.

"What are you making? It smells fantastic."

"Baked pasta with jar sauce, but I've got canned tomatoes. Next time, it will be even better. I'm going to make onion soup for dinner. And something even better. Lift that lid over there." I point at the large bowl.

She lifts it and jumps. It's exactly what I thought she would do. "Bread? You're making bread?

"Oh, something even better than bread."

"What's better than bread? It's round and—" Her eyes dilate. "Pizza?"

"Pizza, yes. If that's okay with you?"

She jumps into my arms. "You are a god among men." She kisses my neck.

"Good. I'm glad to know I can cook my way out of trouble." I wiggle my eyebrows at her. "Don't get too excited—

this isn't going to be New York City street slices. More upscale, I'm afraid. But it will be good. I found wax-sealed Gouda and Parmesan, along with some vacuum-sealed Cheddar."

"I don't care. Bread, cheese, sauce. It's like Christmas. How can I ever thank you?"

I cock my head. "Give me five minutes and I can think of a way."

"Dante? What about the food on the grill?"

"Zane's watching it while he washes off the back of the boat. And by watching it, I mean he lifts the damn cover every few minutes and breathes all over it as he huffs it. He won't let it burn."

"You were really thinking about me back here on your counter?"

"What, Sassy? When I fantasized about you on my counter, it was long before I ever touched you. Back in the before."

"No . . . you didn't like me before the crash. Come on?"

"I did. And don't question my emotions, Sassy. I know exactly how I felt and when I felt it."

"Oh." Her mouth stays in a little round circle. "So, you had a wet dream about sitting on your counter here?" She lays her hand flat on the steel surface next to my onions.

"No."

"Oh?"

"Over here." I pat the section of counter that's in full view of the corridor.

"There?"

"Yes. So what should I do about it?" I'm not going to tell her now that the dream was about me eating her out on the counter. After last night, I want her hot mouth around my cock again.

She takes a step closer and puts her hands on my waist, like she could lift me up there herself.

I smile and, with a quick twist, have her sitting on the counter. And with a quick tug, I have her shorts hanging from one ankle. A quick pull and I have her T-shirt off, revealing a different translucent bra. I suck one nipple through the thin fabric and then the other, leaving them hard and pebbled. "Fuck, Sassy. I do like your new wardrobe."

I kiss down her belly as she leans back on her arms. She's lost weight since we've been on the island, and I don't like it. What I do like is her matching panties. I slide them to the side and fuck, she's wet. "Did Captain give me a head start? I'll have to thank him later."

"Dante." She's scolding me, but that's okay. I like her teacher's voice. Sam isn't ready for me and my mouth, not yet. Hell, most people never are. But not Sassy. Damn, this girl drives me wild.

I give a little pull, bringing her ass to the edge of the counter. And I feast on her clit. She's moaning within seconds. I've definitely been given a warm engine. I push one, then two fingers into her. It's the fastest I've ever seen her come. She slaps her hands on the steel counter, and it rings. Her elbows clatter on the counter, and I reach up and grab her head. This damn table has caused one concussion already; we don't need it to be two.

Her body shakes with little convulsions as I continue to thrust into her. "Dante, please."

I lift my mouth. "That's my aim, Sassy. Always to please you." She slides from the counter, and it leaves a trail. Fuck, it's the sexiest thing I've ever seen.

"Your turn. Get up there, Chef."

"Yes, anything for my Sassy." I've got my pants and T-shirt pulled off. It's weird to be in the kitchen without my chef's jacket, but it's far too warm for my uniform. My hard dick is ready for her mouth. "Do you want some chocolate sauce? I found some in the crew mess. Unopened even."

"You're sweet enough for me, Dante." She swallows me down, and when I bottom out at the back of her throat, I make a noise I've never heard before.

"Fuck, Sassy." I've never had someone take me on like she does. It's unreal. My hand goes for her hair. It's silky and smooth—running my fingers through it makes me harder. I'm over the moon for her. "I fucking love you."

She works the base of my cock with one hand and plays with my balls in the other. When she runs her tongue along the underside of my dick while sucking even harder, I'm lost. "Shit, damn. This is too good. Sassy, I'm going to come in your mouth if you don't slow down."

Instead of popping off, she sucks harder. My eyes close, and stars shoot around my head. I'm pulling at her hair to get me out of her mouth, but she's tugging harder the other way. The tension I feel while pulling on her hair turns me on. Fuck, it's her hair, her head, not even my own, but I know how she likes it and that makes me harder.

She lightly puts pressure on my nuts, and I'm gone. Hot streams flood Sassy's mouth. I'm half done, rockets bursting behind my eyes, when I remember to look at my girl taking my come. She swallows it down. And my cock pops out of her mouth.

"Fucking hell." Sam's standing in the doorway to the galley. His eyes are wide.

The color drains out of Sassy's face. She opens her mouth, but I put a hand on her shoulder. If he even raises his voice half a decibel, we are going to be having more than words. I give Sassy my hand, raising her to her feet. "Sam." I match his tone.

"How the hell is your damn cock that big?"

I laugh and look Sassy in the eyes. "Guess you have another guy who's jealous of my cock."

"Not jealous, just worried about Haley's internal organs. Throat, stomach, hell, maybe even her upper intestines."

Haley turns away from him with a smirk on her puffy lips, but the start of an embarrassed glow rises up her neck. She pulls up her shorts, and tucks in her shirt. I shrug and hop down from the counter.

Sam regains some composure. "Zane took the food off the grill like you told him to."

"Perfect. I'm sure Sassy would like something else to eat." I wink at Sam. "We'll be right there." Sam stares at me, not moving. "Give us a minute, Sam. We'll be right there."

<h1 style="text-align:center">Chapter 23</h1>

<h1 style="text-align:center">Dinner Bell</h1>

Zane

When I open the grill again, just to check it, damn, the pasta smells amazing. It's done, and I take it out, setting it on the counter next to the grill. Back in the before time, when we'd brought the boat from the shipyard and moved to port where we picked up Easton, I'd been the one making a lot of the crew meals. But I certainly never made anything like this on a grill before. Cheese oozes out, bubbling around a golden crust. I'm worse than a dog—I'm absolutely salivating.

Sure, everything Dante has made us has been amazing, but I can't wait to dig into this. It's weird, though. We've been eating nothing but fish and fruit. You'd think I'd feel weak or off eating the same thing over and over, but I don't at all. I'm spot on—I feel better than I ever have. Like, ever.

Dante said after I take it off, it would need to sit for a while. I fasten the aluminum foil back over the top of it. Penny's around here somewhere. I push the dish to the back of the counter to keep it out of her temptation zone. I don't know where Easton's gone off to. And after barging in on Haley and Sam in the wheelhouse, I'm going to let them have their peace. I'm in a flap about what might happen. I've known the captain for a while now, and on an average day, I'd never think about competing with him. What would be the point? He's like one of those fit models you see in those underwear adverts on billboards. I'm not minging, and since I started yachting, I've gotten proper fit, but I'm nothing to look at. But damn, I'm confident our Little Bird won't hurt me and forget about me. I think.

I dash inside, pulling the doors closed behind me. I like Penny, but I don't want her to get to lunch first. I'm through the salon down the main stairs. I weave around, looking for Easton. Damn, I miss radios. The Rock Candy's massive. There's no yelling from one side of her to the other. "Easton." I project down the corridor, but there's no answer. At least I know where Calvin is. I head to the engine room and knock on the open door. Bloody hell, it's humid down here. Captain mentioned a patch he made to the hull.

That's when I see Easton's bum in the air. He's mopping up the floor. "Hey."

Easton stands up, smacking the top of his head on a pipe. The thud echoes through the room. "Fuck."

"Shit, are you okay?" I grab his bicep to steady him.

Easton's holding his head. "I think so." He lifts his hand, holding it to his face. There's no blood.

"You're sure, man? Let me see."

"Yeah." He tips his head to the side—no blood.

"Right, well, lunch is ready on the back deck."

He takes the rag and wrings it out into the bucket. "Great." I'm not sure why, but I expect him to toss the rag into the bucket and leave them on the floor, but he doesn't. He grabs both the towel and the bucket and heads out.

"Green said to dump it into the slop sink, since the water might have oil in it. But I don't know where that is."

I nod. Every day, Rockwell shows me he's not what I thought he was in the beginning. Although, I still can't fathom having even a one-nighter with Brianna. I shiver internally. "That's the way to do it," I say about the sink. I'm always protecting the water, and even more so here. We can't poison the land that's feeding us. "Where is Green?"

"He went out back to check the crash patch." I lead Rockwell to the laundry room, where he dumps the bucket and hangs the towel next to a couple other muddy-looking ones.

"Water's pressurized if you want to wash your hands," I tell him. "It's cold but . . ."

"Thanks."

I wait until he's done washing, then I take him through the toy hauler room to the back swim deck.

"It's like a secret passageway." Easton waits while I check the tender floating next to the boat. It's good. We've got a few more hours before we need to worry about it scraping on the reef.

We head up the swim stairs to the back deck. Haley's laying out plates; Captain and Dante are following behind her with silverware and napkins. She's even found some shells and stuff to put in the middle of the table. It's proper pretty, like they do for guests.

"There you are," Captain says as soon as our feet hit the top step.

"It looks nice, Haley." I kiss her cheek and watch the dash of pink zip up her neck to her face.

"Force of habit. It looked so naked without anything in the middle of the table."

Dante laughs. "But we like naked, Sassy."

I give the captain a sideways glance to see his reaction. He shakes his head and sits at the table, the napkin on his lap taking up all his attention.

Haley smiles at Dante. "I'll be right back. I want to get us some drinks." She stops at the entryway to the main salon. "It's Italian—do we want red wine? Or should we wait until tonight?"

I close my eyes. A glass of wine would be amazing, but then we've got a lot of work to do. "Tonight's my vote."

"Okay. I'll grab some waters and some other things." Haley moves into the main salon.

"I'll help you." I chase after her.

"Thanks, Zane. There's a lot still in the stew pantry. I think Sam took most of the water and sodas from the bar area." She pulls open the door to the pantry. There are boxes on the floor, and some of the cabinets are open.

"Captain said he searched most of the boat, looking for batteries and emergency supplies," I add.

"Yeah." Her face drops. Haley likes order. I saw it all those months ago when she came on board, and then on the beach. The way she wove mats and has learned how to make baskets . . . Neat and tidy. "It's nothing. I'll have the boat looking great soon. I can fix it in between helping get the major systems up and running."

"I know you can, Little Bird."

She moves two boxes out of the way and pulls open the lower door. "Bingo."

There are at least a dozen cases of water and boxes of American sodas. I pull out a tray and hold it down low for her while she makes a sampling, but there's a lot to choose from. It looks like every type of soda ever invented. There's so many there's no way to take them all.

"What do you want?" Her neck twists, and she looks back at me.

"I don't care. I've always been more of a water kind of guy, but then, it's been a long time. A cola sounds good."

"Got it." She puts it on the tray, and I turn.

"Thank you, Zane." I'm about to step out when she places her hand on my arm. "Are you okay?"

"Of course, right as rain, Little Bird."

"Good. I . . ." She looks away.

"This is a lot. It's not something I ever thought I would be into. Like, ever. And I'm not going to lie to you and say that if I could have you all for myself that I wouldn't. When we get back to the mainland, I'm in it with you. Whatever happens with the other guys, that's . . . it doesn't matter. I'm here." I smile at her, and I lean over the tray and kiss her on the lips. I push the tray to the counter and pull her against me. I brush her hair out of her face and deepen the kiss. Another second, and I won't be able to walk out of here. Her hand eases under my crew shirt. It's clean, but I've been scrubbing in the sun for the last few hours. I want to tell her I love her. But in a closet isn't the place; when our lunch is hot on the table isn't the time.

"Zane." She blinks up at me. "I'm glad . . . I think I was more worried about you than anyone else."

"I'm not going to break, Little Bird. I'm tough."

"I know you are."

There's a slap on the outside of the pantry door. Easton's here, his arms resting on top of the doorway. "I thought it was taking a long time, Firefly." He leans in around Haley and takes the tray. His chin scrapes along her neck as he does. "Carry on. I've got the service for you." He flicks his eyes back to me, and then he's gone.

"I'm not going to lie, that asshole is growing on me."

Haley laughs. "Easton's not an asshole. He's just been pigeonholed by what he does . . ."

"And who he is, or I guess was." I bend my neck and kiss her again. I don't want to use my little alone time with her thinking about another guy. I pick her up and flip her so her bum is sitting on the counter. Her legs wrap around my waist, and I'm in my own version of heaven. I never played any of those games as a teen—spin the bottle or seven minutes of heaven in a dark closet. But then, I've never been as attracted to a girl as I am to Haley. She rubs herself against my hard cock, and I have to laugh because her stomach rumbles and vibrates against me. "All right, Haley, let's get you properly fed." I carry her out of the pantry, with her clinging to me like a koala.

She slides down my body, and it's torture. "After lunch, if you can stand the heat, you and I should make sure there isn't anything we need for camp in one of the guest cabins." She winks at me and saunters away.

"That's a date." I pinch her bottom.

Out by the table, Dante glares. "Right, let's get started." He's holding a big spoon at his side, and I'm not sure if he's going to spank Haley with it or serve lunch. But when he scoops the pasta onto the first plate, we all gasp. The stringy cheese trails from the spoon to the first plate, and Haley jumps up, clapping. "Are you crying, Sassy?"

"Tears of joy."

"No tears in the food. It's perfectly salted." He hands her the first plate. She tries to serve it to Calvin, who's sitting closest. I hadn't even noticed he'd appeared from somewhere. "No, Sassy, that's your plate. It's the best of the lot. The damn Viking probably won't even chew before he swallows it down." Dante laughs, and Haley reluctantly sits. "And don't wait for us. Dig in."

Haley takes the first bite as we all watch. Her lips are against the fork, her eyes closed. She makes a noise that's as close to euphoria as possible. Damn, my cock hadn't even calmed down and now it's going hard again.

"Dante, it's divine." She smiles.

"Of course it is, just like you." He hands me my plate. Fuck, he's right. It's so good. The table goes silent. We never eat in silence, but we don't normally have a big sit-down meal for lunch. But this is a special occasion.

"They say it's bad luck to have a toast with no alcohol, but an alcoholic wrote that proverb, so raise your cans." Dante stands. "To a new chapter, to enjoying the moment and not overthinking, to enjoying the day, the hour and the minute." He raises his energy drink to the sky. "Salud!"

"Cheers!" goes around the table.

Calvin chugs his drink. His eyes catch mine, and I swallow hard. He's got that look that never ends in anything good. "I need to tell you about what I found," he says.

Chapter 24

Diamond Knot

Calvin

That got their attention. I stare at my plate. There's still some sauce on it. I pick it up and lick down the center of the expensive china—it's probably worth more than I make in a week. I lick around the rim. And when I put it back down, they're all glaring at me like I've grown a second head. "Right, sorry. Food was solid, Chef."

"Thanks, that's high praise from you." Dante scrapes the last bits from the platter onto Haley's plate.

"Yup, it was good," I confirm.

Dante clutches his chest. "This is the big one. I can die now. Green gave me a compliment. See what you're doing to him, Sassy? You're making him all happy and human. Tsk-tsk. But good job." Dante kisses Haley on the top of her head.

"Right, what I found. Well, I don't like thinking we're screwed, but without a machine shop, I don't know how I'm going to get the engines back online."

"Why did it happen?" Haley asks.

I glance at Sam and he nods back. "Someone did it, on purpose."

Easton's eyes go wide. "What? Why? What did they do?" I know Sam hasn't ruled Rockwell out, but I have. No way would he have put his sister in danger. And why would he want to take out his father? Neither one of Rocky's kids want his money. Hell, Easton's got his own cash from endorsements and things, and he doesn't want to run the tire company. But killing yourself and your sister in the process? There are simpler ways of getting out of being a CEO. No one around this table did anything to the Rock Candy.

"They've done plenty around the ship, but this isn't the saboteur. This is plain old salt water. It's corrosive as fuck. There's rust all over the crankshaft. The zinc anode is used up. And without the power, there's no way to fix it, because I need to grind."

"There's a grinder in the toy hauler room." Zane licks his fork.

"Fuck, you serious?" I chew on the side of my tongue. Pressure always makes me think better. "That's a start. I might be able to rig something up. But we don't have power. And even if I can get the solar panels running, there's not going to be enough amperage to run a grinder."

"Well, we'll just have to figure out how to increase the efficiency of the solar panels." Haley takes a sip of her soda. "Sorry, that's probably not possible. I'm not a mechanic."

I blink at her, and I can see the worry in her growing. It's like she thinks I think she's said something dumb. But that's not the case at all. "Chiefie, that's a brilliant idea. If I can get the battery rack online, then reconnect the solar panels, I should be able to get enough power to get the grinder working."

"What about the radios?" Easton stands and clears some plates.

Sam glares at me.

"It's really a matter of time. Either way, I need to get the solar power up and running before I can do either. But I need to flush the engines first so they don't go downhill anymore. Then we can decide what our priorities are: engines or radio."

Haley stands and clears along with Easton. I don't think she even knows she's doing it. She's on autopilot. And I have to push down a smile. When she comes to grab my plate, I try to take the ones she has instead.

"Clearing I can do. You're the one with the expertise, Green."

My chest goes firm. Chiefie doesn't like being kept out of the loop. But that's something I don't like either. My eyes flick to Sam. I'm thinking about Sam wanting to keep secrets from them. His lips are pursed, and he shakes his head no. I don't fucking care what he thinks. This is something that has to be said, and I can't not tell her or Easton and Dante anymore. They deserve to know the truth. "Sam, we've become a democracy. And this isn't something I'm willing to keep from any of the others. You need to tell them."

I've known Sam for a long time. I've pushed back once or twice on his decisions. And it's always been for safety reasons. I should have pushed for not leaving the shipyard. But then there's always kinks to work out on a new ship. I didn't give a flying rat's ass about the interior. If the guests wanted to be surrounded by boxes, that was up to them. A few flicking lights didn't seem like a problem, and maybe if someone hadn't tampered with the major systems, it wouldn't have been an issue.

He's not happy with me.

"Sam? What do you need to tell us?" Haley lets me take the dishes from her, and I put them on a tray on the side counter.

"Yes, what are you not telling us? Do you know why the wreck happened?" Easton's got his game face on. If I didn't know him better, I would be suspicious of him like Sam is. "It's sabotage. We all know that. You're not telling us anything new. We've talked about it plenty around the campfire."

"It's something else . . ." Sam shakes his head.

"Sam?" Haley's eyes are wide.

"Before I hit the reef, I saw a boat, lights off."

Easton leans in. "I saw it too."

"Really?" Sam cocks his head at Easton. He shakes it off. "It was a while before I landed on the reef. I was trying to fish from the swim deck. Fuck, if it wasn't for Penny knocking the flare gun out of my hand, I would have signaled them. But when I came back with another gun and my binoculars, I saw that their running lights were off. On the aft, hanging over the railing, a guard sat with an automatic rifle. Luckily, he was more interested in his cigarette break than keeping a lookout. I faded into the night. I'd been trying to use the ham radio, but I stopped. The chance of someone hearing it that could help was too slim, while the odds of a pirate hearing it were too great."

"So that's the thing. If we can get the radio working, we should be able to contact help." I nod at Sam across the table. "But will help come fast enough, or will we be sitting ducks? Ducks that are a lot closer to the pirates than we are to anyone who would want to help us."

"What's your take on it, Green?" Easton leans on a chair. Only Zane and Sam are still sitting.

"Get the engines at least limping along, so we can have a shot of avoiding the pirates, and then work on the radios."

"There's nothing saying we can't work on both at the same time." Sam stares at me.

"Other than we can't clone Green," Dante growls. "And thank fuck for that . . . We couldn't feed two of them."

"We're not helpless. Calvin can teach us what needs to be done." Haley grabs at my arm. "Can't you?"

I can try, but there are some people mechanics doesn't click for. "Sure." I smile down at her. "I'll do my best."

"What do we do first?"

"Well, the first thing I'm going to work on with Sam and Zane is replacing the crash patch. You did a good job, Sam, but having more than one set of hands will help make a tighter seal."

"Pirates are one thing, but what have you learned about the saboteur?" Easton's not giving up.

Sam talked about the pirates in the hopes we'd drop the reason why we're here? We're not toddlers who can be distracted that easily. "Saboteurs," I say. And I ignore Sam's scowl because he'll come to understand that Easton doesn't have anything to do with it. "There's no way one person caused all the damage they did. How they did it when Anders and I were tracing issues with the ship's electrical, I don't know yet."

"That seems like a pretty simple answer." Easton raises his chin to me—meaning Anders.

"A simple answer?" Sam's tone has dropped. Easton's reputation isn't secure to Sam, but Anders has been Sam's FO for at least five years. Long enough that he should have left and had his own boat by now. But I talked with the guy. He liked the flexibility of being able to take time off. Not something you can do as a captain. He's got some things going on back at home, things he barely ever talked about. Even after the years I've been on different ships with him, I'm not sure I even know where he's from. He's mentioned Maine, California, Florida. I guess I always thought he was an army brat, but I never asked. Weird things you remember when it's too late.

"Anders isn't the saboteur—no way." Sam stands.

Zane stands too. "I'm thinking the same thing, Easton. No way would Anders be involved with something as sinister as this. Plus, you didn't see how we were working trying to fix all the issues on the boat."

"Acting—it's a thing." Easton shrugs.

Sam shakes his head. "Did either your ex-stepmom or Emily send you the crew talent show from two years ago?"

I'm shaking with laughter inside.

"No." Easton's face is scrunched up. "Well, maybe they sent me a lot of things." His face drops.

"Well, if you'd watched it, you'd have to know that Anders couldn't act his way out of a paper bag. Whatever that means." Zane's holding his side. "Do you remember when one of the stews shot him, and he had to fall to his death? For fuck's sake, that man can't act."

Easton's not convinced. It's fine. I see the way Sam is looking at him. I'll have to tell him later to cool it. The last thing we need is for Sam to waste time thinking that Easton did it. And if Easton points a finger at Anders, it makes him more guilty in Sam's eyes for sure. I glare at Easton. I can see he wants to push back at Sam.

Instead, he says, "I suppose it doesn't matter what happened—it matters what we're going to do about it now. The crash patch? I can help mop up water. Taking it off will have to make it leak more."

"Thanks, but we've got it for now. We'll need help later,

and every day after, keeping the engine room as dry as possible," I say.

"I can do it." Easton takes the extra napkins from the table and tosses them on the tray. "I'll help wash up." Easton, Dante, and Haley disappear into the main salon.

I look directly at Sam. "What else aren't you telling me?"

Zane's neck twists between the two of us like he's at a tennis match. "Calvin?"

"What? There's something he's not telling us. There's a reason he thinks Easton is guilty, and it's not that Rockwell thinks Anders is a good actor." Something was off with this entire season, even before we took possession from the shipyard. And it's only now that I've put it together.

Sam scrubs his hand over his chin and glances at the open sliders that separate the main salon from the back deck. "Rocky wanted to get underway when we left port. He'd picked up a diamond necklace for Candy. His security team wanted to bring it back to the US, but Rocky wanted to give it to her on the trip. When he said no, they wanted to come on board. Rocky found that hysterical. What could happen to it in the middle of the ocean? Right. Fuck. I remember him laughing about it to me over the phone. It wasn't until last week I went looking for it, thinking maybe this whole thing was a ploy to get it off the ship. Was someone supposed to pick up the rafts? In the chaos of being rescued, could the necklace have been passed off to the would-be rescuers? Was it done for the insurance? Was Easton mad about his father spending his inheritance?"

"Easton's got his own money. And honestly, I don't think he cares about money much." Zane grips the back of the chair.

"He bought the damn diamond?" Easton's standing in

the salon, an empty tray in his hand. "I told him he was nuts. Emily and I were planning on talking him out of marrying Candy. Or at least reworking the prenup. That damn diamond . . . it's cursed." Easton flings the tray onto the counter, and it rings like a gong.

Chapter 25

Crosscurrent

Easton

The tray rattles around in a circle on the counter. I don't throw things. Letting my temper out isn't something I allow. Not since I lost a spot on team USA for the Beijing Olympics. I was sixteen and thought I was hot stuff. I was, but that year there were twenty other guys faster than me. They also didn't have the same temper I did. I watched most of the Olympics from the wide screen TV at my father's Fort Lauderdale mansion. While swimming laps. A few Christmases ago, Emily did the calculations. I don't know if I believe her math, but she said I've spent five years of my life in the pool or gym. Honestly, it was only ten months ago I decided my body wasn't going to be able to rebound enough to make it to the 2024 Paris games. I'm a man now. Not going to Paris was hard, but I didn't throw anything. Fuck, what headspace would I be in if I hadn't already given up the idea of Paris? No, this trip was supposed to be the beginning of my future. Taking the bigger step into my father's company. Something I didn't want to do unless Candy had a harness on. The thought of having to deal with her on a daily basis . . . Damn. Now she's gone, but I certainly didn't want it to happen that way.

My eyes flick over to Sam. I get it. He didn't want to tell me about the diamond. I'm sure my dad was adamant about what he wanted done and who he was supposed to tell. Things click together in my brain. Part of me wants to tell him to fuck off—this is my family's boat, and withholding information from me isn't going to fly. But that's the sixteen-year-old kid scratching at my skin.

"Sam." I clear my throat. "Captain, do you really think I would put the lives of everyone on board in danger? Fuck it. Forget everyone. Do you think I would put my sister in danger? Until recently, she's been the only damn person on the planet I really gave two shits about." I take a step toward him. "You've met her. How many summers?"

"Five or more." His tone is low.

"And?" I ask. I feel Firefly come up behind me. I don't stop, though. Anything I have to say, I can say in front of Haley.

"Emily's a really nice girl. Her boyfriend, though?"

"Fucking Brick's a piece of shit. He's just as bad as Candy. He was pissed when Emily made a will, giving her portion of the Rockwell estate to charity. She did it as a test. I might have suggested that he wouldn't stay with her if he didn't have access to her money. Unfortunately, I was wrong. He was upset but didn't leave her." He probably thought he could get her to change her mind.

"I've never gotten a good feeling from him." Sam crosses his arms over his chest.

"He's cut from the same cloth as Candy. The first time I met him, he asked me how much my watch cost. After three drinks, he asked if I knew how much I could sell my gold medals for." I shake my head. That's the thing when you come from a wealthy family—it's always hard to know who your friends are and who wants a seat at the table with bottle service. I was sure Brick was using Emily, but when she gave her money away—something she'd planned to do since she was little—he didn't vanish. "Tell me everything. Because I had nothing to do with any of this. I loved—*love*—my sister, and I would never want to harm her." It's been driving me crazy. When I close my eyes, I see her in the other raft. I'm a good open water swimmer. But they were right, trying to get to the other raft would have been foolish.

Sam nods. "Getting the Rock Candy from the shipyard was part of your father's idea. An excuse to have the yacht in the South Pacific. At first, he said he had something to pick up, something he would feel better about having his yacht bring back—"

"And bringing the Pink Phoenix back into the States without anyone knowing it . . . Fucking hell. That's the dumbest thing I've ever heard. No wonder he didn't tell me or Emily. They were planning to fly back, but I'm guessing the crew was going to bring the Rock Candy back to—"

"We were going to sail her all the way to South Africa, where they would have met back up with us for three weeks, and then again when we got to the Med, and then a skeleton crew was going to take her home to port in Fort Lauderdale."

"Sorry, Pink Phoenix?" Zane asks.

"Yes, it's a named stone. It went up for auction last year. Candy was all excited about it. She drove Emily crazy with it, sending her texts and articles about the sale. It was predicted to go for between 55 to 65 million."

"Shit," Zane grits out.

"That's high, but not unheard of for that kind of stone."

"That kind?" Zane tilts his head.

"The Pink Phoenix is a pink 51 carat diamond from a mine in Western Australia. A mine that's no longer in operation. Pink diamonds have been skyrocketing ever since the mine closed."

"Are you into the diamond market, Rockwell?"

"Only when the chief financial officer of my family's company calls me and alerts me that the new girlfriend has expensive taste. I'd been thinking about turning my father down on helping run the family business. I was still training. The Pink Phoenix got me on a plane from the training facility in Colorado Springs. So yeah, I know a bit about diamonds." I hadn't beforehand. It was also when I decided that if I ever did trust a girl enough to marry her, I wouldn't be putting a diamond on her hand. "My dad promised he wasn't going to buy it. The auction came and went. It went to an anonymous buyer for 55 million dollars. The day of the auction, I even went into the Rockwell offices just kind of to make sure my dad wasn't going to bid on it. But it sold, and when I joined them at dinner that night, I expected Candy to be sulking around the mansion. She was anything but upset. She was bouncing like a kid. I asked her about it. She said she had a new horse coming to the barn." She did. I checked, but my gut said it was more than that. I should have listened to my gut.

"A large pink necklace?" Haley says.

"Yes, did she show it to you?" Part of me wants to be wrong. But so much of this is falling into place.

"Well, yes and no. She was trying to take jewelry with her when I woke them up the night of the wreck. I told her to drop it, and your dad backed me up. She dropped the jewelry bags. I didn't get a good look at any of them. There might have been something pink. I was thinking about other things at the time." Her blue eyes glisten.

"Yes, thank you for saving my life." Without her opening my door, I might have died. Or I guess I would have spent a good long time with Sam.

"But she didn't take any jewelry bag with her. She left one on the dresser. I think the others were on the floor."

"My dad didn't pick it up?"

"No." Haley shakes her head.

My stomach goes cold.

"Are you okay?" Haley grips my arm.

"I'm not sure. Someone did this to us." And now I can't help but wonder if it was my own father.

"He was just trying to keep Candy safe. Every second counts." Haley rubs my arms, and I can't help but lean into it. Has she come to the same conclusion as me? That there's a chance my dad had something to do with this?

"Right, but if you had a small bag you could fit in your pocket lying at your feet? Wouldn't it be human nature to grab it? That's a lot of money, 55 million. No offense to your family, but that's crazy." Zane circles around the table. "I get safety and all, Haley, but 55 million dollars, for one second to scoop down and pick something up?" Zane drops a napkin and snatches it from the ground. He has a point. I don't care about money, but that's a lot of money.

I stare at Zane, and his brow furrows. I shake it off—there's no way my dad planned this out. "I get it, but that's not how my dad operates. If he bought the Pink Phoenix, he did it because he thought it would make Candy happy. Against the advisement of his CFO, his daughter, I'm sure his best friend, and me. He loves making people happy. It's the reason he started buying yachts in the first place. Susan, his ex-wife, loved boating. So he bought her one, then a bigger one, and a bigger one after that. Granted, he loved yachting, too. He used to laugh at me and say he'd rather be on the water than in it any day." I hate this. "Someone on board did this, right?"

There're nods from around the deck.

"It's not Rocky," I say.

Haley gasps. "Wait! What? I'm coming in late. Are you trying to say that Rocky set this whole thing up?" Haley's got her hand on her hip, and her eyes are focusing on Sam.

Sam peers back at her. "Right, I think you were still in the galley when I said I searched the primary suite and there weren't any jewelry bags in the room."

"There have to be. Easton and I were the last ones up. Well, I guess technically Dante and I were the last ones out."

Sam shakes his head. "I searched. There's nothing there."

"That can't be. I took Rocky and Candy to the stairs. That's when I met Emily and Brick in the hallway. I told them I would get Easton out, and they all left." Haley takes my hand in hers and squeezes. "They went up." She pinches her lips together. "But . . ."

"But?" Sam raises his eyebrows at her.

"My back was turned when I was working on getting Easton's door open. And there is the back staircase."

"It's like a damn poltergeist made its way around the ship," Sam growls.

"I'd still like to go and search." There's one thing my dad told me about the ship that no one knows. He had a little something built into his cabin.

"Have at it," Sam says.

"I'd love to go treasure hunting, but I've got a crash patch to replace. You ready?" Calvin asks Zane and Sam.

"That leaves the two of us." Haley pivots and gives me a hug.

Chapter 26

Dragging Anchor

Haley

Sam, Zane, and Calvin head down the stairs, taking the back way through the toy hauler space to the engine room, while Easton and I finish cleaning up the back deck. Dante's singing in the kitchen. I spend a minute leaning up against the doorjamb. Our chef is lost in his happy place. I momentarily think of inviting him on our search but change my mind. Dante's having too much fun. I pivot back to the stew pantry. Easton is wiping down the plates with a bucket of seawater. We'll wash them later, using as little fresh water as possible. He's really focused on it, but it's obvious by the order he's doing things he hasn't washed many dishes in his life. I stay back and watch him.

I've thought about how I got Easton out of his room more than once. There's a bunch of things that bother me about it, starting with why was it only his door that jammed? At first, I thought it was just a coincidence. The longer I mull it over, the more I think maybe it isn't. I don't have any family anymore. Just my best friend and a dad who's barely part of my life. But I'd like to think that if I was stuck in a sinking ship, they wouldn't listen to a stew who said she was going to get the door open by herself. His dad and Brick didn't even put up a fight—they just fled to the top side. When I think back on it, I think Emily was pulling on Brick. But if she said anything, I don't remember what. It's weird—my adrenaline during that night has made things both clear and blurry. It's like when I watch true crime shows and a witness says that something absolutely happened that couldn't have. Like there's some sort of proof yet they won't back down. I can totally see how someone could have a false memory placed. There's no second-guessing though. Easton's dad didn't fight to get him out of the room. His focus was on getting Candy out.

Easton tosses a towel on the counter. "I think I'm done until we wash tonight with some hot water. It's a crazy concept, right? Hot water."

"Yes! I can't imagine what taking a hot shower would feel like."

"Well, we'll have to conserve water, that's for sure. I'm willing to share my hot water with you." He wiggles his eyebrows at me.

"I'd like that."

"Do you want to go down to the primary cabin?"

"Yes. This is going to sound sexist, and I'm sure Sam did a good job searching—"

"But you think he missed it?"

"No, I'm not saying that, but my ex could look directly at the ketchup bottle in the fridge and still not see it. Not that Sam is anything like my ex."

"I imagine not. When we get back to Florida, for his own sake, I hope I never meet that sack of shit."

I smile at Easton, grabbing his arm. There's a thought

I'm not sure about. Would I want the guys to meet Steven? I cling to Easton's arm. I don't even realize I'm holding on so tight until he winces. "You know, I think I wouldn't mind it. Have him see how amazing all of you are."

"Not as amazing as you are." He kisses my neck. "Come on, let's go. It's only a matter of time before I need to start swabbing the engine room again." We head down the main staircase to the guest cabins.

Easton's a few steps down the hallway when I call out to him, "Wait, I want to see something in your room first."

He pivots back. "What do you want me to show you in my room?" He wiggles his eyebrows.

"No, not that. I mean, maybe later." I give his arm a playful swat. "I want to look at your door."

"I've blocked it open with one of the remaining horse statues I found in the closet."

"Right, I want to look at the jamb, like, was it made that way? Or did someone change it?"

"You think my door sticking was done deliberately?" His lips twist to the side and back. "It could be." Easton runs his hand up the inside of the fitting for the door. "Here, look." He points to a spot and steps out of the way. "Run your hand along it."

I do, but it feels the same.

"No, higher. There's a bulge."

"A tiny bulge like in your pants?" Dante appears beside me.

"Yes, I feel it. A huge massive bulge." I turn and glare at Dante because if they were all like him, I'd be dead. "No, but seriously. There's a bump right here." I take Dante's hand and put it on the trim.

"Sassy, you're right."

Easton shakes his head. "After we search my dad's

room, I'm going to pry the molding off. There's something under it causing it to bubble out."

"But that had to have been done at the shipyard. They weren't putting in moldings on the way to the port to get guests, were they?" I ask. But neither Dante nor Easton would know—they both came on after me. Shayla had gotten stuck in here, as well as Easton once before the night we abandoned ship.

"I know they were chasing issues, but not carpentry. The squirrel deckhand, the one with the hair—what was his name?" Dante slaps his hand on the side of the door.

"Ryder or Waldo?"

"No, Mitch—Waldo—they were like one interesting side character together to me."

"Dante! Mitch was soft-spoken, with longer hair, and an engineer. Waldo had worked on tugboats." I put my hand on my hip. There are times that Dante's chef-ness really comes out. I worked with a chef who called me the short one for a four-month charter. I'm five-ten, but the chief stew was six feet and a former model. I stayed out of the kitchen and off service as much as I could for that season. House-keeping and the laundry room lacked the drama that the rest of the boat had.

"Damn, Sassy. I don't know. The one with the pointed nose and the man bun."

"Mitch."

"Mitch, then, was grabbing grapes out of the walk-in all the time. He was complaining about having to help Calvin instead of working on deck. I just ignored him, like a squeaky mouse. I've got zip empathy for complainers."

"No," Easton says in mock shock.

"I heard you're doing some sort of treasure hunt. I want

to help. I've got another hour while my secret for tonight does its magic." Dante winks at me.

"Secret?" Easton scowls. "But Haley knows?"

"Sassy hears all and knows all." Dante makes a face at Easton.

"You'll tell me, won't you, Firefly?" Easton wraps his arm around my shoulder.

"It's a good one. You're going to love it. You'll need to wait for the surprise." I kiss his thumb. Pizza and some beers really are going to do great things for the guy's morale. Actually, for my morale too.

"Okay, okay. Let's go hunting for a fucking diamond. I might have a surprise of my own." Easton leads me down to the primary suite.

"All right, Rockwell. You better not be talking about your dick," Dante scoffs.

Easton laughs. "I'm not, but now I wish I was." He kisses the side of my neck.

The thought of someone running around the ship actively trying to basically kill us all makes my insides quiver, but being with these two lightens my day. My fingers tingle with excitement. When I was little, I wanted to be a detective. That was before I found out how dangerous it was, that plants were a lot safer. Then again, I've never done anything with my botany—including finishing my degree.

The doors to the primary suite are closed. They're double doors for twice the entrance. It feels like yesterday I found Shayla behind them, buried in horse boxes. Crap, thinking about her makes me so worried again. I really want to get home and find her safe. Her and Emily mostly, but everyone. Heck, I even want whoever did this to us to be safe. Mostly so I can see them punished.

I push the doors open. Things are all over the floor. But then this is kind of like how Candy left it any time she waltzed out of the room. Use a towel, drop it. Wear a shirt for an hour and leave it puddled on the bathroom floor. This is worse, though. Everything from the dresser tops has rolled against the starboard wall. The sheets are hanging off the side of the bed, and a bunch of the pillows are still in place, while ten or so others are on the floor. "Right, we need a plan of attack. First, we search the bed, then we can pile things on top of it."

Dante laughs.

I turn and point at him. "By searching the bed, I mean searching the bed."

He nods. "Got it. You're right. This is important."

We strip the bed, look through the mound of pillows, and even move the mattress off its box spring. Then we search through the ton of clothes on the floor, shaking out each one. Horse sweatshirt after horse bathing suit—I never imagined that there were bras with horses on them, but there are.

"Where was Candy when you told her to drop the bags?" Easton tosses a pair of his father's pants on the mounded bed.

I triangulate the position. "Between the bed, dresser, and sofa." The sofa's a fainting couch. At least, that's what my old chief stew used to call them, the kind of thing you see in old movies, when people go to see a therapist. "Here." I stand on the spot. We've got everything off the floor and the dresser, and the nightstands are empty too.

Dante moves to me, circles me, and then drops to the floor so suddenly I squeal. He presses his head to the floor, turning it to one side and then the next. Then he rolls a full tumble and does it again. Easton and I are just glaring. "I don't see anything, Sassy."

"Well, Sam did a good job. It's just weird. There was more than one bag. Where did they go?"

Dante rolls the other direction and props himself up on his elbows, his amber eyes glowing at me.

"I guess that's it." I peek at Easton, and he drops his hands to his sides.

"Maybe we should check the safe."

"It's empty." I pull out the drawer of the dresser that houses the safe. It's where Candy had pulled all her jewelry out of when she was panicking after I woke them up.

"Right, that's the regular safe. My dad had another one built into the room. He told me about it, but I don't think anyone else knows it exists." Easton removes the bottom drawer on the other side of the dresser. From the bottom, he lifts off a wooden base. There is the top of another safe. It's closed, of course, because the drawer and panel are covering it.

Dante rolls to the drawer. "Whoa. But how are you going to get in? You don't have the key, and there's no power for the electrical pad."

"Right. I have the combination if we can get power. I know my dad, though. He's hidden the key around here somewhere too."

"Well, it's not on the floor." Dante stretches his arms above his head, tilting his head to the ceiling. "But what's behind the door?" He rolls and stands in one move. For a guy who doesn't like hiking, he's physically fit. Dante closes the door closest to the wall. "Damn."

Chapter 27

Drop Keel

Dante

In my palm, I hold a pink jewelry bag. It's not heavy. I show it to them and empty it out. The deep gold of a delicate chain pops against my skin tone. It's a small necklace with a rosebud in a vase. It's dainty. The vase portion's made from a pearl, and the flower itself is some kind of gemstone. "I'm guessing this isn't the diamond we're looking for?" I hand it to Haley, who holds it up between her pincher finger and her thumb.

"No, it's not. But it was my mom's." Easton glances back at the pile on the bed. "I'm not sure why Candy would have had it." It doesn't look like something the platinum blond woman would wear.

"Why would she have brought it with her?" Haley holds it up.

"I don't know? None of this makes sense."

"True." I close the other door, but there's nothing behind it.

"Someone came in here while I was in the galley getting you." Haley nods. "What's that?" She drops to her knees, her delicious bottom high in the air. Damn.

"What did you find, Sassy?"

She has the carpet pulled back off its tacks. "There are diamonds. Here." She hands me three sizable diamonds, and another ten smaller ones. All loose, until my palm sparkles.

"Looks like your dad at least bought something." I hand them to Easton; he's sunk to the side of the messy bed. He stares at them and then back at the safe. "I need to get in there."

I pass over the bag the delicate necklace came out of. "You think the key is in the room?"

"Maybe? Or he took it with him."

Haley shakes her head. "He didn't take anything."

"Then it's on the ship someplace."

"He used the desk in the main salon a few times. And the humidor off the side of the salon has a desk too. I think I saw him taking a call there the day we launched. I remember Shayla being upset because we hadn't had time to put the room together yet, and there were still boxes piled up in it."

"It's worth a shot. I should go through all the clothes again, and the ones still in the drawers. His toiletries. But yeah, starting with the desk isn't a bad idea."

There's a knock on the door. "Hey, Little Bird. You guys are still at it? Whoa, that's a lot of clothes. No wonder it took us so long to bring all their luggage on board."

"Zane, do you think one of your deckhands might have gotten back on the ship while I was getting Dante to our raft?"

"No chance, Little Bird. I told them to launch from the other side. The five of them were off. Fuck, remember, we never saw them again, even when we had a visual on the raft with Shayla and the engineers. I fucking hope they made it. I know we don't talk about them a lot, but my guys were solid."

"But we didn't see them after the launch. What if they came back around and circled in?"

"There's no way of saying they didn't. I'd only worked with those guys for a short time, but I got good vibes from them."

"Sam was right. There's nothing here. Someone came back down." Easton put all the diamonds in the bag and is holding the necklace around his hand, the charm inside his closed fist.

"Looks like something." Zane cocks his head.

"This? This isn't worth much, not to anyone but myself or Emily. These? I'm sure they're worth something. But nothing near what was in the other bags. And certainly not what the Pink Phoenix is worth. If that was even here."

"I was coming to see if you would be willing to help dry up the engine room with me."

"What?" Easton stuffs the necklace in the bag and pushes it into his shorts. "Sorry. Yeah, I'll be right there."

"Easton?" Haley puts her hand on his chest. "Are you okay? Maybe you should just lie down and take a break." Haley moves things to the middle of the bed, giving Easton space to lie down, and he does.

"I'm fine, Haley. It just took me by surprise. I haven't seen it in a long time. My mom wore it every day. My dad bought it for her on her first Mother's Day. I wasn't even born yet. I'm coming now." Easton swings his legs around the side of the bed and hops up. "Really, Haley, I'm good. It's game time. I've got things to do. I'm the water-boy."

Haley nods once, stepping out of his way. But she's got that I'm-not-impressed stew face on. It's a cross between a smirk and her you've-been-a-naughty-boy school teacher look. Easton gives her a quick kiss as he leaves the room, but she grabs his arm. "I'd like to talk about this later. I don't think stuffing your feelings in your pocket is going to help you in the long run. Because it's not."

"I know. You're right." Easton smirks.

"What?" Haley's eyebrows rise, and I sink to the bed. Damn, I love good drama.

"It's just, I've never had anyone care enough to call me out on things before," says Easton. "It's good. It's hard, though. Thank you for caring."

I groan.

"What?" Easton and Haley say.

I shrug. "Nothing. It would have been more fun if you got yourself into trouble, that's all."

"Dante?" Haley scowls.

"Who's the one in trouble now?" Zane grins, heading for the hallway.

"Me, but then I like being in trouble." I pull at Haley's shorts.

She shakes her head at me. "You really are the king of trouble."

"It's my middle name."

She cocks her head.

"What? It's how I like it, Sassy." I glance at my wrist where my watch isn't—weird how I didn't look for it at all the entire time we were at camp. This feels almost real but not. "It's stifling in here. I want to finish cooking dinner."

"I suppose if they don't need me for something else, I can work on cleaning the main salon."

"Or maybe you do an Italian-themed table?"

Her blue eyes light up. "I suppose we could all use a little levity."

"That's the spirit, Sassy."

I'm shredding cheese when Sassy comes into the kitchen holding two separate plates, one a checked red and white and the other an onyx black. "Cute or classy?" She waves them at me.

"Which way are you leaning?"

"Not sure? The red and white is fun."

"Pizza's a serious business." I laugh.

"Right, the red and white one it is." She sashays out of my galley.

And I'm about to turn and follow her when I realize I've got things to do. I'm working on getting a chocolate cake together. I've got to get it in and out of the grill before I turn the heat up for the pizza stones. I'm not sure it will work, but why not try?

Two hours in, and I'm almost done. I'm not going to do this every day. I know there are things I could be doing to help the Rock Candy be seaworthy again. Unlike Easton and Haley, I've done some work around boats before. But we need to celebrate, and a celebration needs food.

I've snuck the cake back to the galley without Haley seeing. It's a bit of a mess, but it's not burnt, and with the canned frosting from the crew galley, no one will notice. I'm not one for using boxed food, but it's here and shelf stable.

It's hotter than hell in the decks below, but the galley has a bit of a cross breeze, so I risk it and frost the cake. I've got a friend watching me. "Chocolate is bad for dogs." I lower my head to Penny and give her a stale cracker. Then I put a large bowl over the cake to both hide it and keep it safe from the dog. She goes down on her belly, her soulful eyes begging up at me. "No. No chocolate for you." I take all the supplies for the pizza on a tray, and she trots after me. "Hey, Sassy. Are you almost ready? I've got the last pizza on the grill now. Holy crap on a cracker, that's amazing."

Haley's done the table up in a cozy Italian restaurant style. There's a garland of leaves and fake lemons along the middle of the table, surrounded by mini tea lights, their fake flames flickering. In front of the checkered plates are wine and water goblets.

"It's so weird how I hadn't missed ice, but now I can't stop thinking about it." Haley straightens a water goblet.

"It's the glasses, and it's a lot warmer on the ship than back at camp."

"True."

"Have you seen anyone else?" I ask. "I'm ready if you are?"

"I think so." She's staring at the table. "I haven't seen anyone. They must all be in the engine room. I'll go grab them." Haley heads down to the swim platform, taking the back way to the engine room through the toy hauler space. I remember what Zane said about his guys taking off from the aft. I have no clue what happened after the boat listed hard and I bashed my head. The next thing I remember is waking up to the smell of fish guts on the raft. But I do remember flying across the galley. If we were listing that hard, I can't see how anyone could have made it through the toy hauler garage. It's full of large bulky things, most with sharp edges, and fuel cans. Fuck, no way would I have gone through there. No matter how much money it was.

I made three pizzas. Honestly, I wasn't sure the yeast was going to work, and I didn't want to waste flour turning it into a brick if the yeast didn't proof.

"Damn." Zane's the first to the table, but the rest of the guys aren't far behind. I've got one eye on the dog, the other on everyone sitting down.

"Wow, Firefly, this is amazing." Easton gives her a quick kiss. "How did you do this so fast?"

"Thanks." She hugs him back. "How's the patch look?"

Sam trudges up the steps. "Good. Calvin's getting changed out of his wets, then he'll be right up."

"Do you want me to go get him?" Haley looks at me.

"No, Sassy. You're the last person who should go get the Viking when he's changing out of his clothes. I'll do it. Pour the wine and watch the dog." I'm down the stairs and at his cabin. "Green, hurry up," I say. There's a weird noise coming out of his cabin. The door's cracked. I give it a light tap, and it eases open enough that I see Green sitting away from the door, his shoulders hunched. He's crying—or at least, I think he is. I back away through the crew galley to the back stairs, and this time I come down harder, hitting each step as I do. When I pass the laundry room, I slam the door. "Hey, Green, when you're ready, I've made pizza. We're having wine and beer, and I'm surprising Sassy with a chocolate cake for dessert." I stop short of his door.

"Great, good. I'll be right up." His voice echoes through the hall.

"Don't take too long. Haley will miss you."

He laughs. "I'll be there. You can start without me."

"Nope, we're family, we eat together. Get your ass upstairs."

His dark blond head ducks out of his door. "Thanks, Dante."

"For what?" I nudge him with my elbow.

He nods and takes the stairs two at a time.

Chapter 28

Grog

Sam

"Want me to help pour the wine, Haley?" I ask.

"I'll get the water, Little Bird." Zane stresses her nickname back to me.

"Okay, so what's the big surprise, Firefly? You can tell us, since Dante's not here."

"I wouldn't steal his thunder. He's worked really hard."

"We're here." Dante and Calvin come in from the main salon. Calvin's holding a half-dozen beer bottles by their necks between his massive fingers.

"You brought enough to share." Zane reaches for one.

"These are mine. But I guess I can let you have one." Calvin holds them out for Zane to take one and then lines the rest up in front of his chair. It seems we have assigned seats now—we're sitting in the same order as lunch. Haley's sitting between Calvin and Dante. Next to Dante is Zane, then me. Easton is on my left, next to Calvin. At least I can look directly at her. I want to finish, or at least continue, what we started in the wheelhouse. And not being able to touch her is going to unlock a new level of torture during the meal.

"Sit, everyone. You too, Sassy." Dante goes to the grill and comes back with two giant platters.

"Hot damn, is that pizza? You can't be serious. Honestly, mate, you are the best chef on the whole fucking planet."

"Relax, Zane, you haven't tasted it yet."

"Doesn't matter what it tastes like, does it? It's the idea of the thing."

Dante walks to Haley. "Sassy, do the honors of taking the first slices." She smiles and takes one. "Take two. Once it gets to the Viking, who knows if there will be anything left?" Dante makes a face at Calvin.

"I have manners, Chef. I'd never take food out of Haley's mouth."

"Of course you wouldn't." Dante furrows his brow and turns away. He makes his way around the table and holds the tray between Zane and me.

The table goes silent, just like it did at lunch. Damn, lunch was good, but pizza? Actual pizza. I'm not going to ask where he found the cheese. "Truly, this is some of the best pizza I've ever had. I'm not sure what magic you used to make it."

"Sold my soul." Dante lifts his wine glass. "Again." He laughs. "To found family. The best kind."

"Hear, hear," Zane says and we all clink. Or mostly all clink. I can't reach Haley's glass. She lifts it, and her blue eyes connect with mine. Fuck, this girl . . . If there's any magic around, it's her.

Penny slumps at my feet. I didn't feed her dinner, but she's not asking. Chef must be sneaking her treats again. I take a long sip of the wine. Damn, that's good. I twist the bottle to read the label. My eyes shoot up. Even when I was consoling myself with the expensive tequila, I didn't touch this case.

"Relax, Sam. I opened it. You can have the other bottle if you want." Easton shrugs.

"Château Lumière Éternelle 2015." Shit, I know a little about wines and I knew enough to leave this case alone. It's pricey.

"If my dad's going to buy 55-million-dollar necklaces, we can drink his forty-thousand-dollar bottles of wine."

Zane, unfortunately, is taking a sip when Easton says the price of the bottle, and he starts choking. I slap his back until he stops, and he guzzles his water down. Zane picks the glass back up and holds it to the light. "It's good. But honestly, I don't think it's worth all of that."

Easton shrugs. "It's my dad's favorite. We can raise a glass to his health, wherever he may be."

"To Rocky," I say. Easton gives me a nod. I really did— do—like Mr. Rockwell. Sure, he's a rich ass who knows what he wants, but he does have a down-to-earth side. But also, terrible taste in women.

Easton stands and opens another bottle of wine. He has three lined up like Calvin's beer soldiers. Easton fills all the glasses around the table, but Zane puts his hand over the top of his.

Easton laughs. "Don't worry about the price. Here, the bottled water and shampoo have more value."

"I'm not worried about the price. I'm thinking we should have one sober person to pilot the tender back to camp tonight."

"Oh, good point." Easton pulls the bottle back.

"Unless you all stay the night?" I ask.

Heads snap to me.

"As much as that sounds appealing, Cap—Sam—we've got a cat to feed, a fish weir to empty, and a tender that needs to be kept off the reef." Calvin raises his beer to me.

I raise my now empty glass back. Calvin leans into Haley and whispers something. She laughs, and my dick goes hard. Because it's a real laugh, one without reserve for what others think about her. When she stops laughing, she finishes her wine. "Dante, that was amazing. Thank you."

"Oh, that's not it, Sassy. Sit still."

"More, okay." She beams at him and watches as he jogs to the galley.

"Oh no you don't. No peeking. Make sure she's not looking." Dante points.

"Done." Calvin wraps his hand around the back of her neck and devours her in a kiss. Calvin ends the kiss and moves his hand round and in front of Haley's eyes. "No peeking. You heard Dante."

Dante's almost out of the salon with a lopsided cake on a platter. He stands behind her and places it in front of her. "Okay, open."

"Oh . . . oh," she says. "Oh?" Her tone is more inquisitive now. "Wait, how did you know? I mean, thank you!" She jumps up and pivots in the air. Her arms cling around Dante's neck. "You not only knew it was my birthday, but you baked me a cake. You hate baking. How did you know it's my birthday?" Haley's back is to me, but I can read his face as clear as day. Dante had no idea it was her birthday. I certainly didn't.

"You must have mentioned it," Zane pipes up.

"I think we've talked about birthdays. Haven't we? We had that talk about astrological signs. I'm still not sure if I'm a Scorpio or something else."

"Sagittarius, Easton," Haley tosses to him. "And no, I've

never said when my birthday was. In my head, I guess I decided if I didn't mention it, we'd be home by now. And then I woke up yesterday and realized what the date was . . . I didn't want to make a big deal of it. But this is so special. Thank you, Dante." She gazes up at him, and I see the second she realizes he didn't know. "Oh shit . . . I—"

"Happy Birthday to you . . ." Zane starts loudly, and we all pick it up. Of course, when we get to the part where they should say "Haley," they all say some damn other thing— Sassy, Chiefie, Little Bird, Firefly. I'm not going to be outdone, so I sing "Haley" loudly.

She shakes her head. I'm not sure if she's happy or frustrated. Zane raises his water glass when we finish singing. "To the best damn woman on the planet."

"Hear, hear," I say.

"All right, thank you now. Can I have some of this cake?" She pulls the cake platter closer to her.

"Yes, Sassy. Here you go." Dante hands her a silver cake knife and a plate.

When she takes a bite, we're all watching again, just like we did when she took the first bite of pasta. "Mmm." She pulls the fork out slowly. "It's so good everyone. Eat."

The rest of them all dig in, but I can't stop thinking about how it's her birthday and she didn't tell anyone. My ex had hers on every calendar, sent me a daily text countdown, and was never happy with a single present I bought her. I feel the bubble inside of me, and it's more than food or the sugar. I'll admit there were five cans of frosting, but somewhere during my tequila week, I ate one with a spoon. Which is why I've got the smallest piece of cake on my plate. The way my gut is clenched, I realize, is left over from my ex. It's Haley's birthday, and I don't have a present. Forget that we're on a rock in the middle of nowhere. She deserves more, with all that she's been through.

It's then that I notice Calvin is eating with his right hand when he is left-handed. He takes a bite of cake, puts his fork down, and then takes a swig of his warm beer—bottle down, and he repeats. Haley, on the other hand, has stopped eating all together. Shit. I catch her eyes and hold them. Am I an asshole for letting her know I know exactly what's going on under the table? Possibly. Probably. I don't fucking care. There's a pink tinge going up her neck.

"Dante, this cake is really moist." Calvin nods, putting a large bite in his mouth. "Isn't it moist, Haley?"

She makes a gurgling sound that might be interpreted as a yes.

Dante's eyes flick up and down Haley and land on her lap. "I do like a moist cake." Dante takes Haley's fork and feeds her a large bite.

I'm hard and fucking conflicted. But I didn't tell her no. And I don't think I can. That's what this means. Easton and Zane are watching now. Their own plates are clean.

"Right, well, that's a good cake." Calvin takes his left hand and licks his fingers. Haley's shoulders drop. She glances at the other guys. No one says anything about it, but there are a lot of smiles going around the table. "Happy Birthday, Chiefie." Calvin leans over and kisses her cheek. "We should play some games before we head back." He stands and clears the table onto a tray which he puts on the counter behind the table.

"Games?" Dante growls. "Like Monopoly or charades?"

"What are you, ten? Let's age it up a bit, middle school. We've got what? Like an hour before low tide? Let's cele-brate Chiefie's birthday with some fun."

"Who are you and what have you done with Green?" Dante laughs.

"I've had some beers, Jones. This is what happens when I drink. I forget I'm a fucking mess."

"You're not a mess—"

"Rule number eleven, Little Bird, never argue with a drunk person."

"Still, Calvin's not a mess." She stands and holds on to his arm. "You want to play a game? I'd like that too. What game?" She bounces on her toes and takes Dante's hand.

"Into the salon!" Zane races a few feet. "Right, what's this game? Whatever it is, I'm sure I don't know it. Is it knocking down the ginger or stuck in the mud?"

Calvin's eyebrows shoot up. "Yeah, no. I have no fucking idea what those are, but I'm questioning the safety of your childhood."

Zane laughs. "You're not wrong, mate."

Haley drifts away from the others and comes up to my side. She whispers into my ear. "Are you okay with this?"

"It's your birthday, Haley. You get to pick. I'll play if you want me to. Of course, Green will have to sober up enough to give us the rules."

"I'm not drunk, Sam. Tipsy? Yes. Not having a drink for months will do that to you. But it takes a lot to swing me over to drink—drunk." He snorts. "Or not." He spreads his massive arms out. "Right, guys, sit in a circle." He hands Haley his empty beer bottle. She immediately takes it and moves toward the bar. "No, Chiefie, you're going to need that."

"Oh."

Green puts his hands on her shoulders and moves her into the middle of the room. "Sit." Penny's the only one who does. "Good dog. But the rest of you, circle, floor now."

"We've got furniture, Green." Dante takes a small ottoman and puts it in the circle.

"Fine, whatever, just sit. This is modified spin the bottle and truth or dare. Rules are simple. First round, Haley spins the bottle. Whomever it lands on, she asks truth or dare." Calvin holds up his finger. "Second round, Haley spins the bottle. Haley can ask a question, but if the guy doesn't want to answer, the last guy who the bottle landed on makes up the dare. Sound good, Chiefie?"

"Yes, I like that! I don't have to do any of the dares. And I only have to come up with one idea. Dares always feel so mean, you know?"

Calvin smirks at her and plops down in the circle. I take a chair from the table and sit between Calvin and Dante.

"Give it a good spin, Sassy."

Haley spins the bottle. She's got some real torque on it . . . It wobbles and then eventually slows . . . pointing to Zane, then Dante, and stops on me.

Chapter 29

Sea Chanty

Haley

I watch as the bottle inches to a stop in slow motion. It might stop at Zane. Zane would be a good way to start. He'll take it easy on me. But then it passes him and slows more at Dante. Dante would be good—funny. We'd have a laugh. But no . . . no, no. It has to go and stop on Sam. Right. I was almost starting to have the smallest, tiniest inkling at dinner that maybe this could feel normal, and then Calvin slid his fingers into my underwear.

The bottle wobbles and stops.

Sam's lips clamp together, but he's got a smile going. There's no way in the stratosphere that he'd choose to play modified spin the bottle on his own. But he's here. He said he wanted something with me, and he hasn't flinched in his chair—at least not yet.

"Sam," I say, hoping my voice doesn't crack.

"Haley." His voice drops low.

"Truth or dare?"

"What's the truth?" He leans forward in his chair.

"Wait, wait, hold on now. He gets to ask what the question is before he picks?" Zane cocks his head at me.

"Um. Right, that's not the normal rules." I turn to Calvin.

"Makes it more interesting. Give him a question." Calvin sits on the floor with crossed legs, leaning against the sofa.

I nod, and a thousand things go through my head. *What's the sexiest text message you've ever sent? What's the most embarrassing thing you've ever done? What's your biggest regret? What's your favorite part of your body?* And finally, *why do you like me enough to go through with this?* But I don't say any of that, no . . . I blurt out, "What's your favorite color?"

Sam laughs. "Payne's gray. It's almost blue." Sam winks at me. "Okay, Haley, spin again. I think I like this game." He takes a sip of wine from his glass—his glass that's full again. Easton's shaking his head.

"Haley, Little Bird, come here . . ." I walk over to Zane. "Bend down." I do. "That's not a truth or dare question. It's your birthday, so we'll let this one slide." He laughs.

"Got it." I nod, picking up the bottle. "Ready?"

"Spin it, Sassy." Dante's voice echoes around the salon. I give it a good spin, and this time, it lands on Zane.

I put my hands on my hips and cock my head. "Ready, Zane?"

"Do your worst, Little Bird." Zane smiles. He's relaxed for the first time since he finished the treehouse platform.

Easton winks at me, and I'm nervous. I can do it. No more easy questions. "Right. One question, two parts." There are some groans from the guys. I shake my head. "Tell me about how you lost your virginity and how long you lasted."

Zane roars with laughter and slaps his leg. Then he goes completely quiet, turns to Sam, and with a straight face says, "I'll take the dare."

Sam scrubs his hand over his chin. "Okay, give Haley a lap dance—"

Zane jumps to his feet and almost knocks me over as he races by Sam to get a dining room chair. "Easy."

"Wait, I wasn't done." Sam grins.

Zane puts the chair next to me. "All right then, what's the rest, mate?"

"Zane, you have to sing Old Macdonald—and make it sexy." Sam raises his eyebrows at me.

"There you go, Cap, there you go." Easton rolls to his side in laughter. "That's the spirit."

"You think this is funny, Rockwell?" Zane asks.

"Yeah, yeah, I do."

"Fine, I'll need music. You sing," Zane says.

Easton shakes his head at Zane. "It's not my dare."

Zane glares at Easton and flips his attention back to me. "Have a seat, love. You ready to have your socks and your knickers knocked off?"

I know I'm blushing. I can hardly look at him. He wiggles his eyebrows at me, and I can't help but giggle. "You don't have to." It comes out breathless.

"Oh, Little Bird, but I want to. I can do this, and it's going to be fabulous."

Easton groans. "Fine." And he jumps up. "I've got you." He rushes to the side of the main salon, next to the cigar humidor. Pillows fly from where they've been piled up on the piano. A yank and the heavy cover slides to the floor. The brass anchors shine in the waning light, the only thing that kept the piano from sliding when the Rock Candy listed so hard. Easton runs his finger down the keys in a glissando. I don't play, but it's not hard to tell it's completely out of tune. "Ready."

The first chords almost distract me from the fact that Zane's stripped off his shirt. He slides his hand from the nape of his neck down to his abs. And I have to lean back. I'm giggling.

"I think Sassy likes it. Keep going." Dante claps on the beat, and the other guys join in.

"Old Mac had a farm." Zane puts his foot on the chair in between my legs and thrusts his hips. Slowly, out of sync with the piano, he sings, "E, I, E, I, O . . . O."

"That's not how it goes," Sam says.

I turn my head to him, and when I do, Zane leans in and places the bulge in his pants against my cheek.

"Horse." Zane neighs. "With a neigh-neigh here." He thrusts his hips and then flips around, grinding his—he would say "bum"—in my face. "Neigh-neigh there." He thuds to the ground on all fours, pushing his nose into my crotch. "Everywhere a neigh-neigh." It's muffled by my legs. I run my fingers through his hair. His nose rubs up and down the seam of my shorts. Then he's gone, standing. "Old Mac had a farm. E, I, E, I, Ooooo." And then he licks down the side of my neck. I shiver. I'm undecided if I'm grossed out by the lick or turned on.

Easton does a little trill on the upper keys that sounds like glass breaking.

Zane throws his hands in the air. "You can't out-dare me." He points at each of the guys. Zane gives Easton a slap on his back. "That piano should be shot and put out of its misery."

"Agreed." Easton slides back to his spot. And I'm left in the middle wondering if I'm going to survive the night.

"Okay, Chiefie, spin again." Calvin waves at the bottle.

I slowly stand up. "Thank you, Zane. I think?"

He winks at me, and I move the chair out of the way. I pick the bottle up from where I kicked it when Zane startled me. I clutch it to my chest.

"Spin the bottle, Haley." Sam's warm voice coats me with comfort.

"Okay." My lips turn up in a smile. This is supposed to be fun. I can make this fun. I give the bottle a good turn. I haven't had that much wine, but watching it makes me dizzy with happiness. I'm kind of both hoping for it to land on Sam and for it not to land on him. But it slows and lands on Calvin.

"Dare." He nods and kills another bottle of beer.

"You don't want to know what the truth is?" I cock my head at him.

"No, Chiefie. You can ask me anything you want in front of these clowns or in private any time you want. Dare." He nods. His eyes tell me something different, though—his eyes tell me he wants to get his hands on me. And I'm hoping for the same thing. "Do your best, Morris."

Zane laughs. "Right, then." Zane paces around the circle, like he's about to go into a round of duck, duck, goose. Heads turn and follow him.

Easton laughs. "Come on, Zane."

"Right, it has to be balanced, fun for all but Green."

"That is the general idea." Dante grabs one of the cushions that was swept to the floor from the top of the piano and leans back on it. He looks like a Greek God.

"Maybe you should have taken the truth." Sam's laughing, his wineglass to his lips.

"You have to take Haley's shirt off," Zane says.

Calvin laughs. "Are you sure you know how this works?"

"Wasn't done. With your teeth. And if you touch her with anything but your teeth, you have to strip and stand with your hands in the air until the bottle lands on you again." Zane laughs. "And no help from you, Little Bird." He points at me.

I nod. "Okay."

Calvin's green eyes flash at me. "You ready, Chiefie?"

"Sure." I smile. "Do you want me to put my hands in the air?"

"Yes, please."

I lean into him. His eyes are so compelling. "Stand still, Chiefie."

"Did you set a time limit, Zane? For fuck's sake, Green, hurry up," Sam growls. All heads turn to him.

"I can understand your impatience, Sam. They are some superb tits." Dante flips over to his other side, his fists on his head.

Calvin kneels and bites down on the hem of my shirt. He stands up with such force that my shirt is now around my eyes on one side. I can't see much, just a bit of light through the right armhole. I put on a thin pink lace bra today, one I've been dying to take off. It's not made for this kind of weather. But then, somehow I'm thinking I won't have to worry about that for much longer. "Do you want me to—"

His hair tickles my side. But that doesn't count as touching, right? I'm not telling on him. Although, I do like looking at Calvin naked. He's like a sculpture carved from marble. An oversized one.

There's a tug on the folded bottom of my shirt, and he pulls it almost over my head, not quite letting me see. "Sit down, Chiefie. The chair's behind you."

I sink onto it.

"Put your arms up but bent." His breath warms my wrist. And then he tugs it overhead and down the other side. I blink at the darkening room. The shirt hangs from the other arm. I'm expecting Calvin to bend down and tug it off, but he doesn't. He grabs the back of my neck and pulls me to him, taking me in a deep kiss. When his lips leave mine, I'm panting and I lean forward, following him.

"*Fuck*, Green, now we have to stare at your junk," Easton groans.

"Worth it. I got to kiss our girl." He's stripping his clothes off. Shirt, pants, underwear are all gone. His hard cock points at me. He rests his hand on a beam on the ceiling, elongating his muscles. I've lost the ability to speak. "Look at her—she can't take her fucking eyes off me."

"You could have added that he couldn't talk." Dante lifts his head. "Why the hell did you decide to stand right next to me?"

"It's my spot."

"Who are you? Sheldon from the *Big Bang Theory*?"

"Yeah." Calvin wiggles his eyebrows at me. "Spin the bottle, Chiefie. I've got ideas."

Chapter 30

———

Message in a Bottle

Sam

The bottle spins slowly, and fuck if it doesn't land on me again. I stare at the bottle and then glance up at the naked engineer. He's focused on Haley, with a shit-eating grin on his face. It's like he's asking her how hard he can go. Her eyes flick to the floor and then back to Calvin's face. She gives the slightest of nods. And fuck me. She's given him permission to do his worst—or best. I guess that depends on whose perspective I look at it from.

My heart thuds, smacking against my ribs. Am I really going to go down this path? I want her. Fuck, I've never wanted anyone so much in my life. When I was with my ex, we didn't even hold hands in public. This is another level.

Calvin's hanging on to the beam in the ceiling, naked. Then again, he played football. He's used to being naked in front of other guys. Damn, I'm not shy, I've never been shy, but this is more than I ever thought I'd do. I'm not one to back down, though.

What am I doing? I've never succumbed to peer pressure before, never drank until I was . . . well, I was nineteen, but that was old by the standards of my neighborhood. I've never done drugs. But fuck. Haley's a drug. She is the most amazing kind of drug. And I'm addicted.

"Sam." Haley's blue eyes light up the room. "Truth or dare?"

Shoulders back—I'm not taking the easy way out. "Dare." My heart thuds in my ear, and I stare at Calvin's face. His eyes flick to mine and back to Haley.

"Right, okay, *Sam*," Calvin stresses my name. "Drop your pants and sit in the chair in the middle of the circle."

My forehead furrows.

"Calvin?" Haley whispers.

"What, Chiefie? He wants to play, he needs to follow the rules."

Dante chuckles, reclining on the floor next to me. "You going to spell out the rest, Green? Or are you letting Sassy take the lead?"

Calvin gives half a shrug, and Haley's eyes are glued to his abs. She shifts back and forth on her heels, then sucks in her lips, thinning them. That pink bra of hers doesn't cover much.

"You want to play, don't you, Sam? I mean, if you don't want to, I'll take your torture for you," Dante bellows. "He hasn't spelled it out, but—"

"No offense, Sam, I'll take your place." Easton wiggles his eyebrows at me. He holds on to his glass of amber liquid.

"Same," Zane says.

I unfurl and stand tall, every vertebra in my spine clicking into place. With slow steps, I move to the chair. Locking eyes with her, I unfasten my belt, let my pants drop to the floor. I've had plenty to eat, but I've lost weight since the whole thing went down. I'm not ashamed of my body. I'm lean, fit. But I'm also not twenty-five anymore.

Calvin whispers in Haley's ear but it's loud enough for me to hear. She nods. Her blue eyes sparkling.

"Shirt, too," Haley says. Her eyes travel the length of my legs. She inches closer to me. I'm not afraid. I want this. I've dreamed for months of her touch. Crazy, that's what this is, but I want to do it. I need to do it. It's not much of a dare, having the woman I've been thinking about for what feels like eternity take my dick in her mouth. Yeah, but then I wasn't thinking it would be in a circle of her other boyfriends.

"You heard Little Bird. Don't be slow." Zane cocks his head at me.

I pull the hem of my shirt over my head and let it drop behind me. Haley's got the cutest little smile on her face. And all I've got on is my underwear.

She steps closer, latching her fingers around my neck as she leans in, her warm breath soft on my ear. "You okay?" she whispers.

"Better than okay." I take her lips in mine and kiss her. Her lips are soft and warm. She tastes of chocolate and—

"Sit, Sam," Calvin barks.

Haley breaks the kiss. Her eyes are dilated, and through her pink bra, her nipples are hard. I sit on the Italian leather dining chair that's become the center of the circle. My brother Charlie once did modeling for art students at the local college. He said you get so used to taking your clothes off that you forget about it. When there are dozens of eyes staring at you, it helps to pick one person to look at. But then, Charlie also took home plenty of art students to his boat for a private session.

I'm focused on Haley and only Haley. I hold my hand out, and she takes it and lowers herself to the ground.

"Catch," Zane says. He throws a thin horse pillow at me. I catch it with my free hand and place it on the floor, moving my feet to either side.

Haley slowly moves between my legs. Her hands trail down my sides, leaving wakes of goosebumps.

I close my eyes for only a second, taking in the deliciousness of her touch. It's something I want to always remember.

"Make sure not to get that precious pillow dirty, Sam." Dante laughs again. But neither Haley nor I turn.

"You are so beautiful." I run my hand along her neck, tilting her chin up to me. Now she looks away. "Really, Haley."

There's a rustle to the side of us. Easton's moving closer. "He's right, Firefly. Nothing compares to you."

Her shoulders round. Damn this woman. If it's the last thing I do, I'm going to make her understand how special she is. This isn't about her being here; this isn't about anything other than her.

She lifts her fingers and trails them around my abs, inching closer to my groin. My cock jumps toward her touch. And I have to grit my molars to keep from coming before her lips have even hovered over me. I'm wired to go in an instant.

"Sam?" She runs her finger over my abs.

I have them gone in an instant. I sit, and my cock jumps at her.

Her head bows, and she licks up the underside of my cock. I'm shivering and hot all at once. When her lips close over me, my eyes drift shut and I have to force them open to watch the goddess on her knees in front of me. I'm not worthy of her—none of us are. She's amazing. She has one hand around my waist, and the other grips the base of my cock. Each thrust into her mouth is tantalizing.

"Fuck, you're doing such a good job," I grit out. The air scorches my throat as I pull it in. Her hand wraps tighter around the base of my shaft as she works me into her amazing mouth.

"Damn. I bet she's wetter than the ocean. We need to check," Dante says.

My eyes snap open and over to him. Fuck, I almost forgot they were even in the room. My vision stops when Haley stops.

"No," Calvin says, his eyes wide. "This is a dare; wait your turn, Chef."

There's noise in the room, but she's the sun. Her blue eyes water as she pushes me deeper down her throat. Her tongue swipes along the underside of my head, and I'm gone. My hand in her hair, I hold her snug to me. Taking me down. I don't even hear how she's gagging. A snap of my consciousness and I let her head go, giving her the ability to pull back. She doesn't, though. She sucks harder, and my back arches in the chair, vibrating. My vision blurs on the ceiling, my arms hang loose at my side, as I twitch with the electricity of my orgasm. I'm gone.

She doesn't stop until every ounce of me is spent. I slide out of her mouth. Somehow, I right myself. Her blue eyes are glued to mine.

Zane gives her a cloth, and Easton hands her his glass. She tips it back, drinking it down, and her shoulders shudder when she hands it back to him, still on her knees. She straightens, watching me as she does. Her ponytail is a mess; her lips are swollen and red. I thought she was beautiful before, but I've never seen someone so enticing. She's spun sugar in front of me.

"Look at you, Sugar." I rest my elbows on my knees and pull her to me. Kissing again. Taking the thirty-year-old Scotch from her lips.

"Dare complete," Calvin growls.

Haley steps away, a smile on her lips. I reach out and pull her back to me until she's sitting on my lap. "I don't know if this is fair. It's Haley's birthday, after all."

She wraps her hands around my neck. "I'm having a good time. This is a lot of fun. Don't you think?" She gives me a quick kiss and jumps from my lap, snatching the bottle from the floor. Message received. Earlier in the wheelhouse, she told me that she wasn't going to give them up to just have me. I need to share.

My lips purse as I stand. I'm getting hard again already. I drag the chair out of the middle of the circle. "Give it a good spin. If it lands on me again . . . I won't mind," I say.

She laughs. "Everyone needs a turn."

"Birthday girl rules." Zane tugs on her hand, pulling her onto his lap, kissing her quickly and setting her on her feet again. "Give it a good spin, Little Bird."

She holds the bottle above her head and walks around the circle with slow steps. "Ready?" Her wrist flicks, and the bottle spins. It wobbles and slows, Easton, Zane, Dante, me, Calvin . . . I think it might land on me, but it keeps going. It almost stops on Calvin, but then, like a magician's rigged show, it jumps and stops on Easton.

Easton's face lights up. "All right," rolls off his tongue.

"The bottle has spoken," Dante says.

I reach for my pants, but Dante hooks them with his big toe and tosses them across the room. I'm about to say something when Haley moves to Easton. "Truth or dare?" Haley asks. Her back is to me.

"Dare. I'm an open book. You can ask me anything anytime, Firefly." His eyes roam over her.

She steps to the side.

Easton inclines his head at me. "What's it going to be, Sam?"

"I already said I don't think it's fair that the birthday girl is doing all the work."

"I thoroughly agree. Firefly?" He takes Haley's hand and leads her to the center of the circle. With a flash, he drops down in a low squat. His hands trace up her legs. With a hook of his thumbs, he pulls her shorts down to her ankles.

Haley's got one hand in his hair, the other gripping her breast.

Easton grabs her sides, and she leans backward into his embrace. It's intoxicating, an acrobatic show that's more practiced than spontaneous. He lowers her to the floor— Zane's ready with a pillow at her head before she hits. Easton rocks off his toes to his knees. He pushes up her bra, getting it out of the way.

I find myself tilting my head to get a better view. But when he lifts her leg around his back, her toe points, and fuck if I'm not going hard again already.

Chapter 31

Brewing Storm

Haley

Easton's a champion at more than his scissor kick and butterfly stroke. His tongue has my vision blurred. I'm so worked up from everything that's already gone on: having Zane dance for me, Calvin taking my shirt off, then touching Sam. Dante was right—my panties are soaked. And Easton's tongue is teasing me in the right way. I'm on fire. I can't believe how much I need to release. How much I want to break apart. What he's doing to me has my hips vibrating. I raise my head and will my eyes to look at him. My fingers run through his silky hair, and I lift myself to get closer to his glorious mouth.

It's so good.

My lips part, and I turn my head to the side. Zane's bright smile fills my soul, and then he winks at me. It's like he flicks a switch and zaps of electricity fire around my body. Heat builds.

"Oh, she's close, Swimmer Man." Dante laughs.

And I want to laugh at how Dante has aged up Easton's

235

nickname. But I can't get my mouth to work. I'm jelly, pulsing at Easton's will.

"She's amazing." Sam's voice shakes with me.

"Right? It's as good as having your own orgasm, watching her. Fuck." The carpet moves near my head as Calvin steps toward me. I peek up at him. He's hanging on the beam still. The crinkles at the corners of his green eyes are there. And it fills me.

A finger enters my pussy, one, then two. Easton moves them with his tongue. The fluttering starts. Then Easton slows, and the release I'm chasing moves away again. I lift myself, bridging my back. I might not be a gymnast or an Olympic swimmer, but I can hold a position long enough to get what I want.

Dante laughs next to me. He's closer now too. "Give her what she wants, Easton."

And Easton sucks my clit so suddenly that I fly upward, thrashing as he holds me down, licking every last drop out of me until my legs hinge shut around his head.

I close my eyes but then force them back open. Five attentive men stare at me.

"That was amazing, Haley," Easton says first.

"That's my line." I push up onto my elbows.

His blue eyes are glowing at me. I roll over onto my stomach. I'm definitely not done. "I want more."

Dante's laugh rolls over me. "Of course you do, Sassy." Dante has already peeled off his shirt. His shorts are gone in a flash.

"Fuck." Sam kneels on the carpet next to me. "I've got a sudden urge to protect you from the monster he's got between his legs."

"Exactly." Easton trails his hand around my stomach. I grab his hand and suck his finger into my mouth.

"Game on." Dante's on one side, Zane on the other. But Calvin is still looming over us. His powerful body is a threat and a promise. I'm not sure I can take it.

The bottle's by my head. I turn it till it points at Calvin. He's had enough punishment. And I have too. Staring at Calvin's sculpted body for the last hour has been driving me crazy.

"Dare." His voice rumbles through me.

"Fuck me, hard." I want them all, but his hands drop from the beam.

"Gratefully, Chiefie."

Zane's got one of the beige horse pillows in his hand as he lifts my shoulders up, pushing it underneath me. And another one at my lower back. The angle has my lower half higher than my head.

Calvin's thick finger runs over my stomach, down to my core. He slides one in. I'm still tender from flying on Easton's tongue. But I want more. He taps me on my hips, and I lift my legs, allowing him to settle in between them. When the tip of his cock pushes an inch into me, I'm ready to fire off.

"Hold steady there, Chiefie." He sinks into me. "Okay?"

"So much better than okay." It's weird. I know the other guys are here. I feel them. Sometimes it's like we're all in it together. But then other times, I'm focused on just one of them. I don't know if it's wrong. I'm done assigning that word to things. I have to give that word up. Let it go. All I know is that every day, I'm more attached to each one of them. When this is all over, it's going to break me.

But I shove that thought out. In a way, when it's over, that would be a good thing, right? It means we're home. Back with family. They're back with family.

I slam the door on my traitorous brain. I hook my arms

over Calvin's neck and kiss him. Beer and pizza. Home. His tongue battles with mine. I tilt my pelvis, and he jerks his head back.

"That's the way you do it, Sassy." Dante ducks his head and takes a nipple into his mouth. It's like a wire is attached to my clit. I'm so close already. There's something about the air here. I've become a sex goddess. I want more. So much more.

From the corner of my eye, I see Zane stripping, and I reach for him. "How are you doing, Little Bird?"

Words are hard, but I push out a . . . "Good, so good."

Zane runs his thumb over my lip. It's so him. It must activate some mythical pressure point when he does it, because a wave of shivers cascades through my body.

I scan down his body. And he moves around to my side —kneeling, bending forward, the tip of his cock near my lips. I circle it and suck him in. My eyes close. Zane fucks my mouth, slow at first, but when I run my tongue along the underside, he breaks loose, speeding up the pace.

Easton and Dante play with my breasts, timing their assaults for when there is room, while Calvin's thrusts push me up the cushions.

It's a lot.

I'm so full.

It's amazing how much I love this. I'm in control—while I'm not. I'm not sure why it turns me on so. I need this. I'll never be the same after. There's no after for me. I'll never survive without them. I need them here, but I'll need them more later. Shit.

I slam the door on my overactive brain, sucking Zane down, maybe too hard. He shoots off in my mouth with sudden force. I swallow down as much as I can.

"Bloody hell!" His cock slips out of my mouth, hot

streams of his cum coating my shoulder. His body jerks beside me. I'm watching. It makes me feel so powerful, like I can do anything.

Calvin's thrust is deep. "Chiefie." He breathes in, and his barrel chest expands even larger.

I reach past his chest, wrapping one arm around his back. And the hold on his pace doubles. He grabs my hips with one hand and tilts me. And he hits the spot. The spot that until recently I thought was a myth.

Dante slides his finger between my body and Calvin's. Two flicks of my clit and all thoughts of world domination vanish. All thoughts disappear. There's no overthinking; there's only existing. Vibrations roar at me. My back arches as stars fill my vision. My neck bends, sending the top of my head to the floor, as if I'm about to do the backbends I was never able to do, back in gymnastics in elementary school.

"Haley!" Calvin comes hard with me.

I'm shaky and sweaty. I open my eyes.

And there's Sam.

Upside down Sam. The door to my rational brain opens again. Taking in clues, trying to process what I think he's feeling. Is his brow furrowed? Is there judgement in his eyes? Does he think less of me? My stomach seizes up. Too much wine. I've had too much wine. Two glasses over three hours. No, it's not the wine—it's fear. Fear of loss. Losing the guys, not having a chance to see what things are like with Sam. It's too much—

"Hey, Firefly?" Easton's lips are on mine. "You're fucking beautiful and amazing. Stop thinking so hard." Easton smooths his fingers over my forehead, like he can smooth out my worry lines. "You're fine. We've got you." I know he's talking about him and the guys from the beach. And I know it's true for as long as we're here. Beyond that?

Again, I try to slam the door shut and forget I ever thought about it. Tonight is big. It's too important to wrap a blanket of insecurity around myself.

My lips turn upward, and I give Easton a smile. I push all the way up and twist, bringing Sam into view. He hasn't run off, so that's a good thing. I only hold his gaze for a few seconds before I have to look away. He's too handsome, too classy and sexy for me. They all are.

Easton laughs. "You have no idea, do you?" His finger is on the backside of my hair. The palm of his other hand covers my breast.

"No." I get what he's saying. I need to let go of my racing thoughts. They've never helped me. They're not my friends. It's a fight.

"Let me help you see the truth." His gentle kiss tastes of patience and kindness.

The tips of my fingers trace down his abs. If Calvin's made of sculpted stone, Easton's cast of steel, his taut muscles so defined the sinew ridges cut into each dip of his skin. I trail light touches around him. My eyes close. Easton tastes of a beginning, slow, calculated with care. Calvin's beside me too. His nose nudges at my neck.

Chapter 32

The Tide Waits for No One.

Sam

Calvin kisses her nose, then her cheek and ear. It's a big contrast to what he just did to her. I'm hard again already, and I almost came from watching her. I couldn't keep my hands off my cock. I wanted to touch her too. But there was something about the way they moved around her. They're comfortable and practiced. It's how Dante skimmed his hand down her chest to her core, triggering her like the firework display in Hong Kong on New Year's Eve. The way Zane ran his finger over her lips . . . It's a lot.

Damn. I'm learning about myself. Things I had no idea I . . . I like. Or might like. Or don't hate. I've always been in charge when it comes to sex. I'm not one to be ordered around. This was different. Dante might think he's the conductor, Calvin the boss, Easton the maestro, and Zane the caregiver—but Haley's in charge. When she raises her chin, the four of them move around us like points on a compass. They stay out of the way. This isn't about them, this is about what I could have with her, what I want with her. I'm in it this far. I'm ready to take it all the way.

My chest expands, and they blur into the background. The only thing I see now is her loose blond hair hanging over her dark red nipples. She's an angel with the sunset glowing from the window behind her.

All my euphoria slips away. "The tide!" I'm about to jump to my feet—

"Fuck." Calvin sprints out the sliding door to the back sun deck, his white ass flashing by us, the rest of the guys zipping out of the salon too.

I resist every ounce of training I've ever had, and I hold Haley's arms, keeping her from moving. I peck her on the cheek. The reality of it is that whatever has happened to the tender has already happened. Our moment is over, the bubble of intimacy in the room gone. And I'm the one who destroyed it. Fuck.

Her eyes flick to the sundeck and back to me. She wants to go too.

"Later." I growl out the promise and let go of her arms, a light red imprint of where my hands were vanishing from her skin.

She nods. "Yes."

I'm out the back door. I race across the sundeck and down the back stairs to the swim platform. The damn reef is peeking through the water, the white sharp teeth of the sun-bleached tops protruding out. Calvin's in the water. Zane's already hauling the motor on board. Easton and Dante hold the lines.

Calvin swims next to the reef. The Rock Candy made its way through the opening. In normal operations, I'd stay back, let the crew do what they needed to do. But this isn't normal. It's four mostly naked males yanking on the thing we need the most. It's the lifeline we have between here and the beach. The yacht has a lot of fresh water, but not enough for us to stay on board for as long as it will take to get the engines running again.

Calvin bursts up through the water. "One small hole. But you can lift it without risking ripping it anymore. Damn." He pushes himself up onto the side of the platform.

He really is one of the smartest sailors I've ever met. The natural inclination would be to pull the tender right onto the swim platform, but that could have split it down the middle. My eyes flash to the gash on the side of Calvin's foot.

"It's nothing." He takes the corner of the tender from where Easton's holding the rope.

Zane's back from putting the motor in the toy hauler room. We pull the raft onto the platform.

"Flip it toward me," Calvin barks. It smacks the deck, and water pours out from the ropes around our feet, a trail of red circling Calvin. "Here." He points to a small tear in the plastic.

Dante tosses Zane a drying rag.

Zane runs his fingers over the rip. "I can fix that. But I'll want it to dry for at least twelve hours before we put it back in the water. The glue says two, but it's not like we can run to port and get endless patches if it fails."

"Agreed." I frown at the tender. My gut tightens. This could have been a hell of a lot worse.

"Not your fault, Sam," Easton says. His shoulders are next to mine.

"We all need to be more vigilant. The simplest mistake could hurt any one of us."

Penny barks from where Haley is holding on to her collar on the sundeck at the top of the stairs.

"Let's move it all the way to the toy hauler shed. We're going to have to stay on board overnight." Calvin bends and takes the bumper rope in his hand.

"Go sit down. I can move a damn boat—and put your damn foot up. I want to take a look at it." Easton takes the rope from Calvin, who limps over to the deck chair at the edge of the toy hauler garage. We move the tender, giving Haley a view of the red-tinted ocean water spreading over the platform.

"What the heck?" She takes the stairs two at a time, Penny flying along on her heels. "Calvin!"

"I'm fine." He's pressing a drying rag to his foot, which is no longer white. "Or I will be. It's just a little cut."

"Let me see. Feet can be so dramatic." Dante crouches next to Calvin. "Oh, damn."

I glance to where Haley was, but she's gone.

"Back away from him, Chef." Easton has two towels in his hand. He squats next to Dante, the towel spread over his legs.

"It's not that bad. Seriously, I'm fine. I just need a Band-Aid or something. It doesn't even hurt. Stings, but it doesn't hurt."

Easton makes a face I've seen his father make many times over the last five seasons. It's the *I'm-not-happy-with-what-you're-telling-me* face. "Fine, if that's all you need, I'll put one on. Let's get it cleaned up, though."

Calvin picks up the cloth. My stomach lurches, and I'm not squeamish. The cut on Calvin's foot is larger than the one on the tender. And deep. This is not butterfly bandage material.

Haley's back down the stairs, Penny with her. "Here's the big first-aid kit." She glances at Calvin, stepping closer. "You doing okay?"

"I'm fine. It's nothing."

There's a slight flinch when Haley looks at Calvin's foot. Less reaction than I had. "What do you need, Easton?"

"Are there needles and sutures in there? And to not be drunk. But if he is that will help some."

"Listen, Rockwell, I'm good."

"Not yet, you aren't." Calvin might be drunk, but he's far from good. I turn to Easton. "You've given stitches before?"

"I was a sports medicine major in college. Mostly to piss Rocky off that I wasn't going into either of the family businesses. But yeah. I had to do a rotation in an ER and at a bunch of road races, marathons. I've done it enough. Nothing as deep as this, though. You?"

"I've stitched up a few cuts, but the same. Sounds like you have more experience than me. You want to move him up top so we can get him lying down?"

Easton nods.

"I'm right the fuck here. And I can fucking hop up the stairs. So you can stop talking about me like I'm a damn toddler."

Dante laughs. "I was going to go get him some whiskey for the pain, but I think that's taken care of. Stand up, Viking. Put your arm around my shoulder and I'll help you peg leg over to the stairs."

Calvin stands and follows Dante's directions. I don't know which I find more surprising: Dante barking orders or Calvin following them. There's a lot I don't know about them. Fuck. There's a lot I don't know about myself yet too.

There's a trail of red as Calvin clings to Dante on the way to the stairs. Then he grips the banister tightly enough that his fingers whiten as he hops up each step.

Penny tries to stay at Calvin's side, but I pull her back.

Haley's got her hands full with the large medical kit. And she's the only one clothed.

"You guys have him. I'm going to work on the tender, flush the motor, and then do the patch." Zane's already wiping down the swim platform.

I nod to him and follow them up the stairs, holding Penny back.

When we're on the top step, Penny pulls out of my hand and rushes to Calvin. He's sitting on a chair next to the lounger, while Dante's pulling the cover off the other loungers.

"How can I help?" Haley asks Easton.

They're all moving around each other like a player who has studied the playbook for the last three months and is finally on the field. I was the coach, but I don't know what I am now.

"You want to flush it with sterile water, or are you going to use the alcohol wipes?" Dante's leaning on the grill.

"Yeah, I know we want to save supplies." Easton turns his back to Calvin. He lowers his voice. He might even think he's whispering, but he's far from it. "But this is the sort of thing we are saving the supplies for."

Calvin lifts the towel Easton had been pressing against the wound. "It's not that . . . whoa." He wobbles. But I've seen big guys go down before. Granted, not as big as Calvin. I push myself to his side, pinning him to the chair.

"Let's get you over to the lounger, Calvin." Easton's got Calvin's other side.

"Nope, I'll get blood on it. The owner won't like it."

"I am the damn owner. Move your large white ass over there."

Adrenaline and alcohol are battling for Calvin's brain,

turning him into a toddler the size of a small Macy's Thanksgiving Day balloon.

Haley puts the kit on the chair next to Calvin and drops to a crouch in front of him. She runs her hand up the side of his thigh. "Calvin, honey, can you please do what Easton is asking? He wants to help you."

"Okay." He smiles and cocks his head to the side as Haley pets his head like a giant golden retriever.

And we all take a deep breath.

Chapter 33

Cabin Inspection

Easton

I'm not a surgeon. Never wanted to be a doctor. But I can do this. I push supplies around in the kit.

"Here," Dante says, pushing a can into my hand. It's an energy drink. Unlike other athletes, I never touch the stuff. But this is exactly what I need.

"Thanks." I down it. I'm just hoping it doesn't make my hands shake.

"We've got a couple more kits with other supplies," Sam says.

"Good, but this one has everything I need." Fuck. I put on gloves. And the snap of the vinyl on my wrist clears some of the thirty-year-old Scotch out of my head. Muscle memory is going to be my friend. I can remember how to do this. It wasn't that long ago. Fuck, ten years. It's fine. I've got it. "You ready?" I hope to hell the drunk giant doesn't pick me up and throw me over the railing after the first stab of the needle. I tilt my head, trying to convey that thought to Dante, but it's Firefly who picks up on it.

"Is it okay if I sit next to him?"

"That's a great idea, Haley," Sam says. "Sit there, and I'll steady his leg."

"What in the hell do you think I'm going to do? I've had stitches without being numb before. And I wasn't drunk then. I sure as hell am now. I sliced my hand wide open on a barbed wire fence. Fucking cow charged the fence and I tried to stop her. The cow won, the fence came in second, and I sure as hell lost. Come to think of it, I was drunk then too. My grandma was a nurse. She said if I was dumb enough to try to stop a bovine from going through a fence, I deserved every ounce of pain I got." He lies back and crosses his arms over his chest.

And I'm struck by a couple of things. How did he just fuck Haley? He's drunker than a skunk. And two, how did he not drown, let alone swim under the tender checking it for holes?

I've got what I need to set out. I turn to Dante on the other side. "You got him?"

"I'll do my best, which is always perfection." Dante nods at Sam.

"A little pinch," I say.

"What the fuck?" Calvin scowls at me. Then he drops his head to the cushion. "Just kidding. Do your worst."

I brace myself while I flush the wound with disinfectant. I hold it up, waiting for Calvin to react. But he doesn't.

Haley's running her fingers over his hair. She's keeping him calm.

I take the first stitch and pause. He doesn't so much as flinch. Then the next, and more. I'm on the twelfth stitch when he snorts. I freeze. Then keep going. It's got to hurt, but I need to just get it done. I'm only halfway finished.

Haley raises her eyebrows at me. "He's out."

Eighteen stitches in all, and I tie it off. I coat it with an antibacterial salve and gauze it up. How in the hell is he going to keep this clean, let alone dry? I have no idea. "How is he like this?" I still don't get it.

"After you left the bottle of Glendronach on the floor, the two of us decided to give it a taste test. I had a sip. He had a bit more. That was right before Sam noticed the tide. The alcohol hadn't claimed his wits yet," Dante says.

"Ah, that will do it. I remember being eighteen and just having come home from training. The stuff isn't meant for slamming back, for sure. The worst hangover of my life." I glare at the giant. His mouth is hanging open. "We can't leave him here. He's likely to sleepwalk off the side of the yacht."

"Let's get him to bed. Zane, how's it going?" Sam calls down to the swim platform.

"Coming up now." Zane takes the stairs two at a time.

We're gathered around Green like a family at a hospital bedside, all of us staring and no one saying anything.

"How are we going to get him to a bed?" Haley runs her fingers around Calvin's knee.

"You know, I helped a boxer friend of mine hide one of his passed-out teammates from their coaches. We rolled him onto a blanket and carried it like a giant sling." I leave out the part where we dropped him—twice. Hard, once, on his head. Come to think of it, I was drunk then too.

"We could put this back under him." Haley lifts the discarded lounge chair cover from the deck.

"I never understood how the nurses in the hospital could change the sheets with someone still laying on the bed. Let's move him over," I say. The cover on the lounger next to Calvin is still in place, and I push it next to him, lifting his limp arm out of the way. Then I try to lift his shoulders. He's like a rock. "Yeah, this is going to take all of us." I stare at Dante, who's sitting at the table, staring at the seagulls swarming the cliff of the island. "Can you help?"

Dante grabs Calvin's other shoulder. Zane and Sam each grab a thigh.

"I'll guide his feet," Haley says. The white of the gauze catches my eye. It looks like a kindergartener set out to make a mummy. I hope for fuck's sake that I did a better job on the inside.

"One, two . . ." Even with his size, we easily slide him over. I'm surprised we actually got him over without bashing his head.

Zane un-cinches the underside of the cover, and we each take a corner again. Sam and Zane are in the lead. We travel back through the main salon.

"Where are we going?" Zane slows at the sofa.

"Primary state room." I'm hoping I don't have to re-suture him tomorrow. "The light is better there." The main salon where the sofas are has windows on one side and the study on the other.

Haley runs down to the cabin ahead of us. When we get there, she has the bedding pulled off. "Give me a second." She gets a clean bottom sheet on, and we roll Calvin into bed.

"What the fuck?" He groggily wakes, but Haley's got a blanket over him. He rolls onto his side and sighs.

"I'll stay with him tonight. I don't want him walking on his stitches." Haley's picking up things that she tossed onto the floor earlier.

"If you're staying in here, Sassy, this is where I'm sleep-ing." Dante sits on the side of the bed.

I stare at Calvin. It's a big bed. But not big enough for six adults. My bedroom is down the corridor, but I'm not giving up a single night with Haley. Not a touch, not a minute, not even a sigh. "I should stay in here to watch Calvin."

"Same," Zane says.

The captain grips the headboard. "I've thought about sleeping down here before. The cross breeze will make it the coolest cabin below deck. But . . ."

"We can bring another bed in. This cabin is big enough for three king-sized beds," Haley says. She takes off down the corridor to my cabin. "Let's drag the mattress to the primary."

Zane and I carry it back to the primary suite.

"Fuck no. I'm not sleeping on the floor if there's a perfectly good bedframe down here," Dante says. He walks out of the room, and I'm not sure why most of us follow, but we do. He turns into my old cabin. "That's a good bedframe."

"Then sleep down here," Zane counters.

"I said I sleep where Sassy sleeps." Dante pushes the mattress out of the way. "Only four bolts holding it to the wall. We move the mattress and the frame and make one huge bed."

Zane drops to the floor. "I'll get the ratchet set."

"Good. Call me if you need help. I've got a galley to clean." And Dante's gone.

And that's how we spend the next hour: sobering up and then fighting, pushing, and pulling the mattress to the primary cabin, following it up with the frame.

"Do you need help?" Haley asks. "I would have come down, but I didn't want to leave Calvin alone."

"No worries, Little Bird. There were lots of words you didn't need to hear."

"That bad?"

"Easton dropped the wrench on my leg twice. I'm fine." Zane laughs, and Calvin stirs.

We all freeze, staring at him. When the bed is set back up, Haley has it made. And damn if it isn't big enough for us all. I've got to admit, if it wasn't for the white waving bandage on Calvin's foot, I'd toss Haley on it right now to try it out.

"I'll stay with Green if you want to take a break?" Zane says.

Haley nods. "Okay. I should go help Dante wash dishes."

"On your birthday? No way. I'll go help Dante." And Zane's gone before she can tell him not to go.

"I'll stay, Haley. You go. Have you even checked out your cabin yet?" I push a clump of her hair back from her face.

"No, but . . . it's fine. I was thinking we should search some more for the key."

"We've gone through everything." I turn to look around the room. The last search we did was pretty thorough. We found my mother's necklace. But then I spot the closet. "You know, I looked in the bottom of the closet, but I didn't search the pockets of the clothes in there."

"That's a good idea. I'd never think to look for a key in clothes hanging up." Haley stares into the closet, her hand on the handle. Her shoulders slump.

"What?"

"It was one of the last things Shayla did on the boat. Candy had her re-iron all her clothes after Rocky gave Shayla a compliment on the drink she made him."

"She really was an ass," I say.

Haley sucks at her lower lip. "My mother always said never to speak badly about the dead, but in this case . . ."

"Warranted."

She pulls open the closet door.

"Where are my dad's clothes?" The entire closet is full of nothing but Candy's gross gowns and leather pants. The entire trip they were taking was tropical, and the majority of the clothes in the closet look like something you would wear to a winter ball.

"His clothes, along with Candy's extra clothes, are in the next suite over, the one we hadn't finished setting up. It was a big beef Candy had with us. But the Captain told her we were overworked as it was."

"Right. I suppose we should be thorough, though."

The hangers glide across as I pull them. Most of the outfits have more sequins, bows, and crystals than they have pockets. I pat down the fabric because I don't want to start thinking, later, that I might have missed something. There's nothing but price tags in most of them. I hold a tag out for Haley to see.

At the end of the closet is a garment bag. A big one. "What's in there?" I ask.

"I don't know, but I'm guessing that's the wedding dress Shayla talked about. She said it was hideous. Candy told her that was the only thing she didn't have to touch in the closet. In fact, she made a pretty big deal about not touching it."

"Not touching it? Not showing off my father's wealth to someone who she thought would fawn over it? Yeah, that's suspicious." I pull the zipper down on the bag, and a white and pink silk gown with feathers and crystals sparkles at us. Oh, for fuck's sake. The crystals aren't crystals. They're actual diamonds, and they're in the shape of a horse's head on the back of the train.

"That's . . . Wow! That's like the ugliest wedding dress

I've ever seen. And it doesn't look cheap. Are those real diamonds?" Haley lifts the side of the dress and taps at them.

"I'm not an expert, but knowing Candy, the answer is yes."

"Wow, no wonder she didn't want Shayla to open the bag." Haley pauses. "I guess Shalya did open it, since she said it was ugly . . ." Haley cringes a little.

"Firefly, you don't need to worry. I would have opened it too."

Her blue eyes widen. "Were they planning on getting married on board? No one told me. I certainly didn't order supplies for a wedding."

"Also yes." My stomach flips. Emily and I had planned to talk Dad out of the whole thing. Emily had even made a PowerPoint about how Candy was just using him. And how it was going to come back and bite him in the ass. That if he wanted to play with Candy, that was one thing, but binding himself to her forever was a piss poor idea.

I pat down the side of the dress. It's huge.

"We should take it out. There's too much fabric," Haley says.

"Right." I take the monstrosity off the hanger and pull and pull the length of the dress out of the bag. There's a thump. A very non-fabric-like thump.

Chapter 34

Rocky Outcropping

Haley

Easton and I freeze—the only sound in the room is Calvin's snoring. "You don't think . . . ?" We both fight with the voluminous dress, getting it onto the empty bed. Out of the garment bag, it's even worse than I thought when it was in the bag. I tussle with it, shoving it out of the way, and drop to my knees. Easton's on the floor too.

"Do you see anything?" I'm reaching under the original bed.

"No. But it's dark under there. Whatever it was could have rolled under the new bed."

"Right, I'm going in." I drop and I inch in, slithering in an army crawl and then patting out in front of me. My knuckles bump into a cloth pouch about the size of my fist. I've found something. I pull it to myself. Through the cloth, I can feel something large and hard and some smaller things too. They shift as I grasp the bag. I start back the way I came in, but it's not as easy. It's been a long time since I've crawled underneath a bed. That's how I watched scary movies at my grandmother's house. I can still smell the must and see her mauve dust ruffle.

I hand it out to Easton and push myself the rest of the way out. "Is it the diamond?"

His eyes flick to the package and then to me. He slides it back into my hand. "You open it."

My heart thuds. It's heavy, and the surrounding bag screams *I'm important!* I'm not sure I want to hold a 55-million-dollar diamond in my hand. I close my fingers around the bag. "If this was the reason the Rock Candy was sabotaged, why is it still here?"

"And what's in the safe? But we're not going to know unless you open it up, Firefly."

I clutch it closer to me and step back until my thighs hit the mattress. I sit down on the edge. Then I lay the white bag on the bed and untie the ribbon, holding it shut. It's going to be the diamond. It's like the thing is vibrating. Calling out. Inside, there's a piece of jewelry on top of another bag. I pull out a diamond necklace and two large teardrop earrings.

Easton's eyes narrow. "Those were my mom's first real flashy diamonds my dad bought her. I only saw her wear them once. At the wedding of my dad's business partner."

He leans over, and I pull out the other bag and open it. I hold up the diamond. It's stunning. The evening light catches it and sends a pink spectrum over the top of Calvin's white blanket behind me. It's magical, but it's also—

"A little underwhelming for 55 million dollars?" Easton holds out his hand, and I place it in the middle of his palm.

Fireworks shoot through me. "Exactly. Think of all the

good that money could have done. All the schools it could have built, the children it could have fed."

"You're very right. But that's not something Candy ever thought about."

I shake my head. "Why would Candy put this in her wedding dress bag?"

Easton wraps it back up in the first bag, but he doesn't put it in with his mother's jewelry. He places both in the top drawer of the dresser next to us. "I don't know. But if she told Shayla to stay out of her wedding dress bag, I'm guessing she told Rocky to stay out of it too."

My brow furrows. "He bought her the diamond. Why would she not want him to know where it was? I mean, you can't *steal* something like that. It's got a name. My college roommate loves jewelry. She spent hours watching videos on crowns and tiaras. They're not stolen often because you can't sell them."

"Unless who you're selling them to doesn't care about wearing them. Unless they're collectors."

"Right, but why would she want to take it? Rocky already gave it to her."

"Unless she was planning on leaving him. That would have been 55 million well spent."

"Really?"

"No. But it doesn't matter now." Easton drops into a crouch. "I still want to get into the safe. I just think there's something in there. Something we should know about."

"We can keep looking," I say as Calvin snores. "I think it's okay to leave him for a while. Your father's clothes are in here." I lead Easton across the hall.

"This place is massive. I still haven't been everywhere." Easton yanks open the closet doors. His father's closet isn't something I've even seen. Shayla said Rocky hung up his own clothes. There's what you would expect for traveling in the South Pacific: a lot of linen, some tropical print shirts— that had been his staple when he was on board. And at the end of the closet, pushed to the side, a tuxedo in a garment bag. "I guess Candy wasn't the only one planning for a wedding." Easton pulls it out and tosses it on the bed. The room isn't finished, but Shayla made the bed. The white duvet still has her signature tight corners in place. Easton unzips the garment bag and pulls out the tux. He searches each of the pockets.

I'm holding my breath while he does. There's no reason why the key to the safe would be in Rocky's tuxedo just because the diamond was in the bag with Candy's wedding dress. "Anything?"

Easton pulls something out of the inside of the breast pocket. "No key. But an index card with the initials R H and a quickly scrawled 5.2 b."

"His Royal Highness needs 5.2 birds?" I cock a smile at Easton. Mostly because he looks so serious.

"Maybe, but Dad's business partner, the man who owns the next highest amount in the company, is Roger Harding."

"As in Rockwell and Harding finance?"

"Yeah, it's the company Dad started after he made it big with Rockwell Tire."

"And 5.2 b isn't about birds."

"I'm guessing billions."

"Was Harding trying to buy out your dad? Or was your dad trying to sell him his part of the company?"

"I don't know. I used to think of Roger as an uncle, and then I grew up. I don't trust him. He's been trying to get Dad out of the way for a long time. He's one of the many reasons why I never wanted to take over the firm."

"That might have been in his tuxedo forever. It might

not have anything to do with Rock Candy at all." I lean my head on Easton's arm.

"True, but it hasn't been in here for long. Dad and Candy came straight from New York City. The house manager at their penthouse . . . she's a perfectionist. Dad used to joke that you had to keep your belt fastened or she would strip your clothes off as you walked by to send them out to be cleaned. No way this was in there long. He probably wore it the night before they got on the plane. He's a creature of habit. He has a dozen tuxedos, but he always wore his favorite one for special occasions."

"Like getting married."

"Like getting married, and whatever it was he went to the night before."

"It's too bad we can't figure out where he was the night before they left New York City." I put my palm out, and Easton hands the card to me. I hold it up to the waning light in the porthole, but I can't see anything new.

"We might not be out of luck. My dad keeps a paper planner. It's got to be on board somewhere."

"The cigar room, with the little desk." I'm three steps out into the hall and almost to the stairs when Easton calls out.

"I'm going to check on Green."

I skid to a stop. "Right." Heat rises up my neck.

"Don't, Firefly."

"Don't what?"

"You don't have to feel guilty because you are excited about chasing a clue."

"I'm . . . It's kind of a habit."

"I'm sure. I know Calvin's fine. I'm just . . . I was fucking drunk or drunker when I stitched him up, and I want to make sure he's doing okay."

"You didn't look like you were that drunk."

"Unfortunately, that's a skill I've had too much practice in. The not looking drunk thing, not the stitches."

"Well, your hands were steady, and it looked like you had done it a hundred times. The stitches were neater than my grandmother's embroidery."

"Thanks." He smiles down at me and peeks into the primary cabin. "He must really be out. He doesn't normally snore. But then sometimes it's like he never sleeps at all. He's always on the watch for danger. It's horrible what happened to his foot, but I'm glad he's sleeping."

"Yeah, the sleep will do him good."

Easton feels Calvin's forehead. "No fever. Let's let him rest." We close the door and head up to the main salon.

I haven't been in the cigar room since we got back on board. "Your dad had the Rock Candy built custom, but the entire time he was on board, I never saw him smoke a cigar."

"He gave it up a while back. But I'm sure he put it in the plans with the intention of using the yacht for meetings. You know, that's one of the good things Candy did for him. She hated cigar smoke."

"No one's all bad." Not even my ex.

Easton cocks his head at me. "She was darn close." He opens the seal of the door. And it's humid all right. "Damn, that's like a furnace blast."

The computer and papers that Rocky had out on the desk aren't there anymore. But then, the yacht was more like a sailboat with its stabilizers gone. We could really have tipped over because of the imbalance of the fuel and water tanks with them down. The desk has even slid to the far wall. The leather sofa hasn't moved, most likely because it's latched in place. The two leather wingback chairs are lying on their sides as well. Easton picks up one, and I get the other one. There are papers underneath the one I picked up.

"Do you see a little black book? That's what Dad uses as an agenda."

We both crawl around the floor gathering computer printouts. Under the sofa I see his missing laptop, but it's so far under that with the sofa attached to the floor, I can't reach it. "His laptop is under there."

"It's out of battery for sure and password protected." Easton's straightening the papers.

"I don't see the agenda, though."

"If his laptop's in here, it's got to be here somewhere." Easton pulls the desk away from the wall. There's a lot more paper there. We gather it up, making a pile on the desk.

"I didn't see his agenda in the bedroom, either. I would have remembered it from when we searched the primary the first time." I sit on the leather sofa. It's like butter—well, hot melted butter. The faster we can get out of this room, the happier I'm going to be.

Easton's going through the papers.

"What are all those?"

"End of the quarter reports on both Rockwell-Harding and Rockwell Tire. But something's off. I had a copy of these reports . . . well, not these reports. One of them isn't correct."

"What's off?"

"In my copy, Rockwell Tire was doing great. Earnings were up. Like, way up. In this one, the numbers are the reverse. It makes Rockwell Tire look like a piece of shit."

"Which one's doctored?" I lean forward, looking at the spreadsheets.

"I . . . I don't know." Easton flips from sheet to sheet.

And I get a flashback of Rocky sitting right where I am,

doing the same thing, only with two fingers of his favorite scotch next to him on one side and the stack of papers on the seat beside him. I slide my hand between the cushions. My fingertips hit something hard, and I pry it out. "Is this it?"

"Fuck, yes."

Chapter 35

Watch

Zane

I'm walking through the main salon when Easton yells something from inside the cigar humidor. I have no idea what, because the thing must be designed to be soundproof.

"What's going on?" I say as I yank the door open.

"We found my father's agenda." Easton inclines his head at Haley.

Haley holds up a little black book.

"And did he miss his dentist appointment or tee time?"

Haley scrunches up her forehead, but her blue eyes sparkle with excitement. "Zane . . . no. We found . . . we found lots of things, actually. The Pink Phoenix and—"

"You found the diamond? That's amazing! So the saboteur wasn't trying to steal it. It's still on board." I'm both excited and confused. Do I like the idea of someone trying to off us all? Hell no. But it's 55 million dollars. That's a hell of a lot of money. Not that I would sink a boat for it.

"I don't know about that. We found it in the bottom of Candy's wedding dress garment bag, and then we found a note that seems really suspicious in the pocket of Rocky's tuxedo. Which is why we wanted to know where he was the night before they got on the plane."

I nod. Because while this part doesn't make sense to me yet, I'm sure it will.

Haley hands the agenda to Easton, and I have to admit I want to know what sorts of things a billionaire writes in his little book. Like, does he have phone numbers for famous athletes or the direct line to get him into a Michelin-star restaurant? Not that I care, I'm just curious.

I move behind Easton, and he opens the book up. My heart sinks. It's a generic calendar. Like the ones my mum gets for free for sending money to the children's home or one you could buy at the chemist. "Well, what does it say? Was he at the Met Gala the night before?" I lean over Easton's shoulder. Mr. Rockwell has loopy cursive handwriting that reminds me of my grandmother's.

"Met Gala?" Little Bird laughs. "Why would you ask that?"

"Isn't that what everyone does in New York City?" I straighten up.

"How did you know he was in New York?" Easton puts the book down and twists his neck to see me. And I don't like the look on his face, or the accusing tone.

"Because his luggage tags said he started in JFK and I'm the one who carried all five thousand pieces of Candy's luggage down to their cabin."

"Oh, right, of course. Sorry."

I want to punch Easton in the neck. And unlike Green, I haven't had that desire before. "I noticed because last year his bags came straight from Florida. I like reading luggage tags. They're in code. When I was a kid, I memorized two hundred airport codes."

"That would have come in handy for my roommate; she once booked a trip to Manchester, New Hampshire instead of Manchester, England," Haley says.

"That's funny. But better to be in New Hampshire. Manchester City is an overrated football team. So, what did you discover about your dad?" I ask.

"He and Candy were in New York for the week before they came to the port. The night before is just labeled 'gala.' Not that helpful. In the front, he has notes. But then, he never writes anything out all the way." Easton holds up a section in the front where there's just two letters in a series, page after page, dates and letters.

Haley shakes her head. "I'm not sure you're going to be able to figure much out of that. It looks like gibberish."

"I don't know. There's an awful lot of repetition going on. The letters R H."

"Rockwell-Harding," Easton says.

"And R T—that's Rockwell Tire. Look, here there's R C. That's either the boat or he's referring to himself and Candy. Right? And this here? May I?" I motion to the book, and Easton hands it to me. I move over to the sofa and sit next to Little Bird. "This here, see this sequence of numbers? It's on page number ten and then on page twelve . . ." I cock my head, but the two of them are looking at me like I'm nuts. "You don't see it?"

"No. I have no idea what you're getting at," Easton says.

"He's numbered the pages in the top right-hand corner." They look at me blankly. "But on the other pages he's numbered them on the bottom right-hand corner. But if this is page ten, this one should be page fourteen. These aren't page numbers; they're what you need to multiply this number by. If you multiply this number by ten"—I flip to the other page in question—"and this number by twelve, they're the same number."

"How in the world are you doing that math in your head?" Haley's eyes are wide.

Easton has found a pen and is doing multiplication on the back of the printout. "He's right."

"Of course I'm right. This whole thing is a code."

"Maybe it has something to do with this?" Easton hands me a ripped index card. On it, in Mr. Rockwell's loopy handwriting, is $R\,H\ 5.2\,b$.

"There must be something in here. I'm sure. Do you want me to keep at it?"

"Hell yes. There's no way I would have ever made the connections you already have." Easton taps at his math on the paper in front of him.

I'm deep into the agenda when it occurs to me that I haven't asked about the safe. "Did you find the key?"

"Not yet. But it's got to be around here somewhere. I've got a feeling there's something in the safe." Easton glances away.

"He definitely didn't take it with him on the night we abandoned ship," Haley says.

"It's weird how he told you about the safe but didn't tell you where to find the key. Do you think he thought you would know where it was?" I ask.

Easton freezes, and his eyes go wide. "No, how . . . I'm fucking stupid." Easton races out of the room, and we charge after him. The fresh air from the main salon hits me across the face. "Back to the primary suite." He's taking the stairs two at a time.

Dante comes out of the kitchen. He only had a few things to clean up when I left him. "What's going on?"

I glance at him because there's too much to tell him. I

don't slow down to explain to Dante, but Haley does. "We found the . . ."

I skid around the corner to where Calvin is snoring like my old man. Easton is already on his knees, opening the compartment in the bottom cupboard. "I want to see if I'm right," he says, "but where's Haley?"

"I'm here. I was just filling Dante in."

"Right, well, Dad had . . . I suppose it doesn't matter. Dad had this safe built for the house in Maine. It looks like this complicated thing, but it's not even locked. You just have to know where to press. At his house, it's not a real safe but a bar. Susan didn't like him drinking, so he had the room installed. What if this is like that? There's no key needed."

My stomach flips. Rich people make no sense. "No key for something that costs 55 million?"

"Sometimes you just have to look tough, not be tough. You don't always have to be the best, but you have to make others think you are," Easton says.

"That's some motto." I've got my own rules that I live by. Things my dad said to me before he passed. Rules I've made after I've been hurt by something, someone.

"It's one of the many things my dad likes to say." Easton's hands hover over the dark wood.

"What are you going to try?" Haley drops to her knees next to him.

"What do you think?" Easton cocks his head at Haley.

"The lock is flush, almost like a button," Haley says.

I'm still gripping the planner. "Did your dad have a favorite number?"

"Yes." Easton's blue eyes flash up at me. He pushes the lock. And it clicks open. "Holy hell," he says. The lid swings open, but we can't see what's in it.

"How is the diamond in there?" Haley glances back at me.

Easton stands and opens the top drawer, from which he pulls out a bag and unwraps a pink diamond the size of a small egg. It matches the one that is sitting in the safe. "They're identical." Easton takes out the one in the safe and the one from the bag and sets them on the dresser side by side.

"Identical, but one's a fake," Dante says.

"But which one is the fake?" I ask. I might be able to see patterns in numbers, but the two pink blobs in front of me look like the same damn thing.

Dante reaches around me. He takes the one sitting on top of the bag. "This is the real one. Look at the depth of color in the inclusions. This other one's good, but lab grown. It's a good fake, though. I could use the real one to scratch the fake if you want? But it's pretty enough on its own."

"That's okay, I believe you," Easton says.

"Candy was stealing her own diamond?" Haley pushes at the one on the dresser.

Dante puts the diamond back and sits on the end of the bed next to Calvin. His snoring stops. We all stop and stare, first at Calvin and then at Dante. "What? He's not going to wake up."

"Candy caused the sabotage?" Haley shakes her head. "That doesn't fit. I don't think she could fake how upset she was that night. And if she knew, why wouldn't she have had the diamond ready to go? As it was, she didn't take either of them. That doesn't fit. It really doesn't fit with someone who would go to the effort of making a fake diamond. This must have cost a lot to make as it was."

"That's worth at least twenty thousand," Dante says, crossing his ankle over his knee.

"How do you know so much?"

"My uncle. He owned a little bit of everything in town. A construction company, a restaurant, and a jewelry store. That was my favorite summer job. The jeweler who ran it liked to teach. While I wasn't there long, he did teach me the basics, but I might be wrong. If I didn't know one of them was a fake, it's not as obvious." Dante yanks his shirt off. "All the time on the raft and then in the treehouse . . . I really was looking forward to sleeping in a bed. But it's stuffy as hell down here. It's better than the crew cabins, but damn, I'm glad we're not going to normally stay here. Where on the bed are you going to sleep, Sassy?"

We've got a little schedule. It's not official, but it's becoming, well, official. But then, we've got to throw Sam in the mix.

And just like that, Sam appears at the door. "How are things going down here?" Penny's at his side. She trots into the room and jumps on the bed. In all the seasons I've been with her, I've never seen her jump on a bed. She puts her head on Calvin's back and sighs. "Get down, Penny." But Calvin wakes up enough to put his hand over her head. She turns and looks at Sam. "Fine. You can stay for now." The sigh that comes out of the dog is longer and louder. "I haven't been keeping watch on the horizon for a while. But now that we have more people, we could." It's more of a suggestion than an order, and I'm put off guard.

"Sure, I can take first watch," I say. As much as I want time in bed with Haley, the energy in the room is off. The awkwardness is more palpable than the dog's sighs.

"Thanks. Wake me in four." Sam hands me the binoculars.

"I'm going to go get cleaned up." Haley eases around the group of us, into the hall.

"I've got a flashlight, Haley, if you're going to get things in your crew cabin. I'll come along." Sam leaves with her.

"I'm not giving up my turn," Dante says.

Yeah, awkward as fuck. I follow Haley and Sam out, then head to the back deck when they turn down the crew stairs. But then I remember I haven't told Haley her story for tonight, so I pivot back to the cabin.

Chapter 36

Recommissioned

Sam

My stomach is shaking. There's the possibility that I'm more nervous than when I had my first date at the junior prom. Then again, there weren't four other guys in the back of the sedan I borrowed from my dad.

I pull the flashlight out of my back pocket. I try not to use them too much. I've only got one solar battery bank to recharge them with, so I'm in the habit of fumbling around the ship at night in the dark or just waiting until morning to do whatever it is I need to do. "Can you see?" I smile over at her.

"Yeah, thanks." Her blue eyes are gray in this light. We're three steps down the crew stairs when she stumbles into me. I'm holding on to the rail and catch her.

"You would think it's my first time on a yacht. Thanks for getting me." She holds on to my arm. Her lips are plump. My heart beats erratically.

"I've got you. I'll catch you anytime you fall."

"I know you will." We're standing still on the stairs.

"We should get going. I like to conserve as much of the flashlight as I can."

"Yeah, sorry."

"No need for sorry, Haley." We're through the crew galley and down to her cabin. "What do you need?"

"I . . . I don't know?" She opens a drawer, and I shine the light into it. "I guess a shirt." She takes one, and a few other things, then grabs her pillow but drops it. "The ones in the guest cabins are a lot better."

"They are." I took one a few weeks into my drifting for my nest in the wheelhouse.

"Most of my things are already at the tree house."

"Including your suitcase." I wiggle my eyebrows at her. There are several things in her suitcase I want to see again. But this time on her, or in her.

"Sam Miller, did you have fun with looking inside of it?" She cocks her head to the side.

I gaze straight into her blue eyes. "Yes, I did. I apologize for invading your privacy. It was wrong."

"Whoa. I mean, wow."

My stomach twists. I guess I'm shocked that she's so upset by it. I honestly didn't think I was ever going to see her again. Of course I hoped. I dreamed of it. I dreamed of her finding safety, of both rafts being rescued, but—

I shine the light on her so it illuminates her face more than the dresser in front of us.

"That is the most amazing thing," she says. "You not only took responsibility for what you did, you apologized." Her hands wrap around my neck, and she presses a kiss to my collarbone.

I'm taken aback.

"You, Haley Brewster, haven't been around the right men."

"Not until now. That's true." Her lips hit mine, and I'm lost in her. She pulls back, her eyes wide, and a switch flips. She excitedly shakes her hands. "I didn't tell you about what we found—"

Penny jumps up, a paw on my leg and one on Haley's. Penny whines. "It's potty time, girl?"

"I'll tell you about it on the back deck." Haley takes my hand and walks with me outside—she finishes telling me about the diamonds, and everything else they found, while we wait for Penny. It's almost domestic, like an after-dinner stroll. Our weird version of normal.

Haley squeezes my hand as she finishes up. "Crazy, huh?" She yawns.

"Yes." It's a lot to take in. And I'm too tired to make sense of it all now. I follow her down the stairs, watching her ass on the way to the primary suite. There's shouting. "Not the green menace, Zane. Have some mercy on us." Dante punches a pillow, fluffing it. "Ah, Sassy, there you are. Tell Zane he can skip over Hulk Two because it's shit."

"I don't know. I think I need to hear them all." She steps into the bathroom with her new shirt as Dante groans.

"Sassy, you're killing me." Dante moans and holds up the sheet. "We have a system, Sam. You don't get to jump the line. But on the bright side, it's easier to get up and go to the bathroom if you don't have the Viking's damn calf thrown over your leg."

"The fucker's leg weighs a ton," Easton says.

"Does not." Calvin's eyes are little slits. "Why the hell are you all yelling?"

Haley crawls into bed between Calvin and Dante. She

smooths Calvin's hair back, but I can tell she's checking for a fever. "How are you feeling?"

"Like I haven't drunk a case of warm beer and sliced open my foot in a while."

She presses a kiss to his forehead. "You want to sleep on the edge so you can get up easier?"

"No." He pulls her to him, and Dante puts his hand on her hip.

"You have a shirt on." Calvin's got the hem, and it's gone before she can answer.

"You need to sleep some more, Calvin."

His hand is on her breast, and I can't look away. I should get ready for bed or at least move my dog. But I'm just standing here staring at them. Easton settles next to Calvin. Penny's between the two of them.

Haley lifts her head. "You coming?"

"Come on, Captain. I promise to not spoon you. At least not tonight." Dante laughs.

Zane sits on the side of the bed. "Little Bird wants Hulk. She's getting Hulk. After the opening credits we see our hero David Banner working in a lab—" Zane stops and stares at me. "You ready, Sam?"

"Right, sure."

Dante pushes a pillow at me, and I take it. It's a really good pillow, but so are the sheets. Damn, I hadn't thought of taking some of these before.

"Ready?" Zane asks.

"Yes." The bed is really comfortable, and as Zane drones on, I remember how much I like movies, and he's really good at describing the scene. I can almost remember the smell of the theater I saw it in with my brother Charlie. And this bed is a hell of a lot more comfortable than sleeping on the wheelhouse floor or even on the bed in my cabin. But it's something else. Knowing that Zane is going to go take a watch, that there are others around me, that I don't have to do it all . . . I drift off to Zane's voice.

I'm disoriented when I open my eyes and see the carved beams on the ceiling. It takes me a minute to realize where I am. I'm pretty sure I haven't moved at all since I drifted off. I stretch. Haley's next to me, and Calvin's on the other side of her. But Easton, Zane, Dante, and Penny are all gone. Haley wiggles back, stretching, and as she does, she wiggles into my crotch. My morning wood was already there. With her bare back and little underwear, I'm even harder. Her hand comes around and lands on my thigh.

I put my hand on top and lean over her. "Morning." It's then that I see Calvin's eyes are open. He's watching us.

"Sam." His voice rakes low. "Chiefie." He leans in and gives her a kiss.

"Are you doing okay?" Haley asks.

"Like I have stitches. But nothing else. There's no throbbing. At least, not in my foot."

Haley laughs, and fuck if it doesn't make my dick jump. "Do you need me to get you anything?"

"Always such a good Chiefie. Yes, Haley, I do need something."

"What?" She moves to get up, but his arm swings across her body to my arm. He pins her to the bed.

"You," he says. And his lips are on her neck. He pulls her underwear off in a swift motion.

I'm frozen. But then she takes my hand and wraps it around her, placing it on her breast. She pushes even farther into me. My cock settles between her ass cheeks. My hips take off by themselves. My brain shuts off, and my body takes control. Between my thumb and forefinger, I roll her nipple. And she makes the most delicious mewing sound.

Calvin lifts his lips from hers. "She likes a little pressure. A little nip of pain. Don't you, Chiefie?" His loose hand moves between the back of Haley's hand and mine. He gathers her hair and tugs her head back. It's then I realize his other hand is between her legs.

Her hips are vibrating between his hand and my cock. It's fucking amazing. The noises coming out of her are enough to make me want to come. Calvin takes his hand out of her and licks his fingers.

Haley groans and instantly flips to me. Her kiss is full of hunger, and I'm not going to deny her. She pushes on my shoulder, and I go flat against the bed. Then she's on top of me, straddling my waist. She rolls her hips, grinding up the length of my cock once and then twice.

"Haley, fuck."

Her lips turn up in a smirk. Her blond hair is sticking out in every direction, but with the morning light behind her, she's a damn angel. "That's exactly what we should do."

"Do it." I grab the base of my cock, and with one move, I'm in.

She tilts her head back, rolling her neck, before her bright eyes shine back at me. "Sam."

"You feel incredible."

She tips her hips, and I slide in even deeper. And my eyes roll into the back of my head. I grip her hips. And damn if Green isn't right. The tighter I grip, the more she flutters around me. I'm controlling the pace, but damn if watching her isn't the most erotic thing I've ever experienced. Her eyes are closed, and when her tongue darts out of her mouth, licking her lips, my cock jumps inside of her.

She tries to change the pace, lifting her adorable ass higher and slamming back down into me. But I need this to last. I need for her to get everything she needs too.

The bed dips next to us. Calvin's sitting, his bandaged foot jutting off to the side. Even with her on her knees, he's taller than her. His lips are on her neck, and she turns her head to the side, giving him better access.

All I can think is that Dante was right: watching her get pleasure from someone else is something I could become addicted to.

Calvin moves his massive body until he's behind her. My legs are running through his. His knees are against the sides of my thighs. His hands wrap around the front of Haley, covering her breasts. She leans back into him, and damn if it doesn't sink me deeper into her. I'm not going to last. With my eyes gripped tightly shut, I release her right hip, trailing my fingers to her pussy. But Calvin's hand is already there. My eyes spring open and down to where we are all touching. She's fluttering.

"You're close, aren't you, Chiefie?" Calvin growls into her ear.

"It's so good." Her hips bounce on me, and the pressure of Calvin pushing on her clit has her flying.

She grips me and I'm lost. Stars blur my vision. My back bounces on the mattress. I'm yelling as I come. Words that aren't even English, a garbled mess. "Haley," is the only distinct word I get out.

Her shoulders slump onto my chest, her hair around my neck and arm. As aftershocks take me, our lips find each other like magnets, and I'm sucking on her tongue. Until she starts rocking again. She lifts her head, and our eyes lock. "Sam." She chuckles.

"Haley," I say.

I didn't know how I would feel after sharing her. But Calvin's lips are pressed to her shoulder. And when she bites her lip . . . she inches forward, sliding off me. She pushes Calvin to the bed. But she doesn't straddle him. They kiss. I wait for the pang of feeling less. But it doesn't come, and that confuses me more.

Chapter 37

Math

Calvin

"Chiefie." It comes out as a command.

She lifts her mouth from my cock, and I'm wondering why in the world I'm complaining about what she's doing. "Calvin." She licks around the tip of my dick with those blue eyes focused on me. I've got to admit, I'm wondering how Sam is taking all this. "Is your foot okay? Do you want me to stop?"

"My foot is fine. But you've got to be hungry and dehydrated from last night."

Sam slides off the bed, and I expect her to follow. But then he's back from the coffee bar in the dressing area of the suite, a bottle of water in his hand. "Hydration is important." He cracks the seal and hands it to her. She downs a few sips. "I'll see you when you get up." Sam smirks at me and then kisses Haley on the cheek before he heads out of the room.

She smiles, waves, and when the door clicks shut, she leans back over me. I'm not going to complain. And if there's one thing that can shut my brain the fuck up about the problems in the engine room, it's Haley's mouth, pussy —fuck, it's anything Haley.

My hips press up, and she swallows my cock down to the back of her throat, and fuck me. "Haley," I growl a warning, but it's too late. I'm shooting off. My hand roughly holds the back of her head. I'm half pulling on her hair, half holding her down. And when I settle, she looks up at me with mischief in her eyes. Fuck. "I love you, Chiefie."

My heart explodes when she winks back at me. Damn, Dante has it right. She is Sassy. I don't even care that she hasn't said it back yet. How can she not without putting pressure on everyone else? And that's not how Haley works. If there were a patron saint of empathy—which I'm sure there is, but I have no idea what their name is—for me, it would be Haley. It's amazing she hasn't been crushed under the weight she's carrying. It's even more amazing that her father sounds like a piece of shit stuffed into a business suit.

I lay my head back on the pillow. I have to get up. I have . . . well, everything to fix. But last night, I decided that getting a local radio up and running would be the best thing. Sam said he saw pirates, and I believe him. I think we did during the first few nights on the island too. Which means they're around. And I'd rather know when they're around.

The engine is going to have to wait. Not only do I have to deal with the sabotage but the damn saltwater in the generator too. And the VHF radio is something I can do up on the bridge. Let my foot rest for a little while.

There's a knock on the door, and Zane's there. With a tray.

And I'm staring. "Is that an egg?"

"Yeah. So, don't get mad."

I have a feeling I'm going to get really mad.

"Right, so I was up early. Dante and Easton too. We were looking at the WaveRunners at the top of the boat."

My gut is clenching. But Haley puts her hand on my shoulder, and I try and relax a little.

"Okay, so I'll start with nothing else being broken. Kind of. Nothing important, that is."

"Zane?" I growl.

"Right. Easton took the second shift. Sam was out. I don't think I could have woken him if I tried. But then I couldn't fall asleep, so I went up with Easton to the top deck, and then Dante came up right before sunrise."

I grunt. "The Three Stooges—"

"Maybe fast forward, Zane." Haley slides out of bed, looking for her clothes.

"The front WaveRunner was up top, and the crane wasn't attached to anything. Since they launched the transport during the evacuations—"

"Fucking stupid," Zane and I say together.

"When I stood on the edge of the antenna platform, I could reach the sling for the crane. It was high tide and—"

He was damn right to be wary about telling me. I can already see where this is going. The WaveRunner could have crashed into the side of the boat. "Fucking hell, you dropped it off the side?"

"Yeah, but it's fine."

"What did Sam do?"

"He made the same face you did, ate the egg, then went to the wheelhouse and slammed the door." Zane's not standing close to the bed.

"That is the stupidest thing you've ever done. You could have ruined everything. I don't even know who you are anymore. Even my fucking stupid engineers Mitch and Waldo wouldn't have done something so asinine."

Zane's eyebrows go up in surprise. "Mitch wasn't stupid. Same goes for Waldo."

"What? What does that even matter now?"

"It could mean a lot." Haley has found her shorts and is running her fingers through her hair. "We're looking for who could have done the sabotage. If Zane says that both Waldo and Mitch were hiding their intelligence from you, that could mean it was one of them."

"They both barely passed the test I gave them," I say.

"Failing a test is easy," Zane says. "Waldo had a lot of experience on tugboats. He was a deckhand. Said he'd even been a bosun once or twice off the Maine coast. But he wanted to try his hand at engineering."

"Fuck, it could be one of them. Part of me was hoping it was just Emily's boyfriend, Brick. But when would he have found the time? And when would he have even known what tanks to put those damn stickers on?" I'm staring at the tray. And then I realize I've gotten side-tracked. "Wait. How did you drop the damn WaveRunner over the side of the boat?" I have to take a breath. I'm starting to feel sorrier for my dad and all the stupid things Jared and I did on the farm in the name of saving time. "How did it end with eggs?"

"Sure . . ." Zane's bouncing on his toes, and if it was anyone else telling me this, I would have already exploded. It ticks in the back of my head. That's why Dante and Easton sent Zane down to tell me. "After I righted the WR and checked it over, making sure the lines were good and no gas was . . . right, I took it for a little spin. I zipped along the cliff away from our beach camp. The opposite direction of the cliff doesn't go that far. In fact, there's a cave. But that's not where I found the eggs. The beach on the opposite side is exposed. And there were chickens. I followed one, but I couldn't catch it. I did, however, find a nest with some eggs. And I came back. Chickens! How amazing is that? I'm thinking it must be kind of near where you found the Pomelo trees. I didn't see any signs of anyone around. But I didn't stay for too long. I wanted to get back." Zane's back to smiling.

My foot is throbbing now. And my brain hasn't caught up with everything he said. "Back up. You said you almost didn't damage anything. What did you damage?"

Zane's bouncing back and forth on his heels. "The sling. We got the WaveRunner in the sling, then forced it over the edge. I put on a harness. Easton belayed me, and I cut the sling while pushing the WaveRunner off. I suppose that was stupid. But now we have eggs and a machine that doesn't use as much gas as the tender."

"And how are we going to get it back on the yacht at low tide when the surrounding reef is practically cutting through the water? The fact that the Rock Candy found this space in the reef to settle is lucky."

"The cave isn't that far. It's got a shelf. We tie it up in the cave and swim back and forth. Or we drag it up onto the tiny beach on the other side of the reef. Or keep it back at the treehouse beach."

I purse my lips because they're answers. They might not be the answers I like, but they're not bad. Okay, they're fine.

"Look at that, Little Bird. He's speechless. Dante has an egg for you, Haley, and wanted to wait to make sure you were ready for your egg. Want me to tell him you're up?"

"That's okay. I'll go chat with him in a minute."

Zane puts his arm around Haley's shoulders. "Thanks for calming him down." He wiggles his eyebrows at her.

"I'm glad you didn't get hurt," Haley says.

"Me too. He took it much better than I thought."

"That's not what I'm talking about, Zane." Her tone drops, and she glares at him. Now it's me who is happy that he's getting a scolding. Disappointing Haley is probably better than me taking it out on him, anyway.

I push the pillow back to the headboard and move the tray onto my lap. The last time I ate breakfast in bed, I was twelve and had strep throat. My grandparents and I were in deep quarantine. I read and listened to music for four solid days. It was awesome, but that's not going to happen here. I need to get to the wheelhouse to work on the radio.

Haley sits on the edge of the bed. "You want anything else?" she asks.

I hold up a bite of the egg for her. It's remarkably good. I thought what I would miss most was pizza and beer. And last night was fun, although maybe no more beer for a while. But there's nothing better than a fresh egg.

"That's yours," she insists.

"One bite." I hold the fork out, and she takes it, her lips closing over the tines.

"Mmm. It's really good." She leans in and kisses my cheek. "Do you need anything?"

"I'm not staying in bed. I've got shit to do. I should have been up already." I wipe up the rest of the egg with the pizza crust that Dante has sliced open and grilled with something. "I'm getting up."

The door swings open, and Easton steps in. He's got the medical kit under his arm. "No, you're not. At least, not until I take a look at your stitches." He hands me a little cup with some pills in it.

"What's this?"

"Just a couple of normal pain killers."

"I don't need that. We should save them."

"The yacht has enough for a couple of years. We don't need to skimp on them anymore."

I frown at the cup but then toss it back and chase it with the rest of Haley's bottle of water.

"You need me?" Haley asks Easton.

"Unless he's going to take the WaveRunner incident out on me? No."

Haley gives me a quick kiss and is out the door.

Easton drops the medical kit on the bed next to my legs, and my foot bounces. A zip of pain shoots up my leg. I glare at him.

"That's what I thought. How bad does it hurt?" He unwraps my foot and pokes at the bottom of it.

"Not bad until you started jostling me around and poking at me."

"I'm on your side. It's just I had a feeling you're the sort of guy who acts all tough and doesn't let the wound heal before trying to do too much."

"What more do you want from me? I'm lying in bed."

"Exactly. And that's where you should stay."

"I can't. You know that."

"We've been stuck for a long time. A couple more days isn't going to hurt us. We've got more food. Medicine. Seriously, Green. What we don't need is you getting your foot dirty and getting it infected. Stitches, I can do. Amputations? Not so much. I mean, I suppose if I had to . . ."

I'm glaring at him. He's got my heel in his hand.

"I'm still shocked. I think these are the best stitches I've ever done."

My forehead furrows. I have no idea why he's trying to give himself a gold medal for stitches. Seriously. "Thanks."

He laughs. "I'm just glad I didn't fuck it up. I was drunker than you last night."

"I doubt it."

Easton cleans the bottom of my foot and wraps it back up in gauze. He's found a giant sock and pushes my foot inside it. "I'm a quiet drunk. Right until I pass out. Which I was ten seconds away from when the Captain—Sam— called out the tide. You want to get up and use the bathroom?"

"Yeah, that would be good." I swing my legs around and stand, and *holy mother fucker*.

Chapter 38

Charting the Stars

Dante

I'm wiping down the main galley island when Sassy appears. "Good morning, Sassy. How did you sleep?"

"Great. I heard you were up early and causing mischief."

"Guilty as charged. How did the Viking take it?"

She cocks her head at me. "How did Sam take it?"

"About the same, I imagine. But do you want an egg?"

"Yes, please." She pulls a stool from the stew pantry into the galley and watches as I get things ready to take to the back deck.

"Did Zane talk to you about Rocky's notebook?"

"No, he was focused on getting out of the primary cabin without Calvin exploding all over him."

"Fair enough. While we were watching the horizon, we bounced ideas around about what some of Rocky's codes could be about."

"Did you come up with anything?"

"Nothing that doesn't sound crazy. So, no. But we got

chatting about all the deckhands and the engineers who left on the other raft. Easton hated Emily's boyfriend, and he wants to blame as much of this on Brick and Candy as possible. You know where the evidence is. Candy switched the real diamond with a copy."

"Or someone else did."

"Right. Someone else could have done it too." I cock my head at Sassy. She's not going to like what I have to say. "Like Shayla."

"No way." Her eyebrows rise. "Plus, Shayla was on the old boat last season, right? She worked her ass off to get the boat ready."

"Okay, so not Shayla. We've searched the primary cabin. There's still Emily and the one that Brick moved into. Plus all the other crew members." I pick up the things I need for the back deck and take them out with me. A few seconds later, I'm enjoying the noises coming out of Sassy's mouth as she cleans her plate.

Things are washed, and after the two of us make a quick visit to the engine room, I realize there's nothing we can do to help them. They're trying to figure out how to make a grinder work.

I turn to Haley. "You want to go play Nancy Drew?"

"Oh, I had a Nancy Drew computer game. I seriously loved it. Yeah, let's go investigate. I'll get a notebook." She jumps up. "And we'll need to find a flashlight."

And now I'm trying to forget the crush I had on the actress who starred in the remake on some cable show.

"Take good notes for me," Zane calls out from under a pipe.

"I will," Haley says.

And we're out in the corridor. "Where do you want to start?"

"Shayla's cabin. So I can prove to you she has nothing to do with it." Haley's down the crew hall to the crew mess. From out of a cubby next to the crew day board, she takes a notebook. "My list of things to do. Look . . ." She shows it to me. "Find somewhere to store the extra box of horse statues Shayla found in the back of Emily's closet."

"I'm guessing Sam already found something to do with them."

"Yeah, they're trotting with the fishes." She laughs.

"Notebook found. Shayla's cabin?"

Haley nods. The place is immaculate, and the bed hardly looks slept in. Haley pulls open the first drawer and picks through the carefully folded clothes.

"What if she's stuffed something in between them?"

Haley glances at me and frowns. "Right." She pulls each piece of clothing out, shaking it. There's not much to be found but a box of melted candy bars hidden in the bottom drawer under her jeans. No photos or much personal stuff. But that's the thing with working on a yacht. The more you work, the less you bring. Only the most important stuff comes with you. Because it's a bitch when you have to leave. It set me up for van life. For the stint I did a few years ago.

"Across the hall or next door?"

"I'm next door. I mean, if you think you need to search my room, go ahead." She holds out her arm like a game show assistant.

"I think we're good. My cabin's next to yours. Do you want to shake out my drawers?" I grab her around her waist.

"Dante?" She laughs, but her soft lips hit mine. My dick hardens in my pants, and I'm thinking I don't care about who might have done anything to the ship. But Sassy pulls away. "We need to keep looking."

"Right."

"Over here?"

"Let's do it." This cabin is a pigsty. It looks like someone has already searched it. But then I remember walking past it when we were on board, and it was kind of like this.

"Oliver and Cruz." She picks up a few pieces of clothes and puts them on the top of the empty dresser. It's hard to tell whose things are whose. "They both sure are slobs."

"Yes. But other than clothes, a collection of colognes that together probably total more than five gallons, protein powder, and enough vapes to last a year, there isn't much else." I lift the mattresses.

"Oh, that's good. I didn't even think to do that," Haley says.

"All right, next cabin. Who lives here?"

Her blue eyes shine at me. "Zane and Luke. We should wait to do that with Zane."

"All right. Last cabin on this side is Anders and Calvin." That I knew. "You want to wait for Calvin too?"

"I think that would be polite. Let's go back down the other side of the hall."

I point to the next one. I didn't have much time to figure things out on board before we abandoned ship. I was still trying to learn the galley and praying we had enough provisions until we got to the next port. But Haley had done a good job of ordering things for me.

"I'm not sure about these two cabins. Mitch, Waldo, Ryder, and Daxton were here, but they were switching around. Waldo snored, and there was some argument. So I have no idea who ended up in which cabin."

"I'll take the top bunk while you take the lower berth."

"I thought I would be able to figure out who was sleeping in which room by looking at the clothes. But I don't think anyone had moved their clothes yet." This drawer has a mixture of differently labeled crew shirt from Daxton, Mitch, Ryder, and Waldo.

"Ryder was the quiet deckhand with the pointy ears, right?"

"No, that was Mitch, the engineer."

"Right, I knew that," I say.

"Okay, so anything we find in these two rooms at least narrows it down to the four of them. Waldo was quiet. I don't think I got two words out of him the entire time we were on board. Not that I had much time for socializing."

"Right, same. Okay, you take the bottom and I'll do the top bunk." There isn't much. A bunch of dirty socks inside the sheets which, after being left there for months, have developed quite an odor.

We're through. I even pull the lid to the tank of the toilet back in each of the rooms, but there's nothing in them but stale water.

"I think we can call the first room," Haley says.

"I agree."

The next room is a lot more of the same. I pull the sheets back, and between the mattress and the wall is a stash of magazines. I try to push them back, but Haley catches sight of them.

"If I had to shake out Shayla's underwear, you can pull out the deckhand's dirty magazines."

When I pull out the first magazine, two pictures flutter to the floor.

Haley bends. "What are those?"

It's two black and white photos. One is of a girl in her early twenties, with dark hair. She's sitting on a bed, the kind you might find in a summer camp you don't want to be at. A cross hangs on the wall behind her. The other photo is of the back of a girl wearing a backpack. It might be college, boarding school, or even a high school. It's hard to say.

Haley looks at me. "This is weird. Are these old pictures? I mean, who has black and white pictures anymore? Unless you're trying to be artsy?"

"If this is art, then so is boxed mac and cheese." I shudder.

"Maybe it's some sort of photography contest?"

"For the worst photo? This one's barely in focus." I tap the picture of the girl on the bed. "And this one? What the heck is it even of?"

Haley cocks her head. "Are they the same girl?"

"I don't know. With them being black and white, it's hard to tell. They could be. But they're modern. Look at the clothes and the backpacks. That guy is wearing one of those Only Good Vibes T-shirts that are really popular right now. Or at least they were popular when we left."

"Did Waldo, Ryder, Daxton, or Mitch have a girl-friend?" she asks.

"Hell if I know. But these pictures say 'I'm a stalker' more than 'I'm going to ask you for a date.'"

Haley nods. "Yeah."

"Let's see what else is around." I shake the rest of the magazines, but nothing else comes out. Then we search through both rooms again. We find an address book under the frame of the built-in bed.

"Whose is it?" Haley asks.

The front page lists Waldo's name and his 207 phone number. "Waldo. I didn't think Waldo was from Maine?"

"Why do you think he's from Maine? Oh, wait, the area code. That makes sense." She taps the front page, where Waldo has his number printed in sloppy handwriting.

"That makes a bunch of the crew from or tied to Maine:

Anders, Waldo, Mitch, and Daxton. How weird is that? Plus, I think Easton lived in Maine for a while too." I flip through the book, but there's nothing else of value. There are stars next to girls' names and some detailed notes of what they are willing to do. It's nothing but the desperation of a twenty-three-year-old dude-bro who clearly doesn't know the value of a relationship and has never had a quality woman in his life. You don't rate women in a book. Not without having it come back to haunt you. That shit needs to be locked up tight. But the Maine thing tumbles through my head.

"I was hoping we would find something more. Besides some photos and a phone book."

"Yeah, me too." I close the address book. "We should put this with Rocky's notebook. Maybe Zane can find a correlation between one of these phone numbers and something Rocky has written down."

"Yes. But do you really think 'Janie five star wow, wow' has anything to do with Rocky's notebook?"

"No. You never know, though. Maybe Janie is into some weird shit." I wiggle my eyebrows at her.

"Just your type of girl," Haley says.

"You are my only type of girl, Sassy. And don't you forget it."

Her smile lights up the dark room. "You are so full of yourself."

"I like it better when you're full of me."

"Dante?" She tilts her head back and laughs. Leaving her long, delectable neck available for me to kiss. "Whoever put those stickers on the tanks to make them look level? They must have had a second set. What would they have done if the first one went crooked?"

"We didn't find any."

"Right, because they put them on and they worked. But what would they have done with the other ones? If they had extras? Thrown them away, right? We need to search the trash."

"The trash?" Trash is a big deal on a yacht. Rich people tend to make a lot of it. It's the first thing we deal with when we get to port. "I made linguine for crew dinner with chicken that night. I watched Shayla clean up. If that trash was still in the crew mess, we wouldn't be able to stand in here."

"Sam must have gotten rid of it. But did he put it in the pit on the bow, or did he pitch it overboard?"

Chapter 39

Down and Dirty

Haley

It's almost lunchtime when I head to the engine room. Sam and Zane are working on the engine. It's hot and muggy and super hard to breathe. I've only been in here a few minutes and I want out. Everywhere below deck is warm, but here . . . In here, it's become unbearable. Sam and Zane both have their shirts off. Their backs are smeared with grease. "How are you guys doing?"

"Little Bird! Better now that you are here." Zane steps toward me. "Wait, don't touch me. I'm absolutely filthy." I give him a kiss anyway. "I don't want to get you dirty. Well, at least not this way."

Sam groans. I turn and kiss him on the cheek too.

I'm not sure how he's going to react. But he smiles at me in the dim light. "We're making progress. Not as fast as if Green was here, but he saved the tender from a bigger tear, thanks to his sacrifice." Sam clears his throat. "And we still have a fucking starboard outer wall too." He shoots a look at Zane.

"Yeah, I did the math. The arc of the WaveRunner wasn't going to hit the boat. There was a small possibility that it might have hit the reef instead of the deep pool of water that it fell into. But I get you. I get the point. Things might not have gone how I thought they would. I mean, they did. Because my math was right." Zane flashes me a smile. "But they might not have. Pass me the wrench, Sam." Zane ducks back down under the . . . generator? Maybe. I wish I had a better understanding of yacht mechanicals. Then I might be more helpful.

"Dante said lunch will be ready in ten. It can hold, so whenever you get hungry, come on up."

"Thanks, Haley," Sam says. "I'm not hungry. You can go eat if you need to, Zane."

Zane pulls out from under the equipment. "I'm good for another hour at least."

"I almost forgot," I say. "We found some things. But I would like to go through the galley trash from the night we left. Did you take it out?"

"Yeah, it's in the bow pit. I started to go through some of the trash, taking out the food waste and dumping it into the ocean. The rest, I put back. But that grew old really fast. I double-bagged most everything to keep the smell from coming up."

"Okay, great." It comes out of my mouth out of habit. Because am I actually excited about going through garbage that is months old? No, no, I am not. But I want to know why this happened to us as much as any of the guys do. And since they haven't come up with anything for me to do yet, I'm going to do it. I pivot and head out of the engine room.

I'm down the corridor when Zane calls out to me. "Little Bird, there are hazmat suits in the toy hauler room."

"Great, thanks." I wave.

"If you wait, I can help you later," he calls to my back.

"You've got more important things to do. I can pick through garbage."

He stares and then nods and heads back to the engine room.

The toy hauler room is full of everything. But after opening a bunch of cabinets, I find a box of white suits. I take out a couple and head up to the galley because I have a feeling I'm not going to want to eat afterwards. "Hey."

Dante puts his knife down and lifts his arm, calling me to him. "Hey back at you, Sassy."

I put the suits on the side counter, give him a hug, and slide into my chair. "Can I help you with anything?"

"Nope. I'm almost done. What do you have there?" Dante asks.

"Hazmat. Sam said most of the trash is double-bagged in the bow pit."

"Sounds like a party for after our food digests."

"Agreed."

"Do you mind telling Easton and Calvin chow is on? They're in the wheelhouse."

"No problem." I head down the hallway past Sam's room, where Penny lifts her head at me. I can't help it; I have to stop and pet her. I scratch her ears until she thumps her legs on the bed. "That's the spot, huh?"

Is it weird I feel like she's smiling at me? That's when I hear Easton and Calvin. They're arguing about something. "I've got to go, Penny. I'll be back." She's got to miss running around. She's been on board for such a long time, with only the little strip of sand to stretch her legs on.

I knock and walk into the wheelhouse at the same time. "What's going on?"

"He won't sit the fuck down." Easton points at Calvin.

"You don't have to stand for what you're doing. You're just being obstinate because you fucking like it."

Calvin furrows his forehead and steps toward me. But I see the grimace on his face when he does. "My foot is fine. It's my fucking ears that are bleeding from listening to his griping all day." His foot isn't fine.

"Am I going to have to separate the two of you?" I flick my eyes from Calvin to Easton and back.

"Please," Calvin says, throwing his hands up in the air. On the table in front of them lie several circuit boards in parts.

"Yes. I'll leave. Can you do me a favor?" Easton grunts.

"Sure." I rest my hand on Easton's arm.

"Keep him from making his foot fall off if you can." Easton yanks on the port door, but then he stops. "Thank you, Firefly." He leans down and kisses me.

I grab his hand. "Dante said lunch is ready when you want it."

He gives me another kiss and shoots Calvin the middle finger. "Thank you." The door bounces behind him.

I cock my head and jump on the back bench that runs the length of the wheelhouse. "He's trying to get you healthy."

"I know. And I'm fucking grateful. Just don't tell him that. But I've got to get at least one thing working. Being down in the engine room right now isn't going to work. Because honestly . . . ?"

"Always." I hold his gaze.

"It hurts like a motherfucker," he says through gritted teeth.

"I'm sorry."

"It's my own damn fault for drinking. If I wasn't drunk, I would have been smart enough to either grab flippers or at least not stand up on coral. Damage is done. But what's almost undone?" His smile lifts in a half smirk.

"What?"

"Connect that wire to the solar battery pack over there." Calvin puts down the tool he's using and points. "Just pull that wire off, then that red wire . . ." I do what he asks and hold up the red wire. "Connect that where you took the other one off. I combined two radios. This one, the antenna wasn't working, and this one, the circuit board was broken. They're not the same. This one was the primary, and this one was the secondary. But the fucker who did this to us knew enough to damage both just a little to make neither of them work."

I plug it in, and static comes over the radio. "You did it. You fixed the radio."

"I did, but don't get too excited, Haley. I didn't fix the high-frequency radio, the one that can communicate over thousands of miles. This radio is going to give us about twenty miles. But still, it's a good thing. It's like the radios we use on board, but with a little more power and more channels."

"But this is fantastic. Right? If we see a ship, we can contact them."

"Or not." Calvin's jaw twitches.

"Pirates?" I know they don't want to talk about pirates in front of me. It's something my mom was always scared about. But then, when she was alive, I was only doing charters out of Florida in the US coastal waters. There's a pressure in my chest. I've heard stories about pirates. Everyone who's worked in yachting has. You know someone who knows someone who had their yacht attacked. But I've never met anyone who actually has been in an attack.

"Yeah, there is a chance we might hear a cargo ship."

Calvin moves things around on the table. The radio isn't inside the case.

"We'll need to set up a watch."

He laughs. "I feel a list coming on. Yes, and we'll need to be careful when changing channels. I've fixed this, but too much jostling and it could be broken again. It's beyond fragile from combining the two of them together."

"Let me help you to lunch, and then I'll come back and listen." There's a stick by the door—looks like part of one of the little sailboats. I try to hand it to him.

Calvin shakes his head and smiles. "Or . . . you could get me some food and I'll take the first shift. I'd like to come up with a process. If that's okay? I can go get food myself, Chiefie."

"No, I'm happy to help. I'll be right back." I dash to the galley, where Easton and Dante are eating. "Calvin got the VHF radio working!" I'm ignoring that it feels like Calvin is acting like the VHFs are more pirate protection than a means of finding help.

"Seriously?" Dante drops his fork and glances toward the wheelhouse. "That's fucking fantastic, Sassy."

I avoided it as long as I could. But I really wanted to know if there's something in the garbage. Did I really want to dig through the trash? No, but now I'm dripping sweat in a paper suit.

Dante's down in the hole with a shit ton of bags. He's opening a bag and doing a quick scan. If he's confident that it's from his kitchen, he's tossing it to the side. And if he thinks it might be the galley trash from the last night, he hands it up to me.

In theory, if Sam hadn't tried to get rid of some of the trash, we'd have a stratigraphy to work with, but it was smart. Sam did a lot of things when he was drifting on his own that the average person would never think to do. But now the newest garbage isn't on top. Well, that's partially true. The bags from Sam being on board by himself were easy to toss to the side.

We're halfway through our third bag. Penny would like to help, and I've had to push her out of the way more than once. But she's stopped putting her nose into my bag and is sitting patiently beside me.

There's nothing like garbage that has baked in a pit for months. I turn my head and cough.

Dante's pushing things around that look like pasta noodles. "Eureka! Leftover Carbonara. I have the right bag." He holds it open for me to see.

"That's it." I try not to gag, which only makes me cough more.

Dante hands the bag up and hops out of the pit. We spread the tarp out flat again from the last bag. "Let's dump it."

This is my least favorite part, but Penny's tail is going strong. Dante rakes the pile out, moving the wet parts out of the way.

I crouch down. Part of the mound is fairly clean. I push stuff around. A broken hanger, a good ten chocolate wrappers that I remember being mine and Shayla's—we were stress eating chocolate. And there, under an empty granola box, are three little sheets of clear plastic. Two with stickers still in place and one with the stickers missing. Next to it is a wet notecard. There was something written on it in pen, but the ink has run.

"Holy crap." I hold it up to Dante.

"Holy crap is right." He tosses the last bag back into the pit. "Holy crap. You found it."

"We found it."

Chapter 40

Set a Course

Zane

Dante, Easton, Haley, and myself are gathered around the dinner table. I've showered the grime of the dank engine room off in cold water, but it was still a shower. Even a quick one is better than scrubbing in the ocean. We stopped for the day because our flashlights have been drained and need to recharge. Now that we're using the solar power for the VHF radio, it will be a few hours before we can head back down to work on the generator some more. But we've called it for today. Sam—under Calvin's guidance—carried the VHF to the sideboard in the dining room so the two of them could work on the wiring around the corner from us in the main salon.

Like a murder mystery, in the middle of the table are:

Rocky's agenda.

Waldo's phone book.

The empty sticker sheet and the unused ones.

The note from Rocky's tuxedo.

The real Pink Phoenix and the fake one too. *Not that I can tell them apart.*

The two creepy stalker photos and the adult magazines they were found in.

The broken motherboard.

The note from the trash, with the unreadable smeared-ink writing.

"It's too bad we can't fingerprint things. What else are we missing?" Haley's got her notebook out and is chewing on the end of the pen. She pulls it out of her mouth and looks around the room. "Bad habit, sorry."

"Not that bad." Easton kisses the side of her neck.

We've finished an early dinner and are taking just a few minutes getting things together before we head back to the beach.

"What about Easton's sticking door?" Dante points at Easton.

"Right. We should rip off the door and see why it's sticking. No time like the present," Easton says.

"You've got a toolbox in the toy hauler room?" Dante asks me.

"Yeah, want some help?" I push back.

"No, you keep working on Rocky's notes. Golden Wonder and I have this." Dante hangs his arm over Easton's shoulders. They take off down the back stairs, leaving Haley and me laughing. Calvin and Sam are around the corner, muttering about the wires they're fixing, and there's a low static hum to the VHF radio on the side table behind me.

I pinch my forehead and copy some of the notes from Rocky's book. There's a lot of numbers. Easton left the stack of printouts on the table too. I've scanned them, but I can't find anything that lines up.

Haley's switching between looking at the pictures and

at Waldo's book. "Sam, you have copies of our passports, right?"

He ducks his head around the corner. "Yes."

"Can I grab them? I just want to look at the pictures."

"I mean, normally no. But at this point, sure. I'll get them." Sam puts down his wire snips.

"No, I can do it. Are they in the file cabinet in your cabin?" Haley's up.

"Top drawer. It's unlocked." Sam nods and is back at work already, with Calvin directing him.

Haley returns with a pile of folders. She pulls everyone's picture page—that is, everyone who's not here—out. "I'm just wondering if I can match one of the girls to someone. What if it's not some crazy stalker but a relative?"

"Yeah, I've got a sister. She'd be gutted if that was the photo I took with me to hang in my cabin. It's not really a flattering photo. But it's worth a look. The girl on the cot has a distinctive nose."

"I guess you're right." Haley spreads her pictures across the table, then holds the photos up next to each passport photo. I watch her for a while, but then I'm back to Rocky's numbers.

Dante and Easton thunder up the stairs, and Easton drops seven large washers into the pile. They roll and then wobble until they are flat, lying amongst the diamonds and stickers.

"What the hell are those?" Calvin's leaning back in his seat, peering around the corner.

Dante steps closer to Calvin and Sam. "Those were built into the doorframe of not only Easton's room but Emily's too. Someone was trying to keep them locked in their rooms. The ones in Emily's room had slid, causing the door to not stick. But the other room, the one Easton was sleeping in, those were jammed in there tightly. We pulled a couple other doorframes apart, but they're all fine."

"Someone was trying to kill my sister and me." Easton's eyes narrow when he sees the passport photos. He jabs at the table. "One of these people."

"Hold up," Calvin says, leaning back in his chair again to see around the corner. "Those were most definitely there the whole time. I or someone else would have noticed the finish work of the yacht being off."

Sam ducks around the corner. "I did a full walkthrough with the shipyard. One of the many things on the checklist was checking all the doors. They all passed. But we didn't take possession until the next day. They were still working on trying to get as much of the interior furniture placement done."

"So it happened after the checklist and before you left the shipyard." Easton runs his hand through his hair. "But this was intentional."

"Yes, it does seem like you were targeted. I agree. But Shayla got stuck before you were on board. This is bigger than just an on-board sabotage. I think we can say that for sure." Haley's holding the photo of the girl on the coat next to Ryder's passport photo. Not that anyone looks like their passport photo.

I don't blame Easton. I'm raging about this, but he was the direct target. It's got to hit even harder.

Haley takes the pictures. She holds them up to the waning light. "There are some bumps on here. Look." She passes the photo to me.

"There is. It's writing." I angle the sheen of the photo left and right, but I can't make anything out.

I ran the sequences and letters in my head as I lay on my back in the muck of the engine room, trying to sand away by hand the corrosion the saltwater left behind, while we figured out how to make the power tools run. There's a pattern, I can feel it, just out of reach, but I haven't been able to touch it. It's proper annoying.

"There's something seriously wrong with those photos," Sam says. His hands are inside the wall. "They're not photos you bring to work with you."

"Not unless you're seriously fucked up." Calvin hands Sam a pair of pliers. When I hand back the photos to Haley, she's smiling.

"Oh, he's right. I'm just glad Calvin's sitting." Little Bird holds them up again. "I can't make anything out. But you know, I think both this and the blurred mess on the card might match. And it's not printing but cursive."

"So then, who did it? Has to be someone older." Easton's got the diamonds in his hands and is moving them around the table like he's going to play three-card monte.

My eyebrows shoot up. "Why?"

"Because they don't teach cursive in schools anymore," Haley says.

"In America." I shake my head. "That's why all of you have handwriting like doctors. In Britain, we get a proper education." I'm poking the beast.

Dante throws his hands up in the air. "You're not wrong."

"True," Easton says.

"So the saboteur is someone from Europe or older . . ." It feels wrong coming off my tongue. "Or the person in charge of the sabotage is older." I turn to Haley, and she nods.

"Well, that doesn't help us narrow down the list." Haley's staring at the photos again. "I just feel like I know this building. Look at this part here. I think it's a university. It has a plaque to the right of the door. And this girl is not the one the camera's focused on. But this one here, to the side, she's wearing a midriff shirt. There can't be many high schools that allow that. What do you think that plaque says? It's too small to read."

"Hold on." Sam strides across the main salon, past us in the dining room, with Penny at his side. The dog flops down at the edge of the room, stares at the wall and barks. Sam stops and turns back to us in exasperation. "It's gone, Penny. There was a spider there like a month ago, and she won't stop barking at the wall." In a minute, Sam's back with the map magnifier. "This should help." He hands it to Haley.

"Thanks!" She hovers it over the photo of the girl outside the school building. "Holy shoot! Does that say Clapp, Langley?" She pushes the photo and lens toward me. "Right there?" She points to the plaque.

A guy with short hair stands in front of a plaque, and I can make out the C L A and then the next word starts L A N G before it runs behind him. "It could?"

"This is the biology department building at the University of Pittsburgh. I spent way too many hours in it. Yes, this is definitely Pitt, my alma mater." Haley taps the table next to the photo. "East coast university. I don't know if that helps narrow things down? I mean, people come from around the world. But really, most of the kids are from the east coast."

"It might." Easton's pacing now, the diamonds in his hand. If he starts juggling them . . . I guess he can do whatever he wants with them. They are his family's, or at least the real one is.

"On the other raft were Emily, Rocky, Brick, and Shayla. I think we can rule out all of them knowing how to mess with the stabilizers, the fuel, and electrical." Haley writes their names down in a column on her notepad. "Then we have the two engineers, Waldo and Mitch. Anders, the first officer." She writes their names on the other side. She turns to me and bites her lips. "Cruz, Luke, Ollie . . . Help me out, Zane."

"Daxton and Ryder. Luke's from Australia and, if I remember right, an only child who's never been to the states." Haley puts an X next to his name. "Oliver's from England, and Cruz is from Santa Barbara. I don't remember them talking about family." I squint and stare at Little Bird's neat printing of Daxton and Ryder's names. "Daxton's from New York City. He had a lot of siblings. Luke and Cruz's cabin was a pigsty. Wait, Cruz did say he had a sister, I think? And Ryder is from New Hampshire. But I also don't remember anything from him. Let me stew on it. Something might bubble up." Bubble up? That's an expression my Nan used to use.

"What about Waldo and Mitch?" Haley leans back to look at Calvin.

"I didn't talk to them about family. This is a job, not a social club," Green says. Which isn't shocking.

"They both have sisters. Waldo was born in Youngstown, Ohio, and Mitch is from Erie." Sam ducks his head around the corner. I raise my eyebrows at him. He wasn't the sort of captain who hung with us around the galley table. "Waldo was leaning on his radio, and a conversation came through."

Little Bird has drawn a question mark next to Daxton, Ryder, Waldo, and Mitch. "It's the same four the pictures could belong to."

Dante's flipping through Waldo's address book. "The phone number in the front is Maine."

"I'm pretty sure that's where he lived before coming

out. Honestly, he's the only person around my age I know with a paper address book," I say.

Dante doesn't look up. "There's been more than one time in yachting when my phone was dead or didn't have service and I would have loved to have been able to look up a phone number. This one time in the Maldives when I wanted to call my aunt to see if she would . . . Never mind, that's a story for another time. The point is, I didn't know her number. So maybe it's not that strange. But there's no numbers from Ohio or Western Pennsylvania. Not that area codes mean much anymore with cellphones. But everything in here has area codes from New England and New York City." Dante tosses the book in with the rest of the clues.

And the VHF radio on the side table crackles. It takes all of a minute to adjust to the sound. A garbled voice . . .

Chapter 41

Radio Signal

Easton

We're all silent, gathered around the radio. Sam's sitting in a chair next to Haley. We're waiting. So far, we haven't been able to make anything out. If we hadn't seen what appeared to be pirates . . . I would have been the first one to grab the mic and let them know we're here. But we're sitting on an expensive piece of salvage. That's without them knowing about the diamonds. It occurred to me once or twice that I could try and leverage myself by giving a finder's fee reward to them. But there's so many ways that could go wrong. So many. I shiver internally at the thought of anything happening to Haley.

And then it crackles again. Words with breaks in between them. It's not a language I know. Something Asian, not Japanese, but that's the limit of my knowledge. My head snaps to Dante. He was at least able to identify the language on the bottle we found on the derelict.

"I have no idea what they're saying, but it's Filipino.

The most I can do in Tagalog is hello, goodbye, and bathroom. I was only there for a few weeks."

The speaker slows and then says, "over."

Someone else starts, "Kamusta . . ."

"That's 'hello,'" Dante says.

"Great, we can at least be polite," I say.

Sam's next to the radio, his hand on the mic, when the second speaker says, "over."

And another one begins, but this one is throwing in a lot more English words. Cargo, sick, and payment are all mixed into the five minutes of Filipino.

"Fuck," Calvin says when the radio goes quiet.

Sam crosses his arms over his chest. "We need to keep a log."

"I'll grab an empty logbook from the wheelhouse." Zane takes off down the hall.

"And we need to keep a better watch." Calvin's trying not to limp as he moves to the table. "We're all in agreement —we stay quiet until we know more about them."

"Fuck, yes," Dante says.

There's static on the line again—it's stronger this time than last time. "Are they getting farther away?"

"Yes and no. Each of the speakers could have different types of equipment, and even just having their antenna pointed in a different direction could increase the static. They could be changing course, moving to a point away from us. But the best equipment out there can give thirty nautical miles, depending on conditions," Sam says.

"But sitting on the ocean, two to two and a half miles is the farthest you can see," Zane says.

"I know the answer, but I'm just going to go out on a limb and say we're not going to risk that they might not be pirates and broadcast. What if they're actually a hospital ship and they need payment for their sick . . . ?" Stern faces stare back at me. "I'm going to shut up now."

"No, Easton, you might be right. That's why we need to keep a log. I definitely saw a pirate ship. That doesn't mean that these guys are pirates, but let the evidence lead us to the answer," Sam says.

"Agreed," Zane and Dante say together.

"Right, Calvin?" Haley touches his arm. "We need to keep an open mind."

"What we need to do is get the damn boat fixed," Calvin growls.

Zane cocks his head at Calvin. "True, but we've got weeks of work—"

"Weeks of work if we had power and the right tools. Months without power tools, if ever. And the rainy season's going to get going soon. It's going to get a lot harder to get back and forth between the beach and the boat, and a heck of a lot more uncomfortable on the beach." Calvin straightens his leg under the table.

"Until the rainy season starts, we need to conserve water." Sam's still looking at the radio. We all are.

"What about the regular radio—what's it called again?" I ask.

"The VF radio's dead. I don't have the parts to fix it." Calvin pulls on his foot.

My eyes follow his leg. "You doing okay?"

"Good enough."

I nod at him. "You should stay on board for a few days. Let your foot stay as clean as possible."

"That's a good idea. I'll need someone else to help monitor the radio at night, and we should keep a lookout too," Sam says.

"We'll use the map tree for the lookout. It can see a heck

of a lot farther." Calvin takes my dad's agenda from in front of Zane and flips through it. From inside, a piece of paper floats to the ground.

I pick it up. My eyes widen.

"What is that?" Zane stands and moves next to me.

"Haley, can you please hand me the note from my dad's tuxedo pocket?" She does. "Thank you." I hold up the two pieces of paper, and they fit together.

Haley jumps up. "That's an exact match."

I haven't shown anyone the other side yet. I'm jumping to conclusions, but H could stand for Harding. My dad was doing it? Was he selling the family business to his partner in the finance firm?

"What does it say?" Haley asks, and I put it on the table. She reads, "R. T. to H 3.1 B."

Dante's eyes flash to me. "Rockwell Tire to Harding for 3.1 billion?"

I nod. "That would be my take on it too. What does our resident cryptographer think?"

Haley passes the two slips to Zane. "The thing with codes, shorthand, is that it's usually the simplest answer, except for when it's not."

"But why did he rip it?" Haley pushes the two pieces apart. "And why did one end up in his book and the other in his agenda?"

"Sound questions that I don't have an answer to." I take the agenda and search the inside folds and cover, but there's nothing else there.

"Mr. Rockwell is a complex man who has some trust issues." Zane swallows when I look at him. "I'm not being rude. A man with his wealth has the right to be secretive. He's got to have some enemies."

"I'm not offended, Zane. You're right, my dad did have

trust issues. But as far as enemies? I'm not sure. He's even still friendly with Susan. She made out well in the divorce. Honestly, I don't know anyone who doesn't like my dad." And I'm not just spewing out shit to make Zane feel better. It's true. My dad might not have been emotionally available to Emily and me, but that doesn't mean he didn't go to great lengths to provide us with the best of everything.

"Three billion," Zane says.

Haley shakes her head. "Three point one billion."

"Shit, that's worth killing someone over. Or in this case, a lot of someones," Dante says.

My stomach turns. Of course this whole thing is happening because of money. My family's money. I hate it. Emily's right: money is shit if you don't have it and a whole lot of shit if you have too much.

I've been to Harding's house. Went to his wedding. Celebrated Christmas with him and his wife. I taught their kids how to swim. What in the ever fuck? It can't be them. It's Candy. She's the one who had the diamond in the bag of her wedding dress. She's the one who wanted the damn diamond so much. She's the one who pursued my dad. Not a man who I think of as family.

Fuck it. I need to get off this boat. The heat of the enclosed space is suffocating me. I'm drowning. "Do you have a spare set of binoculars? I'll take a watch at the top of the tree tonight. It looks like it's going to be clear." I have no idea if it's clear out there, but I need to get away.

"Okay, good. Dante or Zane, which of you want to cover the radio watch?" Sam's in captain mode.

"What about me? I can take a watch." The irritation in Haley's voice rings.

"I thought you would want to take care of Pepper. From

what Calvin says, she likes you better than anyone," Sam says.

"Oh, uh . . . yeah. I do. I was worried about her all last night. She's never had to catch her own food. She's a little teenager cat now, but I still worry about her."

"I left lots for her, Sassy. She's going to be angry, but she definitely won't have starved. But I'd like to go back. I want to take care of the fish weir."

"I'll get the tender . . . Wait, you could use the Wave-Runner and we could give the adhesive a little more time to cure. We put three people on WaveRunners all the time." Zane glances at Haley and Dante. "Do either of you know how to drive one?"

"Zane, I grew up on a lake before we moved to Florida, with a stepmom that I tried to avoid as much as possible. I can drive a WaveRunner, a powerboat, go-cart, four-wheeler—if it had a motor and carried me away from the house, I asked for it and received it. Emily used to say she thought Susan was hoping we'd get injured and be out of her life."

Dante laughs. But Haley gives me the I'm-sorry-you-had-horrible-adults-in-your-life-growing-up look.

I smile back. "The point is, I can ride it back to the beach."

It's a good two hours of getting ready before we're sitting on the damn machine.

"This is the emergency gas shut off." Zane's standing above me.

"He's got it, Zane." Dante's holding on to the back seat, and Haley has her arms wrapped around me. We all have on new life jackets, and Zane has given us the safety briefing twice.

"We'll see you tomorrow morning," Calvin says from the top deck.

Sam's already said goodnight. He's on radio duty while he's working on the wiring.

"Okay, we need to go before it's time to come back," Dante says.

Zane pushes us away from the yacht.

Haley's arms are tight around my waist, and her cheek is pushed into my back. I head straight out through the reef to deeper water. Haley's calves scrape against mine. Her mouth comes to the side of my earlobe. "Can we take a quick swing around to the caves and beach on the other side?" Her voice trails on the wind.

"Do it. Better to ask forgiveness than permission with those protective bastards," Dante yells.

I glance back at the boat, and what the hell, Zane made it sound like it's not far. We've got the water with the tide for another hour. I'm sure he'll be watching, but Dante's right. I turn the WaveRunner toward the caves.

"Is he watching?" I ask Haley over my shoulder.

"Yeah. He's not happy. We better make it quick."

The waves aren't as big as we round the bend away from the Rock Candy. The island juts out in front of us again, just like Calvin said it would. I don't know why I pictured it as a round island, but it's not. The wall to the right of us protrudes out into the ocean.

Haley lets go of my waist with her right hand and points at the cliff. "There, it looks like a cave."

I slow and pull in, and the temperature drops a good ten degrees.

"Whoa," Dante says. "This is seriously cool. How did Zane even see it? It's really camouflaged."

"Can we get out?" Haley asks in a normal voice, but the cave absorbs it to a whisper.

"We'll have to save exploring for another day. I'm sure Zane's having a nervous breakdown." I turn the Wave-Runner around and head back out. "Make sure you blow Zane a kiss when we go by the yacht."

"You think he'll be watching still?" Haley wraps her arms back around my waist.

"I'll be shocked if he hasn't pulled the other Wave-Runner off the top of the yacht with his teeth, Sassy."

"Oh, we should get back."

As Dante correctly predicted, Zane and Calvin are on the back platform, scowling as we ride past them. Haley lets go of my waist with both hands and waves. The terror on Zane and Calvin's face is both funny and relatable.

"Sassy," Dante growls. I'm not looking, but I'm guessing he's holding on to her.

The waves coming into the shore are bumpy but nothing we can't handle. Dante helps Haley off, and we all push and pull the machine far above the tide line.

"I'm going to get some palm fronds to cover it," Dante says.

"I'll help." There are old palm fronds from when we slept in the raft nearby, and it doesn't take long to cover it up. It's still strange hiding our camp. When we got here, we were doing everything to be seen. Now with the VHF seemingly confirming our theory? We need to be more vigilant.

Dante takes off the backpack he brought—it's stuffed. "What's in there?"

"You know, some more things." Dante pushes some palm fronds around.

From the edge of the forest comes a loud meowing. Pepper runs straight to Haley. "There you are, our little girl." Haley scoops her up. But Pepper's not done with her scolding. "I'm going to go get her some food." They take off.

Dante follows them, but I'm not letting him get away that fast. I put my hand on his shoulder. He stops. His eyes flick back to Haley trailing up the path. "Sam sent the gun with me."

"The flare gun?"

"No, the pistol from on board. We're going to keep it with whoever's with Haley. You know how to fire a gun?"

"I've shot but never at a person or even an animal. I've gone to the range with friends before."

"Right, then I'll be keeping the gun with me."

Haley has her towel on her lap when Zane and I get back to camp—Pepper sits on top of it. "I thought I was going to go for a dip at the waterfall. Pepper seems to have other ideas."

Zane sweeps in. "I've got you. Hey there Pepper, how about a snack?" Pepper jumps with enough force that the towel flies off Haley's lap in the other direction. "Problem solved. She didn't get you?"

"No," Haley says.

"Give me a minute and I'll come with you," I say.

She smiles. "I'll wait."

I toss my pack up on the living room platform and grab a towel. Having my own towel will always be a luxury from now on. "Ready."

We sit on the big rock and take off our shoes. Shoes also aren't something I'll always think of as a luxury. Having them for our walks in the forest has been a game changer. I strip my shirt off, and soon as I do, Haley puts her head on my shoulder. Peeking down at her, I see her eyes are closed. Her chest heaves in a light sigh.

I put my arm around her and squeeze.

She looks up at me, and her blue eyes shine in the dappled early evening sunlight. "What do you want from life?"

I run my fingers over her hair. "That's a big question. For most of my existence, it was to win a gold medal. Then it was to win more gold medals. Now? After this? I think it's to be normal. Or as ordinary as I can be. Maybe get a dog like Penny."

"A cat like Pepper," she adds, and her blue eyes flick up to mine.

"Just like Pepper. What do you want?"

A tear hits my chest. "A family."

"Haley," I growl, pulling her up into my lap. "You have us."

She nods. "Right."

"You have me." I lift her chin to mine.

She smiles, but this girl . . . she doesn't believe me. I want to tear the men in her past apart, every single one of them who has let her down. Her ex, her father—damn them both.

Chapter 42

Shore Leave

Sam

"How's your foot?" I'm on the back deck with Calvin. We've got what I hope are most of the cut wires spliced back together. Getting the major systems from the portside helm reconnected would be a win, as none of those wires were sliced. But we need to get the generator and the engines up and running. Calvin's eating breakfast, and Dante's taken the VHF into the galley to listen while he finishes cleaning up the dishes from last night.

"It's good. Easton took the stitches out last night before he went back to camp."

Dante strolls in. Calvin and I stare at him. "What? There hasn't been a sound on the VHF for ten days, and what we heard then was barely anything. It can hang in the galley for a minute. I want to talk to the two of you."

My eyes flick to Calvin and back to Dante. "Okay, shoot."

"We need a day off." He sits and leans back in the chair. "Not even a full day off. We can go on a fucking hike and collect pomelos. Or brainstorm on how to get the power grid strong enough to run more current. But we need to be together all in the same place. And that place needs to not fucking be here. Because here we're all going to be thinking about how the hell to get the ship up and running."

"Like spending the night in the treehouse?" I ask.

"Yes, we need bonding. We haven't done anything but focus on getting the Rock Candy running since Haley's birthday, and that was what? Like three weeks ago?"

"Twenty-seven days—almost a month," Calvin says.

"I know you're worrying about Penny on the tender. Or is it something else and you're using your dog as an excuse?" Dante leans forward.

Penny, of course, picks that moment to stand up from where she was asleep next to me and walk over to Dante. She drops down on his feet.

My chest expands, and my vision focuses on the horizon off the back of the yacht to the ocean. It's high tide, and waves crash against the alcove wall. I'm slow to respond. I want to get us all out of here. I want Haley safe. I've been pushing us all to get as much of the ship fixed as fast as we can. We have some things complete—not enough but some. The crash patch is perfect now. The engine room is dry. The wiring is pinging current traveling through it. When we get the engines up, we should have limited operations routing it to the port controls on deck.

But we're not machines. It's something my mom used to tell Charlie and me in school. We'd be signed up for every activity, sport, and club. Then we would fall asleep on our textbooks at night—she hated that we were both so driven. Now, I've been pushing too hard. "You're right. We're not machines. There's a lot to do, but it will still be there tomorrow."

"You're going to skim right by my other question, aren't you?" Dante raises his eyebrows at me. Damn the man. I might be older than him by a few years, but he's wiser in a way and fucking cocky as hell.

"Are you sure you're not a therapist?" I ask.

Dante smirks. "I was a bartender for a while."

"That counts," Calvin says. "We should go now." He stands, and while he says his foot is good, you can see the effort he makes with each step to keep from limping. When Haley's around, he tries a heck of a lot harder.

"Now?" I turn to Calvin, who's already at the door to the main salon. "As in, to the beach, now?"

"Yeah, it's high tide and not raining. You know Penny would like to have a good run. If we wait until tomorrow, it could be raining. And fuck me, I don't want to have a repeat of the time I took her to land when we were anchored off St. Lucia."

I shudder. That wasn't a fun night. Logically, what Calvin's saying makes sense, but I'm not being logical. My throat tightens. Penny does great on the yacht, but she hates water so much. And the tender gets bumpy. "Sure. Let me get things for her and stuff for tonight." I haven't been back to the beach. It just didn't make sense for me to go. My stomach flips.

"It will be fine, Sam. The yacht will be here when we get back," Dante says. "And better than that, we'll all be with Sassy. That's something we've been missing out on."

I'm not a flincher. That's the thing with being a captain or a leader of any type—you have to keep your opinion to yourself.

Dante huffs out a half-laugh-half-scoff. "You still don't get it. But you will."

He's right. I don't get it. If the lot of them bowed out, I'd be thrilled. Yes, that one night during her birthday and the next day, I liked watching her with them. I'm still processing it. But I'd much rather have her all to myself. And part of me has been wondering what the plans of the other guys will be when we get back to land. Because we are getting back to land. We're going to make it happen. Sure, we can take a break tonight, and it won't hurt us too much. But we can't get lost in our lust. I'm not even sure if that's what's causing me . . . "Has she said something about it to you?"

Dante shakes his head. "This isn't high school. I'm not inserting myself into your relationship with Haley. Plus, you're not stupid. We're all busy. Even Easton's become a pro at splicing cable and grinding on that damn corroded wheel in the generator. But Haley . . ." He raises his eyebrows at me.

I've been trying to keep everyone safe, but mostly Haley. It's not a feeling I've had before, but I'm not the only one. And keeping her safe means keeping her off the boat as much as possible. Sure, we haven't heard anything on the radio for a long time, but her being on the island is a hell of a lot safer than her being on the ship. The Rock Candy is a beacon for anyone who knows how much she's worth to salvage. Haley not being on the ship is the best thing.

But when she's on the boat, she takes the lead on listening to the VHF, which has meant listening to nothing for a long time now. She helps Dante with food and has taken Penny to the strip of sand out front of the ship, when the tides line up right. But it's not fulfilling, and I've been . . . I've been avoiding her without even realizing it. I've always thought I was great at the big picture, but lately I've been hyper-focusing for sure.

Calvin's holding on to the door. "Sam, it's one night.

Pack your shit, get the stuff for Penny, and meet us on the swim platform in ten minutes."

I don't move.

"Fuck, Sam. The ship will be here when you get back tomorrow." Calvin pivots and moves into the salon. "Of course it will. The motors aren't going to start themselves." Green shoots me the middle finger and disappears around the corner to the main stairs.

We've been using mainly the WaveRunner to get back and forth. We've got lots of fuel, but it uses less. And since we have no idea how long every—

Those words echo through my head a thousand times a day. I'm fucking sick of them. When will we run out of water, food, fuel . . . ? I nod at Dante, who's still glaring at me. "I'll pack some stuff. If we're taking the tender half full, we should bring more canned goods too."

"Yup, I'm on it," Dante says.

I set my bag down and walk up to Penny like nothing's amiss. But her ears dart back immediately. She knows. "It's all right, girl." I've got Penny's life vest behind my back, but she already knows. She hates lots of things, but this vest is top of her list. "Sit down, Penny."

Penny drops to her haunches and takes a few steps away.

"Do you want to go see Haley?"

Penny cocks her head to the side and then drops down on to all fours. She's not making this easy for me, but I wrestle her into the vest the way I imagine a toddler has to be wrestled into a snowsuit. A sixty-pound toddler with an attitude and odd haircut. I've never been great at cutting her hair, but I've had to do it. Otherwise, she'd be looking like a sheep by now.

I pull up the zipper on the back and attach the leash.

"Let's go," I say as I pick up my backpack. Calvin has the tender ready. It's not that hard to drop into the water by yourself. Pulling it out, though? That's a pain in the ass. Dante has two medium containers of canned goods and other things on the dock.

I hop into the tender, and Dante helps Penny. It's more of a push as she whines. Her amber eyes glare at me. She's not happy. Dante pulls the ropes and we're off.

It's the first time the Rock Candy's been empty since we left port. Sure, I went to the beach once, but Penny stayed behind. Not that she would have protected the ship. She would most likely have licked the pirates into submission. The waves are rough, and Penny lies on my feet, her head tilting up at me with each wave. Like, why in the hell did I choose to be a captain, anyway? There are moments I wonder whether I should have left her with Jenifer. Then I remember what a horrible, selfish woman Jenifer is and push the thought out.

We pull up onto the beach. There's no one waiting for us. But then, why would there be? They had no idea we were coming. The WaveRunner's not in sight. Which is good. I have to scour the tree line to find it covered in palm fronds.

"We'll come back down and move the tender later," Calvin says.

"No, let's move it now." I lift Penny from the tender, and she freezes. She looks back at me like this must be a dream. Then she levitates, jumping straight up, barking over and over again. "Hold on. Let me get your vest off." I set my backpack above the tide line in dry sand and wrestle the life vest off her. She glares at me and then shakes, sending the small amount of water on her fur all over me. I glare back and toss her vest in the tender. Calvin's got the motor. "Let me help you." It's at least eighty pounds.

"I've got it," he says.

"I'll just run up ahead and let Haley—"

"Fuck, here, take half." He twists, letting me grab the housing. We walk it up to the WaveRunner. Penny zooms up and down the beach, away from us until I can barely see her behind the big rocks and back. She's prancing. And damn if it doesn't make my heart lighter. She needed this.

Calvin and I grab the tender and pull it next to the WaveRunner. Once the palm fronds are spread over it, I turn, but Penny's not zooming back. "Fuck, where did she go?"

"She followed Dante." Calvin grabs his bag from next to mine. "Up the path to the treehouse. This way. We've been working on camouflaging the path better."

It hasn't been that long since I've been here. At least, it doesn't feel like it to me. But if I wasn't following Dante's tracks in the sand, it would take me a while to find it. The trail goes into the forest but cuts to the right and then zigs again, creating a blind. We head up the path, and that's when we hear the commotion.

Chapter 43

Liberty Call

Haley

"Pepper?" I call down from the platform. I'm back from my bath at the waterfall with Easton. Things are still swirling in my head. But he was so tender with me, so kind. It's something I'll cherish for the rest of my life.

Penny howls again, and it's followed by a long hiss.

"Penny?" How is she here?

Zane and Easton have gone off to the stream to collect water. I've been sweeping out the sleeping platform and tightening the rain flaps. Zane's improved our windows a lot with panels from the back of the Rock Candy that snap into place over the swim platform. They were for letting people fish while staying out of the rain.

Pepper hisses again.

"Pepper?" I head down to the living platform and then down the stairs. Penny barks.

"Hey, Sassy, we're home." Dante puts two boxes down in the kitchen area, tucking them out of the way.

Pepper's back is arched, and she slowly moves backwards as Penny inches forward. I ignore the danger of her scratching and biting me. She might look like a full-grown cat now, but she's still a kitten to me. I scoop her up. "It's okay, Pepper. Penny is our friend."

Penny barks.

"You're not helping." I crouch down. I'm not sure if that's what I should do, but it feels right, letting Pepper see Penny face-to-face.

Pepper lets out a warning growl but curls up in my lap. Penny inches closer and lies down at my feet, her nose dangerously close to my leg and Pepper's claws. She lets out a long sigh.

"It's hard to make friends, I get it." I risk Pepper fleeing when I take a hand off her and run it over Penny's face, stopping to scratch her ears. For a second, Penny closes her eyes and I feel Pepper relax. "How did you get here?" I pet the sleeping dog again. It's a silly question; I've already seen Dante. I turn to him. "Did Sam and Calvin come too? Is everything okay on the yacht?"

"Everything is fine. We were just missing you, Sassy."

My heart dances inside my chest. It's more than the rain that has been bringing me down. Not having all of us together every night is . . . odd. I know that's a weird thing to say. *Oh no, only sleeping with two or three guys instead of five.* But it's not even the sex. It's like a piece of me is missing when we're not together. I don't like it, not at all.

I've been wondering if we should all start sleeping on the ship together. It's not something we've done, not since my birthday. And it's almost the holidays. Whatever that means. Thanksgiving, Christmas? They both still hurt. It makes me miss my mother so much. I never understood how people didn't like the season, but for the last few years, it makes so much sense. "I was missing all of you too. I know we just left a bit ago. But yeah, I'm glad you came. And I've been waiting for Pepper and Penny to meet."

Sam's staring at Penny. "She's always loved cats. But it takes a special kind to know that her licks are of love and not from hunger."

"Well, that hasn't happened yet," I say.

"Pepper's tough. She'll let Penny know if she oversteps," Calvin says.

I hug Pepper closer. "I think they can be friends once they work out some of their fears." My eyes flick to Sam, and he smirks. The correlation between Penny and Pepper and Sam and the guys might not go over his head.

"Sometimes a little dose of healthy fear is a good thing," Sam says.

"And sometimes fear can stop you from doing the thing you want most in life." Dante kneels next to me. "You want friends, don't you, Pepper?"

"It's true. She's seemed off when there's only a couple of us on the beach." I look up at Dante.

"She's been lonely. It's okay to be needy," Dante says before popping up. And now I'm wondering if he's talking about me. It's Dante; he's definitely talking about me. "We should get camp buttoned up. We'll be lucky if the nightly storm holds off much longer." He bustles around the kitchen area, which now has a rain shelter over it. It's camouflaged. It had been ordered for Emily as a wildlife screen. Apparently, she's a really good photographer.

"Are you going to bring Penny up into the treehouse?" I ask Sam.

"I hadn't thought about it." He skirts around Penny and loops his arm around me, pressing a kiss to my neck. "I'm glad to see you. Although, it's only been a few hours." Sam rubs Pepper behind her ears. Her round eyes gaze up at him before she rubs up against his chest, reaching for his beard. My little feline friend has a thing for facial hair. And I've got to admit it, while I wasn't sure at first, their beards, both thick and scruffy, are sexy as hell.

"I've got just the thing." Zane's got the lid to one of his tool tubs open. "I knew eventually we'd have her here, so I made a sling to attach to the bucket rope and pulley."

"I don't know about that." Sam takes it from Zane's hands. "You think she'll sit still to be hauled up a rope? I can barely get her in the life vest."

"Is she good for the night?" Calvin's leaning against the tree. "Like, has she done her business?"

"Yeah, back on the beach." Sam's eyes flick to Penny.

Calvin picks the dog up like she's a small child and climbs the ladder.

"Or we could just do that," Zane says, the bewilderment in his voice felt by all of us.

"There you go, Penny." Calvin sets her down and tosses his legs over the opening next to the ladder. "She doesn't jump off the boat. Don't see why she would do it here."

Penny puts her head on his shoulder.

"That's got to be the cutest thing I've ever seen. Wish I could take a picture." There've been plenty of times since we had the treehouse that I've thought the same thing. "Do you think I could charge my phone enough to take some pictures?" I'm looking up at Calvin, since he's the one who rigged up the second solar pack here. We needed a way to keep the binoculars charged for their night vision. Although, there have been a few days in the last weeks that the rain has kept them from charging much.

"I don't see why not," Sam says.

On the beach, we all refer to Calvin when we have a question, and on the yacht, we go to Sam.

"You know that little proverb you dropped a few weeks back, Dante? It's easier to ask for forgiveness?" Zane puts something in the basket and lowers it down. "There you go, Little Bird. I charged my phone last week after the binoculars were done. There's no signal, but you never know when Cellnex Telecom is going to take over the South Pacific." He laughs. "Passcode is 18741982. There's no signal. I did check. That would have been mental if our cells had signals all this time."

I hand Pepper to Dante and take Zane's phone from the basket. I turn it on and type in the code. "1874?"

"The year Aston Villa Football Club was formed, and 1982 is the last time they won the European Cup." Zane wiggles his eyebrows at me.

"Naturally." Dante laughs.

"This feels so weird. Hold still, Calvin." I take the picture. And now my heart is soaring. I want to go snap pictures of everything. Penny tilts her head on Calvin's shoulder like she knows exactly what I'm doing.

"My ex had an Instagram account for Penny. Penny knows how to pose."

Penny sits up behind Calvin and puts her paw on the other side, effectively giving him a hug.

"You're not kidding." I snap a few shots.

When the thunder rolls out over the ocean, Pepper lunges from Dante's arms and scurries up the tree, leaps to the sleeping platform. I'm sure she's ducked right into the little sleeping cubby that Zane made for her.

"We've got a few minutes before the rain pours down," I say to Sam. I push Zane's phone into my pocket and bustle around the camp, getting ready for the downpour. Things stay pretty much dry as long as we get everything in. We're a well-oiled machine, with everyone taking charge of a certain area. Dante does the food tent, Zane and Easton get the windows in the sleeping area tightened down, Calvin secures the firewood, and I make sure that there's nothing on the secondary platform that can't get wet.

I'm up the ladder and tackling the living room platform in no time. We ate dinner up here when we got back from the boat. Zane spent the day at the treehouse standing on the observation platform, watching the never-ending empty ocean.

"Easton, here, take Penny." Calvin hands her up to Easton. I move up to the other platform, gathering some cushions I had out earlier, tucking them back into their containers, and I have the empty dinner dishes in a basket to go down to the kitchen later.

When I look down at Sam, he's standing there watching us all. His blue eyes catch mine. He gives me a small shrug and turns to Dante. I don't know what he says, but Dante hands him a bucket, and he heads down the trail.

On the sleeping platform, Easton is watching me watch Sam. "He's getting water," Easton says before he turns back to helping Zane with the window.

"Right, but he's only been to camp once," I point out. "Maybe I should go with him?"

"He's not going to get lost, Firefly. The trail is pretty trampled."

I nod. He's right. "But I think I should still go."

Lightning flashes through the trees. Crap, I hate it. Even after months of the rainy season, I still hate it. The noise, the flashing—all of it. I always have. But as much as I hate it, I don't want Sam to, I don't know, feel unwelcome.

When Easton moves to the other side of the sleeping platform to help Calvin, I climb down the ladder and run along the path. Easton's right—the path to the stream is really worn down and not from animals but from us. Sam should be at the first turn of the stream, but he's not there.

"Sam." I cup my hands and call out to him. I stop speed-walking and wait to see if he answers me, but there's no reply. Now I'm full-on running. Easton said if you stay on the path, there's no way to get lost. But if you head into the jungle because you see something . . . My heart pounds in my chest. "Sam," I call again, but there's no answer. My steps thud on the wet path. It hasn't started raining yet, but it also hasn't dried off from the last storm.

I stop. This isn't how Calvin taught me. Observe, look, and listen. I push against my panic, panic of not knowing where he is, of not knowing about the storm. He's only been out of my sight for a few minutes. I'm being silly.

"Sam," I shout. The wind is picking up, and while the rain hasn't started, the palm fronds are throwing the water from the last storm down on my head. I push down the path, way past the point where we stop to get our water, and I keep going.

The rain starts, small droplets at first, but I know what's going to happen; they're only going to get bigger. I'm almost at the waterfall. I don't think I've ever come this far, this fast, or by myself. I turn back, and there are two black eyes peering at me.

Chapter 44

Right of Way

Sam

Even over the rush of noise from the waterfall, I hear something. Haley! I drop the bucket and race down the path. Did she follow me? There's no way I could hear her from all the way back at camp. Dante told me to be quick and that the waterfall was far, so it would be best if I just got water from the first bend.

My legs strain as I race toward Haley's cries. I see the light brown-blond of her hair in the distance through the trees. "Haley."

"Sam, stop. Don't come any closer. There's a boar." Her voice is calm now. "It's staring me down. Or I'm staring it down. I don't know."

I keep going. What in the hell is she thinking? She's got a stick in one hand and a log in the other.

"Haley, Sugar . . . back up toward me. Slow steps. You're doing great." She's right: if I get too close, whatever trance she has the wild animal in is all over. I move slowly and take the knife out of my waist holster. I've only thrown knives once with my brother when both of our boats happened to be in the same port in the Bahamas. But this is a whole different level. I keep it on me in case I have to cut a line more than anything. I've used it mostly for opening bags of potato chips.

"Sam, I don't know what you're thinking, but we need to climb a tree. I'm going for the one to my right. I think I can grab the lowest branch." She pivots and takes a small step backward.

The boar grunts.

"I'm going to run on three. Are you ready?" Haley asks.

It's not much of a plan, but me actually killing a boar on the first throw with the knife doesn't sound like a good plan either.

"I'm good. There are two branches. I'll push you up." Which means I have to put my knife back in its sheath.

"Okay." Haley's whispering. "One. Two. Three—" She flings herself toward the tree, and I make sure I'm between her and the boar. She's right; the beast is on us. The sky lights up, and thunder claps as Haley reaches the tree. She jumps for the branch, her fingertips barely ringing the thin tree. I push her ass up as the boar comes at me. With another shove, she's straddling the branch. I, however, am not. And if I turn, he's going to gore me from behind. His tusk grazes the side of my leg. Pain shoots up my calf. The rain sheets to the ground.

Thunder cracks, and lightning hits the top of the island. The boar squeals, running toward the waterfall.

"Fuck." I reach up for Haley. "Let's get out of here." She takes my hands and slides out of the tree into my arms.

"Sam, did it get you?" Her eyes flick to my leg.

I look down too. "It's a scratch." It's more than a scratch, but it's not horrible.

"Right." The tone of her voice lets me know she doesn't buy it at all.

"It really isn't bad," I say.

"Why did you come out here on your own?" She's shouting into the storm, her arms crossed over her chest. Her discarded stick is back in her hand.

"I wanted to see the waterfall that you all talk so much about. I thought I'd make it back before it started storming. Why did you come after me? Wait, don't answer that. First, let me say thank you. If that boar had come all the way to the waterfall, there wouldn't have been anywhere for me to climb, other than jumping into the pool. Not only that, but I was mesmerized by the beauty of the place. I wouldn't have noticed it. And I was crouching. It could have hurt me badly. So, thank you."

"Are you mad at me? No, wait. I'm going to do the same thing you did and say don't answer that. I get it, you've gone back into captain mode. You want to get the Rock Candy up and running. Get us back to safety."

"Get you. I want to get *you* back to safety. And I suppose I wasn't avoiding you so much as keeping you safe." I laugh into the rain. "And somehow I imagined the beach camp as safe."

"It is, besides the boars. And that's only the second one I've seen down here. But then Calvin said their pattern would change as the rainy season drags on." There's a clump of wet hair stuck to the side of her face. "I've missed you."

Lightning flashes across the sky, lighting up the dark clouds, and Haley jumps. "Sorry, I'm not a fan of storms."

"I know. Let's get you out of here, Sugar." I wrap my arm around her, and we huddle our way back to camp. I've been warned about how much she hates storms, but this is the first time I've been with her during a big one. By the time we get close to camp, the rain is slashing our sides. Calvin and Easton are standing under the kitchen tent. I'm not sure who is holding who back. But there's definitely a debate verging on a fight going on between them. So much so that they don't notice we're here.

"Where the hell did you two go?" Somehow, Calvin appears even taller than normal.

"I went to the waterfall like I told Dante," I say.

"He told you to go to the stream."

I mimic his stance. Arms crossed, feet shoulder-width apart.

"Calvin, it's fine. We're back." Haley places her hand on his arm, water dripping from her fingers. Calvin glares at me as if I'm the reason it rained.

"It's storming. We were worried that you might be scared," Easton says.

"I wasn't worried, Sassy," Dante's voice booms from the top platform in the treehouse. "I know you can take care of yourself. It's the damn stream, not the red-light district in Karachi. You're sweet, but you're not going to melt."

"If you're done with the interrogation, can you let them come up?" Zane says.

"Fine," Calvin and Easton grunt together.

I see Haley's eyes flick to my leg. It's bleeding, and I want to clean it up. But I get that she doesn't want to tell the others about the boar, not now. Letting them cool off will be better for all of us. I follow her and take the rungs built into the tree, doing my best not to show off my glorified scratch.

Zane's holding open the flap to the sleeping platform. And I'm taken aback. I'd forgotten how nice the place is. It's dry, comfortable, and even smells good. Clean earth with citrus. They've added so many cushions that the whole floor is practically a bed. Penny's lying on a towel in the corner of the room, nosing at a box. A box with two blue eyes glowing out of it.

"Has Penny caused any problems with Pepper?" I ask.

"No, she wants to lick her. Which Pepper isn't sure about." Calvin runs his fingers around the cat's head, and it purrs loud enough to be heard over the rain. Penny looks at me and drops her head. It's Penny's overtired look, her I'm-going-to-sleep-for-ten-hours look, and I couldn't be happier.

"You're bleeding," Easton says, and he smacks the side of my calf.

"I got a scratch. It's nothing."

"Take off your wet clothes. They go in the box by the door." Zane points. "I brought your pack up. It's over there. You want anything out of it?" He lifts it.

I reach for it and take it from him. "Thanks. This is a really well-built treehouse. It's amazing what you did with so few tools." They really surprise me—every person here. Without their talents and grit, we wouldn't have lasted as long as we have.

"Thanks." Zane pulls the rain flap around the door closed. "It's even nicer on a clear night when we open the windows."

Easton's got one of the medical kits out. We've split a lot of the supplies. When the rainy season kicked in, I was worried that the reef could rip another hole in the hull and we'd have to risk getting enough supplies off the ship. But the more I heard of the pirates, the more I wanted to keep the surplus safe.

Haley takes my hand in hers, and I kiss it. "I'm fine."

Thunder booms in the distance. Haley shudders.

The storms are rolling over us, but we've all been here

long enough to know there will be another one right after the first one. The rainy season can't be over soon enough.

I hold her eyes long enough for the two of us to make a silent pact of not telling the rest of the guys about my wound.

Easton glares at my leg, then Haley, then me. "A little scratch? So how did you get this little scratch?"

"Things happen. I'm fine."

Haley puts her hand on his knee, and Easton purses his lips at me. "It's not bad, Sam. You don't need stitches, but it's going to leave a scar. Let me get it cleaned out, well, because things happen with bacteria."

"Scars are sexy, right, Sassy?" Dante's lying down in the middle of the bed already.

"As long as you're healthy, you're sexy to me." She leans over and kisses the side of my ear.

Easton has my leg bandaged up quickly, and then the dance of moving around the space to get to the right position in the bed begins. Having the three of us return from the ship has set the normal routine into a tailspin, apparently. Not that I've been part of the rotation since the night of Haley's birthday.

I clear my throat. "I'm pulling rank and taking my turn next to Haley."

"Ho," Dante chortles. "Rank, is it? Well, how about we let Sassy decide? I'm also not moving. I'm comfortable."

Haley smiles at Dante. "Ready?" she asks.

A chorus of "Yes" and "Always" fills the treehouse. From a small tub, Haley finds dry clothes. She doesn't put them on; she places them on a shelf at the center of the bed. Then she strips off her wet clothes and hangs them on the line above the tub. All eyes are on her. Mine, too. And I wonder how I could have stayed away. I'm a damn fool who has to learn things over and over again.

Haley lies down next to Dante, her back to his chest. His arm pulls her to him. When she tilts her chin up to me, it's like the first time I kissed her in the butler's pantry—the one kiss that sealed everything for me. I'm drawn to her. Fighting it is pointless. I want her, and if they come with her, so be it.

I strip my shorts off; they join my shirt in the bin by the door. And then I walk up to the mattress and wedge myself between Easton and Haley.

"Shouldn't I have rank over you?" Easton laughs, but he rolls over.

"There's no rank, not with me." Haley's blue eyes blink at me in the soft light. She leans forward, and her soft lips hit mine. I'm lost. My brain blurs, and all my responsibilities are washed from my skin. This girl, this woman, does it for me.

Dante pulls on her shoulder, and Haley lands flat on her back. Easton's up on his knees and has positioned himself at the head of the mattress. With my eyes closed and Haley's lips controlling my brain, I turn off my natural desire to pick out where everyone and everything is on the platform.

Her fingernails run through the hair at the nape of my neck. It's my favorite thing. My cock twitches between us.

Chapter 45

Mess Hall

Haley

I've thought about this for weeks. I've sat on Sam's lap in the wheelhouse while we were listening to the radio. We've made out. He's had his head between my legs, and I've done some interesting gymnastics squeezing between the back bench and the map table. But we haven't done anything with one of the other guys again. Mostly because it seems every chance they get, they keep me here on the beach and Sam stays on the ship.

The way they're touching me, it makes me want to purr. It's so easy to forget the storm raging on all around us, the dangers we face simply going to get a bucket of water.

"Little Bird?" Zane rubs his fingers over the top of my forehead and follows it with a kiss.

I smile up at him. He's right, he always seems to know when I'm getting too deeply introspective. He always knows how to bring me back out with just a few words.

"Zane." I reach around his neck and pull him into the mix of Dante, Easton, Sam, and me.

Dante has my nipple between his fingers. I tilt my head backwards, capturing Dante's lips. Our necks twist together. Sam ducks his head, and his kisses trail down my chest. His tongue swirls around my clit, and a zip of electricity jumps through me.

"Our girl is on fire tonight. Sam, keep it going." Calvin hovers near my knees.

Through my closed eyes, I see a flash of lightning. I freeze. But then there are hands on me everywhere. My hair, my feet, my breasts, my neck.

Dante's fingertips run over my shoulders. "We've got you, Sassy."

All the while, Sam's working my clit. Easton moves behind my head and lifts my shoulders up. He eases my back onto his knees. My hands slide behind me, grabbing his hips. My body elongates, but more so, I can see everything Sam's doing. He pushes his middle and ring finger inside my pussy. His eyes lock with mine, and then he finds a spot on the inside of my wall.

My hips jerk up and land against Zane's hand. But there's more there. He's got my vibrator from my suitcase.

"You caught me, Little Bird." His sweet voice sings with laughter, and I turn my head to him. He flicks it on, and his expression turns serious.

Sam's hand moves with precious motion, but then Zane joins him with the toy focused on my bud. The vibrations travel to my bones. It frazzles my brain. I really am on fire. I'm going to need to stand in the rain when this is all done to keep organs from cooking. The vibrator pushes in a little.

"You doing okay, Little Bird?"

I mumble something. I'm sure it's not English, or words at all.

Dante laughs. His hands swim over my skin. Calvin's

lips latch onto my nipple, and my view of Sam and Zane vanishes. My hands go to his blond hair, I push on his head, and he sucks harder. And Easton's fingers run through my hair.

"Look at that. You're so demanding, aren't you, Sassy? She likes a little nip with her pleasure." Dante grips me harder; Zane joins him in holding me down.

The pressure of them pushing on me, holding me down, makes me jerk harder. The balls of my feet press on the cushion. I'm a giant tethered with the ropes of my lover's hands. I'm flying like a hot-air balloon. Behind my eyelids, the clouds part and stars light up my night. I'm screaming. I have no idea what I'm saying. Their names pour from my constricted throat. *Sam, Dante, Calvin, Easton, Zane.* Over and over again until I'm hoarse. My head thrashes from side to side.

When I turn my head, Easton's cock jumps behind me. I'm bouncing as I come down. I'm not sure how I can come harder than I just did, but I know I will.

Dante and Zane's forceful touches turn tender. Sam pulls his hand back and licks his finger. My glazed-over eyes blink, and energy rushes back into me. I'm upright. Easton's behind me. Sam and Zane are in front of me. Calvin and Dante are to my left and right. But sitting up so quickly, I've shocked them into silence. If I didn't have a plan, it might make me laugh. They're all so doe eyed. I'm chewing on my lower lip when I put both hands on Sam's pecs and push him over backward, then straddle him.

"Hey there, Sugar." His voice rumbles through me, and shivers roll up my sides. He could ask me to do anything in that tone and I'd obey.

"Hey." I've wanted this, and now is the time for me to take it. He's naked. Like all the guys, when it happened doesn't matter. I'll count myself lucky. I wrap my hand around his velvety cock. His eyes close; his lips part. "I want you, Sam."

"Then take me, Sugar. I'm yours." His eyes open. "We're all yours."

"Damn straight," Calvin growls.

I lift my hips and position Sam, then I sink slowly, slower than I ever thought I had the ability to, until I'm completely seated. I hold him there, absorbing everything that is Sam. His hands are on my thighs—fingers gripping me tight. He thrusts up, pressing into me even more. Hitting everything. I'm so full.

Sam hisses. "Sugar, you're . . ."

"Home," Zane says. His fingers glide over my spine and down to my bottom. The vibrator turns on, and he eases it into my ass.

Sam's fingers dig into my skin. "Yes, home."

"Relax, Little Bird. Don't clench up."

I can't help it, but he's right; it's so much better when I relax. Dante's lips are on my neck, and he moves to the tender spot behind my ear, the spot that makes me forget how to think. My brain turns to mush, but my hips take off on their own. Sam's setting the pace, but I'm the one with gravity working for me.

The vibrator stops and is replaced with Zane's lubed finger, one first and then two. The pinch of him stretching me makes me gasp, my eyes popping open.

Sam freezes, and his eyes snap open. He cocks his head to the side. "You okay, Sugar?"

"I'm good." It pinches, but I know it's worth it. The heights that Zane and Sam are going to take me to are worth it.

There's a remnant flash of lightning from the passing

storm, but it doesn't send fear through me. Seeing the tension and ecstasy on Sam's face sets me off. I'm jerking and thrusting onto him.

There's a smack on my right butt cheek. "Slow down, Little Bird." Zane pushes another finger into my ass.

I huff in a breath through my dry throat. I bear down and still. Both Sam and Zane groan. And then Zane's fingers are gone. The tip of his cock pushes between my cheeks. "Easy, Little Bird." Zane rubs his hand around my buttocks. "You've got a beautiful ass."

I twist my neck and gaze back at him in the dim light. His normal smile is replaced by complete concentration until he sees me looking at him and his face lights up. His smile could win awards. It's crazy what it does to me. I can't help but smile back. "There you go." He pushes in slowly. "It's easy when you let it be. Rule 17."

I want to ask him how he has a rule about anal or am I misunderstanding, but he grabs my hips and seats himself all the way.

"Damn," Sam says. "That's tight."

Easton and Dante are on either side of me, and Calvin's next to my head. My eyes flick back to Sam.

"Fucking amazing." Zane's driving into me. The pace has my eyes watering. It's so much. There's so much going on, but I want more.

I'm holding myself up with one arm, and with the other, I take Calvin's dick in my hand. I flash my eyes down at where I'm holding him and lick my lips. It doesn't take but a second before the head of Calvin's cock is in my mouth. I'm moving too much from Zane's thrusts to be delicate or precise. Instead, I suck and rub him as much as I can. Calvin's growling. It's his own way of purring. He's close.

I'm close. From the noises that Zane is making, he's even closer.

Dante leans in and kisses me behind my ear again. His other hand squeezes between Sam and me. He finds his way to my very swollen clit. Sam groans. It's a lot. Dante is touching me as much as he is Sam. For a second, I panic, but Dante sucks harder on my neck and the thought of Sam being uncomfortable vanishes. Dante flicks me once and then a second time, and I'm done.

I suck Calvin hard as I come.

"Chiefie," he cries. Thick streams fill my mouth until he pulls out.

I'm twitching, and it takes both Zane and Sam over the edge at the same time. Sam's fingers claw into my hips. I don't care that there will be bruises tomorrow, that I'll have red spots and black and blue fingermarks over me. Not when they came with such passion.

We've broken through. It's us now. Not them and Sam. Us.

I collapse onto Sam's chest and stare into his sleepy blue eyes. There's so much I want to say. So much I want him to know.

"Are you done being stupid?" Dante cackles next to me. He pops his finger into his mouth, licking it clean.

"What?" I lift my head.

"Not you, Sassy. You couldn't be stupid if you tried. I hate that word, don't know why I use it. My uncle used to call me stupid. I'm not. What I'm getting at, *Sam*—" he stresses.

"What he's trying to say is teamwork makes the dream work," Zane says, pushing up onto his elbow.

Easton groans and pushes a pillow over Zane's head. "That's not exactly romantic."

"It's not *not* romantic." Zane shrugs.

"It's not romantic," Calvin says.

And through it all, Sam hasn't taken his eyes off me. "I wish I could give you a night in Rome. That's romantic."

"Rome is overrated. Santorini, Greece. I ported there once during a Med season. Primaries rented a pavilion overlooking the ocean. Thousands of candles, so many it was practically daylight. He proposed to her with a giant diamond. Not as big as the Pink Phoenix . . . but it was nice." Zane kisses my shoulder.

Dante's voice tickles my neck. "Greece is nice, and Rome, you can't go wrong. But Morocco. Oh, I had the best meal of my life on a rooftop terrace at Riad El Fenn in Marrakech."

"Nope, you're all wrong," Easton says.

Dante shakes his head. "All right, Swimmer Boy, what you got? A penthouse in New York City with a view of midtown?"

Zane waves his hand. "No, a jet to Paris for the weekend."

"Always fun, but no. Lewiston, Maine. There's a restaurant that does farm to table in a historic barn. I'd rent the whole thing out. Haley's favorite foods. Lots of chocolate." Easton leans over and kisses me.

"Macarons," Zane says.

"Italian food, gnocchi with extra bread," Calvin says.

"Brussels sprouts fried in maple syrup with pecans." Sam squeezes my hand. I forgot we talked about brussels sprouts on one of the first days. I can still taste the way my mother made them.

"Brussels sprouts? That's good to know, Sassy."

"I'm sorry, but you're all wrong," I say, blinking up at them.

"Really? What is it then, Haley?" Sam pulls me all the way onto his chest.

"Here, right now. Comforting me in the storm. Showing me how you've listened to my endless drivel about food. What I like. Because I would like all those places. Rome, Paris, Morocco, Maine—"

Zane cuts me off. "What about you, Calvin? You didn't say where?"

"I can't say now. But when we get the engines running and get back to the mainland, any mainland, I'll just have to take Chiefie there." He winks a green eye at me.

There's another flash of lightning, but it is far off in the distance. The storm will pass soon. Zane hands me a cloth from the cleaning cubby he made last week. And Easton reaches up, getting my sleeping clothes. Zane and Calvin move around, cracking open the louvers, and the post-storm breeze blows in. It's going to be a good night for sleeping.

The guys were all so wonderful, so kind, loving, but that horrible little gremlin in the back of my brain clicks on. It's the feeling of *I left the stove on* or *I left the car running*, but this is far, far worse: How can this last when we get home? When they have the rest of the world of girls to choose from?

Chapter 46

Buried Treasure

Easton

My gut clenches. It's Haley's turn to stay at camp with Pepper and Penny, and none of us like the idea of her staying here by herself for the day. Every time her turn has come around, we have made up an excuse to have one of the guys stay with her.

Haley walks away from the treehouse down to the outhouse, and Zane turns to me and asks. "You want to stay?" I've been helping with the wiring, but that's almost done. Really, Dante's a bigger help with the things they're doing down in the engine room. I do know how to swab an engine room floor now. Although, now that the crash patch has been fixed again, there's hardly anything to mop up. "Yeah, I'll stay with her. But we need an explanation."

"I've got you," Dante says.

I cock my head at him. "And?"

"Don't worry about it."

I wasn't worried, but now I am. I sit in one of the director's chairs we've brought over from the yacht and sip at a cup of island tea—leaves from the pandan plant that Haley found a few weeks ago. It's not coffee, but that's long gone. We've all gone through caffeine withdrawal a second time. And honestly, I don't think I'll ever pick it up again. But I've come to like the pandan plant's vanilla-like flavor.

Haley's light footsteps patter back down the trail. She loops her arm around my shoulder. "How's the tea?"

I lean over and kiss her cheek. "It's good." It's not a classic tea, more like warm, flavored water. But I've become quite fond of it. I pull her into my lap, and she nuzzles into my neck.

"I'll miss you today," she murmurs.

I give her a squeeze and wait for this grand plan of Dante's, the one he hasn't shared with us yet. He has cleaned the counter and has the fire going in the wood stove. His back is turned to Haley and me when he sighs loudly. I cock my head at him because there's no way she's not going to see through his middle school drama performance.

Haley gets up from my lap. Dante better pull his plan off. She puts her hand on Dante's shoulder. "What are you doing?"

"Getting set up to smoke some fish for when we come back."

"Okay, I've helped you a bunch of times. I'll do it today."

"Sassy, you should go to the Rock Candy for the day. I'll stay." What in the hell? He could have just said that to start with.

"And do what, exactly? Work on my tan? You've been helping with the engine. It's my turn to stay at camp and keep watch. With the new viewing platform that Zane made, I can do it. I can even drive the WaveRunner now." She turns to Zane. "I did a good job last week, didn't I?"

"You did, but . . ." Zane runs his hand through his hair. Calvin and Sam were on the ship last night. Calvin's been working nonstop in the engine room. He's not close to getting it going. At least, that's what he says. But he's closer than he was back in September.

"Oh no, not you too? What if I want to hang with the girls and have a spa day? Just me, Pepper, and Penny." Haley purses her lips at Zane.

"I . . . I don't see why not," Zane says. "She can handle it. Make sure you strap in when you go to the platform—"

"Easton should stay too. The two of them can take turns working on smoking the fish and getting the fish weir cleaned out. That okay with you, Swimmer Boy?" Dante barks at me, like I'm going to put up a fight.

"That's good with me. My delicate hands are getting calluses from all the mopping." I hold up my very not callused hands.

Zane loops his arm over my shoulder. "Ah, poor guy. Guess you'd never cut it as a deckhand."

"You know it," Dante says with a smirk.

They're teasing me. It's weird; I had guys I swam with for a long time, but as I got better, they dropped away. At the Olympic level, sure, there are people you see over and over, but it's not the same. These men are my brothers. Which is weird to say because they're not brothers . . . Yeah.

"We should get the fish smoked sooner rather than later," I say. The fish weir is still pulling in a decent haul, but it's not like the first month we had it up. We need to be more cautious with the resources we're using. The pomelos are done, but there are other trees coming into season. And the other side of the island, while a long hike, has a good amount of coconuts.

Haley cocks her head at me. "I can stay by myself. I can do the smoker."

"Sure, but now you can do the watch and I'll do the fish." I take her hand and position her back between my legs.

Her eyes widen. "Oh, okay."

I raise my eyebrows at Zane and hope to fuck he understands that in no way are we telling either Sam or Calvin that Haley's the one up on the platform. Even if she's strapped in, those two would burst an appendix. Sure, it's up high, a lot higher than a high dive platform. But she can do it.

Haley, Penny, Pepper, and I walk Zane and Dante down to the tender. Dante and Zane hop in, and Haley and I push them out.

They're a little past the breaker when Dante cups his hands. "I'm bringing family dinner back tonight." We've been doing family dinners once a week. Sometimes on the Rock Candy. Pepper really likes the yacht. Beds and pillows and endless places to hide from Penny are her jam. The tender isn't her favorite, though, so most of the time, we have family dinner at camp.

Haley and I wave, our arms wrapped around each other. I kiss the top of her head. She gets sad anytime any of us leave. And I get it. Nothing is guaranteed. Look at Candy. Hell, the fact that Roger Harding seems to want us dead. Well, Emily and me at least. Everyone else was an innocent bystander. Not that we've cracked any codes yet. But we're working on it.

Her blue eyes blink at me. "Sorry you have to babysit me."

"I'm not babysitting you. But you know how Sam and Calvin worry."

"If we were going to encounter pirates, wouldn't we have already?"

"I don't know, Firefly." And that bothers me. Calvin and Sam are both uber worried about someone finding and taking Haley. But there are more days than not that I think we should just try to talk about the VHF. I'm not naïve. I know there are bad operators in the world who want to use us or anyone for their own profit, but there are good people out there too. Maybe not here, though. Maybe not the voices on the VHF. And for now, we're good. We're making progress on the yacht, and that's all that matters.

"Having you not stay here alone isn't about you, Haley. It's about our own insecurities. We need to be needed. We've got fragile egos."

She stands on her tippy toes and yanks me in for a delicious kiss. "You're so full of it. But I lo—like you a lot, anyway."

I freeze. I thought she was going to say she loves me. Because I sure as hell love her. Zane, Calvin, and even Dante tell her they love her all the time. I haven't said it. I do love her, but I see she hasn't said that to the other guys—not that I know for sure. It's not that I need her to say it to me first, not at all. I just don't want to put pressure on her. Pressure does horrible things to a person, makes them reactionary. I can wait. I know she loves us all.

"You are the most special person I've ever had in my life, Haley Brewster. You make me happy. Everything about you brings me comfort and joy." I move a tendril of her hair away from her forehead.

"You are amazing too, Easton Rockwell. Are you really okay with me up on the platform?"

"As long as you're safe and use the harness."

"Of course. I don't have a death wish."

I watch as she gets into position. "You good, Firefly?" She's locked in, with the binoculars around her neck.

"It's beautiful up here. I really missed out on my tree climbing years as a kid."

I laugh and get ready for my day on land. When I get the fish smoker up and running, I'll have a little time to examine the metal lock box we have with our collection of clues. Zane likes to study them at night. They've been at the treehouse for a long time now. In fact, there's a lot of the ship here now. It's come over one trip at a time. We're working on getting the ship up and running, no one as hard as Calvin. Individually, it's like we've all come to the realization that we might never leave. And being as comfortable as we can at the camp makes sense.

I stoke up the smoker. Pepper and Penny keep me company while I watch it. "Come on, girls, let's see what Haley is up to." They both follow me up the path. "Hey, Haley?" I call to her. She's up on the platform.

"Easton. How's it going down there?"

"Dante left us lunch. Are you ready for it?"

"Yes, coming down now."

When we're done with lunch, I know I have to ask her. "I'm glad you're here with me." I have the Pink Phoenix in one hand and the fake one in the other. "I've thought about this for a while. And I don't want to see these anymore." I've been using them as worry stones.

She's got her stew face on, but I'm not sure what it means. "Okay. And what are you going to do with them? Throw them into the ocean?"

I laugh. "I'm not nuts. 55 million isn't something I'm going to trash in a childish rage. No, I want to bury them. And I want you to know where they are." I take her hand and the shovel from the tool bin.

"Let's do it." She takes the shovel from me.

And damn if I don't like this woman more. There's no second-guessing me. No *Are you sure?* Just *Let's go.* I smile at her. This girl.

"Where are we going?" she asks.

"Someplace special."

"I know just the place." The trail to the big rock near the waterfall isn't as stomped as others. She stops at the rock, right where we had our talk about what we want for the future.

There's some clear-ish ground near the side of the waterfall, empty enough to get a shovel in.

"Here?" she asks.

"Exactly where I was thinking." I hand her the bag of mostly diamonds and take the shovel. I dig a hole a foot deep, deep enough that the bag should stay put. I raise my eyebrows at her, and she holds the bag back out to me. "Drop it," I say.

"No, you should do it. It will be therapeutic." She holds it out closer to me.

I'm nodding as I take it. She's right. I place them in the hole. And a little of my pain disappears. My pain of not knowing what's happening to my sister and dad.

Haley and I stare at the bag. "I'll see them again," I say. "When we get out of here."

The dirt sprinkles over the white bag, and it's starting to feel a lot like a funeral.

"This is one buried treasure I'm not making a map for." I stamp down the earth and place two round, fist-sized rocks on the spot to mark it. They're a slightly different color than the surrounding ones.

I want to tell her I love her. I know she loves me, loves

all of us. But the future scares the crap out of her. It does me, too. I'm not going to pressure her. I can wait.

Chapter 47

Loot

Calvin

We're another two months into the rainy season. You'd think that would be a quarter of the year—three months each for winter, spring, summer, and fall. The fucking rain should get three months. But that's not how things work here.

The treehouse is holding up. It's solid. And it's better than stressing over the Rock Candy's water and sewage. The treehouse has something the Rock Candy doesn't—a cool breeze. Zane and Dante have rigged up louvered window covers, so the wind zips right through it at night. I've also grown fond of the noises of the jungle. The ocean is just loud, whereas the jungle has a melody to it.

The most important part of the treehouse, though, is that it's a hell of a lot safer for Chiefie. With our watch up on the top platform, I'm a lot more comfortable sleeping through the night—something I haven't been for a long time.

But not tonight. Tonight, I'm hanging out on the ship.

"If we all work on it tomorrow, I might get the crank to move," I say. "Maybe a centimeter."

"Fuck, yeah." Zane lifts the water bottle in a toast. "Then we all work together to get that shit moving. It's too bad the tide is taking half of our day today."

I slap him on his back. "It's fine. I've got enough to do on my own."

Sam beams at me. Getting the crank to move is just the first step. There's a lot of other work we still have to get through. "Tide's going out. We need to launch the tender. You two okay staying?"

Easton nods. "I've got the radio tonight, and Calvin's going to sleep early."

"Good luck with that," Sam says. No way I'm not going to use all the time I have.

"There's food for you in the galley." Dante climbs into the tender and holds Haley's hand. She doesn't need it, but she takes it. With the funky tides today, we left the observation platform back at camp empty.

"Thanks. It's much appreciated," Easton says.

I've worked for another hour in the engine room when Easton knocks on the door. "I'm taking the WaveRunner back to the cave for the night."

"Fine."

"Do you want to watch?" Easton asks. It's a safety protocol that Zane put in place. When anyone takes the WaveRunner to the cave—usually Easton because he's the best swimmer—someone stands on the back deck and watches.

"I'll be right there." I grab a rag and wipe my hands, then head out back. He's waiting on the swim platform. I cup my hands and yell, "Take the damn vest."

"Right." He puts it on but doesn't latch it up.

I roll my eyes at him, but what am I going to say? Give him Zane's safety talk? Yeah, I don't think so. I want to get back to the engine room, but Haley would have my hide if I didn't wait until Easton was back on board. Easton takes off on the WaveRunner as I watch.

I'm sitting on a lounger, almost enjoying the sun on my skin, when it clicks. This is the first time I've been alone since my hike all those months ago when I found the pomelos. And now I'm craving pomelos.

It's not long before Easton's head appears in the distance. Typical—he's left the vest back at the cave. Whatever. I'm turning into my dad. I go down to the swim platform and put out my hand to pull him up from the water.

"Oh no, I left my vest back in the cave."

"Ha ha. I'm going to tell Haley on you."

"Fucker, you wouldn't."

"Maybe I would. Maybe I wouldn't." I shrug.

"I'm not trading my time next to Haley for your silence," Easton says.

"Damn straight. I don't play games with the woman I love."

Easton dries his hair with a beach towel as we head up the backstairs, through the main salon, to the dining room where the VHF is sucking up battery power. I haven't been able to get enough current running to plug anything big in. No computers, hair dryers, or power tools, that's for sure.

"I'll listen all night. Go get a good ten hours of sleep." Easton pats me on my back.

"Yeah, you know, sleep and me don't work that way." I flop into a dining room chair and put my feet up on the back of another one. I really wish I could get some sleep when I'm on board. That would be freaking fantastic.

Easton opens the logbook. He's got a handwritten copy of the notes from the back of Rocky's journal on the table.

"You going to stare at those numbers all night long like Zane does?"

"Why not? Nothing else to do." Easton shrugs. "Hey, why did you take that panel off and put it back?" He points over my shoulder.

"What panel?" I crane my neck.

"The one on the far side. Over there."

I raise my eyebrows at him. I certainly haven't put any panels back in place. What would be the point? If—*when* we get the ship running, we're going to want easy access to any of the areas that were damaged. We're not going to be throwing a cocktail party. "We haven't ever removed that panel," I say with firmness. "There are no systems behind it."

Easton stands up and moves around me. He taps the wall. "This here? It looks like the marks we made on the first few panels when we took them off."

"You worried about the finish on your boat? I'm sure insurance will pay to have it buffed out. The hole in the side of the Rock Candy's hull? Not so much." I laugh. Most of the wall panels around the main salon are off and stacked on the other side of the room. All the way from the wheelhouse back to the galley, all on the side with the mechanicals.

"Fuck you, Green. Look here." He taps the wall.

I stand. He's right. I should just go down to the primary cabin and get some sleep, but Easton has a pry bar in his hand. "Fuck, Rockwell, if you're going to do it, do it right." I take the tool out of his hand and pop the bracket that holds it in place. I move it to the side, giving Easton a view of the inside I don't have.

"Holy shit!" Easton cries.

"What?" I'm walking the panel to the other side of the main salon to put it with the others.

"It's like someone went to Best Buy and loaded up on electronics." Easton's holding a box in each hand, both from leading manufacturers of yacht electronics. A red Simrad box and a black Digital Yacht box. "I'm guessing these might be replacements for the snap boards in the wheelhouse?" He hands me one.

"These are exactly what we need. What else is in there?" I duck my head in, hoping for some engine parts, but it's just boxes of electronics.

"I'm guessing this isn't normal storage for duplicates? Something the shipyard forgot to tell Sam about?"

"No. This . . . this makes that box of clues Zane keeps obsessing over even more complicated." I slap the wall.

"The saboteur was after the yacht? Not the diamond, not trying to kill Emily and me . . . and everyone else along with us? This is . . ."

"Amazing. Right now, I don't fucking care how any of this shit got here. I only care about installing it." My brain is whirling.

"Yeah, no way either of us is going to sleep now."

"Fuck no. Help me get the rest of the boxes out." I grab three red boxes and stack them on the table. A few hours later, we've got ten boxes of components, and fuck me, I only knew seven of them were damaged. Which somehow pisses me off even more. Most of the parts are plug and play. Which is fabulous. But the high-frequency radio, the one that could get us some actual help? There are no parts for that one.

"Something else must have gone wrong." Easton's pushing the trash from the boxes into a bag. I've got sweat running down my back and one of the last parts in my hands.

"What do you mean?"

"Why put all these parts in the wall if you weren't going to come and claim the yacht?"

"We were in a weird current with the storm. The other raft got yanked in the direction we should have been."

"So you think whoever was going to put all this back in found my sister's raft?"

"I don't know anything anymore, but yeah, sure. That sounds plausible."

"Don't get snippy about it. We're talking about my sister and my dad. Now I'm not sure it's a good thing if they were found."

"And Anders, Shayla, the rest of the crew. I'm not snippy. I'm never snippy."

Easton glares. "You're the definition of snippy, grumpy, whatever you want to call it." He's got that *I'm counting to ten* look. The one my dad used a lot. Huh. Right, well, maybe I am snippy. "Whatever the fuck you want."

The VHF radio on the sideboard crackles, and excited voices come over it. Voices that sound remarkably clear.

"Kill the light." I grab the manual binoculars and flare gun. Easton moves to go to the back deck, but I grab his arm. "Up top, stay low."

We fly up the stairs, and when we get there, we're only there for a few seconds before Easton turns to me. "There's too many of them."

Chapter 48

Seized

Haley

I roll over, and Sam's blue eyes are watching me. "Morning, Sugar," he says.

"Sugar?" Zane laughs from the platform below.

"You good to get going? I know Calvin's anxious to get working on things."

I put my head on his chest. "I know Calvin won't say, but do you think he's close to getting an engine to turn over?"

Sam presses a kiss to the top of my rat's nest hair. "I think so. It damn well feels like things are really close. But then, really close could be another month."

The tender's loaded for the day. Dante is staying back today to work on smoking more fish.

"Ready?" Zane pulls the lines and jumps in. Sam has his hand on the motor's tiller. Dante gives us a good push and we're away. Penny runs along the beach, following us until we can't see her anymore.

"What a blue sky," Zane says. "I think the rainy season might finally be over."

"I hope so." I tilt my face to the sun. I have absolutely no idea what I'm going to do on the ship today, but I'm going to try and be as helpful as possible.

The waves next to the bluffs are calmer than normal. It's one of those days where, back in the States, it would be hard to go to work.

We turn the corner, and my hands fly to my face, covering my mouth. There where the Rock Candy should be is nothing but cut ropes floating above the reef. My throat burns from my cut-off screams. I can't breathe. I want to throw up.

"Haley." Zane wraps me in his arms. His hand covers my head, pulling me to his chest. "Get us out of here, Sam." The thudding of Zane's heart echoes in my ear. "Go." But the tender slows. "What are you doing?"

"We only have so much fuel. And we need to search. You want to know everything we can, right? Haley?"

I lift my head from Zane's chest and nod. "Yes, Sam's right. We need to find out as much as we can."

"What if the pirates are still here?" Zane barks.

"If they've seen us already, what does it matter?" Sam fires back.

I stare into Sam's eyes. In the bright light, they are so blue they blend with the sky.

"Sam's right. We need to get all the facts." I'm shaking.

"I'd just like to get the facts when you're safe. But I suppose you're right, we only have a couple of ten-gallon cans of fuel at camp."

My eyes flit over the reef. My stomach turns. I can't think of Calvin and Easton as dead. They can't be.

"Little Bird, I see you. Don't do that to yourself. They're

rugged, smart men. They can handle a lot. Don't count them out."

"I'm not. I'm not," I say, but I don't believe it.

Sam points the tiller through the cradle opening in the reef that the Rock Candy sat in for months. When we get to the sand, Zane hops out and pulls us up onto the little strip of beach. It's high tide, so there's not much of it.

Sam pulls off his shirt and tosses it into the tender. We all follow his lead. Then we're in the water, swimming over the reef. I turn and realize that Zane's there, but he's swimming great. He waves at me. All the months with a great coach, he's really got it now.

I have no idea what Sam wants us to look for, but I've got my eyes peeled for anything might give us a clue to what's happened to Calvin and Easton. And whether we'll ever see them again. My stomach twists and I clench my core. Will I ever see them again?

Want bonus stories from the island? I've got some free micro episodes here.
https://BookHip.com/TMHTASF

Unmoored is available now.

XOXO
Ellie

Also by Ellie Pond

Dark Wing

Resisting the Bear

Claiming the Wolf

Courting the Bear

Redeeming the Dragon

Tempting the Bear

Defying the Dragon

Chasing the Wolf

Dark Wing Series, Hidden Valley Wolves

Hidden Heart

Brilliant Heart

Bewildered Heart

Mated (completed series of Hidden Valley Wolves)

Mermaid Why Choose—Enchanted Elements

Wicked Water

Rugged Rock

Western Winds

Fire Falls

Veiled City

Captured by the Dark Commander

Tempted by the Forbidden Mate

Caged by the Ruthless Thief

Bound by the Golden King

Seduced by the Mermen: Men of Stele

Claimed by the Mermen

Dark Wing Series, River Divided

Crafting Love

Fighting Love

Dark Moon Rising

Guard

Protect

Honor

Wrecked

Adrift

Uncharted

Unmoored

Wayward

Revenge and Surrender (Emily's series)

Savage Vow

Stolen Promises

Scandalous Devotion

About the Author

Ellie's had many professions, including costume designer, contract archeologist, organic farmer, fabric store owner, and airline gate agent. She's happy to be a full-time writer now. She lives in New England with her three teenage sons, husband, and father. It's a lot of testosterone. When time allows Ellie likes to travel. You can follow her on social media for her travel adventures, and more.

9 781956 083118